# Graywullf

## Book One of
## the Dragonspawn Trilogy

### Thomas Rottinghaus

AuthorHouse™
1663 Liberty Drive
Bloomington, IN 47403
www.authorhouse.com
Phone: 1 (800) 839-8640

Published by AuthorHouse 2/2/2015

ISBN: 978-1-4969-6751-0 (sc)
ISBN: 978-1-4969-6752-7 (hc)
ISBN: 978-1-4969-6750-3 (e)

Library of Congress Control Number: 2015901526

"If the powers of Light and Dark do not merge,
evil will prevail."

Alana, Mistress of Aard

# CHAPTER ONE

_L_YNCH WATCHED THE SMALLER man trailing him from the concealment of a frozen clump of oak brush. His eyes were sunken in the sockets from exhaustion and hunger, and sharp lines cut through the stubble of beard that covered his haggard cheeks. The duster he wore, the pitifully light pack across his thin shoulders, even his shoulders themselves which had been capped with muscle before he started this journey, all bore the evidence of a tremendous ordeal. He was a tall man, normally lean and sinewy, but now he seemed almost cadaverous. The hunt had been abnormally long, and prey and hunter had reversed roles more than once. At the moment, he was once again the prey. Or was he? Indeed, had he _ever_ actually been the prey? It made no difference. His smoky gray eyes betrayed more than a hint of the necessary savage cruelty of a born predator. But for now he merely waited.

The twigs of the brush he hid behind, forged in ice, were curved and hooked like the claws of a Dragon. That image dredged up memories from deep within the sediment accumulated throughout centuries within Lynch's mind, and for a moment he actually forgot where he was. A branch snagged the threadbare sleeve of his duster and the thin cloth tore with a small, apologetic ripping sound. The sound jerked Lynch back to the present. That tiny whisper of ripping cloth made a statement, bold and clear. _End it now._ This ruse had gone on for far too long and it was rapidly becoming an exercise in futility for the DarkWizard. How much strength could he gain from the ceremony? Would he even rebuild his power to its former levels? But he found he still could not abandon his plan.

He glared at the tear ruefully with a slight shake of his head. Such pitiful garments were not befitting a Wizard of the stature Lynch had attained. Even a Dark Wizard, he thought, should be deserving of more than rags. He turned his attention back down the trail. The churned up snow where he had walked, coupled with the plume of steam from his breath in the frigid air, pointed out his location like a giant flaming beacon. The smaller man who trailed him had stopped four hundred yards away and was staring in his direction. Somehow that pleased him, that his adversary was so utterly competent in his task. This one was better than all the rest. He had been pursued relentlessly over a period of time and space that would only confuse most mortal minds, and still the man in gray followed him. And now he had no choice but to let the hand play out. He lunged out from behind the brush and broke into a purposely awkward run through the calf deep snow.

Some perverse instinct that allowed him to survive despite countless efforts to prematurely end his existence warned him and he jerked his head to one side. He felt the passage of the bullet before he heard the report. It whipped through the hood of his duster, tore a shallow furrow from the bone of his skull and took a chunk from his right ear. It sounded like a cannonball had detonated inside his head. He catapulted forward to his hands and knees and pitched face first into the snow. He lost his vision completely for several seconds, and when he regained it black spots danced across his frozen surroundings. His ears rang as he reached around with agonizing slowness to tentatively explore his wound and he simultaneously raised his face from the stinging iciness of the melting snow where he had fallen. Warm blood ran in rivulets down the side of his head and neck and an alarming amount stained the snow in the indention left by his face. He was hit and he was down. Yet that also pleased him. He had been hunted before, but this one was truly amazing! The smaller man's breath came in great clouds of escaping steam from the last mad dash up the trail and he still had almost pulled off an impossible shot. But the man who called himself Lynch was also pleased because he knew there would be no more near misses. He had watched that very morning as his pursuer had ruefully tapped the last grains of powder from his horn and then sat studying the last of the round lead balls from his possibles bag. He had no more bullets and no more powder to stoke the long rifle he carried. Now they were on even ground, and as he lay there bleeding in the snow, Lynch grinned his feral grin.

Lynch cocked his head at the pale yellow sun as it arced across the cloudless sky. The timing was not quite right. Soon, but not just yet. He gathered his strength, struggled to his feet and bowed with a flourish, even though that made his head swim alarmingly and blood cascaded down his neck. He rocked forward and dropped down to one knee again, and as he did his vision went blank once more. The Dark Wizard felt a momentary thrill of fear, then his vision returned. He laughed mirthlessly as he struggled to his feet and resumed his torturous run, giggling maniacally and weaving like a dockside drunk.

"Son of a bitch," the smaller man blurted in amazed disgust as he watched Lynch escaping yet again. "May the gods damn his black heart!"

He spat into the snow and tried to calm his racing heart. Now it was his turn to ruminate. How in the name of Aard, the Mountain God, did that bastard keep going? But he knew. Oh, yeah. He knew. It was the Dark Magic which fueled his quarry's body and gave him unnatural endurance. Even so, he felt enormous respect for the Dark Wizard Lynch. He had hunted down more than his share of hardcases but Lynch was by far the hardest of the lot.

He stared at the place where he had spat in the snow, and hated it for the bright red around the edges of the tiny hole where it had melted through the top layer. He had resorted to Dark Magic himself, even though it was strictly forbidden. Just one simple spell, when he realized this was the last leg of a terribly long race. And he'd had the bastard in his sights and let him get away. Now the Dark Magic was showing its price. Was it worth it, he wondered, to give up his own life to end another? His chest ached so badly he could barely sleep even when he allowed himself the time to do so, and he awoke at regular intervals when sleep did overtake him, coughing up bright red splashes into the snow. That one spell was eating away at his guts as surely as a wolverine on a fresh kill. The price of Dark Magic was high, for one who didn't give themselves entirely to it. Perhaps it was even higher for those who did embrace it and received near immortality, only to lose their soul. Whatever, he thought. It didn't matter any more. Nothing mattered except this last hunt. He muttered the rune from memory, and felt strength flow back into his muscles like molten metal. Then he resumed the chase.

Lynch glanced back only once, just to make sure the man in gray hadn't given up. That would not suit his plans at all. Now that the hunter behind him had lost his ability to end the chase at long range, Lynch wanted him to persist. The man in gray had something he wanted. All he needed was the right place and the right time. Two agonizing miles further along, he found it.

The snowy plain came to an abrupt end, interrupted by a massive glacier towering hundreds of feet into the air. It ran several miles in each direction. But what interested Lynch the most were the fissures ranging from six inches to six feet wide that burrowed into the bowels of the glacier. After another glance at the sun, he entered one of the wider ones and ran onward. Sound from the outside was curiously muffled, while sounds from within were amplified. The glacier creaked and groaned like a living thing, and Lynch felt a moment of unease. He had a brief but extremely vivid vision of being digested by some massive creature while he was still alive. He stopped, and peered upward. Far above he saw a sliver of blue sky and a shadow that flickered over the chasm. Fear, usually a foreign emotion to the man called Lynch, wrenched his guts. He paused. His overdeveloped sixth sense was working at a frantic pace now. There were worse things afoot and on wing in the World than he, even though they had given him a wide berth to this point in his career, and Lynch had no desire to meet any of them at the moment. His hands were full with the bounty hunter on his trail.

Shards of ice rained down on him. He lowered his gaze and plunged ahead. After another three hundred yards the chasm took a right turn and Lynch stopped, his lungs working like a bellows. Sweat beaded his brow. His head ached and his ear stung like fire and blood stained his cheek and neck. He fumbled within one cavernous pocket and withdrew a limp bandana, which he tied over his mangled ear. Then he drew his sword with trembling hands and waited.

The ritual he intended to complete had certain requirements, and one of those was that the kill must be fresh, and it had to be completed by the light of the moon. Kill too soon and it would all be wasted. But he had waited for so long for this moment he had to force himself to be patient. A giddy excitement overtook him, and he felt a stirring of physical arousal.

He heard the man in gray long before he could possibly have been that close. The ice canyon played tricks with the sound and Lynch became more agitated by the minute. His eerie gray eyes darted from side to side and his breath came in short, silent gasps. Finally he could take it no more. He darted back around the corner, his sword held at the ready. And he nearly dropped it in surprise. Two small children skipped along the bottom of the chasm, hand in hand, laughing as they came. Their eyes were bright and full of life and their cheeks were rosy from laughter. Lynch was astounded. The children drew even with him, and their eyes turned a fiery red and their rosy cheeks elongated into narrow snouts lined with sharp teeth. They lunged for him as he fell backwards, his legs flailing against their thrashing bodies. He slammed into the wall of the ice chasm and needles of pain shot up from his thighs as they chewed through his breeches. Razor sharp, sparkling white teeth ground into the flesh of his thighs and chewed upwards towards his balls. He threw a desperate punch into the side of the nearest one's head, and as it fell he slashed his sword across the second one's throat. Warm blood sprayed up his forearm and, for a moment, the child's face returned. But these creatures didn't know who they were dealing with. Lynch drew his blade back and skewered the second without a moment's hesitation as it, too, turned back into a childlike being. He grunted as he rose to his feet, anger blazing through him as he saw his tattered leggings with his own blood seeping through them. The children's bodies shimmered against the glaze of ice then began to shrink. In moments two field mice scampered between his legs as Lynch stared. Suddenly, his head was forced back from the sudden pressure of an icy cold blade. Lynch dropped his own sword and coolly regarded the man who held his life in his hands. The man in gray's mouth was rimmed with red, and a tiny rivulet of blood seeped down the whiskers on his chin to drip silently onto the pristine ice. His eyes burned with single minded intensity, and just a touch of madness.

"Gotcha," he said hoarsely.

Lynch gave an almost nonexistent nod. He indicated the passage of the field mice with the barest glance and uttered one word. "You?"

The man in gray nodded. "Transfiguration spell. I have to know one thing before I kill you. Who are you?"

Lynch didn't answer.

The blade slipped under the skin of his throat as the man in gray increased the pressure on it. "I really don't think I have much time. Who are you?"

A coughing fit wracked the man in gray, but his blade hand was steady. The blood running from his mouth was now a thin steady stream.

Lynch grinned. "You used the Dark Magic to catch me. Bravo! I applaud your determination."

"Shut up." The man in gray wheezed. "I ask, you answer. Who are you?"

"Since I am about to die, what can it hurt? I am Lynch, Warlock and Executioner, Dragonrider and Thief."

"You killed my family," the man in gray stated in a voice that was already lifeless.

"Perhaps," Lynch acknowledged. "I kill a lot of people."

"Why?"

Lynch considered that for a long moment, then shrugged. "It's just what I do. And," he added as an afterthought, "I'm good at it."

"Now you'll die for it," the man in gray said coldly. He steadied himself for the final thrust.

"Wait," Lynch said.

It was more of an order than a request. Despite the hatred which burned in his eyes, the man in gray stayed his hand.

"Since I am about to die, I'd like to know who you are."

The man in gray snorted, and blood erupted from his nose in a fine spray. Flecks of it stained the worn lapel of Lynch's duster and peppered his cheeks. He didn't flinch.

"I just want to know who killed me, that's all. Before…"

The man in gray nodded in understanding. "Before I die and my name dies with me. You know the Dark Magic will kill me soon enough."

He hesitated, and Lynch thought he had lost that last gamble. Then the man in gray blinked back tears.

"My family name is Roark. I was hired to hunt you down, but I'd have done it for free. I'm Ned Roark"

"Ned Roark," Lynch repeated very softly. He slowly raised his left hand and laid it on Ned Roark's grizzled cheek, and Roark knew he had lost. With his thumb Lynch tenderly wiped away the tears which trickled down through the beard stubble and washed a trail through the grime.

"Ned Roark," he repeated. Roark felt the crushing weight of the spell which Lynch cast using his own name. Lynch casually reached inside his cloak and withdrew a long knife, then plunged it into Ned Roark's stomach. Ned tried futilely to slide his sword home, but he found he couldn't move a muscle. A long, sighing moan escaped his trembling lips. Lynch angrily knocked Roark's blade aside, ignorant of the gash it tore in the side of his neck.

"You're a fool, Ned Roark. Never tell anyone your true birth name," he slammed the smaller man backwards into the opposite wall and held him upright. "Tell me, Ned Roark, who hired you?"

"Elander," Roark groaned. He looked down at the haft of the knife which protruded from his stomach. All his strength ran out with his life's blood. Tears of frustration welled up in his eyes. "Goddammit. Thirty years I trailed your sorry ass. But it don't even matter that I failed. They'll keep comin' forever. One of 'em will nail you, you murderin' son of a bitch."

A shower of ice rained down on them. Lynch glance upward, irritated. He caught the flash of a shadow as it hurtled over the abyss and disappeared. He grunted an obscenity, then grabbed Roark by the collar and dragged him out of the chasm. To his surprise, the smaller man was still alive and conscious when they reached the snowy plain. A crimson trail marked their passage.

Roark's words in the chasm cut through the fog in Lynch's brain. The smaller man had said "they" would keep coming. He released Roark's cloak and the smaller man dropped to the frozen snow with a lifeless thump. His head lolled to one side. Lynch frantically shook him.

"Who will keep coming forever?"

Roark smiled a sickly smile. He whispered something. Lynch bent down closer to hear

"Who are you? I mean, who are you, really?"

Lynch threw back his head and roared with laughter.

"Tell me who you are," Roark whispered. "And I'll tell you…"

Roark sagged onto the carpet of snow, and Lynch bent low over him, cursing under his breath.

"You won't die on me yet, maggot." He touched his hand to Roark's brow and let some of his life force flow into the mortally wounded man, though it weakened him alarmingly. Roark's eyes flew open in sudden agony.

"You'll tell me what I want to know," Lynch said. "Or I'll keep you just barely alive until you starve to death."

He slid three of his fingers through the cut into Roark's stomach.

"Sweet Mother of God!" Roark whimpered.

"Tell me," Lynch demanded.

"The *magii'ri*." he blurted. "Elander called on the *magii'ri*. I'm *magii'ri*. The Gray Hunters are comin' for you. Please god, just let me go."

Lynch released his hold on the smaller man and suddenly stood. So King Elander the Good had called on the *magii'ri,* the race of Warriors and Wizards chosen by the gods themselves to uphold their laws. He was in the big time now. The Gray Hunters were the most ruthless mercenaries in the World. His thoughts were interrupted by a sound from Roark.

"Who are you?" the dying man croaked.

Lynch grinned. "You don't give up, do you?"

"I'm dyin'. What difference would it make?" Roark begged.

Lynch sat behind the smaller man and almost lovingly took his head in his hands.

"Exactly. You're dying. Why should I tell you?"

As the moon rose, he casually broke Roark's neck and held the smaller man's head to his chest much as one would comfort a restless child, until he quit struggling. Lynch sat there until the last vestige of sunlight disappeared and under the full light of the moon he sliced open Roark's chest and removed his heart. He muttered the necessary words, and while the pale stars winked at him from the distant heavens, Lynch ate it.

He awoke later beside the burned out ashes of his campfire and sat shivering in his bedroll. The light of the moon reflected off the stark whiteness of the snow covered tundra to give the landscape a surreal glow. Branches extending from fir trees became the curved claws of Dragons, and distant clumps of oakbrush seemed to shift position like a pack of wolves closing in on their prey. Lynch blinked his weary eyes. The chase had taken much out of him, physically and emotionally. The ritual at the end of it was designed to replenish his strength and make him even more powerful than before, but he didn't feel it. As a matter of fact, he felt strangely diminished. His mind was fuzzy and he found it difficult to think clearly. Things he had known for a hundred years eluded him now. He wondered for a moment if eating the heart of the fallen *magii'ri* Warrior had the opposite effect of what was intended, and even now he felt that his power was draining out of him and he had no way to stem the flow. The moonlight paled noticeably, and Lynch cast a curious eye heavenward. The night was still cloudless and nothing obstructed the moon, but the darkness grew more oppressive by the minute.

Lynch grudgingly shrugged out of his blankets and rose to gather fuel. The frigid night air hit him like a solid wall and he cursed through his clenched teeth. The truth was he was tired. He couldn't argue that. He was tired of running, tired of scheming, and goddamned tired of freezing his ass off on that godforsaken frozen plain. And, he thought, maybe that bullet had scrambled his brains a bit. He laid the wood in a haphazard formation and stirred up the coals under it. As he did, a shadow swept over him, and he froze. His eyes darted from side to side, but he saw nothing. He casually stretched and glanced overhead. A whisper of a shape floated across the face of the moon, and he relaxed.

Smoke rose from the pile of wood while Lynch waited impatiently for it to catch. He huddled back under his bedroll. He needed to make water, but he was loathe to leave the warmth of his blankets again. He wanted to be gone from this place, back to a city, any city, where he could have a hot bath, a hotter woman and a meal he didn't have to cook himself. A bed would be nice too, he thought, maybe with two or three women to keep him company. Another shadow flickered over him, and Lynch distinctly felt a light whiff of displaced air. The fir branches didn't stir. He leaned forward and blew on the embers of the fire. He could strike it with magic, but that would drain the strength he was only gradually rebuilding. A guttural croak made him lurch to his feet and unsheathe his long sword.

*Just a raven,* he thought. But it was still hours until dawn, and whatever made that noise had sounded bigger. A whole lot bigger. He turned a slow circle and scanned the sky. Just as he had begun to chide himself for behaving like a schoolgirl his survival instinct kicked in once again. He dropped on the hard packed snow and rolled, then thrust his sword upward as the moon was blotted out by a triangular shape at least a dozen feet across. The shocked Wizard slashed at the black shape and felt the jar of steel against bone and sinew, and warm black blood rained down upon him. The creature above him bellowed in pain as it swooped skyward, then faltered and dropped a hundred yards out in the clearing. Lynch didn't bother lunging to his feet. He simply rolled through the snow and frantically hurled a spell at his smoldering fire. It burst into flames as more than a dozen of the hovering creatures squawked in alarm and rose, wings flapping, into the night sky.

Lynch expelled a great sigh of relief, but his relief was short lived when the creature he had wounded advanced upon the camp. The Wizard grabbed a pine knot and commanded it to burst into flame, then held his flaming torch aloft. The beast hissed in alarm and backed out of the circle of light thrown by the torch. The beast was careful to stay well out of the light, and all Lynch could see was the gleam of light reflected in its eyes. His fear was rapidly being replaced by a deep, burning, unreasonable anger, and when he was enveloped in the throes of such a mood the Wizard Lynch was a formidable adversary. His lips curled in an answering snarl each time the beast hissed at him.

Lynch thrust the torch at the beast and it hissed loudly and jumped back. As it did, a gout of fresh blood erupted from the wound in its chest, leaving an obscene trail in the virgin snow. The beast was weakening and Lynch's desire for retribution was strong, but he felt exposed when he gauged the distance to his fire. He retreated, and the beast sank down in the snow. Lynch dragged a good sized log back to his camp site, all the while swiveling his head around to keep watch.

He built up a roaring fire, and watched as the wounded beast dragged itself farther out into the deeper darkness. It was barely visible in the fading moonlight, and Lynch watched it closely. He sat down on his bedroll and raised his shaking hands in front of his face, then laughed and lowered them to his knees. His laughter died on his lips seconds later when more of the beasts began dropping from the night sky. The night was filled with the whistling of wings and the guttural calls of the beasts. But they did not attack. Instead they advanced upon the wounded beast. It heaved to its feet then promptly fell over. The others rushed it, and in seconds the night air was filled with a hideous crunching sound accompanied by growls and shrieks of rage as the hapless wounded beast was devoured by his comrades. Some devilish vagary would occasionally cause the firelight to flicker brighter, and one or the other of the beasts would raise a bloody snout to glare with red eyes in Lynch's direction before it lowered its head to resume feeding. Lynch gritted his teeth and settled in for a long night.

He held his sword at the ready position with both hands while the beasts enjoyed their grisly meal. After the initial rush of adrenaline subsided, Lynch analyzed his situation. He was utterly alone, thanks to the relentless pursuit of Ned Roark, hundreds of miles from another human being. And even if he had stumbled onto other people, it was highly doubtful they would help him. He actually wasn't sure he would, or even *could* ask for help. Not after the way he had lived his life. He also had no idea what kind of adversary he faced. They were nameless, faceless predators that dropped from the sky, but he knew that he should be able to identify them. He wracked his brain and several times felt that he had the answer on the tip of his tongue, only to forget it again.

Lynch chuckled. The sounds of the feeding frenzy stopped briefly, then immediately resumed.

"Out of the frying pan," Lynch whispered and chuckled again.

What the Hell, he mused. He had no one else to blame for the position he was in. He had gotten sloppy, that was when Ned Roark picked up his trail and he couldn't give him the slip. He had also become greedy, and that was when he decided to absorb the strength of Roark's spirit instead of just killing him. It was a mistake he didn't intend to repeat. The next time he would kill anyone who came hunting him at the first opportunity that presented itself, and if the opportunity was right, he'd perform the ritual. Otherwise he'd just have to be content with killing them. But he had to find a way out of his present situation first.

One of the beasts abruptly wheeled away from his dinner and stalked gracefully around the perimeter of Lynch's camp. It was careful to stay out of the light, following the edge of light like a physical boundary. In moments it was joined by several others. Lynch lunged to his feet and clutched his sword with whitening knuckles. He turned a slow semicircle in time with the dim shadows that circled his camp, waiting for an attack. It became quite obvious the beasts would not penetrate the circle of light that ringed his camp. At least not just yet.

Lynch grinned, and it was a frightening, inhuman sight. They thought he was helpless. They thought he would cower in fear until they chose to attack. They had no idea what kind of enemy the Dark Wizard Lynch could be.

With an inarticulate battle cry bursting from his lips Lynch shrugged out of his duster and charged across the barren snow. The beasts looked stupidly at the man running across the snow as if they couldn't comprehend being attacked by such an insignificant creature. Lynch bared his teeth and delivered a vicious backhanded blow with his sword that completely severed the wing of the first beast he encountered. A guttural croak burst from its jaws as it fell sideways, vainly flapping its one remaining wing. Those closest to it dove upon it, driven by mindless bloodlust. Lynch spun and drove his blade upwards into the throat of the next beast. He wrenched the blade free with a loud grunt, then suddenly dove to the ground and rolled to avoid the wide open jaws of one of the recovering beasts. It drove its pointy snout into the snow, milliseconds behind the frantically rolling Wizard. He sensed a slight hesitation in the attack and thrust his sword skyward just in time to drive it into the beast's open mouth and out the back of its skull. His sword was wrenched from his hands when the beast reared up on its hind legs.

"Oh, shit," Lynch whispered.

Once again he lunged to his feet and sprinted back towards his fire. One of the enraged beasts lurched after him, then recoiled with a bellow of pain as he neared the fire. The skin on the beast's face and neck shriveled and blistered from the light of the fire and it fell backwards into the snow. Lynch dropped to the snow next to his fire and rolled onto his back, steam billowing from his open mouth. The blood was singing in his ears and a strange exhilaration filled his being. His insane laughter echoed from the scrubby trees. He rolled to his hands and knees and tried to catch his breath as another paroxysm of laughter shook his body. Lynch slowly regained control of himself as he felt what little strength he had left seeping from his body. He collapsed into his blankets and lay there shivering through the remainder of the night while the surviving creatures devoured their fallen brothers.

The flock of bloodthirsty beasts took to the air and circled once then flew to the west before the first rays of light brightened the east. Lynch sat huddled in his blankets, bleary eyed from fatigue and with a massive headache pounding his temples. He forced his tired brain to function.

What were they? Where did they come from? In all his many years, Lynch had never even heard of such a creature. Or had he? He did know what they were, he just couldn't place it. So why did they surface now? To harass him? Or was he just a target of opportunity? Deep inside he knew that he should know those things, but it felt like pieces of him were missing.

He fashioned a bowl from green bark and scooped up snow to melt for tea. While the snow melted he walked out to examine the remains of the beasts. The hair on the back of his neck stood up and gooseflesh rose on his arms as he neared the kill site. Bits of leather-like skin were scattered about and a few fragments of bone protruded through the snow. The trampled snow was a deep, oily black. The carnage at the kill site was even more complete than he had imagined. The only remains of the beasts were the skulls and the backbones. He paced from one end of a carcass to the other. From head to tail, it had been over ten feet long.

Lynch retrieved his sword and wheeled around to return to his camp, but before he had gone two steps he reversed his course, dropped his breeches and urinated on the remains. Only then did he return to his fire. He hastily gulped his hot tea and squandered more of his magical energy conjuring up a spell for endurance. He wanted to get as far away as possible before nightfall. As he packed up his meager camp, the gleam of his captured long rifle caught his eye. Ned Roark's rifle, crafted for the Gray Hunters by the most skilled craftsmen in the World. He thoughtfully hefted it then reluctantly wedged it in the crotch of a tree with a scrap of fur concealing it. It was a beautiful weapon, but totally useless without powder and lead. He had neither, and in all his years of searching he had not found the formula to make gunpowder. He was nothing, if not practical. He took only what he had to have to survive and abandoned the rest.

Lynch walked directly towards the south. Early in the morning he fought the urge to break into a run, but by noon he no longer had the strength to either run or fight the crazy urge to do so that still lay within his mind. He slogged along through the snow in a dazed state, shedding layers of clothing as the day grew warmer and sweat beaded his brow. He stopped often to drink from his waterskin and to fish out another piece of dried meat to chew on. An hour before dusk he was thoroughly exhausted.

As he gathered fuel for a long night, he calculated the distance he had walked that day, and figured he had walked roughly fifteen miles. Fifteen miles! Gliding along on the air currents the bloody beasts could travel that distance in less than an hour! Anger flared up within him, and when had unloaded his last armful of firewood he made one more trip into the densest forest to gather ten long, slender poles. He built up his fire and sharpened one end of the poles, then tied a crosspiece on each end to make a picket. He laid the pickets in the snow and tied a long length of rope to each then counter weighted them with a log suspended from a nearby tree. When he tripped it, the pickets would rise to a forty five degree angle. They could harass him and keep him from sleep, but it would cost them!

At midnight Lynch sat morosely brooding in his blankets, adding wood to the fire at regular intervals. His supper of a thin soup made with dried meat sat soddenly in his stomach like a lump of uncooked dough. He longed for a thick juicy steak, piled high with steaming mushrooms and sweet potatoes with a hot apple pie for dessert. A sudden spurt of saliva erupted in his mouth, and he slammed his tin cup down in frustration. How in the Hell had he gotten himself into this mess? He sighed. He had chosen his path five centuries ago. As a youth he had longed for eternal life, to drink in the pleasures of the flesh while his peers withered and faded away. And his wish had been granted, but at a terrible price. The sensations he had experienced, the tastes of life he had indulged in, were all addictive and he longed for more until it consumed him. His life had become a rat chasing its tail. His tastes grew more exotic, his demands more extreme with each passing decade. And no matter how much he indulged, he always wanted more. He laughed bitterly. How ironic was it that he, Lynch, now sat in a goddamned snow bank and yearned for something as mundane as a hot meal?

The next thing he knew he was lying face down in the snow with a ringing in his ears and something warm and sticky running down his neck. His head buzzed and his vision blurred. The bastards were back! Then it hit him. They were losing their fear of fire. Rage flowed through him.

"You sons of bitches! You want some of me? Come on then!" He leaped to his feet and found his counter weight ropes.

"Come on," he said under his breath. "Come on back for another piece of ol' Lynch."

He searched the night sky, and finally saw a few flickering shadows wheeling and darting among the stars. Several of them split off from the group and headed his way.

"That's it," he pleaded. "Just keep coming…a little farther. A little more…come on."

Two were gliding in on a perfect plane. Lynch grinned. This was better than a goddamned steak! He gauged the distance and released the counter weights. His first picket slammed into position and Lynch actually laughed with glee as the beasts flared their wings in a vain attempt to stop. Both impaled themselves as they went down squawking amid the sound of splintering wood and thrashing wings. The points of the pickets penetrated the beasts completely as their struggles destroyed Lynch's newest weapon and they wheeled away from each other, biting futilely at the main beams which still protruded from their chests. They turned on each other in their agony, and with each graceful dip of their slender necks blood spurted from a newly opened wound. Lynch watched eagerly until neither beast moved any longer. Only then did he allow himself to explore the wound on the back of his head with trembling fingers, and he still kept a wary eye out for more attackers. He found a goose egg the size of his fist and a three inch gash which still oozed blood. No matter, he thought. He'd bagged two more of the bastards. A little blood was a small price to pay.

As before, the remaining creatures circled like vultures, then spiraled down to feast on their comrades. Lynch thought briefly of slipping away while they fed, but as soon as he stepped out of the circle of firelight one of the beasts hopped into the air and circled that side of his camp. He hastily stepped back into the light. So, he thought, they are intelligent, at least to some degree. That revelation did nothing to improve his mood. Lynch spent yet another sleepless night mentally sorting through all the creatures he had heard of in reality and in myth. His thoughts were accompanied by the hideous crunching, tearing sounds as the beasts polished off their fallen comrades. *Dragons? No, not dragons. Not gryphons, either. Giant bats? Maybe, but still not quite.*

He felt that the answer was right on the tip of his brain, but just out of reach. And even as hardened as he was, Lynch had no desire to delve too deeply into that convoluted mass. What he needed, he finally decided as dawn streaked the eastern sky, was a library. Too bad there was no such thing within a thousand miles. Nearly delirious from lack of sleep, Lynch laughed at that until tears rolled down his cheeks. The beasts glared at him one last time and he thrust his middle finger skyward in a timeless gesture of contempt. The beasts flew back toward the west. He broke camp and staggered off to the south

By midday the snow was noticeably shallower, and the air held a hint of warmth. But Lynch knew his progress was pitifully slow. The melting snow sucked at his booted feet and sapped his energy even faster than before. He had to rest. Rest, or go mad from sleep deprivation. His mind wandered. Once, in a different time, he had seen a man go nearly mad from lack of sleep. The men of that time traveled impossible distances in horseless carriages and guns and ammunition were commonplace. There were Demons there, but most of the people walked with blank faces, unaware of the evil that ran rampant right under their noses. Unaware, or maybe they just didn't care. Demons of a different sort than those he now faced, and they made his own skill at starting trouble pale by comparison. He chuckled. At least these Demons attacked a man face to face. They didn't hide behind catchy slogans or false promises. With a start he realized he was sitting on a snow free boulder warmed by the spring sun which had just reached its zenith. He built a fire and banked it with a huge fallen log, so big he could barely roll it into the fire. Then he slept.

He slept hard, so deep in slumber a passerby might have thought him dead. The chill of the evening awoke him, and he huddled deeper into his blankets. Then he bolted upright. Sundown. Dark. The Slayers would be back. His fire still smoldered, and he piled smaller branches on it until it crackled and roared. The sleep had done him good, but he felt logy and a headache settled in at the base of his skull.

*Wait just one goddamned second.* The Slayers. He knew what they were. He had no idea how he knew, but he did know. He involuntarily thought back to the *other time*, the time which he didn't know was coming or had already passed. That man, the one he had watched go crazy from lack of sleep, had told him many things. He wasn't actually supposed to talk to anyone, but Lynch had never been one to respect another's rules. The man was already twitchy by that time. The slightest noise would cause him to lurch around and stare with bleary eyes. Finally he had just laid down and couldn't be roused. Lynch wondered absently if he had died like that. What had amazed Lynch then and now was that the man *knew* him. He shook himself. What the Hell was he thinking?

He faded away again, and when his senses returned it was dark. His befuddled brain took that in and processed it. He forced himself to concentrate. He needed sleep, which he would never get at night. The solution, therefore, was to travel at night with the protection of a torch, as long as that lasted, and sleep during the day. He would regain his strength, and with his strength he would regain his power. And when he had regained his full power, *nothing* could stand in his way.

He clambered to his feet and found a couple of solid pine knots. He lit one from the fire and resolutely started out again, leaving the fire burning. Perhaps, he thought hopefully, the Slayers would be attracted to the firelight like moths. But that hope was dashed when he heard the telltale whistling of wings in the air above him. Panic rose within him, but he choked it down and forced himself to hold his course towards the south. But he had only gone perhaps a mile when he heard the rushing of wings and a light breeze ruffled his hair. He involuntarily ducked his head, and the bulk of the beast whooshed over him. He quickened his pace, and another beast dived on him, so close he could feel the heat of its body and smell the fetid odor of decay that clung to its leathery hide.

Lynch broke into a trot, holding his torch high like one of the champions he had heard of from yet another time. His breath came in gasps and sweat plastered his clothes to his body. It was an impossible pace to maintain, yet the beasts easily kept up. Another one dived for him and clipped the torch with its talons. It squawked in pain and rose again, but Lynch could sense that it was not seriously cowed by the flames. His legs were filled with molten lead and his lungs burned with each labored breath. The words sprang to his lips without conscious thought, and Lynch muttered them, even if it be the death of him. The power of the Dark Magic exploded within him as another tiny part of him died with it.

Strength radiated out to his extremities, and the burning in his chest was quenched. His legs pumped like twin pistons, spraying mud and snow behind him. Conscious thought deserted him. He was a machine, fueled by Dark Magic. His eyes noted when the scrub brush turned into dwarf trees and his brain processed the information, but it meant nothing. He heard the beasts crashing through the uppermost branches and sensed their anger, but still his legs beat their staccato rhythm. The whistling of their wings became fainter as they gained altitude to clear the trees, and still Lynch ran on. He ran on long after a mortal man would have crashed to the ground, vomiting blood, with his muscles twitching in death throes. Exposed roots clawed at him, rocks sliced his boots to shreds and low lying branches whipped across his face. He ran on all through that hellish night and was totally unaware when the dwarf trees slowly gave way to the towering pines and firs of a black timber forest. Finally, as morning approached, Lynch became slightly aware again. The next thing he knew, he was falling.

He awoke with a ringing in his ears and the brassy taste of blood in his mouth, lying face down on a bed of springy moss that smelled faintly of mold. He tested each of his extremities with a groan of pain and found that he could still move, but his muscles ached with a frightening intensity. Lynch groaned loudly and rolled over. Far above him there was a small square shaft of light. Where the Hell was he? He closed his eyes and tried to remember.

He remembered running like he had never run before, farther and faster than any mortal. And he remembered falling. He sat up and looked around him. He had been running from something totally unnatural, something so fierce it defied description and even now dread ran fingers of ice along his backbone. Then it came back to him. He remembered falling, and thinking at the last second that he was about to die a disgraceful death in some accident that wouldn't even be discovered for a thousand years. Then he had struck something which yielded to his weight. There had been the shrieking of a rusty pulley, his descent had slowed, then he had crashed to the ground and everything went black. He stared at the shattered remnants of a hand elevator scattered around him. One beam was still securely tied to a tattered hemp rope. He looked upward again. Impossible. It was at least three hundred feet down. A pebble struck his shoulder, and dust wafted down the shaft.

Lynch felt his breath catch in his throat. They were there, and they knew where he was. A faintly familiar, guttural croaking sound echoed down the shaft accompanied by an eager whine. The scrabbling, grating sounds of steel hard claws on solid rock supported his sudden fear. They were trying to dig into the shaft.

He had once considered himself nearly fearless and superior to anything he might encounter. But now his self confidence was shattered and his amazing ego lay in tatters. He had never encountered anything like the beasts that trailed him. They were totally unrelenting, nearly without fear, and savagely skilled at destruction. Lynch grinned. They were kind of like him. He groaned loudly and stood up. He had one thing in his favor. They had no idea who they were messing with.

Lynch studied the opening in the shaft and gauged it against the outlines of the writhing bodies of the beasts as they tried to dig in. He estimated they would have to double the size of the shaft before they could resume their hunt. Claws and teeth against solid rock. He had some time, now he needed distance.

The first few steps were exquisite agony, and Lynch made a mental note of it to apply that principle to his own keen interest in torture. He found one of his torches where it had landed after the flight down the shaft and cast an illumination spell. Even that effort left him winded, and Lynch once again felt the thrill of fear. His power was nearly exhausted.

"This may be the end of the road, old boy," he muttered half aloud. "What a waste. What a colossal fucking waste!" He clenched his fists in impotent rage.

He was close, so tantalizingly close, to the crowning glory of centuries of destruction. All of his plans were coming together, his allies were firmly in place and growing in power. He had spent hundreds of years honing his own skills just for the moment nearly at hand, and it was going to be spoiled by a handful of brainless creatures driven solely by instinct and bloodlust. Kind of like some people he had known. Lynch giggled. *Dammit, I'm going loopy*, he thought.

A larger fragment of rock struck the floor of the cavern with a dull thump. Lynch stared dully at the dark shapes of the beasts as they busily enlarged the opening into his hole. Why had his plans unraveled? It was so hard to think! A name kept floating about just out of reach. Then he had it. It was because of…Roark. Ned Roark. Before that, everything had been fine.

"Well, Mr. Ned Roark," he exclaimed into the gloom. "You are going to pay for this. Or did you already? No matter. I'm going to hunt down your entire family, no, I'm going to hunt down every single person you ever associated with and wipe them off the face of the World. That, Mr. Ned Roark, is a promise!"

Lynch smoothed down his hair, straightened his disheveled clothes, and resolutely walked into the overpowering darkness. As he stumbled along, he focused on one thing. *Roark*. He had no way of knowing that, far above him, the light of the moon was steadily growing dimmer.

# CHAPTER TWO

**F**OR THIRTY YEARS I had wandered from the Eastern Provinces to the Land of Ice, seeking knowledge for the great Warrior King Elander. I was the seventh of seven Scribes, sent out to gather every scrap of knowledge discovered by the various inhabitants of the World. It seems a daunting task now, even to me.

Perhaps I should explain. Scribes are not men, nor Warriors, nor Wizards. Neither are we elves or dwarves. We Scribes are an anomaly, a race apart. To be blunt, we are an accident of nature, freaks, neither male or female, slight of stature and mild in manner. We also possess an enormous capacity to assimilate, comprehend and store knowledge, and knowledge is the most heady elixir which King Elander found he could not live without. After the First Ogre Wars, Elander uncovered one of my kin in the rubble of a burned out ogre encampment, badly injured but alive. He nursed Trib back to health and learned from him. In due time, he discovered all of us, and bade us swear fealty to him. It seemed like a good idea at the time, to trade our services for protection. I am Nish, the Seventh Scribe.

I was working in a basement library deep beneath the Hall of Tombs in the Land of Ice, led there by my nose, one could say. I often walked through the Hall, picking up scraps of knowledge from the decaying memories of those great men preserved in sheets of crystal clear ice. It is not well known, but memories live well beyond the death of their owners, and we Scribes have a talent for finding them. As I said, I went there often.

On that particular day, I was tracing down a faint bit of information from the tomb of the Warrior King Bern, a great bear of a man killed by the ogres at the start of the war some five hundred years earlier. It wasn't much to go on, and I'm quite proud I could decipher it. I stood there gazing into King Bern's limpid brown eyes, which, it was rumored, were the main reason he was able to spread so many pretty sets of feminine thighs. And that was the reason he had sired such a great number of heirs that the country was thrown into total chaos after his untimely demise at the wrong end of a giant's lance. But I digress. The memory which floated about that day was that of a library. I saw a clear picture of it in my mind and was able to determine the type of stone in the walls. I knew immediately it matched the stone of the Tombs. From there it was only a small matter to pick out the clues and find a tiny fissure in the living rock of the Hall. From that crack in the stone issued the scent of parchment and leather. It was the intoxicating scent of books that had lain unopened for centuries, books filled with the knowledge of history, prophecy and swordcraft, and the most delicious scent of all; *magic.*

I found the trigger which opened the door to reveal a long, winding staircase carved into the rock itself and descended to sate my appetite among those glorious stacks of books. I spent three years there, and when I was done feasting on knowledge I felt as gluttonous and bloated as if I had feasted on exotic meats and rich pastries the entire time. The servant boy sent to be my assistant brought me the final tome, and I examined it with relish, like one receiving a fine liqueur or a particularly delicious dessert after a heavy meal. I was anxious to report to Elander, for this had indeed been a rich find. But something about this book was not quite right. I looked at the front. No title. I looked at the back and the spine. Nothing. Then I ran my hands down the fine leather of the jacket and the words leapt into my mind with a flash brighter than summer lightning. *Prophecies of Alanna, Mistress of Aard.*

Suddenly it was as if I had fasted for months and this book was a seven course meal and fine wine combined into one. My mind fairly ached to devour it. I read and re-read each page lovingly, caressing the parchment like a lover's skin. When I finally laid the book down, two full days had passed in an instant. My skin was suddenly clammy and cold, drenched in a fine sheen of sweat. The book contained everything about the one man who would finally defeat the ogres and their allies, including the half-men of Haan, the giants and Wizards of the Dark. Even the Black Queen Mordant would be defeated. And there was more. The book contained information about another being, a Warlock who had slipped from memory hundreds of years ago. He was a powerful man who fed off the power of his victims until he was nearly invincible, one with the shadows. He was even more powerful than the Black Queen. Even he would be defeated. But that would never happen if the book fell into the wrong hands. It was with great sorrow that I ripped the pages from the book and fed them into the fire one by one, until only charred ashes remained. Oh, another Scribe could have read the ashes, but all the Scribes were loyal to King Elander, the Good. This find I would report to him in person and the words were burned into my memory.

*A time of sorrow and despair will cast a heavy shadow across the land. Evil will surface hidden by an innocent face and many will lose their lives. The End of the World will seem close at hand through famine, fires, floods and the greatest destruction of all, war. But the blood of the Ancients will be refreshed in a time of dire need, and a hero will come forth. Look to the brigands and the highwaymen, for only those who live in the shadows can understand the Darkness.*

I turned to leave as a shadow fell over my table. There was an instant of pain and a bright light, and my world went dark.

I awoke with a throbbing in my oversized skull and complete darkness around me. I thought for a moment I was blind. I tried to run my hand over my face and realized that I was hanging by my arms from something not even visible above me and my feet were bound with chain. A faint shadow swept in front of me, and I drew the scent in.

Not good. My catalog of scents revealed the shadow to be a Nightrider, servant of Haan, the Keeper of the Abyss and a footsoldier of the Black Queen.

"You know who I am?" the voice was dry and lifeless.

I scented again. "A High Priest to the Black Queen."

He chuckled. His eyes glowed red. "Yes. Do you know how long I searched for the book which you destroyed?"

I was asked a direct question which had no visible ramifications to my King. "Eleven years, and two hundred sixteen days."

I never saw the blow coming. Sudden pain exploded deep in my abdomen and radiated outward. Dark spots floated across the lightning which flashed over the inside of my closed eyelids. Scribes were never meant to be fighters.

"That's right, freak. Eleven goddamned years, and you burned it to a crisp when I was so close I could actually taste it. Now you're going to tell me what was in it."

"No."

"What?"

"I cannot. That is a direct contradiction of my code. I swore fealty to King Elander, only he can assimilate my knowledge unless my existence is in danger. When he is done, then I can divulge more."

"I thought you might say that."

Sparks flew along the stone floor as he struck a light into a pile of tinder, which I happened to be standing on. It did not appear to have been an accident.

"Your existence is damn sure in danger. You burned the book. Now suffer the same fate."

My feet were jerked out from under me as my legs were raised so I hung upside down. I could already feel the heat from the fire as smoke choked me. But, far above I saw a solitary star. Time. I needed time to work the spell.

The Gatekeeper grunted as he released a huge wheel and lowered me with metallic clicks closer and closer to the fire. Sweat poured freely down my face. I focused myself inward. The spell. Where was it? Where had I found it? My eyelashes burned off and my bald head began to steam. I heard heavy bootsteps and a new voice, loud, deep and authoritative.

"Idiot! Raise him up! If you burn his brains his memories die with him."

More metallic clicks sounded accompanied by a blessed coolness as I was raised back up from the fire. The spell I was looking for had come from a dungeon…on the Isle of Serpents. I had it. Now for only a few more moments while I crafted the spell. I was flipped once more, and lowered feet first into the fire. My boots had been removed, and I could smell my scorching flesh immediately. It was so hard to think! I dredged up my teaching from the Dragon Warriors and ignored the pain while my feet cooked. Then I was lifted once again and by some strange wheel like apparatus I was rotated away from the fire. My feet were a full yard off the ground. I drew a shuddering breath and regained my composure. The cavern was well lit now. It wasn't long before I wished for darkness again.

The one with the heavy boots stomped over to me. His face was even with mine, which I calculated made him approximately nine feet tall, and from the breadth of his shoulders, about five hundred pounds. I stared into eyes as dead as the charred flesh of my feet. His protruding jaws flashed wide open as he howled into my face. Flecks of spittle wet my cheeks and stung my eyes. His breath gagged me.

"Nothin' better than the smell of roasting flesh," he said into the deafening silence which followed his howl.

The Dragon Warrior spell was working. I could no longer feel anything below my waist. Now I could concentrate on the spell I really needed.

"You can't eat him!" the Gatekeeper yelled.

That revelation made it difficult to concentrate, even though if all went well I would no longer need my old body. It still bothered me to know that the vehicle which had carried me for two centuries would end up as giant fodder.

The giant spun and struck the High Priest with a back handed blow which sent him flying into the rock wall. He tumbled bonelessly into a heap on the floor, blood trickling from his ears. The giant turned back to me and slammed a hand into my crotch. The perplexed look on his face showed just how little he knew about Scribes, for where he had expected to grab a handful of testicles there was…nothing. Nothing at all. In the next instant I knew just how little that mattered, as he wrapped his hand around my pelvis and began to squeeze.

"What did the book say?"

My pelvis snapped with a sound like a dry branch breaking. It was a totally inane question, with an answer he was surely not going to like. This was not going well.

"Books don't say anything," I whispered. *Goddamnit, what was that spell?* I felt pain now, even the Dragon Warriors couldn't have drowned out that pain. It was quite indescribable.

"I can only answer the question you ask me if it does not endanger my King." I reached out with my mind. The brute's name was Tarlow. That could prove useful.

"Do you really want to play games with me?" Tarlow asked. "What do you know of my people's reputation?"

*By god, would he ever stop asking questions?*

"I am bound by oath, programmed, if you will, to answer the direct questions which you may ask me if it does not endanger my King." I gritted my teeth against waves of pain. "Giant; a race of people so named because of their unnatural size and inhuman strength. Aligned with Haan and his followers, the giants were nearly exterminated by the Dragon Warriors. Those that remain often work as mercenaries, selling their services to the highest bidder." I cast a sideways glance at him and smothered a grunt of pain. "I'd say you work for the Black Queen, and I know of no games we could play."

"You're kinda funny," he said. "I'd almost like to keep you for a pet. I could drag out what's left of you at parties to perform tricks for my guests."

He carefully examined his jagged, dirt encrusted fingernails, then punched me in the ribs three times. My ribs caved in and all traces of air were blown from my lungs. The force of the blows spun me around and he slammed the edge of his hand into my back. Tarlow the Giant watched patiently as I swung there in exquisite agony, trying in vain to drag air back into my tortured lungs. I was quite sure that all of my ribs were broken. I dragged in a breath, finally, and felt a sodden sensation in my chest. A punctured lung, no doubt. It was becoming exceedingly difficult to remember exactly what I was trying to do. I tried to swing my legs and felt a grating sensation in my lower back. My back was broken. That would explain the sudden cessation of all sensation below my waist. It was much more effective than the Dragon Warrior spell, and no doubt much more permanent.

"This is a game we can play. Tell me what was in the book and I'll stop. Then you'll quietly bleed to death. No more pain."

"I can only answer direct questions…"

"This is getting tiresome," the giant growled. He slammed a serrated blade into my midsection and I heard a ripping sound. "What is in the book you burned?"

My vision blurred. I heard a splashing sound and knew he had struck an artery. I had to have a few seconds to focus.

"*The Prophecies of Alanna, Mistress of Aard.* There is a man already sired, who carries the bloodline of Malachi. His spawn will destroy Darkness forever. And," I looked that beast directly in the eye, "one of Malachi's blood will kill you first."

The giant backed away, considering that information. I dredged up the last of my physical strength and finished the spell. I was immediately looking down on everything, including my own battered, bloody body. I rose towards the vent in the top of the cavern.

The giant spun back towards me and with one blow he cut my uninhabited body in two. Then I was free, soaring through the night air, searching for a host as the light of the moon was slowly blotted out as if by a giant hand.

# CHAPTER THREE

Lorn Graywullf shuffled tiredly through the stubby sage and ankle high buffalo grass, at the head of a line of men equally as tired as he. Even though his bones ached from physical exhaustion, he could have dealt with that easily enough. But the fatigue went deeper than that. He felt worn out right down to the bottom of his soul. He stopped and looked back down the line. Each footfall kicked up a puff of dust. A column of the bitter stuff rose like a flag in the still air and hovered over his men, choking them, stinging their eyes and burning their throats. He knew that. It felt like he had a wad as big as his fist in each nostril.

"This is a lovely country," his lieutenant and best friend, Jacob Sipowicz, remarked with his ever present grin tarnished by a smear of dirt.

"Ain't it though," Lorn replied. "Makes you wonder why in Hell anyone would want it enough to fight over it."

"They wanted it bad enough to die for it."

"Did 'em a Hell of a lot of good too, didn't it?" Lorn asked bitterly.

He didn't wait for an answer. He just resumed plodding along. Jake watched him go for several long moments.

"I do believe I might retire here," he said to the next man.

"Yer a crazy bastard, Smilin' Jake," Bill McCurry said sourly.

Jake considered that. "Yer right. But I do enjoy myself. You, on the other hand, don't know a joke if it bites you on the sack."

"What's there to laugh at out here? Goddamn rebels killed sixteen of us, wounded maybe twenty more. Laid siege at us for so long we had to eat most of the goddamn horses and drink up nearly all the water before the Cap'n came up with a plan to roust 'em out. But they wouldn't give up until we slaughtered ever man jack of 'em. Now we might still die out here. What the Hell is so funny about that?" Bill fumed as he continued in Lorn's tracks. "The whole goddamn desert's goin' to be covered with stinking corpses."

Smilin' Jake watched him go as well, until he was nearly out of earshot. "But yer not dead yet."

Bill McCurry ignored him and plodded after the Captain.

Jake sighed and swung around in step with the next man, Jon Duvay, known to all as Ox. He was a great bear of a man with shoulders the breadth of an axe handle and arms the size of sapling trees. He was also the last of the four truebloods on the assignment.

"What do you think, Ox?" Smilin' Jake asked.

"I think yer crazy as a bedbug," Ox replied. He playfully clapped Jake across the shoulders, which nearly knocked the smaller man sprawling. "But it's good to have you along."

"Finally, someone who appreciates my good humor." Jake paused and gestured with both hands to encompass the barren hillside they stood upon. "Look at this view! I really am going to come back and build a little cabin here. Then, when we are all old and gray, you can come sit on my front stoop and look out on the endless, empty sea."

"That's the problem, you jackass," Ox retorted. "It's an *empty* sea. What I wouldn't give to see just one sail out there on one ship full of rancid salt pork and beans and old, stale water. Just one stinkin' sail."

"Like that one?" Smilin' Jake asked innocently.

Jon Duvay followed his pointing finger. "Cap'n!" He yelled excitedly. "A ship!"

Jake roared with laughter, while Ox barreled down the slope towards Lorn Graywullf, who had already spied the ship and was bringing his spyglass around to bear on it. What he saw did not improve his humor. The ship ran up a black flag, which meant that they had been spotted as well. *Spotted by a pirate ship and caught like sheep out in the open,* Graywullf thought. *Ain't life grand?*

He hastily considered his choices. Even the long rifles couldn't match the range of the ship's cannons, so making a stand on that empty hillside was out. There had been a thin line of green visible to his keen eyesight for the last three miles. It had to be a ravine, perhaps another mile or so ahead. It would offer scant cover and the possibility of an ambush if the pirates decided to pursue them. He made his decision.

"Double up the wounded on the horses!" He called back down the line.

Ox skidded to a stop in a cloud of dust. "What the Hell?"

"It's a pirate ship. We have to make a run for it."

"Run? Where the Hell are we gonna run to?"

"There's a ravine up ahead. Put all the wounded on horseback! Light a fire under yer asses!"

Smilin' Jake squinted into the glare of the sun just long enough to make out the garish skull and crossbones on the flag. He sprinted down to Graywullf, grinning from ear to ear, as the common bloods scrambled on horseback.

"How far do you reckon it is?"

Lorn took one look to make sure the common bloods were following orders, then he gauged the distance to the ship.

"Too far. They'll be in range before we hit the ravine."

The four truebloods gathered in a group as the first of the horsemen thundered by. Lorn noted with dismay that they had disobeyed his orders. Some of the horses carried three or four men.

Jake saw the direction of his hard stare. "Nothin' to be done about it now, Cap'n. They'd never have run that far afoot anyway. Last one to the ravine sucks eggs."

They wheeled as a unit and broke into a trot. Lorn noted with satisfaction that each of his friends checked the prime on their long rifles as they ran, making sure they were ready to return fire. The years of training as *magii'ri* Warriors served them well, and they caught up to the men on horseback within the half mile. The exhausted mounts were rapidly fading under the heavy loads they were being forced to carry.

"Don't let 'em stop!" Graywullf shouted. He hit the first mount across the butt with his rifle stock and forced the exhausted beast into a trot. The other three truebloods did the same, hazing and shouting at the half crazed horses to keep them in motion. The acrid dust rose up in choking clouds.

Graywullf heard the whine of the first approaching cannonball, then most of the sounds on that desolate hillside were drowned out by explosions. Two of the horses disappeared in a spray of red tinged smoke.

"Save yerselves!" Graywullf ordered the Truebloods. "Run, damn you! Don't stop!"

The four Truebloods emerged from the smoke and dust at a dead run.

"Don't look back," Graywullf gasped to himself. "Don't look back." He turned his head and saw only four horses running out of the dust. "You looked back." He muttered in disgust. He skidded to a stop and went down on one knee, bringing up his long rifle as he did. It was an impossibly long shot, but he had to try. The front bead danced and weaved with each gasping breath he took. He closed his eyes for a moment and went within himself. His shaking hands stilled and he drew in an easy deep breath, released half of it, sighted down the barrel and squeezed the trigger. The report almost caught him by surprise, just like it should. The heavy rifle jarred against his shoulder, and for several long moments he thought he had missed. Then one of the gunners on the pirate ship threw his hands up in the air and was flung to the deck. *That'll give them something to think about.*

He leaped to his feet and ran after his men. The volleys from the ship were ragged now, and most were wide of the mark by at least fifty feet. The gunners were no longer sighting, they just crouched behind the heavy cannons and touched off their shots at random. With great relief he saw the Trueblood *magii'ri* Warriors dive over the lip of the ravine to safety. Within moments he slid over the edge himself and lay there on his back sucking in great draughts of air. He automatically reloaded his rifle, dumping in a pre-measured charge of powder and topping it off with a conical lead bullet. He rammed it home as two of the horses stumbled over the edge of the ravine. One went down squealing and dumped its riders headlong into the rocks on the slope. It lunged to its feet, but one front leg dangled uselessly. Lorn caught the glare of white bone against the crimson splash of blood from the beast's mangled front leg. One of the riders struggled to his feet, but the other lay still, his head cocked at a crazy angle to his shoulders.

"*Son of a bitch!*" Graywullf shouted. He lunged to his feet and kicked a small bush to pieces. The truebloods watched stoically. They were used to outbursts from their volatile captain, as well as sudden and violent death. The common bloods, however, stared in wide eyed amazement. It was obvious they were close to going into shock.

"Whoever he is, he's going to pay," Graywullf promised. "The captain of that ship is a dead man."

He crawled back to the lip and scanned the deck of the distant ship. Even with his naked eye he could see amazing differences in the size of the figures on the ship. He steadied his dented and scratched spyglass to confirm the hunch he had.

"What do you see?" Smilin' Jake asked at his elbow.

"It ain't good. Looks like they have two, make that three giants on board."

"Aw, shit," Ox blurted with a disgusted shake of his head.

"That's right, Johnny boy," Jake taunted with a huge grin. "Somebody that's actually bigger'n you are."

Lorn steadied the spyglass once again. "Son of a bitch. This is not your run of the mill pirate ship, boys. They also have two mountain trolls on board, the regular crew, looks like, and…a woman."

"What?" the three truebloods said almost in unison.

"A witch," Bill McCurry said darkly. "Has to be. They wouldn't let any other woman on board."

"Magic," Lorn muttered distastefully.

"What about the captain?" Smilin' Jake asked, trying to change the subject.

"It always comes back to bite ya, don't it, Cap'n?" Bill McCurry said gloomily.

"Gods, Bill," Ox interrupted. "That was years ago. There ain't no curse on any of us."

"Everybody just shut up," Lorn ordered. "It don't matter if she is a witch. That ship is our only way out of here. They attacked us first, without provocation. So we're gonna take it."

He stowed his spyglass in a shirt pocket and turned back towards the ravine. A small stream glittered in the bottom. Lorn stood suddenly and caught the wounded horse. Her front leg flopped uselessly and stark white shards of bone showed plainly through the lacerated hide. He slid his knife from the sheath at his hip and drew it quickly across the horse's throat The mare dropped to her knees and slowly toppled over.

"You." He pointed to the common blood who had been riding the twitching horse. "Field dress this critter."

"Aw, shit," Ox repeated. "Horse meat again."

"Ox, you and Bill take all the waterskins and go down to the stream. Make sure it's fresh and refill the skins."

The two truebloods gathered the skins and took off down the slope.

"Come on, Jake. Let's go see what the mouth of this ravine looks like."

The two walked in silence just below the lip of the ravine until they were two hundred yards from the survivors.

"That was some shot you pulled off."

Lorn grunted. "I held four feet high. Must have been eight hundred yards."

"Closer to a thousand. What the hell did you do, double charge?"

"Yep," Lorn answered, matter of factly.

"Yer gonna blow that thing up in yer face one day," Jake said with a shake of his head. "Fowler warned us about that a hunnerd times."

"And who'll miss me?"

"Why, me and the boys would. And good old Marsten."

Marsten. Even the mention of the Wizard's name made a knot as big as his fist suddenly appear in Lorn's gut. He and his three comrades were *magii'ri* Warriors, descendants of five generations of the forgotten holy Warriors who's names were synonymous with sudden, violent death, blind justice, and short lifespans. The *magii'ri* were under the control of a High Wizard, who supposedly answered only to Aard, the Mountain God. But the line had deviated somehow with Marsten. His edicts had become twisted, his rules convoluted to serve his own purpose.

"Marsten," Lorn grunted. He spat to clear his mouth of the bitter taste of bile. "It's his fault we're here."

"Those drifters attacked settlements, killed women and kids and half the miners working here. They might have even killed an *innocent* man or two before we were sent out. That's why we're here."

"And who sent us? Who ordered the ship to pull out while we were gettin' our asses pounded on by three times as many drifters as we were told there was? Why was the map screwed up? And finally, why was it this unit that was sent?" Lorn waited expectantly.

Jake never stopped smiling. "Marsten," he answered cheerily. "So what are we gonna do about it?"

Lorn grinned suddenly. "We're gonna roast some horse meat and drink our fill of fresh water. Then at dusk we're gonna sneak down to the shore and take that ship. Then, after we get back to Norland, we'll see what happens."

They reached the mouth of the ravine. The sides leveled out and over the knee high sage they could see the anchored ship.

"It ain't gonna be easy," Jake remarked. "They'll have at least one giant on each watch with the regular crewmen, and I bet they'll chain the trolls to the mast on the upper deck."

"It's never easy. But, it can be done."

"You got a plan?"

"Yeah," Lorn replied as he dragged himself back across the coarse sand to the cover of the ravine. "And nobody's gonna like it."

Smilin' Jake tilted his head back and laughed soundlessly. By the time they returned to the makeshift camp, Jon and Bill had returned and were preparing to roast some fresh horse meat over a greasewood fire. They ate and drank their fill while the remaining common bloods watched suspiciously. Lorn outlined his plan and the four truebloods prepared to leave. Lorn retrieved his battered pack and withdrew a carefully wrapped package, which he handed to Bill McCurry.

"You been carryin' that all along?" Ox shook his head.

"Yep."

"Yer crazier'n Smilin' Jake." He declared. "What if you'd dropped it, or landed wrong, or if you'd been hit with one of them cannonballs? Hell, we'd all be blown to such little pieces the crows wouldn't even have found us."

"But it didn't happen, did it?" Lorn responded. "Keep it dry, Bill, and remember, only half a stick on board. We have to float that ship back to Norland still."

"I'm not stupid," Bill countered. "I know the plan." He slipped off into the darkness as the other three truebloods trotted down the ravine. In minutes they had reached the mouth.

"Tell me again why I have to go out there," Ox asked.

"Yer the biggest, and if them giants see one big guy actin' crazy the crew won't be able to hold 'em back."

"Why do we want' em off the ship?"

Lorn sighed. "Do you want to fight three giants and two trolls in such close quarters?"

"I reckon not."

"I reckon," Lorn grinned. "So the giants come after you, you lead 'em to us. Boom. Two down, and then Bill drops the hard powder into the crew's quarters.. Boom. No crew. They loose the trolls and we finish it off."

"It has a few loose ends," Smilin' Jake countered.

"Then we improvise," Lorn peered around the sage at the lonely cry of a loon which was no loon at all. "Bill's ready. Stay in the water and you'll be fine."

Smilin' Jake's grin shone in the darkness as he slipped off.

It happened fast, just like it always did. But to Graywullf's trained eye everything seemed to move in slow motion. Ox lurched along the beach singing some godawful saloon song, acting for all the world like a drunken sailor at home on leave. The giants spotted him immediately and began to taunt him. Jon laughed at their insults and hurled back a few of his own. In seconds the two giants on watch were straining at their chains and howling. At a word from the Captain, a crewman edged close enough to unlock their bonds, and they both jumped feet first into the waist deep water. Jon hesitated just long enough for them to reach the beach and broke into a staggering run back towards the waiting *magii'ri* Warrior. Lorn took it all in, and scowled in trepidation when he saw how fast the rest of the crew was roused. They lined the deck to watch the fun of a pair of giants tearing one man into very small pieces. There was no time to worry though, as the trap was sprung.

Ox hurled himself over a small dune and swung his long rifle up before he was even stopped. The first giant crested the dune and for one awful moment he looked right into the bore of Jon's rifle. Lorn saw the spark in the pan, and then the giant was flung backwards with the back of his head blown away. A moment later he heard the report. The second giant topped the hill and Ox lurched to his feet and made an obscene gesture. The giant snarled and attacked, but Lorn had already drawn a fine bead on his chest and when he touched it off, he knew the shot was true. The heavy lead slug tore through ribs and cartilage and ripped a jagged hole through the giant's heart. He dropped to one knee, his mouth working as he tried to draw in air. Ox swung his rifle butt in a short, savage arc which connected solidly with the giant's head. He collapsed into the sand.

Lorn dropped powder down the muzzle of his rifle and jammed home a huge lead slug. He glanced over the dune just in time to watch a trail of sparks cut across the night sky and drop directly onto the ship's deck. The pirate crew erupted in chaos. Shouts of terror wafted across the gentle waves and at least a half dozen men jumped headlong into the shallow water. But nothing happened.

"Oh, shit," Lorn started to leap to the crest of the dune when the hard powder failed to explode, but a massive hand dropped like an anchor onto his left shoulder. He flinched visibly, and for one crazy second considered wheeling around and taking at least one enemy with him. A woman's voice halted that movement.

"Even you're not that fast, Warrior."

Lorn glanced far enough back to see that the giant who held him also held a wickedly sharp sword to the base of his neck.

"That's right," the Black Queen sidled up next to him. "One wrong move and he'll paralyze you, so you can watch as we kill the rest of your mates."

"Magic," Lorn sputtered. "It had to be."

The Black Queen laughed. "Of course it was! How else could we get this close to a *magii'ri* Warrior without his knowledge?"

"So now what?" Lorn asked.

"Now we take a little walk back to the ship. Then you call out the rest of the Warriors, we disarm them and take you back to our friends."

Lorn reluctantly fell into step behind the Black Queen. Despite himself, the situation he was in and her position as his worst enemy, he could not help but notice her distinctly feminine charms. To his embarrassment he became painfully aroused. The Black Queen glanced back and laughed.

"My name is Mordant, Warrior. And yours?"

"Why should I tell you?"

She stopped so suddenly he nearly ran into her. Then she turned and ran her hand over his groin.

"Because you like me." She turned back towards the ship.

Lorn's head felt heavy and thick, and his tongue felt like gauze in his mouth.

"Graywullf. My name is Lorn Graywullf."

"I may have to keep you for myself, Graywullf."

The giant walking behind Lorn muttered under his breath and Lorn could feel his animosity. They reached the dune where Jon stood, his arms pinned behind him by an evil smelling troll with one good eye.

"Sorry, Cap'n," Ox apologized.

Lorn shook his head in dismissal while the troll rolled his one good eye and belched. A fetid odor surrounded the group like a cloud. The Black Queen held one hand to her offended nose and hurried down the beach.

"He surprised me," Ox offered.

"It was magic, Ox," Lorn muttered.

"Figures," Ox replied. "If they played fair I'd have torn his head off." The troll laughed, a hideous, gurgling sound.

"Maybe later," Lorn suggested. "Once I get primed…"

Jon cast a sidelong glance at him, then slowly nodded.

"Move it," the giant prodded Lorn with the muzzle of his own rifle.

They reached the ship. The crew stood at the rail, hurling jeers and insults at the two captives.

"How many others made it to the ravine?" the Captain called down.

Lorn studied him closely. There was something familiar about him, but he couldn't place it and the man kept his face concealed with a hood. "Only two common bloods," he answered. "The other Warriors were wounded by shrapnel. They bled to death minutes after we got out of range."

The Captain grunted an obscenity. "Bullshit. Kill them."

"Whoa, whoa, wait just a minute," Lorn protested. He turned towards the Black Queen. "What was that about keeping me for yourself? If you need blood, you can take this big Ox." He indicated Jon.

"What the Hell?" Ox yelled.

"Sorry, sweetie," Mordant smiled. She patted Lorn's flaccid groin. "You're no use to me in this condition."

In desperation, Lorn returned his attention to the captain of the vessel. "How will you explain this?"

"Explain what?" the captain replied with a humorless laugh. "No one will ever know we were involved. Besides," he laughed again, "shit happens."

The Black Queen and her henchmen hastily stepped aside as the pirate crew readied their own rifles and scatter guns. When they were thirty yards down the beach the Captain stepped forward again.

"One more time. Are you certain there are no more Warriors?"

Lorn nodded his head mutely.

"So there's nothing more you wish to tell me?"

"There is one thing," Lorn replied. He paused for a long moment.

"Well?" The captain demanded impatiently.

"You should have looked behind you."

"Behind…? There's nothing but the sea at my back, Warrior."

"Look again," Smilin' Jake said with a crazy laugh. He dropped a piece of flaming punk into a trail of gunpowder that led to all six of the cannons on board, which he had swiveled to aim at the crew. Seconds later the entire ship rocked with a series of blasts as grape and chain shot swept the deck. Lorn and Jon flung themselves to the sand as another trail of sparks flew through the sky and landed among the Black Queen and her soldiers. Lorn saw the Black Queen raise her hands to ward off the blast before another explosion threw up a curtain of sand and flame. The troll staggered through the flames with his tattered clothing ablaze, howling in rage. He hunched his massive shoulders and his chains parted with a snap. Jon leaped to his feet and met the beast with his own charge. As he did, Lorn hurled himself into the crater left by the explosion of hard powder, groping blindly for his rifle. He was dimly aware of the pelting of grape shot into the sand at his feet.

"Goddamn it, aim higher, Jake!" He shouted as a piece of shot gouged a chunk from his left ear.

Laughter echoed down from the ship in response.

"Crazy bastard's going to kill us all," he muttered as he felt for his rifle in the crater.

"You wanted a piece of me," He heard Ox taunting the troll. "Come and get it!"

The two stood toe to toe and slugged it out, trading blow for blow. Jon's face was immediately bloodied by the hoary fists of the mountain troll. The beast's ragged clothing was totally engulfed with flames which were licking at his greasy hair, but the troll seemed not to notice. Jon ducked low and threw a vicious blow into the troll's groin, narrowly avoiding the flames which licked upwards from the beast's loincloth. The stench of burning hide and hair filled the air. The mountain troll merely growled and resumed his attack on Ox, oblivious to the pain. Ox hastily retreated.

"Damn it, Graywullf," he shouted. "Do something!"

Lorn finally got his night vision back and saw the gleam of his rifle barrel. He pulled it from the sand, praying that the barrel wasn't obstructed, and hastily dumped powder into the pan. He lurched from the crater as the troll picked Ox up and threw him ten feet down the beach. Lorn went within himself, steadied his hand and squeezed the trigger a moment before the troll reached Jon's inert form. Lorn actually saw the strike of the bullet. It slammed into the back of the troll's head and burst from the socket of what had been his good eye. The monster walked blindly down the beach for twenty yards, then fell face first into the damp sand. Fire flared up in his shaggy hair. Silence engulfed the beach.

Lorn watched until Jon sat up, then he returned to the crater. The Black Queen was gone, as was the giant.

"More magic," Lorn muttered to himself.

He turned to look at the carnage. Several of the sailors who had jumped overboard rose from the sea, but an even darker shadow rose behind them. One by one they went down silently then Bill emerged from the shadow of the ship's hull onto the beach and wiped his long knives clean before he ran from the shadows and helped Ox to his feet. Satisfied that his friends were safe, Lorn resumed his observations. The deck of the ship was quite literally covered with the torn and mutilated bodies of the pirate crew. A few had fallen overboard and now drifted with the rising waves.

"What do you say, Cap'n?" Smilin' Jake yelled with a broad grin from the ship's deck.

"You cut that close, Jake." Lorn fingered the tattered sleeve of his shirt, which had been shredded by chain shot from the ship's cannons, then wiped away the trickle of blood from his ear. He surveyed the bodies floating in the rising surf. "Is the Captain up there?" he called to Jake.

"Hold on," Smilin' Jake responded as he hastily searched through the crew. He stepped back to the rail. "No, he ain't here. He ain't down there either?"

"Nope," Lorn replied thoughtfully. "And that ain't good." He clapped an arm on each of his friend's shoulders. "Let's go home."

Several hours later, Lorn watched as the last of the common bloods boarded the ship. He had personally removed the skull and crossbones from the main mast and replaced it with an improvised flag depicting a howling wolf, the symbol of the *magii'ri* Warrior sect. Jon took the wheel and they allowed the light breeze to carry them out to sea. Only then did Lorn Graywullf allow himself to relax, just a tiny bit. But, even though his body rested, his mind ran in circles like a rat in a trap.

It sure looked like Marsten had set them up. Too many things had gone wrong from the moment they set foot on land. It was a tribute to their harsh training that they had even survived. But what did Marsten hope to gain by disposing of them?

"I always liked the sea," Smilin' Jake offered him a mug of strong, sweet tea.

Lorn took it gratefully. "It beats walkin'."

Smilin' Jake laughed quietly. "That it does. So what's on yer mind?"

"Just trying to sort things out."

"Hell, we lived to fight another day. What is there to sort out?"

"Marsten." Lorn replied.

Jake shrugged. "Kill the bastard. There. I sorted it out."

"He needs killin', no doubt about that. But what then? With no leader in line, Norland would dissolve into chaos. The entire *magii'ri* race could disappear, and everything that our fathers fought for, bled and died for, would be gone."

"You think too much," Smilin' Jake countered. "That's what happens when a man has something to lose."

"Yer talkin' about Luke?"

"I reckon. A man with a family, he has to consider the future. The rest of us take it day by day. Look over yonder at ol' Bill."

Lorn followed the direction of Jake's nod.

"Bill's happy right now. We killed two trolls and two giants and a bunch of lowlife scum. Now there he is, just sharpening his knives and not thinking about tomorrow. That's the way a *magii'ri* should be."

"So yer saying I ain't a good Warrior?"

"Hell no, that ain't what I'm sayin'. You an' me, we been all over this part of the world and through some tight scrapes. And I ain't never seen anybody that could best you with gun or knife, or bare hands. Hell, you could probably beat the shit out of Ox an' he outweighs you by a hunnerd pounds. But you got one weakness, and it makes you vulnerable."

"My son," Lorn stated as he realized Jake's point.

"I reckon so."

"So I have a weakness. What difference does that make?"

"It means that even though killing Marsten would remove that problem, it would open up a real can of worms. He ain't alone, you can bet on that. So if we, or you, openly revolt, his followers are gonna come after you. Hard. If they can't get you, they go after your family."

Lorn sat heavily, suddenly exhausted. "Luke's all I got."

"Then take care of him. When we get back, take him to stay with someone you trust, somewhere they can't find him. Then we'll hit them back."

"Yer a good man, Smilin' Jake."

"Put that in yer report," Jake responded as he sauntered over to stand next to Jon. He pointed to a spot on the barren hillside. "How's that for our cabin site, Jonny boy?"

Lorn grinned as he ducked into the Captain's quarters. He ran his hand wonderingly over the cherry wood paneling and the finely carved liquor cabinet, inlaid with gold and silver. A huge oak desk dominated the room. It, and all the other furniture, was securely bolted to the immaculately clean floor. He sat at the desk and rummaged through the drawers. This was no pirate ship. In fact, it appeared to be a merchant ship made to look like a pirate vessel.

There was a map tacked to the wall, and Lorn could decipher that easily enough. His old master Fowler had drilled every map known into their heads with blows that knocked teeth loose. He searched the desk and found a sheaf of papers in one drawer. He stared at them intently, as if he could will the foreign symbols written upon them to tell him the secrets they held. He sighed and called Jake in to join him. His lieutenant entered the cabin and gave him a questioning glance.

"Found these," Lorn handed him the sheaf of papers. "What do you make of 'em?"

Smilin' Jake shuffled through the papers, his lips moving silently as he painstakingly sounded out each word. His expression became grim.

"They're shipping manifests for a ship named *The Gray Goose.*"

Lorn half- rose from his chair. "*The Gray Goose*? You're sure?"

"Yep. That's all I could make out."

Lorn stood and paced once through the cabin when the door burst open.

"Yer gonna be interested in this, Cap'n," Bill McCurry stated.

A few seconds later he stood staring in awe at the contents of the hold. Barrel after barrel lined the hold from front back, and most held the same contents. Gunpowder. It was a miracle they hadn't blown the entire ship and themselves into bits too small for even the carrion birds.

"Where could a merchant obtain this much gunpowder?" Lorn asked in disbelief.

Gunpowder was the closest guarded secret of the *magii'ri*. Only a handful of Wizards knew the formula to make it, and many Warriors had died protecting it. Without it, the Warriors long rifles and revolvers were useless, and in the wrong hands it could be disastrous.

"Where was it headed?" Bill asked.

"The Isle of Serpents," Lorn answered. "Under direction of David Flannery, Inquisitor General of the *magii'ri*. This is his ship."

"Instead it was captured by pirates," Bill said thoughtfully. "I wonder if Flannery was aboard?"

"David Flannery doesn't leave his office unless he has to," Lorn replied. "I doubt he'd have been aboard. But why was he sending a shipment of powder and guns to the Isle of Serpents?"

"This much powder could arm a regiment," Smilin' Jake said thoughtfully. "And a well armed regiment could overthrow the Council, with most of us out on patrol."

"You think Flannery's behind our troubles?" Lorn asked. "I counted him as my friend."

"You said it yourself, there's just been too many coincidences on this mission, and all of 'em have been bad." Smilin' Jake hammered the lid back on an open barrel with the heel of his hand. "Maybe Flannery is in it with that slimy dog Marsten."

"We don't know that," Lorn argued. "The ship may have been taken by pirates. This powder might have been on its way to a *magii'ri* garrison. Hell, Jake, we been gone two years now."

"Maybe," Smilin' Jake agreed. "And maybe Ox is going to sprout wings and fly back to Norland. Do you see any signs of a fight on this ship? The wood is unscarred," he grinned, "Except where I had the cannon aimed a little too low. Besides," he paused, "Like you said, we been gone two year. Hell, we don't know what's going on back in Norland."

"Something's fishy," Lorn conceded. He reached a decision. "Plot a course for the Isle of Serpents. We'll cache the guns and powder in the Citadel at Sylmarin, and play dumb about it later. While we're there we'll find out exactly who was expecting this shipment."

"That's risky, ain't it?"

Lorn turned with a questioning look on his face.

"What if somebody's watchin' for us?" Bill asked.

"They ain't going to be watchin' near the Citadel. Besides, I still think maybe this shipment was legitimate."

"It's still risky. I mean, what if somebody stumbles onto it?" Bill asked.

"Would you go into the Citadel by yerself?" Ox asked. "I wouldn't, and I ain't half as leery of magic as you, Bill."

"That's just an old wives' tale," Bill asserted. No one answered. "Ain't it?" he asked plaintively. "What do you think, Jake?"

Smilin' Jake shrugged. "It's true that a platoon of men were abandoned there and killed by half-men. How should I know if their spirits still guard the Citadel?"

"That ain't the whole story," Lorn interrupted.

"You know it?" Bill asked eagerly. "So is it true?"

"I know it. They were among the first *magii'ri*, before the bad blood was weeded out, under the command of Malachi the Marauder. They were left to protect several members of the royal family while Malachi ferried the Serpent King across the bay. Half-men swept down from the hills and laid siege to the Citadel of Sylmarin." Lorn's eyes clouded over, as if he saw the scene played out. "The *magii'ri* ran low on food and water. Malachi's ship was damaged, and he could not immediately return. He sent a message by hawk, but it was too late. The half-men offered a terrible trade. *"Give us the royal family, and we'll let you live."* He muttered the last phrase in a guttural tone. Jon and Smilin' Jake exchanged startled glances. "To their eternal damnation, the *magii'ri* handed over the King's heirs. The half-men gutted them, ate their flesh and hung the remains on poles. Three days later, half mad with thirst, the Warriors charged the half-men lines. They were cut down to the very last man. Their spirits are doomed to guard the Citadel, waiting for the return of Malachi to release them. No one who has set foot within the Citadel in the last two hundred years has lived to tell about it."

He clamped his mouth shut and climbed out of the hold. His men found him leaning on the railing, staring into the cloudless night sky.

"So what happens to a trespasser in the Citadel?" Bill asked.

"Legend says the spirits of those soldiers will behead anyone foolish enough to disturb them."

"So how in the Hell are we going to cache this powder inside the Citadel?"

Lorn grinned. "We're *magii'ri*, ain't we?"

"What's that got to do with it?" Bill blurted.

"The *magii'ri* find a way. Always. So, we walk right in and find a way."

Jake just grinned and nodded his assent at such a bold plan, while Jon looked confused.

"Would you look at that!" Smilin' Jake interrupted.

The others followed his pointing hand. The full moon visibly darkened, and several huge shapes flickered across the face of it. The dark of the night deepened.

"Did it just get darker?" Ox asked of no one in particular.

"I reckon so," Lorn answered.

"It ain't never done that before." Ox looked genuinely confused.

Lorn shook his head, but he knew what his friend felt. He felt it too. A man who spent the majority of his life outdoors became in tune with nature, but he also took it for granted. There were some things that never changed. The sun rose in the morning and set in the evening. The moon waxed and waned, but it didn't just change in the middle of a cycle. To see the moonlight simply fading away was no small thing.

"Set the course and lash the wheel," Lorn ordered. "Douse all the lights and come below."

The tone of his voice left no room for argument, and the *magii'ri* rushed to comply. It took only moments to do so, but all were out of breath when they ducked through the hatch. Fear was plain in their shadowed faces. Lorn knew what they were going through, for fear of the unknown was the worst fear of all.

"Get 'hold of yerselves," he ordered gruffly.

He cracked open the hatch a scant inch and peered out. The night was deeper in darkness than he had ever seen, but the sky still held a vestige of light. Wraithlike shapes wheeled and danced across the faded black backdrop of the sky. He silently lowered the hatch. The whites of his comrades eyes were visible in the gloom.

"What did ya see?" Smilin' Jake whispered.

"Not sure," Lorn replied. "Somethin' strange is going on. We'll stay below. Where the Hell are those common bloods?"

All four *magii'ri* Warriors exchanged confused glances. They had lost track of the last two common blood soldiers sent on the mission during the confusion of taking and boarding the ship.

"They was right here a minute ago," Bill announced suddenly, and just as suddenly two men appeared from the rear of the cargo hold.

"We're here," a man Lorn knew only as Rayburn called out.

Lorn stared suspiciously for a few moments, certain that the men's pockets were bulging tightly. No doubt, they had helped themselves to the ship's cargo. Not that Lorn cared. These two had been the steadiest of all the common blood soldiers who had been sent on that ill fated mission. They could walk out of the treasury at Elanderfeld with loaded mules for all Lorn cared.

"We should have dropped anchor," Ox interrupted. Genuine fear flickered across his barely visible features. "We might crash on some rocks or somethin'."

"He's right," Smilin' Jake agreed. "Sailin' blind ain't very smart."

Lorn knew what was really eating at Ox. The big man couldn't swim and had a terrible fear of drowning.

"There's somethin' out there like I ain't never seen before. If we'd have dropped anchor and stopped the ship, it would'a known there was someone aboard. This way it looks like the ship's been abandoned, or the crew's all dead. Either way I'll take our chances of crashing on some rocks compared to whatever's out there right now."

"It's that bad?" Bill asked.

Lorn hesitated. "I reckon it is."

The crew fell into an uneasy silence.

"I can't swim," Ox announced. "If this ship crashes, I'm a dead man."

"I looked at the charts," Lorn reassured him. "There ain't no reefs between us and Sylmarin. Come morning, I'll peek out again. I'm bettin' the sun will be rising and we'll make sure we're on course." He stretched his long legs out straight. "Get some rest. Aard knows we ain't had enough of that lately."

The others followed Lorn's example and a nervous night slowly passed. Lorn dozed off several times, only to jerk awake when his chin bumped his chest. He leaned back as far as he could in the cramped hold and finally drifted off to sleep. The Warrior's internal alarms awoke them at almost the same time.

"Must be daylight," Smilin' Jake observed. He playfully kicked Ox's booted foot. "Even ol' sleepyhead's awake."

Ox dealt him a baleful look.

Lorn climbed the ladder and peered out the hatch. It probably was dawn, he observed, but the darkness had barely faded away from midnight. A few stars were visible, and there was a tiny flash of light on the eastern horizon. He lowered the hatch and rejoined his comrades.

"Well?" Ox asked anxiously.

Lorn shook his head. "It's dawn, but it's still dark as pitch out there. I'll go above deck and get a reading."

"I'll do it," Smilin' Jake volunteered. He grinned at Lorn. "Hell, you ain't near sneaky enough."

"Watch yerself," Lorn warned. The implication in his words was not lost on Smilin' Jake. Whatever was out there had the Captain thoroughly spooked.

Jake slipped through the hatch and lay prone on the deck until he was certain there was nothing near. He belly crawled to the bow and searched the blackened sky for a familiar star. The stars in the western half of the sky were visible, but the eastern half was in total darkness. A semi circle clearly bisected the sky, and as he watched yet another bright star disappeared like a snuffed out candle. He hastily set up his sextant and took a reading, making certain they were heading due north. Then he checked the ropes on the wheel and crawled back down the hatch.

"It's fine, Cap'n," he reassured Lorn. "The wheel's lashed good and tight and we're still churning ahead, due north."

"Is it gettin' lighter?" Ox asked.

Smilin' Jake hesitated.

"Is it?" Lorn asked.

"Nope. I think it's gettin' darker."

"What does that mean?" Ox asked. "It ain't supposed to do that. It ain't never done that before."

Bill laid a hand on the visibly shaken Ox's shoulder.

"It'll pass," he said quietly.

"But what if it don't? I can't stay down here in the dark much longer," Ox said. "I don't like closed in places. You know that, Bill."

"It'll be fine," Lorn broke in. "I promise you, Ox, it'll pass. We just have to give it a few days."

But it didn't pass in a few days. Jake sneaked up to the deck and took readings until the entire sky was devoured by darkness and there were no stars to navigate by. By the fourth day the entire squad of *magii'ri* Warriors was clearly worried, and Lorn couldn't keep them below deck any longer. The common bloods elected to stay in the hold.

One by one they slithered out the hatch and found a hiding place on the deck. The air was noticeably cooler than it had been only four days earlier, partly due to the distance they had traveled to the north and partly from the constant darkness. Lorn scanned the sky worriedly, not sure if he could see even if something were directly above them.

"So what did you see earlier?" Smilin' Jake whispered, nearly in his left ear.

"Huge winged monsters," Lorn replied.

Smilin' Jake chuckled, then bit that sound off as his teeth clamped tightly together.

"Yer not kiddin'?"

"I reckon not," Lorn answered. "I don't think it was Dragons, but it could'a been. Whatever it was it looks like they're gone for now."

"So we can stay above?" Ox asked plaintively.

"I reckon so. We should be gettin' close to the Isle of Serpents and the Citadel anyway."

"How in Hell will we know when we do get close?" Bill asked sourly. He raised his hand to his face. "I can't see a goddamn thing."

Jake raised a hand to silence the group. "Ya hear that?"

Lorn strained his ears to listen.

"Son of a bitch! Strip the sail and drop anchor! Those are waves you heard!"

The crew hastened to stop the ship, but before the anchor rope came taut it lurched sickeningly to one side and stopped so suddenly the entire crew was thrown to the deck.

"We're here," Smilin' Jake said in a muffled voice, half buried under Ox.

Ox punched him in the ribs. "This ain't no time for jokes."

"Ow! Who's jokin'?" Smilin' Jake demanded as he dug himself free. He crossed to the rail and peered intently into the gloom. Lorn joined him there.

Lightning flashed in the distance, dimly illuminating the ship for a fraction of a second.

"That was close," Lorn said in an awestruck voice.

Lightning flashed again, and the entire crew saw the sheer, nearly vertical cliffs of Sylmarin, the Isle of Serpents only a few hundred feet away. They were firmly grounded on a sand bar. Another bolt of lightning lit up the sky and was followed by an enormous thunderclap.

"Grab yer personal effects," Lorn ordered. "We're goin' ashore."

The crew gladly ran to retrieve their belongings. Smilin' Jake accompanied Lorn to the hold. Lorn crawled down the ladder and handed up six extra revolvers, a small cask of powder and a bag of bullets. They tossed everything into one of the lifeboats as a few raindrops pelted the deck. Within minutes they had launched the boat and steered a course for land. Lorn hunkered in the bow, staring intently into the darkness.

"See anything?" Ox asked worriedly.

Lorn shot him a perplexed look, then resumed staring into the blackness. If there wasn't at least a strip of land between the cliffs and the sea, they'd have small chance of getting through. Another bolt of lightning ripped through the sky.

"There!" Lorn nearly shouted. "To the right. Looks like just enough beach to make landfall."

The *magii'ri* pulled hard on the oars and slowly swung the boat around. As they did, they struck something with a small thump.

"What the Hell?" Lorn exclaimed.

He bent down just as another flash of lightning crashed into the cliffs above them. A ghostly white hand clawed out of the water, then disappeared. Lorn gritted his teeth against the fear he felt at that sight and plunged his hand into the cold sea. He felt cloth and grabbed it, then lifted the body with all his strength and flung it into the boat.

"Goddamnit!" Bill cursed as he lunged away from the body. "What the Hell are you doin'?" His sudden move nearly capsized the boat and Ox lunged to the opposite side to counterbalance it.

Smilin' Jake bent close to the dead man's face, then felt for a pulse. As he did the man suddenly grabbed his hand in his own cold and clammy ones. He jerked Smilin' Jake close to his mouth while Bill frantically clawed for his revolver. Ox placed a restraining hand on Bill's wrist and stopped him at half draw.

"They're comin' for me," the dark man whispered. "Leave me." Then his head lolled to one side and his hands thumped lifelessly on the deck of the boat.

Lorn suddenly felt very exposed.

"Row, dammit," he ordered though gritted teeth.

The *magii'ri* rowed with renewed energy and struck the sandy beach with enough speed to plow a furrow and firmly ground the lifeboat. They quickly jumped ashore, and Ox lifted the injured man effortlessly and flung him over his shoulder.

"Which way?" he asked.

"Only one choice," Lorn replied.

He led the way up the beach in the same direction they had been rowing at a fast trot. He didn't look back to make sure the others kept up. He knew they were there, and that Ox could carry the injured man all day if need be.

Lorn felt his land legs returning, and his breath came deep and evenly. Sweat dripped down his face, but he kept up the brutal pace. The common bloods lagged behind, but only by a few yards.

"Somethin' up ahead," Smilin' Jake grunted.

Lorn strained his eyes into the gloom, but could see nothing.

"What is it?"

"Prob'ly a whorehouse," Jake muttered. "What do ya think? It's gotta be the Citadel."

Bill skidded to a halt.

"I ain't goin' in there," he stated.

A loud croaking sound floated down from the darkened sky. It sounded like a raven, only bigger. A lot bigger. A vagary of wind swept over the group. The Citadel was visible now, the window ports were dark shadows against the ghostly white stone. The injured man began to struggle violently, and Ox had to wrap both arms around him to restrain him.

"For bein' dead he's a strong little bastard," Ox grunted.

"They're comin' for me," the injured man moaned. "They'll kill us all!"

"Get inside," Lorn ordered. He drew his revolvers as he brought up the rear. Even Bill went willingly. Jake waited only long enough to keep pace with his Captain.

"See anything?" Lorn asked.

"Not yet…" Jake's voice trailed off as a blurry black shape engulfed him. He was knocked flat on his back, and could feel the fetid breath of some unearthly monster against his cheek. Then Lorn opened up with his revolvers in one continuous roll of thunder. The monster squealed in pain as the heavy lead slugs tore through it. It tried to leap back into flight then fell as its life blood gushed from the bullet wounds. Lorn bent and hauled Jake to his feet by the collar. The common bloods had surpassed them as fear sent shots of pure adrenaline flowing through their bodies. Their churning feet sent geysers of sand spraying behind them.

"Run, dammit!"

Smilin' Jake drew as he ran, occasionally firing into the sky. They were almost there, but Lorn sensed another attack. Then Bill and Ox opened fire through the window ports, and several more of the monsters squealed in pain. They burst into the Citadel as the skies opened up and rain pounded the beach. Lorn began reloading. Rayburn dashed through the door accompanied by a ghastly scream.

"They got Hawkins!" he shouted. "Just scooped him up and…" His voice trailed off as at least a dozen arrows flew through the darkness and thudded solidly into his body. His face twisted in pain and he slithered limply to the floor. Bill finished loading his revolver and emptied it into the darkness. Ricochets whined wickedly off the solid rock as Jake tackled him.

"Goddamnit," Lorn shouted into the silence that followed the gunshots. "Cease fire! Are you crazy?" He wiped blood from a gash in his forearm where a mangled lead slug had torn his skin. Nothing happened for several long seconds.

Bill struggled for a moment under Jake's solid weight, then he relaxed.

"Sorry, Cap'n," he muttered. "I thought we was under attack."

"Rayburn's dead," Ox announced. "Poor bastard. He thought he had it made."

Lorn glanced about. "Shit," he summed up the situation with one word. "Did you see it?" he asked Jake.

"Yeah," Smilin' Jake replied as he reloaded too. "It had really big teeth."

"I already know that," Lorn said. "Did you notice anything else?"

"Well, it was dark and I was kinda preoccupied at the moment!" Smilin' Jake said. "They're big and mean and nasty! That's all we need to know."

"They can't get in, can they?" Bill asked.

"I don't think so," Lorn answered. "I think they're too big to get through the doorways."

"So who shot Rayburn?" Ox asked.

"Damned if I know," Lorn answered.

As he spoke, stone slabs to each side of the doorways began to slide shut. Ox leaped into the doorway and pushed back with all his strength until Bill jerked him back into the Citadel. The doors slammed shut with a resounding boom.

"I ain't sure I like that," Bill said.

"Strike a light," Lorn ordered. "Let's see if we can get a fire going and see about this injured man." He finished reloading and holstered the weapons.

Bill struck a light into a piece of tinder from his belt pouch and held it aloft. Driftwood from some violent past storm littered the ground floor of the Citadel, and they hurriedly gathered some and built a small fire in the center of the room. Other than that and some wreckage, the Citadel seemed empty. Ox dragged the wounded man closer to the fire, and Bill McCurry bent to examine him. Lorn and Smilin' Jake took stock of the security of their position. The window ports were much too small for the monsters, but almost as soon as Lorn noted that one began to claw at the opening. The monster's claws shattered against the stone of the Citadel, and as it began to mindlessly bite at the opening its teeth sheared off. Lorn raised his revolver for one careful shot, but before he could squeeze the trigger they all heard a hissing sound and an arrow plowed into the monsters gaping mouth. It fell out of sight, squealing in pain until the rest of the beasts finished it off. Lorn dropped into a half crouch and hastily covered the room with his revolver, but there was no one else in sight.

"Now what the Hell…?"

Silence answered him. The remaining beasts, educated by the failure of their comrade, made no attempt to attack the enchanted stone of the Citadel.

"You said the Citadel was guarded," Smilin' Jake finally said. "I reckon those critters ain't welcome." He indicated Rayburn's body. "And neither are common bloods."

Lorn grunted an obscenity. "Then why ain't we stuck full of arrows, too?"

Smilin' Jake gave him his trademark grin. "Maybe we're just lucky," he replied sarcastically. "It don't make a damn bit of difference *why*, it is what it is."

Bill McCurry stood with his mouth working like a fish, but no sound came out. His revolver was in his hand again, cocked and ready.

"Bill." Lorn said quietly.

McCurry stared at him.

"Holster that piece, Bill," Lorn ordered, "and tend to the wounded."

"Its magic, ain't it?" Bill asked as he found his voice. "Honest to Aard magic."

"It ain't directed at us," Smilin' Jake said.

"He's right," Lorn agreed. "It's workin' for us for a change. Now holster that hogleg and tend to that wounded man."

Bill slid his revolver home in its holster. He tried to speak again then clamped his mouth shut and bent over the man they had pulled from the sea.

"I hate magic," Lorn muttered under his breath. Smilin' Jake grinned in agreement.

"He's still alive," Bill announced. "But this man's been through Hell. He's skin and bones and has two nasty gashes on his head. I don't know what's keepin' him alive."

"Well, we seem to be safe enough for the time being," Lorn said. He drew a few strips of dried horse meat from his belt pouch and tossed that along with his waterskin to Bill. "Boil that up and see if he can drink the juice. Jake, you and Ox keep a watch. I'm goin' to look around a bit." He glanced at Rayburn's body. "Cover him up with sumthin', too."

The Citadel had been carved from solid rock, reaching hundreds of feet towards the cliff top, and according to legend it was protected by countless spells. The *magii'ri* had witnessed firsthand the protection spell of the Guardians, but there were many more. Now lightning played tag among its highest spires and raced in streaks of light among the intricate stonework. Lorn fashioned a torch from a piece of driftwood and climbed the solid stone stairs to the next level, his right hand never more than an inch above the grips of his revolver. That level was deserted as well, and so were the next three that Lorn climbed to. He explored several rooms on each level, and even though some were closed off by wooden doors several inches thick, he found nothing. Finally he returned to the ground floor. His crew had made the wounded man comfortable by the fire, and now they sat around it, talking in hushed tones.

"He took a little broth," Bill offered. "But he's in a bad way."

Lorn glanced at the haggard faces of his men. It was obvious they needed rest almost as badly as the wounded man.

"Get some sleep," he told them. "I'll take the first watch."

The *magii'ri* bedded down, and in minutes they were asleep. The storm broke loose, and rain pelted the Citadel. *They look like Hell*, Lorn mused. But it had been a tough assignment from the very first day. Too tough, as a matter of fact. It seemed that everything that could possibly go against them had done so. And now they had those monsters from above to contend with. He sighed and poured the tin cup full of water and sat it in the coals to heat. When he had made tea he settled back in his bedroll to watch the embers of the fire. They were safe enough in the Citadel, he reckoned. The Guardians would have already killed them if they were inclined to do so. He didn't know why they hadn't, but the reason did not matter in the least. He ate a strip of dried meat and contemplated their situation as he chewed. There was no doubt in his mind that they had been set up, but even the magic of the *magii'ri* Wizards couldn't conjure up an enemy like the flying monsters that still squawked occasionally in the black sky. He was startled from his reverie by the wounded man's voice.

"Who am I?"

The enormity of such a question silenced Lorn for several long moments.

"I don't know who you are," he finally sputtered. "But you're safe enough, for now. Rest easy, you're among friends."

The wounded man huddled under his borrowed blankets.

"You really don't know who you are?" Lorn asked.

The wounded man paused then shook his head irritably. He stared into the fire, deep in thought.

"Do you remember anything?"

"I remember being cold, cold as death. And falling. Then there was a comforting blackness that enveloped me. I was warm again and I saw my father's face. I felt safe in that blackness until I was pulled from it like a babe from its mother's womb, jerked from my only safe haven into the cold danger of the World."

"That was me, I reckon," Lorn said. He shrugged apologetically. "It was me that pulled you from the sea."

The wounded man stared at him.

"You should have let me drown," he said thoughtfully. "Who are you? Do I know you?"

"I reckon not," Lorn replied.

"You seem familiar to me," the wounded man said. "Are you sure we haven't met?"

"Not that I recall," Lorn replied. "And I have a good memory for faces."

"Well, you saved my life, I think. The accepted response for a man in my position would be to thank you." He fell silent again, but only for a moment. "At any rate, I owe you a life debt."

"We just bumped into you," Lorn said with a smile. "Think nothing of it."

The wounded man seemed to relax, and grinned. "Is that where I got this knot on my head?"

"One of 'em," Lorn said with an answering grin.

The wounded man turned sober again. "Where are we? I had a meeting…somewhere."

"This is the Isle of Serpents. Our ship was blowed off course and we hit a sand bar. So we put in the lifeboat and hit you," he grinned apologetically. "Then we ran for the nearest shelter."

"Ran from the storm?" the wounded man questioned.

"More or less."

A strangled squawk reached them seconds before a peal of thunder drowned it out.

The wounded man shrank back into his blankets and edged closer to the fire. "They're coming for me," he whispered.

"You said that in the boat," Lorn said. "Do you know what's out there?"

"Death," he answered. Then he lay back down and turned away from the *magii'ri*.

"That ain't really what I wanted to hear," Lorn muttered. He built up the fire. It was going to be a long night.

# CHAPTER FOUR

## *The Citadel*

L ORN AWOKE TO THE muffled sounds of his crew preparing for a new day, even if that day could not be discerned from the previous night. He rose stiffly and stretched, trying to work the kinks out of his complaining muscles. Pounding rain flickered like diamonds in the firelight through the window ports. He noted with satisfaction that someone had fashioned a funnel from the scattered debris left by the previous inhabitants of the Citadel which collected and diverted rainwater into the interior. They had already filled most of the containers that were salvageable. That solved one problem. The refugee sat morosely staring into the fire.

"I'm getting' too old for this," Lorn said to Jake.

"Ain't we all?" Smilin' Jake answered.

"I ache from head to toe," Lorn said as he sat next to the refugee and began to brew a small pot of tea. "I think it's time to retire, sleep in a warm bed in a dry, tight house every night. I don't want to spend any more time in some forgotten land sleeping on the cold, hard ground."

"Only one problem with that, Cap'n," Smilin' Jake said. "We have to get out of here first."

"I reckon so," Lorn said. "Let's take stock." He indicated the water supply. "Looks like we got plenty of water for at least a few days. That was a good piece of work."

"It was him," Smilin' Jake said, nodding at the wounded man.

"Good thinking," Lorn said. "Maybe you're on the mend?"

"I'll live," he said shortly.

Lorn stared at him curiously for a few long seconds then turned his attention back to the problem at hand.

"Empty your packs. Let's see where we stand on food."

After the *magii'ri* did as he requested, a pitifully small pile of dried horse meat and crumbled trail bread lay on the blanket he had thrown down.

"Well, we been on short rations before," Lorn commented

"What I wouldn't give for a nice thick beefsteak topped with butter fried mushrooms," the wounded man suddenly said. "And baked sweet potatoes, with apple pie for dessert."

The *magii'ri* stared at him.

"Sorry," the wounded man said, suddenly realizing that he had spoken aloud.

"Well, what we got is horse meat and trail bread," Lorn said.

"Aw, shit," Ox said in disgust. "Now he's got *me* thinkin' about thick, juicy steaks."

"Would you shut up about steaks?" Bill said angrily. "Hell, we ain't had a decent meal in months."

Lorn ignored his chattering crew. "Are you starting to remember more?" he asked the refugee. "That memory came from someplace."

"Bits and pieces," the wounded man admitted. "Gods, I'd feel better if we could actually *eat* something."

"There's game aplenty on the Isle," Smilin' Jake interjected. "All we gotta do is get by those winged wolves out there."

"There *was* game aplenty," Bill said. "Those flyin' wolves might have killed everything by now."

"How many you reckon there is?" Ox asked. "We could take out a couple dozen."

"Many more than that by now," the refugee interrupted. "But they are somewhat scared of fire."

"You remember that?" Lorn asked.

"Yep," the wounded man said. "There's more. I think I remember my name." He stared hard at Lorn while he spoke. "I think my name is Lynch." The name tumbled off his tongue in an unfamiliar way.

"Lynch, eh?" Lorn replied. Something bothered him, just a slight tickle at the edge of his memory, but he let it pass. "Mean anything to any of you?" he asked his crew.

Jake began to speak, then shook his head and scuffed a boot through the sand. No one else said a word

"Anything else you remember?"

"It's all jumbled up," Lynch said. "I'm trying to sort it out."

"That must have been one hell of a blow to the head," Smilin' Jake remarked. "Might have scrambled yer brains permanently."

Lynch looked him straight in the eye. "It might have." He said quietly.

Lorn watched the exchange curiously. He and Jake had ridden together for a lot of years, and if Jake found something to be suspicious about, Lorn wanted to know what it was.

"We got enough food for a few days anyway," Lorn said. "What we really need to do is figure out what to do about those flyin' wolves, as Jake called 'em."

"The Slayers" Lynch said suddenly. "They're called The Slayers in books of magic. They have no other name because they are not of this World. They must be called forth by a Wizard of Dark Magic, one of great power. But there is no single Wizard alive at this time with enough power to raise them. Perhaps it was several working together."

"More magic," Bill said in disgust. "Goddamnit."

"And you just suddenly remembered all this?" Smilin' Jake asked. He was not smiling now.

"I did," Lynch replied.

"So how do we know yer not one of them Dark Wizards?"

"I am," Lynch admitted. He was not prepared for what happened next. He suddenly found himself covered by four pistols with very large holes in the barrels. None of the four wavered in the slightest. He hastily added, "But what you have to remember is that we are in the same pickle here. I want to get out alive as much as you, which requires a Wizard. And there is the matter of a life debt which must be settled."

"What's he talkin' about?" Ox asked, looking forlornly at Lorn. "Does this mean there's gonna be more magic?"

"I reckon so," Lorn said tiredly. He heaved a gusty sigh. "Tell us what you know."

"That's all I remember," Lynch responded.

"That's it?" Smilin' Jake muttered. "Kinda convenient."

Lynch stared him straight in the eye. "I'll remember the rest eventually. Right now I need to gather my strength."

"I say we blast him," Jake suggested. "Before he gets his strength back."

"Uh-huh," Bill agreed. "Shoot him now and throw him out to those winged wolves. Hell, he admitted to using Dark Magic and that's punishable by death. What do you say, Ox?"

"Yeah," Ox replied. "Let's shoot him before he can curse us all."

"And Dark Magic is the only thing that can save you now," Lynch said slyly. "You can't kill all of the Slayers, not without me. You are trapped here, just as I am. As a matter of fact, without me, you'll die."

"Goddamnit," Lorn muttered as he holstered his pistol. "He's right. Put those pieces away."

"I could center him right now and be done with it," Smilin' Jake tried one last time. Lorn stared at him until he slid his revolver home in its holster. One by one the other *magii'ri* reluctantly followed suit.

"I reckon this is a new low, even for us," Lorn said. "I can't imagine the *magii'ri* throwing in with a Dark Wizard."

"Is that so?" Lynch replied. "It's been done before."

"I reckon it don't matter," Lorn replied with a wave of his hand, completely missing the significance of such a remark. "You said we need you. I reckon you better explain."

"The Slayers can't tolerate sunlight, so whoever the Wizards are who called them forth have conjured a spell to create eternal night. To defeat the Slayers I must break that spell."

"How do we do that?"

"Not we. Me. I will be the one who must break the spell and I'm working on it," Lynch said shortly. "I think I've forgotten more than most Dark Wizards ever learn."

"I'm not sure you're shootin' straight with us," Lorn said quietly. "Seems a bit too farfetched that you just showed up here."

"Absolutely," Lynch countered. "I starved myself, hit myself in the head several times, then jumped into the sea just on the chance that you'd find me and bring me here. Wherever we are," he finished with a scowl.

Lorn sighed. The situation was becoming too damn complicated. "Yer right. But, you just admitted to knowledge of Dark Magic. Hell, we've all shot men for less than that."

"So we're at a standstill," Lynch said. "I propose a truce. Whatever our previous positions may have been, at this moment we must become allies. What happens later is irrelevant."

Lorn thought for several long moments, then walked forward and offered his hand, which Lynch gripped firmly.

"We have an accord," Lorn said. "Help us get out of here and we'll help you get yer strength back. If we defeat the Slayers then I'll consider your life debt paid in full. When we leave here we'll go our separate ways."

"Agreed," Lynch said smoothly.

Jake spat and muttered an obscenity.

"So, where exactly are we?"

"This is the Isle of Serpents and we are standing in the Citadel of Sylmarin," Lorn replied.

"Jumping rockcats! The Citadel?" Lynch cast a fearful glance all around.

"Didn't expect that, did ya?" Smilin' Jake asked. His old grin was firmly back in place.

"Yet we still live," Lynch said thoughtfully, under his breath. "Do you know what this means?"

"It don't mean nothin'," Lorn replied. "We needed a dry, safe place and took shelter here."

"It means a damn sight more than you let on, my dear Captain," Lynch argued. "I know the curse on the Citadel very well." He stood and paced slowly around the fire. "I have been extremely impolite. I have introduced myself, but I don't know your names."

"That's Jake Sipowicz," Lorn said, despite the warning look Smilin' Jake shot his way. "The dark lookin' gent is Bill McCurry and ol' tiny over there is Ox Duvay. I'm Lorn Graywullf."

Lynch dropped his battered tin cup from his suddenly nerveless fingers at the mention of the final name.

"Graywullf, eh?" he said, trying to sound calm as he bent to retrieve his cup. "That name is not all that common."

"Common enough among the *magii'ri*," Lorn said.

"Exactly," Lynch agreed. "Your name is common *only* among the *magii'ri*. Your *magii'ri* bloodline goes back many generations. Hell, it goes back *centuries*, all the way back to the origin of the curse of the Citadel of Sylmarin, even before it. I remember it well." He stopped and looked guiltily at the floor.

"Well glory be! This must be one of them miracle healings I hear about," Smilin' Jake proclaimed. "Just like a bolt of lightnin' your memories are all comin' back at once." He drew his pistol smoothly and leveled it at Lynch's midsection. "I'm just an ignorant country boy trained as a Warrior, but I ain't smitten with you just yet, like some dumb bastards I could name." He leveled a hard look at Lorn. "I ain't as ready to share my blankets with you like the cap'n seems to be." he added, "So right now the best thing for you would be to cut the bullshit and tell us *everything*, or by gods I'll send you to your maker. Whoever that might be," he added as he thumbed back the hammer of his pistol.

"I'm telling you as it comes back to me," Lynch replied without even a hitch in his voice. "But if that's not fast enough for you, then by all means go right ahead and cut me down. Then you can figure out how to defeat a magical enemy all by yourself." He stared expectantly at Jake. "Go ahead, do it."

Jake's trigger finger began to tense, which Lorn noticed immediately. The man called Lynch was a hairs breadth from getting his guts blown out.

"Stand down, Jake," Lorn said flatly. Smilin' Jake scowled, but he relaxed his grip on the trigger. Lorn turned back to Lynch again. "He ain't gonna shoot you yet. But, if you don't cut to the chase and quit bullshittin' us, he won't have to. I'll do it myself."

Lynch stared hard into Lorn's cloudy blue eyes and saw no mercy there. "I reckon this ain't the time for games," he admitted. "Don't ask me how I know these things, because in most cases I don't know where the knowledge came from to begin with. I know I have lived a very long time, much longer than any mortal man and right now I am weaker than I have been in centuries. I need your help, and you need mine." He shuffled slowly around the fire again. "The curse of the Citadel can be thwarted by only one man, a man who carries the purest blood of the *magii'ri*, the heir of Malachi the Marauder. Malachi's surname was Graywullf." All eyes turned towards Lorn Graywullf. "That is why the Guardians didn't kill us. They need the heir of Malachi to release them from the Curse."

"Son of a bitch," Bill muttered.

"Yer famous," Smilin' Jake said sarcastically.

Lorn shrugged. "Let's just say I buy that, for now. That solves one problem. We can get out of the Citadel, if I break the curse. Then what?"

"You can come and go as you please right now," Lynch said with a slight smile. "Your men and I are prisoners here until you lift the curse."

"So you tell me how to lift the curse," Lorn replied. "I'll do it then we can all go."

"Think about that for a moment," Lynch said. "Right now nothing can get in, and only you can get out. If you hold off on breaking the curse, we have a built in defense. That gives me one element which I need to rebuild my strength: time. And I will need all of my strength to break the spell and destroy the Slayers. Your men are also nearly exhausted, so time to rest will benefit them as well."

"What else do you need?" Smilin' Jake asked suspiciously.

"Food. Nourishment. Much more than a pound of dried horsemeat. The use of magic, Light or Dark, burns up a man's energy stores."

"Goddamnit," Lorn muttered. "You mean a Wizard or Warlock's energy, I reckon. Why ain't nothin' ever easy?"

"Adversity makes you strong," Lynch said with a smile.

"If being a *magii'ri* Warrior was easy, everyone would do it," Smilin' Jake offered.

"Shut up," Lorn growled. He kicked a small pile of driftwood, before turning back to Lynch. "We have an accord, remember? I don't know if you're a Wizard of the Light gone bad or what. You may be a Dark Wizard but even Dark Wizards have a code of honor. If I bring back the meat you need to rebuild your strength, you are honor bound to help us break the spell and return the sunlight. Then we'll let you go your separate way."

"I gave you my word, and I will hold to it," Lynch replied.

Lorn sighed heavily then began refilling his powder horn and bullet pouch. He checked the loads on both his revolvers and bent to fill his waterskin. He slung it from his belt, and when he rose he had one revolver trained on Lynch.

"I reckon since you already admitted to being a Dark Wizard, or something of the sort, you'll understand if I don't trust you," Lorn said.

"I'd expect no less," Lynch replied, but his expression revealed his surprise.

Lorn motioned with his free hand, leaving his revolver stone steady on Lynch's solar plexus. "There's a couple cells back there. Take those blankets and pick one."

Lynch did as he was ordered. Smilin' Jake and the other *magii'ri* followed while Lynch entered the cell and Lorn swung the door shut. The lock clicked as he closed it. Smilin' Jake gave the door a tug and it remained firmly latched. He looked questioningly at Lorn.

"I hate magic and I damn sure ain't no Wizard, but I reckon its working for me right now." Lorn took one last look around the Citadel. "Jake, you're in charge while I'm gone." He indicated Lynch with a nod. "If he gives you any trouble, kill him. Don't argue or beat him or even bargain with him, just kill him. Understand?" Jake nodded and looked at Lynch with his crooked grin.

"There's several more entrances at various upper levels," Lynch offered.

"You would know that, wouldn't you?" Lorn said.

Lynch cast a quizzical look his way and muttered under his breath. Lorn's entire body twitched and it felt like a pool of hot lead had accumulated in his groin and ran down inside his thighs. He stared suspiciously at Lynch then joined his men near the fire.

Lynch watched the *magii'ri* through slitted eyes until they left the cell to return to the fire, then swathed himself in blankets and lay down. It felt good to be warm again, too good for mere words. He was safe here, there was no doubt of that, and that made his current condition much easier to bear. Even now his bones ached clear down to the marrow, and he was nearly too weak to stand. He remembered the hellish march across the frozen plains of the Land of Ice and the constant harassment from the devilish monsters from the sky. He even remembered falling and wandering through the pitch black that only can be found at the core of the World. But his words were true when he told the *magii'ri* that most of his memories eluded him. That thought should have bothered him, he realized. But it didn't. He had been here before, in this position, even in this place. He would prevail, as he always had.

# CHAPTER FIVE

**L**ORN ACCOMPANIED HIS MEN back to the fire. More than once he cast a suspicious glance into the cell where Lynch lay concealed in his borrowed blankets.

"I don't like this," Bill stated flatly.

"We need him," Lorn replied. "I can handle most anything, trolls, giants, half-men, even Dragons. But this...Dark Magic is beyond any of us. You can't shoot it or cut its throat. Lynch knows his way around it, I'm sure of that."

"I think he knows it too damn well," Smilin' Jake agreed. "There's something familiar about him, but I can't put my finger on it."

"I can," Bill replied gloomily. "He's a Dark Wizard, ain't he? It's the curse, comin' back to haunt us again."

"Shut up," Ox suddenly spoke up. "There ain't no curse on us."

"Would you both shut up?" Lorn said in exasperation. "You two cackle on like a couple of old hens. I don't give a damn if there is a curse. I killed that Wizard long ago because he needed killin'. If that cursed anyone it'd be me. And if this one needs killin', I'll cut him down, too."

He looked around one final time to make sure he hadn't forgotten anything. Then without saying another word he wheeled around and began to climb the steeply ascending stairs in the rear of the room. He paused at each of the first few levels and cautiously opened each door. The rooms were all the same, littered with broken furniture and scraps of cloth, and even though the storm raged outside they were as dry as dust. He climbed for what seemed like an eternity, until his thigh muscles burned with fatigue and his breath came in long gasps. He didn't want to admit it, but he and the other *magii'ri* needed that meat as much as Lynch. They had been on short rations for far too long. He could see it in the gaunt planes of their faces as they had stared into the fire when he left. Maybe he had been too hard on them. Maybe not. It didn't matter now.

He leaned against the wall at the next level and slid down it to his haunches. He was exhausted, and he knew the rest of the squad felt the same. Their survival depended on his success, and their death would be the result if he failed. He shook his head irritably. Sometimes it did seem that they were cursed, even more so on this mission than at any other time before. He laughed, but there was no humor in the bitter sound. Cursed or not, they still had to eat, and he knew it would be blind luck to stumble onto any kind of game in the unnatural darkness that hung over the Isle.

He climbed a few more levels and finally found an iron bound door set inside a deep arch. He made sure the tails of his coat were draped over his pistols, then slowly opened the door and stepped outside. The rain had nearly stopped and the air was washed clean. He breathed deeply then realized that he still held the torch. Cursing, he flung it back inside the Citadel as the door swung silently shut.

"Brilliant," he muttered. "Draw them in like a moth to a candle."

The doorway opened onto a sloping trail that snaked the final distance to the top of the cliff. Lorn reached back inside and propped his long rifle in the corner by the doorjamb. There was no way to keep the powder dry, which made it as useless as a club. He hesitated long enough to allow his eyes to adjust to the absence of torchlight then gathered up his courage and stepped out of the doorway. A breeze ruffled the damp hair on his forehead, accompanied by the whistling of wind over leathery wings. He cringed, half expecting an attack from above to send him crashing down into the boulders that lined the surf hundreds of feet below. But the Slayer was below him, cruising on rigid wings as it soared in watchful circles, guarding the entrance at ground level. Lorn screwed up his courage and padded up the trail.

When he reached the lip of the cliff he could see the silhouettes of trees several hundred yards away, and he set a quick course for that dubious cover. He reached the cover safely and paused, panting softly as he kneeled amid the dripping branches. His bracing hands felt the slightly hollowed surface of a trail. He realized he had no better option and should follow it, but a strange lassitude came over him. He felt that he didn't have the strength to stand, so he knelt there in the mud and allowed himself to close his eyes. *Just for a few seconds*, he promised himself. Then he would push ahead. When he opened his eyes and tried to stand his knees popped and groaned and he was chilled to the bone. He began to walk with a stiff legged, clumsy gait, feeling the concave surface of the trail through the soles of his boots. He went slowly, so slowly that it seemed he would never make any distance at all. But haste would be careless, and carelessness meant death. Every ten or fifteen steps he paused, and by the time he had covered a quarter mile he had instinctively cataloged the scents, sounds and the few sights that he could make out in the gloom. He kept his right hand dry under the tail of his coat, ready for a quick draw if the need arose.

He smelled the musky scent of deer before he saw its vague outline, and he snapped his revolver up and thumbed back the hammer in one fluid motion. But the deer was already gone, leaving not even a waving branch in its wake. He cursed, low and viciously. It would only have to move six feet and he'd never see it until it moved again.

Lorn resumed his cautious stalk, but he had only covered ten feet when he stopped suddenly. His caution was rewarded by a tiny whisper of sound from his left. He casually surveyed his surroundings, but couldn't see anything alarming. He moved ahead again, and thought he saw a shadow of movement in the brush, perhaps even one branch that whipped to and fro a few times. He caught a whiff of a faintly familiar smell then it was gone.

"Those things got you spooked," he whispered to himself.

He resumed his hunt, even though it appeared hopeless. It was the *magii'ri* way, to always push ahead. However, after several hours of fruitless stalking he was near despair. A deep contented grunting sound banished all thoughts of failure. It appeared to be coming from farther up the trail, and he thought there might be a small clearing ahead. He bent lower to the trail and abruptly slipped in the layer of muck and landed heavily on his right knee. He muffled a curse even as he heard a commotion ahead. The brush rustled, he heard a thud and a short squeal, followed by a splashing, gurgling sound. He lunged forward into the clearing.

"Took you long enough," a soft voice whispered.

Lorn frantically drew his right hand revolver as he stumbled backwards in the brush.

"Quiet!" the voice hissed. "You attract their attention and we're dead meat for sure."

Lorn finally saw the outline of a slight figure of a boy over the sight of his pistol. "Who are you?" he demanded in a shaky voice.

"My name's Nick, but that don't matter right now." He held out a glistening hand, and after a moment's hesitation, Lorn stepped forward to take it in his own. He almost tripped over the carcass of a wild pig with the haft of a spear sticking out from its spine as he felt the wetness of the boy's palm against his own. Lorn held it up to his face and saw the dark smear of the pig's blood. "I been waitin' for you fer half the day. You make enough goddamned noise for ten men. Help me butcher this pig and I'll take you to a safer place."

"What the hell are you doing out here?" Lorn said, his confidence slowly returning.

"I told you," the boy replied. "Waitin'."

"No, I mean what are you doing on the Isle of Serpents? It's supposed to be deserted."

"No time for that now," Nick said. He expertly sliced open the pig's belly and pulled the entrails out, then cut through to the spine and separated it between the vertebrae. "Are you gonna help me or stand there and gawk?"

Lorn grinned in the darkness. "Help, I reckon." The two made short work of quartering the animal, and Nick stuffed the heart and liver into a burlap bag.

"I can carry this and the meat from the front shoulders, if'n you can carry the hams. I s'pose you're *magiir'i*."

"I am."

"Warrior or Wizard?"

"Warrior," Lorn answered.

"Good," Nick replied. "That'll make it easier. Pa don't have no truck with Wizards anymore. Come on. We got a safe place where you and him can talk."

He stood suddenly and disappeared through a narrow opening in the brush. Lorn hesitated.

"Are you comin' or not?" Nick whispered.

"Goddamnit," Lorn muttered through clenched teeth. He slung a hindquarter over each shoulder and lunged after the boy.

The opening in the brush was another game trail, narrow and grown over to form a natural tunnel. Nick ran along it standing fully upright, but Lorn had to run bent over at the waist More than once he raised his head too high and received a stinging slap to the face from a low hanging branch. A knot of pain formed in his lower back and radiated outwards, but he plunged on, occasionally catching glimpses of his young guide in the gloom. Abruptly they came to a tiny clearing, no more than fifty feet across. A squat stone hut with an attached barn was carefully concealed on one side of the clearing. Lorn could see no window openings and no smoke rose from the chimney. Nick disappeared inside, and with a low curse Lorn followed him.

The smell inside was pungent with the odor of cow manure. A few tallow candles sputtered in various places around the room which opened directly into the barn. A stone wall ran between the living quarters and the cows. Three other people emerged from hiding places. Lorn instinctively dropped the meat and drew his pistols and covered them.

"Easy now. We mean you no harm." The speaker was a fully bearded man of indeterminate age.

"Who are you people?" Lorn demanded. "There's no settlers here."

"And that's the way we want it to stay," the bearded man responded. "I'm called Tully. This is my wife, Sarah and my daughter Beth. You've met Nick."

Lorn glared at the unexpected surprise. One of the cows burst forth in the barn with a sloppy stream of farts, followed by an unmistakable plopping sound. Lorn wrinkled his nose in disgust. The children hid their faces behind their hands and giggled.

"By the gods, why would anyone live like this?" Lorn asked.

"Sit down," Tully offered Lorn a serviceable chair fashioned from tree branches. "I think we have some talking to do."

"I reckon so," Lorn sat, but held one revolver in his lap.

Tully sighed. "Hell, I don't even know where to start. Yer a *magii'ri* Warrior, are you not?"

"I am," Lorn agreed.

"Well the *magii'ri* are mostly to blame fer us bein' here."

Lorn shot him a warning look.

"No, don't be gettin' the wrong idea," Tully said. "I was a farmer back in Norland. It was a good life, hard, but good. Then the *magii'ri* Council started raising our taxes, demanding more and more for the King, so they said. A few tried to refuse payment, and they disappeared in the middle of the night with their homes burning down behind them. Nightriders were to blame, the Council said. Eventually they were takin' so much I didn't have enough left to feed my family. We left our home in the middle of the night after the harvest two years ago. I had heard stories about the cattle and sheep running wild here ever since the Siege, and I thought we had a chance here."

"You didn't fight?" Lorn asked in disbelief.

"I didn't resist," Tully looked defiantly at Lorn as he said that. "I got a family to look after, and I couldn't do that dead. Besides, my quarrel ain't with the Warriors. It's with the Council. But ain't that the way it always is? The rulers always get the Warriors to do the dirty work and they get the profits."

Lorn sighed deeply. By Aard, would this mission never cease to become more complicated?

"But why do you live like this?" Lorn asked.

"This is the end of the line for us," Tully stated. "You wouldn't understand. We have nowhere else to go. The cows have been running wild since the Siege. We trapped 'em, and they saved us with milk and meat. They'd be out on pasture right now if it wasn't for those goddamned Dragons."

"They ain't Dragons."

"Whatever. We live like this because it's the only way we can be free. Shit, I was just a slave to the ruling class anyway. There. Now, if you want, you can clap me in irons and take me back, I guess."

Lorn shook his head. "I ain't here for you."

Tully smiled. "I had hoped it was so. Nick thought you might help, but he ain't as cynical as I am."

"Those things you call Dragons are called Slayers. I have a man with me in the Citadel that can help, but we're almost out of food."

"Let's just say that I give you some food, enough to get yer strength back. Then what?"

"We defeat the Slayers by breaking this spell of darkness," Lorn answered. "My men and I only want to return to Norland. We been gone nigh on two years."

"There's the problem," Tully said. "If you go back to Norland, then the Council's gonna know where we are. We don't have anywhere else to go. The Council took our lives from us."

Lorn's voice nearly broke, and he wondered momentarily at that sign of weakness. "I have a son, a few years younger than Nick. I know what it's like to have a family to look after." He blew out a gusty sigh. "I don't know anything that has happened in Norland since we left, but I give you my word as a Warrior; if you help us now no one will ever know that you are here."

Tully thought for a long moment. "Nick, gather up some smoked meat. Sarah, he'll need trailbread and cheese." He turned back to Lorn. "Ya know, you still have to make it back to the Citadel. How much can you carry?"

"All that you can spare," Lorn answered grimly. "I got a feelin' my man is gonna need all his strength to break this spell."

Tully stopped what he was doing. "He's a Wizard?"

"I reckon. But not of the Council."

"Then he's a Dark Wizard?"

"I reckon so," Lorn replied.

"That's bad."

Lorn shook his head, still incredulous that he had thrown in with a Dark Wizard. Then he had a brief image of Lynch's feral grin. "You have no idea."

Tully thrust a sack of dried meat and another of trailbread and cheese into Lorn's hands. Lorn looked at him in disbelief. "This is too much. You have to eat, too."

"We'll smoke the pig Nick speared after you kill the beasts, and the cows provide the rest," Tully said. "There is one more thing. Right before the darkness began, another ship approached from the South, much like you. They docked on the other side of the Isle."

"The other Dark Wizards," Lorn guessed. "That'll help. And I'm much obliged for the food." He dug out a gold coin and flipped it to Tully, who caught it in midair.

"It's pretty," he remarked. "It's worth a fortune in Norland, and not worth a pile of cow shit on the Isle."

"Keep it," Lorn said. "Maybe one day we can set things right. Then you can buy something for your family."

"I'd like to know your name," Tully suggested.

"My name is Graywullf," Lorn answered.

Nick cast a questioning look at Lorn as he slowly opened the door and peered outside. "It's clear. You ready to run?"

Lorn ached clear down to his toes. "I reckon so."

"Good luck, Graywullf," Tully called softly as Lorn and Nick left the safety of the stone hut. "Yer gonna need it," he added under his breath.

Lorn tried to keep up with Nick on the return trip, but even with the trail burned into his memory the boy easily outdistanced him. He was waiting for the *magii'ri* Warrior a hundred yards from the clearing where he had speared the wild pig. Lorn stopped, breathing heavily. Nick turned towards him and Lorn could see the whites of his eyes. Then he heard the snuffling sounds from the clearing.

"They smelled the blood and found the gut pile," Nick whispered. "We gotta go around."

Lorn nodded, not wanting to chance even a whisper. Once again he followed the boy, but Nick went much slower this time, picking each footfall with care. They circled wide around the clearing, then suddenly cut back onto the trail. Nick stopped when they could hear the surf crashing on the beach.

"Yer on yer own now," the boy said, his teeth flashing with a ghostly whiteness in the gloom. He turned to go back, but hesitated. "Mister Graywullf?"

Lorn turned back from studying his route to the sloping trail that led to the Citadel. "What is it?"

"I gotta tell you this. I sneaked in close to those people from the other ship, and one of 'em has a drawing on his arm, just like yours."

"He has a tattoo?" Lorn asked.

"Yep. Does that mean something?"

"I reckon so," Lorn replied. "It means I ain't the first *magii'ri* to throw in with Dark Wizards. Why'd you wait to tell me?"

"Pa'd beat me if he knew I had been wandering around. Since those Slayers showed up he don't want me to hardly leave the cabin."

"He's right. One bad move and they'll tear you to pieces," Lorn said. "I reckon I owe you fer tellin' me. You risked your life finding that out."

"It ain't nothin'," Nick replied. "They ain't much better'n you on a trail. Amateurs."

Lorn had turned to look at his route, and he snapped his head around with disbelief on his face. But the boy was gone. He couldn't suppress a low chuckle. "Amateurs, eh?" He shook his head and ran for the cliff.

He reached the steep trail and skidded down it, his heart beating in his throat and his blood singing in his ears. A Slayer could have been crouched on the trail and he'd never have seen it before he ran over it. The massive door swung open at the lightest touch, and Lorn wondered briefly about that. Then he stepped inside and relief flooded over him. He felt for his rifle, but his searching hand came up empty. He stepped forward and slammed one knee into the solid stone doorjamb. Pain seared through his knee.

"Sonofabitch," he growled as he dropped the sacks of food and hopped around on one leg. He angrily struck a light with his flint and steel and spied the torch he had thrown in earlier. He crawled to it on hands and knees and struck a light into the remaining pitch. It caught easily, and he scooped it up and turned back to where he had stowed his rifle. It was gone. He searched every corner of the room.

*Maybe Jake had grown bored and retrieved it for me*, he thought. *And maybe not.*

He picked up the sacks of food and half ran, half slid down the stairs to the ground floor. His legs trembled as he saw the faint glimmer of firelight, and a spark of anger leaped into life when he wasn't challenged by a sentry. He stalked up to the tiny fire fully intending to dress down his men. Jake looked up at him with a startled expression.

"By the gods," Lorn breathed.

Jake's face was haggard and drawn, but he still managed a weak smile. "Took you long enough."

"What are you talking about?" Lorn demanded. "I ain't been gone more'n half a day."

"Bullshit," Jake answered. "It's been a week or more."

"Eight days," Lynch called from his cell. Lorn whirled around as Lynch chuckled. "You have a bit of Dark Magic in your own background, don't you?" Lynch asked slyly.

"What are you talking about?" Lorn asked, bewildered.

"You've been out foraging for eight days and yet you're as fit as a fiddle," Lynch answered, "while your men have been wasting away, day by day."

"You're looking fat and sassy yourself," Lorn retorted.

"We gave him the grub," Smilin' Jake interrupted.

"You did what?"

"We decided that you needed him to break the spell, so he was more important than we were. After the fifth day with no grub I was ready to shoot him and eat him. Ox took my damn gun." Lorn couldn't decide if Jake was joking or not.

"Did somebody mention grub?" Ox sat up and leaned on one elbow.

"I'll be damned," Lorn cursed. For the first time he noticed the low supply of driftwood for the fire, and that many of the water containers were empty. He sat down and drew out some of the smoked meat and trailbread and cheese and passed it to his men. Their eyes lit up as if it were a feast. He dug deeper into the sack and found a cloth wrapped bundle with dried fruit inside. His stomach growled and his head swam.

"Eat, Graywullf," Lynch urged. "You'll need your strength. We must leave tonight."

Lorn ate, but after a few mouthfuls his stomach rolled threateningly. He drank three cups of water and lay down near the fire. There was something he needed to ask Jake, but he couldn't remember it. In moments he was asleep.

The fire burned low, and Lorn shifted in his sleep, rolling onto a sharp rock. He sat up, and for just a moment he thought he saw a flicker of movement near Lynch's cell. He climbed to his feet, suppressing a loud groan as his punished muscles nearly rebelled against his commands. He grabbed a handful of meat and cheese and took it back to Lynch along with a cup of water. The Dark Wizard took it gratefully then retreated to the back of his cell to eat.

"What happened here?" Lorn asked.

Lynch grinned. "What do you mean?"

"How can eight days pass and seem like less than one?"

"Remember when you locked me up and I was muttering under my breath?" Lynch reminded him.

"I reckon."

"I placed a spell of endurance and concealment on you, just on the off chance that it would stick. It damn near killed me." He looked at Lorn with an openly mischievous expression. "Only those that are open to it can use Dark Magic and not be destroyed by it. You're not a pure, chaste little *magii'ri* lamb, are you?"

Lorn was thoroughly confused.

"Anything can happen under the influence of Dark Magic," Lynch explained. "Time can speed up or slow down. The user can suffer memory loss, blindness or paralysis. He can even travel through time. But the use of Dark Magic always comes with a price. Sometimes it kills the user, and sometimes the price is not revealed for many years."

Realization slowly dawned in Lorn's clouded mind. "You son of a bitch."

Lynch laughed. "Perhaps."

Lorn stepped back one step and drew both of his revolvers, thumbing back the hammers as he did. The instant the sights aligned on Lynch's belly he squeezed the triggers. The hammers seemed to fall in slow motion and at the last possible moment, a millisecond before the detonating powder would have sent two half inch lead balls crashing into Lynch's guts, Lorn swung the muzzles just far enough to each side to miss his vitals. The bullets plowed bloody furrows along Lynch's ribcage and tore out a splinter of bone on each side. He let out an inarticulate squawk of mingled pain and fear as he stumbled backwards and fell onto his blankets. The other *magii'ri* came to chaotic life around the fire, but Lorn's attention remained fixed on the Dark Wizard.

"That's your last warning," he said coldly. "Don't toy with me."

The echoes of the gunshots reverberated through the chamber as Lynch realized he had never in all the centuries of his storied career been closer to death. The yawning muzzles of Lorn's revolvers looked as wide as a canyon mouth. With a deft spin, so fast even Lynch's eye couldn't track it, Lorn holstered his weapons. He opened the cell door.

"Come on. We got a job to do," he ordered.

The *magii'ri* Warriors, still confused by the sudden gunfire, holstered their own weapons and began to pack their belongings.

"Not you guys," Lorn said quietly. "Your all so worn down you won't make it to the top level of the Citadel, and we gotta go clear across the Isle."

"You found 'em?" Smilin' Jake asked.

"I came across a farmer and trailed him to his home," Lorn replied. "He took me to his home, gave me shelter and all this food. The Slayers tracked us there." He turned to stare hard at Lynch. "They're all dead now. Men, women, even the kids. Slayers got 'em." Lynch was staring at him with his mouth open.

"Goddamnit," Ox swore, shaking his head sorrowfully. "Killin' kids, that's bad."

"I can't speak for the others," Smilin' Jake asserted, "but I feel strong enough for a march."

Lorn was taken by surprise. He studied the men and was astounded at their recovery in a few short hours. Indeed, they did look nearly fit enough to fight again. He turned to Lynch, who merely shrugged and finished binding a cloth around his ribs.

"There," he commented. "That should hold me together." He stepped from his cell and met Lorn's suspicious gaze. "What?" he asked innocently.

Lorn mentally took stock of his own physical condition. He suddenly realized he felt good. Too good. "You did it again."

Lynch stepped back into the cell with his hands held out to ward off another attack. "You're not going to shoot me again, are you? I thought you needed a little healing spell, that's all."

Lorn threw his hands in the air. "Stop doing that! What do I have to do to get through to you?"

"It wasn't Dark Magic that time," Lynch grinned. "So you can't shoot me."

"Wanna bet?"

Lynch watched for even a hint of a smile on Lorn's face, but none appeared. "No more magic," he agreed.

"Until we take on the other Dark Wizards," Lorn reminded him. "If you back out then, I'll blow your head off."

Uneasy silence filled the Citadel.

"I'm starving," Ox's voice broke the silence.

The *magii'ri* Warriors and the Dark Wizard attacked the food Lorn had brought back, and in minutes much of it was gone. Lorn suddenly remembered his rifle.

"Did any of you climb to the top and bring my rifle back?" he asked around a mouthful of bread and cheese.

"We didn't go anywhere," Smilin' Jake said.

"What about Lynch?"

"He was in the cell the whole time," Smilin' Jake answered. Bill and Ox nodded in agreement.

"What about it?" Lorn asked Lynch.

"Don't look at me, I was locked up," Lynch replied.

"More magic," Bill said with a scowl. He spat to one side.

Lorn sighed. "I hate magic." He took a huge drink of water. It was too late to worry about it now. Whoever had taken it was long gone. But how could anyone besides a Wizard enter the Citadel and avoid the Slayers?

"Was it a special rifle?" Lynch asked guilelessly. He popped a dried apricot into his mouth.

Lorn sighed. "No. It was a standard issue *magii'ri* rifle with my initials carved in the stock and a little handiwork to ward off the bad spirits. But you know as well as I do that *only* the *magii'ri* are allowed to have firearms by royal decree of King Elander."

"I do know that," Lynch agreed. "And I have always thought it was strange why the *magii'ri* don't trust their own people with weapons."

"It's the Code," Smilin' Jake replied.

"The Code," Lynch mocked. "That precious *magii'ri* Code which guarantees that you will have superior weapons in every fight, yet weakens a man's ability to defend his own home and family."

"The Code," Lorn said quietly, "is much more than that. It is the guideline for nearly every action we take as *magii'ri* Warriors. By following the Code we are able to carry out an unpleasant duty with honor and integrity."

"That's nonsense," Lynch retorted. "It's just bullshit drilled into your heads by some elite member of the ruling class who is using you for his own gain."

"It's not nonsense," Smilin' Jake argued. "It's the difference between right and wrong. Men have to adopt rules and live by them. That is the difference between order and chaos."

"Rules for right and wrong?" Lynch burst out laughing. "You've all been brainwashed. I have traveled the known World and I can tell you one thing. The fewer rules a society has, the happier the citizens are. You already suspect that your Council is merely using you. So why put your lives at risk? Don't give your life for a false cause. The ruling class of Norland whom you so mindlessly serve, slaughtering thousands in their name, is corrupt. Everything you do makes them fatter and richer and more powerful. With every life that you take in the name of Aard, another coin drops in their purse. Go back to Norland and you'll see I'm right." He spoke with such fervor his hands shook, and he jammed them in his pockets. "Are you so blind? Tell me, Warrior, where have you been for the last two years?"

"We were sent to the Southron Desert to deal with a band of outlaws who drove out the miners who had settled there," Lorn answered.

"What were they mining?" Lynch asked.

"Gold," Smilin' Jake interrupted. "They were minin' gold."

"Did you see any miners or settlers?"

"Damn few," Lorn admitted. "The outlaws drove most of 'em out before we got there, and there was a damn sight more outlaws than we figured on."

"Because they were one and the same," Lynch said. "It was supposed to be an ambush. Those *outlaws* were mining for the *magii'ri* Wizards."

"How do you know that?" Bill asked.

"Where were you before that?" Lynch said, ignoring Bill's query.

"We wiped out a band of opium traders," Smilin' Jake replied. "And before that, we put down an uprising of farmers who refused to pay their tribute."

"And what did you do with the opium and the tribute that you seized?"

"Handed it over to the Wizards," Lorn admitted.

"And before that?"

"We seized a lead mine," Lorn said, despair now evident in his voice. "And before that we arrested several ship's captains who were engaged in piracy and handed the plunder over to the Council."

"I rest my case," Lynch said. "Your Council is rotten to the core. They used you, no, they are *still* using you to make themselves so rich and powerful no one can touch them."

"But how do you *know* that?" Bill insisted.

Lynch hesitated. He stepped back from the fire. "Because I was one of them."

"What are you talkin' about?" Ox finally spoke. "I never saw you before, and we been in Richfeld plenty of times."

"You wouldn't have seen me if I didn't want you to," Lynch asserted. "But I was there. As a matter of fact," he cast a sidelong glance at Lorn, "I was supposed to meet some of the Council here."

"Here?" Lorn couldn't hide the surprise in his voice.

"Aye, but they started without me. I was held up by personal business and it damn near killed me."

"You were supposed to be with the Dark Wizards when they conjured up the Slayers," Lorn said in sudden realization. "What in the Hell were you thinking?"

Lynch shrugged. "It seemed like a good idea at the time. We'd conjure the Darkness and summon the Slayers. They'd kill of most of the population then we'd drop the spell of Darkness, the ensuing sunlight would kill most, if not all, of the Slayers and we'd come along behind and simply pick up the spoils."

"And you just decided to switch sides?" Smilin' Jake asked.

"Maybe you weren't listening," Lynch said. He almost mentioned being pursued by Ned Roark, who had been sent by that same *magii'ri* Council, but held his tongue on that subject. "I wasn't just another Dark Wizard they let in on the plan. It was *my* plan from the beginning, and when I was a little late and in a weakened state they tried to use my own plan to kill me. My own plan! They double crossed me. At that point I decided our partnership was over."

"This is all too much," Lorn said, shaking his head. "You admit to being a Dark Wizard, and a very powerful one at that, and to participating in a plan that would have killed thousands of people. Yet we find you floating in the sea, near death. We nurse you back to health, and now you would have us believe that you only want to help us? Forgive me, Lynch, but it all sounds like bullshit to me." The other *magii'ri* Warriors nodded in agreement.

"You've forgotten one very important point," Lynch said in a flat tone. "They crossed me. No one crosses Lynch and lives. *No one.*" The Dark Wizard sat down next to the fire and helped himself to a cup of tea. He took a long drink then spoke. "I will have my revenge, with you or without you. Now, we're wasting time, and with every passing hour more people will die."

Lorn reached his decision. "Me and Smilin' Jake are going to look for my rifle one more time. When we get back, be ready to go. C'mon, Jake."

Lorn and Smilin' Jake left the others by the fire and began to climb by torchlight. Both Warriors felt renewed, physically and mentally, and the flights of stairs dropped steadily behind them. Lorn had to admit it felt good, magic or not. Eventually they reached the top floor where Lorn had left his rifle. There were no tracks in the thick dust on the floor besides Lorn's.

"He came from outside, then," Jake suggested. "Just reached in the door and took it."

"Goddamnit," Lorn cursed. "It looks that way."

"It's one rifle," Smilin' Jake said. "Man can't do much harm with one rifle, can he?"

"I reckon not," Lorn admitted. "But I sure liked that rifle. Best one I ever had. I carried it for years."

"Is that the only reason you had me come up here with you?"

"No," Lorn admitted. "I don't trust Lynch."

"No shit," Smilin' Jake blurted. "He ain't exactly the trustworthy type."

"I reckon," Lorn answered. "You and me been on the trail together a long time, Jake. Do you trust me?"

"I reckon so," Smilin' Jake answered.

"Good. I need you to close that door and guard it. Don't let no one in or out unless it's me. Got it?"

"What are you gonna do?" Jake asked suspiciously.

"Somethin' Fowler beat the crap out of me for when we were 'prentices," Lorn answered. "Then, when he realized I had the aptitude, he showed me a little the oldtimers all knew. I'm gonna use magic."

"You ain't trained in it," Jake protested.

"I have to have some answers," Lorn said. "And we need the upper hand on Lynch. This is the only way to get it. Close the damn door, and don't open it for anyone but me."

"Alright," Jake answered. "Don't let no one steal your pistols, too." He grinned to take the sting out of the words.

"Just shut the damn door," Lorn growled.

The door shut with a final sounding click and Lorn turned a slow circle to survey the room. His old mentor Fowler had taught them much, some of which was supposed to be off limits to Warriors. In addition, he had taught Lorn a few things that even the other Warriors didn't know. He had caught Lorn in a magical trance once, and had beaten him bloody for practicing magic without any instruction. Then he had recognized the unique abilities of a Warrior who could practice magic as well as any of the Warriors of old, and had dug up a disgraced Wizard to teach Lorn a few tricks. As he had told Lorn, maybe it would be enough so he didn't kill himself. Lorn dug deep into his belt pouch and pulled out a tiny bottle plugged with a bead of wax and wrapped with buckskin. He held it up and the contents reflected the sparkling torchlight. He thought he could see images inside the bottle, fighting to get out. With a deep sigh he pulled the buckskin stopper, raised it to his mouth and tapped it once to dislodge a few grains of white powder under his tongue. The bitter taste filled his mouth and he fought the urge to spit as his blood pounded in his ears. Almost immediately he felt his knees buckle and he slumped to the floor. Angry voices filled his head. The room began to spin, and he put both hands out to try to stop it, unmindful that he dropped the vial in the process. He felt the rough sandstone of a bench with his searching hands and climbed on it then held on to the sides until the room stopped spinning.

"It's about time you pulled your head outta yer ass," a familiar voiced rasped.

Lorn squinted, then cocked his head and cast one bleary eye towards the far wall. The very tall figure of a long, lean man leaned against the wall with his hat pulled down to conceal his face. He raised his head and Lorn recognized him. It was Fowler, the instructor who had pounded lessons into him and hundreds of other *magii'ri* Warriors with a heavy hand. But it couldn't be. Fowler had been dead for years.

"Yeah, it's me," Fowler growled. "It took you long enough to figure out you needed help." He crossed the room in three long strides and sat beside Lorn.

"How can it be?" Lorn heard his own voice ask, sounding strangely hollow.

"I taught you just enough magic to get answers when you truly needed them," Fowler answered. "I don't know how it works myself. I do know you're runnin' out of time."

"Tell me about the curse of the Citadel," Lorn said. And Fowler talked. He told Lorn every fact about the Curse. When he had finished Lorn nodded. He knew what he had to do. "Do you know what happened to my rifle?"

"I reckon so," Fowler said. "It was taken by a *magii'ri* Wizard, just as you suspected."

"But *why?*" Lorn pressed.

"Even the dead can't read what is in the hearts of men," Fowler replied. "All I can say is you're right in your thinkin'. There's a river of blood headed your way."

"Is there any way we can stop it?"

"Not now," Fowler replied. He shrugged. "Believe it or not, it was needed. But be warned," his voice began to fade, "you won't be welcomed in Norland."

Lorn shook his head as his thoughts became clear once again. The image of Fowler sitting beside him was so real he laid a hand on the stone beside him. It was still warm. Then he became aware of voices outside in the hall.

"Stand back, Lynch," Smilin' Jake said in a conversational tone. "Or I'll splatter your guts on the wall."

Lorn crossed the room and flung the door open. Jake stood at the doorway, his revolver at waist height aimed at Lynch's belly. Ox and Bill stood to one side, plainly confused.

"It's alright," Lorn said. He pushed Jake's revolver down until it pointed at the floor.

"I heard voices," Jake said, still keeping his eyes on Lynch.

"I had a visit from an old friend," Lorn assured him. "Fowler."

"So where is he?" Lynch asked suspiciously.

"He's gone now," Lorn said with a shrug. He brushed past Lynch to stand before Ox and Bill. "Are you ready to march?"

"Say the word," Bill replied.

Ox nodded. He looked past Lorn into the room. "Fowler was here? Where did he go?" He took a short step into the room. "It'd be damn good to see ol' Fowler again."

"He's gone, Ox," Lorn said patiently.

"That's too bad. I guess you didn't find your rifle, did you, Cap'n?"

"It's gone too," Lorn answered. "Let's march." He led the way back into the room.

"Ummm…" Lynch stammered. "Aren't you forgetting something? We can't leave until you break the Curse."

Lorn grinned. "Fowler had a lot to say, considerin' he's been dead and buried for years. He told me all about the Curse." He reached for the door but Lynch rushed forward and seized him by the forearm before he could open it.

"Let's not rush this," he said.

"It's time to end it," Lorn replied. "So unless you have something else to tell us, I suggest you let go of my arm before I break yours." His tone was mild and he smiled when he spoke, but it was obvious he meant what he said.

Lynch dropped his hands back to his sides. "Alright, alright. Just don't open that door. We can't use this route again. The Slayers are waiting for some fool to step outside again so they can tear him to pieces."

"And how do you know that?" Bill asked.

Lynch rolled his eyes. "Think about it. Someone came up the same trail and stole a rifle from this room. Therefore, they know Graywullf used this trail once. It stands to reason they'd suspect someone would try to use it again."

"So what would you have us do?" Lorn asked.

"We'll go back down to the main entrance and you can lift the curse. Then we'll climb up the old wagon road."

Lorn shrugged indifferently. "Whatever. One way or another we're gonna end this."

He led the way back down to the main entrance. The fire they had left had burned down, but it still cast enough light to see the dark corners of the room. Lorn once again led the way, this time back towards the entryway.

"You will not pass." The warning sent shivers down Lorn's spine. The stones of the Citadel groaned and creaked against each other. The sound of ringing steel chimed in as the Warriors drew their blades.

"Steel will not harm them," Lynch warned in a hushed whisper, but Lorn noted a tiny smile that curved his lips.

Lorn stepped away from the group. "I command you to show yourselves!"

The Citadel shook and dust sifted down from the blackness overhead. The clinking of leg irons filled the room.

"Sweet Mother!" Bill gasped.

A column of Warriors appeared, dressed in full battle armor and armed with swords and lances. Their legs were individually bound together with heavy chain. No facial features were visible beneath their helms, no hands showed through their gauntlets.

"Who bids us to appear? Who has the power to command the prisoners of the Citadel?" the captain demanded.

"I am Lorn Graywullf, Captain of the *magii'ri*."

A sighing sound passed through the spirit ranks. The captain laughed bitterly.

"So says you."

He drifted across the room, his legs irons dragging behind him, to stop directly in front of Lorn. Smilin' Jake stepped up beside him, but a careless blow from the haft of the captain's lance sent him sprawling.

"Hold!" Lorn shouted, and the captain froze in place. "If any harm comes to me or my men, I'll leave you in this Hell until the end of the World. Harm us and I will never release you."

"Who grants you the power to release anything?" the captain asked. "For centuries we have stood guard here, cursed as scoundrels by those who deserted us!"

"It is my birthright," Lorn replied, anger growing within him. "Your arrogance towards a son of Malachi will not be tolerated. You're like a pack of cur dogs left alone for too long, snapping at anything that draws near.

Hear me well! I am Lorn Graywullf, son of Lawrence, son of Martin, son of Matthew, son of Malachi, the first Warrior."

The captain grunted an obscenity. "The sire of your sires left us to rot. Did you know that? He abandoned us."

A growl of anger rippled through the soldier's ranks. Lorn made no reply.

"We did as he bade us. For twenty days we paid no heed to our own needs. We guarded the royal family, though they treated us like dogs. Every day we scanned the sea with hope rising in our hearts, but the sail of the 'Wullf never appeared. Our food ran low then gave out entirely. The half-men fouled and diverted the water supply out of the Citadel. I sent men, good men, on a desperate quest for water. The half-men butchered them alive. They ate them while they still breathed! Do not dare to lecture me on duty!"

"Men such as us must have our honor," Lorn replied calmly. "Without honor we have nothing. You disgraced your fathers when you gave the royal family to the half-men. You not only broke the Code, you made a mockery of it!"

"The Code IS a mockery!" the captain shouted. "Can't you see that? The Wizards used us just as they are now using you. You don't know what happened here at all. We were counseled to hand over the royal family by one of our own!"

Utter silence followed.

"What did you say?" Lorn demanded.

"Aye," the captain laughed. "Now you're all ears. A Wizard, left here as an adviser, convinced us to hand over seven children to a mob of half-men who had just eaten six of my soldiers." He feigned surprise. "Oh, you didn't know that, did you?"

The *magii'ri* were stunned into silence.

"That's right. A *magii'ri* Wizard used his power to sway us from our sworn duty. He released us from his spell of confusion in time to watch the children die. We saw what we had done, and we attacked the half-men in a desperate attempt to rescue the royal family. They outnumbered us a hundred to one, and yet I still was able to reach the eldest child while he lived. I held guard over him and many fell to my blade that day. We stayed true to the Code, even if it deserted us. We have the honor of trueblood Warriors. We *are* trueblood Warriors!"

"Did this Wizard have a name?" Lorn asked with a gleam in his eye.

The captain replied uncertainly. "After five hundred years, who can say?"

"Five hundred years?" Lorn repeated wonderingly.

"That doesn't matter," Lynch stated. "We live in the present. What do we do now?"

Lorn addressed the captain of the prisoners. "I believe you. History has wronged you, and I will try to make it right. I can release you, but I have one more favor to ask. Stay here yet a little longer, and guard our plunder. I, or one of my blood, will return for it and release you from this half-life."

"Release them now," Lynch hissed. "before they kill us all!"

"How do we know you *can*?" the captain asked.

"We must have proof," one of the soldiers growled. He flitted across the cavern directly at the group. A shot rang out, and a neat round hole appeared in the center of the soldier's forehead. The bullet ricocheted off the far wall and thudded into the drifted sand on the floor at Lorn's feet. But the soldier did not fall. He laughed, and continued towards Bill McCurry, who was hastily reloading his long rifle. Lorn stepped between them and cut the soldier in half. A dark chasm opened up in the floor and the soldier was sucked into it. His clawlike fingers dug furrows in the floor, and for only a moment he was visible as a man of about thirty, with sandy blonde hair and a stubble of beard. His haunted eyes rolled back in his head as he realized his fate. His screams echoed in the cavern as the hole drew closed and all sign of his existence disappeared.

Lorn stared at it thoughtfully for a long moment. "Any questions? I can release you… or send you to Hell."

The captain bowed at the waist, as did the rest of the soldiers. "We are in your service. What must we do to fulfill our duty?"

"No harm is to come to these men," Lorn ordered. "And the cargo we leave here must remain safe and dry. If that is done, an heir of Malachi will return for it and release you."

"I see you have the power, and no harm will come to the trueblood *magii'ri*," the captain responded. "Why won't you release us?"

"I need this favor from you. Besides, you've been here five hundred years. Another twenty surely won't hurt."

A ripple of what may have been laughter went through the column of soldiers.

"We will be loyal to you, son of Malachi, as we remained loyal to the Graywullf for the last five centuries. It will be done as you asked."

The column of soldiers melted back into the stone walls.

"That's something you don't see everyday," Smilin' Jake said. He grinned then spat blood from his smashed lips.

"Why didn't you release them?" Lynch seethed. "We're trapped here!"

"You weren't listening," Lorn replied. "The captain said that all the trueblood *magii'ri* would leave."

"Fine for you," Lynch said. "But I am a Dark Wizard..."

"Who just happens to have *magii'ri* blood," Lorn finished. "As a matter of fact, you were once one of us. A Warrior."

Lynch was silent for a moment then he sighed deeply. "Those times are best forgotten, and believe it or not, I had banished those memories from my mind."

"You were a *magii'ri* Warrior?" Smilin' Jake asked. His voice was heavy with doubt.

"That was a long time ago," Lynch answered. "And I was a different man then. I was about as innocent as a Warrior and Wizard could be."

"This is too much. You're apologizing for being *magii'ri,* like it's something to be ashamed of," Bill said. Lorn watched in silence.

"I am ashamed of it," Lynch replied savagely. "I spent the last few centuries trying to forget that part of my life. And you four misfits had to show up and dredge all those memories right back to the surface."

"You were an outcast," Lorn said suddenly.

"And if I was?" Lynch snarled. "None of that matters now."

"Whatever you say," Lorn said. He turned to his men. "Better eat now. There won't be much time when we set out."

"You're not listening," Lynch interrupted. "I can't leave, and you can't beat the other Wizards without me."

"You'll be comin' with us," Lorn said calmly.

"You're wrong," Lynch began to say.

"No, you're wrong," Lorn turned back to the Wizard so swiftly Lynch thought he may actually get shot. Again. "You want to believe that being a *magii'ri* Wizard was a part of your life that you can just forget, but it's not. Being *magii'ri* is part of you. It never changes. Like it or not, it's who you are." He turned his attention to the last remnants of bread, cheese and smoked meat. "We're traveling light and fast, Lynch, so if I was you I'd eat somethin' before Ox polishes it off."

Lynch closed his eyes and rubbed his temples with his forefingers. "You're right," he finally muttered. Then he said something under his breath, too low for the *magii'ri* to hear.

"What's that?" Lorn asked, his words muffled by a mouthful of bread and cheese. Crumbs dropped from his parted lips as he tried to stuff even more into his mouth. He was suddenly ravenous.

"I said, you're right," Lynch admitted. "I am *magii'ri*."

"I'll be goddamned," Smilin' Jake said in disgust. He took a huge drink of water and stuffed a full slice of cheese into his mouth. Lynch shouldered his way into the group and helped himself to the food. The entire group fed like hogs at a slop trough until all of the food had disappeared. Lorn drank three cups of water and stared hard at Lynch, wondering at the unnatural hunger.

"You did it again," he accused.

Lynch grinned. "I reckon so. It's time to end this, as you said. I thought a spell of concealment would help us up the wagon road without the Slayers spotting us."

"I give up," Lorn said. "You're beyond help. I guess this means you have your full strength back?"

"Not completely, but close enough," Lynch agreed.

"Then what are we waitin' for?"

Lorn and Lynch led the way out of the Citadel. Once they were all outside, Lorn paused. The sea air was wonderfully cool after the close confines of the Citadel, but it bore scents that were strangely intense to his nostrils even after spending weeks at sea. He suddenly realized that his eyesight could pierce the unnatural gloom that had enveloped the land as well. He laid a hand on the stone wall and reveled at the sensation he felt. It was almost like the rock was alive. He cast a questioning glance at Lynch.

"It's part of the spell," Lynch explained. He nodded at the base of the old wagon road. "There's our trail. Look about a hundred yards up it."

Lorn did as he was bid. At least a dozen of the Slayers perched in the rocks lining the trail. Cold fear clamped down on his guts. The remaining *magii'ri* saw the Slayers at the same time and were only a fraction of a second slower than Lorn in drawing their weapons. Lynch grimaced as he quickly stepped in front of the Warriors.

"By the gods are you trying to get us all killed? They can't see us, but if you go to blazing away at them they'll figure it out damn quick. Then we'll all be dead."

The Warriors reluctantly holstered their weapons while Lynch shook his head. "Is that your first reaction to everything? Shoot first, ask questions later?" he asked.

"It always worked before," Lorn replied. "We always figured if we killed the wrong man the gods could sort them out."

"Not this time," Lynch reminded them. "Now you're going to learn to use your brains instead of blowing the Hell out of things and picking up the pieces when the smoke clears. The Slayers can't see us well enough to attack. To them we're just like an unusual shadow, a mirage, if you will. So keep quiet, stay close together and let's get to the top of the cliffs."

Lynch started off up the trail and Lorn hurried to keep up. He didn't look back at his men, he sensed their desire to stay close to the Dark Wizard as strongly as he felt it himself. As they drew closer to the waiting Slayers he could feel the heat radiating from their leathery bodies. Their expressionless eyes bored holes through him, and he felt his balls shrivel and draw up nearly into his belly in fear. If Lynch's spell failed, or if even one of the Slayers noticed them, they were goners. There would be no time to cut them all down before they pounced upon the men on the narrow trail, and there simply was no where to run. Sheer cliffs rose two hundred feet above them and the sea pounded the rock strewn beach hundreds of feet below.

Sweat trickled down between Lorn's shoulder blades despite the cool sea breeze, and he chanced a glance behind him. Smilin' Jake caught his glance and gave him a crooked grin. His eyes danced and both hands were firmly wrapped around the grips of his pistols. If anything went wrong, Smilin' Jake would go to his death laughing with his guns blazing. Ox stared straight ahead, placing each step with exaggerated care, as if by ignoring the threat above he could negate it. Bill McCurry brought up the rear, looking as if he might bolt at any second. But Lorn knew better. When the chips were down, Bill would stand steady and deal death as efficiently as any Warrior born. He hurried to catch up to the rapidly ascending Lynch, and his men hustled up behind him.

The air was sweet and clear to his newly reborn lungs, courtesy of Lynch's indiscriminate use of Dark Magic, and the physical exertion felt good. There was no explanation for what happened next. One second Lorn was striding along, caught up in the climb, the next he was falling even as he heard the sound of splintering rock. He frantically clawed for a handhold and just grasped the edge of the rock. His feet dangled crazily in space as the three truebloods stared stupidly for a moment, as if they couldn't grasp the fact that their captain could die by something as mundane as a fall. Then they rushed forward as one.

"Stay back," Lynch hissed, with a frantic glance back at the Slayers. He pointed to a fissure that separated the staircase from the wider cart road. "I'll go. I'm lighter."

He leaped nimbly across the fissure and landed as lightly as a fly. Smilin' Jake started out to help, but Ox dragged him back to the cart road.

Oddly, Lorn felt no alarm or fear, only disappointment. *So this is the way it ends,* he thought. Then Lynch's bristly face appeared at the edge and he clamped his hand over Lorn's wrist like a steel trap. Lorn swung his other hand up and Lynch caught it also.

"If it goes, we'll both die," Lorn stated as calmly as he could muster.

Lynch expelled his pent up breath in a *whoosh* redolent of garlic and something else that Lorn couldn't identify and a harsh chuckle erupted from his compressed lips.

"Wouldn't that be ironic," he muttered.

He gave a great heave, and yet another unexplainable event took place. The wiry Wizard hoisted up the *magii'ri* captain who outweighed him by more than seventy pounds and literally carried him to the safety of the cart road. The moment Lynch's feet were safely off the shattered staircase another giant chunk calved off the cliff and plunged to the beach several hundred feet below. The truebloods grabbed Lorn and literally dragged him closer to the mountainside.

"That was close," Lynch whispered calmly, even as three Slayers took flight and glided in to examine the crumbling mountainside. "Don't move," he warned even as he tried to will himself to become part of the stone behind him.

They lay with their backs against the sheer wall of the cliff and regained their wind, while the Slayers flew by sometimes within thirty feet of the crouching men. Sweat beaded up on Ox's forehead and his eyes darted wildly from side to side, until Bill placed a calming hand upon his thick shoulder. Even Lorn's hands shook as he rested them on his knees and he willed them to remain still. Only Smilin' Jake remained unaffected. His crooked grin was firmly in place, as if the entire situation were no more than a joke. Finally, the Slayers rejoined the main group, landing lightly on outcroppings of rock. When Lorn stood, his knees felt like jelly. But he nodded to Lynch and they resumed the climb.

Finally they reached the top, and stood for a few moments watching the trail, and the Slayers that still stood watch over it. It was obvious they had passed by unseen. Lorn nudged Lynch and pointed away from the cliff. When they had gone several hundred yards, he spoke.

"That was a good piece of work. I owe you."

"I'll collect someday," Lynch replied with a slight smile. "But we still have a long ways to go. We better pick up the pace."

"Can you handle that?" Lorn asked.

Lynch grinned, "I can. The question is, can you?"

Lorn rolled his eyes. He hesitated, then shook his head and chuckled. "Alright, do what you have to."

He had barely spoken the words when he felt his muscles come alive.

"I could get used to this," Smilin' Jake said. Then Lynch broke into a fast trot, and the *magii'ri* followed.

Six hours later they finally stopped, sweat soaked and wheezing. They had traveled nearly fifteen miles. A half mile farther ahead torches and campfires blazed brightly.

"Guards," Lynch panted. "There's a dome shaped hill beyond them. That's where the Wizards are."

They sat for several minutes, trying to regain their breath and studying the enemy encampment.

"Let me guess," Lorn said finally, "The Wizards will be on the hill, so you need to get past the guards."

"I reckon so," Lynch agreed.

Lorn slid his revolvers from the holsters and checked the loads, then sighed. "How long do you think it'd take the Slayers to reach us?"

"Not nearly long enough," Lynch replied.

"Then it has to be quiet," Smilin' Jake interrupted. Bill nodded his pleased agreement.

"Knife work, then," Lorn agreed.

The Warriors spread out, and in moments the guards fell silently, one at a time. As the Warriors regrouped, Lynch joined them and they stood for a long moment gazing at the dome shaped, barren hillside.

"Can we help in any way?" Lorn asked.

"I'm afraid not," Lynch replied. "This is a very complicated spell, and it requires all of the involved Wizard's attention and energy. However, one or two of the Wizards may actually survive the breaking of the spell, and I am pretty sure they will not be pleased."

"You intend to kill all of them?" Smilin' Jake asked incredulously.

"I do," Lynch answered. "It's a shame, actually. I counted several of them as friends for many years." He shook his head as if to clear it and glanced around. "This seems to be secure for now. Wait here. I'm going to turn the energy of the spell against them, and I don't really know what kind of commotion that may cause." He walked away, muttering under his breath, without waiting for a response.

"You know," Smilin' Jake said suddenly, "he might have made a good Warrior."

# CHAPTER SIX

L YNCH WALKED STEADILY, WITHOUT any hesitation. The path was now familiar to him, after all, he had walked it many times when this had been *his* plan. And in many ways, he thought, it was all to similar to any one of a hundred other paths he had walked which always ended in death. But it was always death for others, never for Lynch. As he walked, the light from a magical fire grew brighter and brighter. He approached within thirty feet. The Wizards were gathered around the leaping flames, seated crosslegged with their hands outstretched, totally oblivious to his presence. Lynch could not resist the opportunity. He walked forward and boldly penetrated the circle. The other Wizards felt his presence and began to withdraw from the magical trance they had placed themselves under. Lynch gave them just enough time to realize who he was.

"Hello boys," he said softly. "Couldn't wait?" The expressions on their faces were priceless, a memory Lynch cherished for years. With a single word he quenched the flames, and the hillside went dark. The Warriors gathered below looked up in sudden fear.

"Lynch!" One of the Wizards shouted as his befuddled brain cleared. "No! You mustn't break the spell!"

The words were no more than out of his mouth when the entire dome seemed to implode. Moments later, streaks of lightning erupted from the crater where it had stood and arced across the sky. The Warriors sought cover among the few boulders that were strewn around the campsite. Smoke and fire and red hot, glowing chunks of granite followed the lightning, along with a high pitched keening. Rocks the size of pumpkins whizzed past and Lorn and his men hugged the ground as several of them plowed directly into the boulders with enough force to disintegrate the smaller rocks.

"I just had a bad thought," Lorn yelled, nearly in Jake's ear.

Jake rolled his eyes, the whites were plainly visible. "Really? How could that be?" he shouted back as another rock slammed into his sheltering boulder with the sound of a cannon going off. He ducked even lower and drew his pistols.

"What if it's really night time?" Lorn shouted as all the sounds suddenly died around them, plunging the hillside into unnatural silence. His ears rang. He took a chance and raised his head just far enough to look up the hill. Lynch walked out of a shroud of dust and smoke, and behind him there was a barely perceptible lightening of the sky.

"Is it over?" Lorn asked as Lynch drew near.

"Almost," Lynch replied. His voice sounded weak after the deafening explosions. "There was one small miscalculation on my part…"

"Don't tell me," Lorn interrupted. "It ain't sunrise yet."

Lynch nodded and pointed down the slope hill towards the sea. In the half light between full dark and dawn, the *magii'ri* Warriors could see a flock of black winged shapes rapidly approaching.

"Get ready," Lorn shouted as he drew both his pistols and checked the loads. He glanced down to make sure the extra cylinders were still in the pouches on his belt. When he looked up the Slayers were almost on top of them. The Warriors began firing in a smooth, drawn out fusillade of lead. The Slayers in the front of the flock were cut down, but as soon as one fell another glided in behind it. Lorn holstered his left hand revolver and smoothly replaced the empty cylinder in his right with a loaded one from his belt. He fired from the hip and a Slayer fell so close to Jake it actually nudged him with it's snout.

"There's too many!" Bill shouted.

"Back to the rocks!" Lorn ordered.

Jake was knocked off his feet and the Slayer atop him dipped its head to finish him. Lorn tried to snap a shot at it, but the hammer fell on an empty chamber. A moment before the beast's jaws snapped shut on Jake's face, Lynch leaped astride it and plunged a long bladed knife into its spine. The Slayer convulsed, throwing itself backwards and dismounting Lynch in the process. Jake was on his feet in a fraction of a second, and fired a shot at point blank range into the ear hole of yet another Slayer as it tried to finish off Lynch. Despite the heroics of every man there, the Slayers were destined to win by sheer numbers.

Lorn's pistols ran dry. He dropped them to the ground and drew his sword, hacking and slashing at every black shape that came near. Then he too was knocked to the ground. He saw in vivid detail the open maw of the Slayer as it plunged its head down towards him. In desperation, he drove his forearm into its open mouth. Pain coursed through him as the Slayer's teeth rended the flesh on his arm. Then, abruptly, the Slayer released him and threw its head back in agony. Lorn stared in disbelief as the flesh seemed to melt away from the Slayer's head and it dropped lifeless to the ground. In moments the only thing that remained of it were stark white bones. Lorn raised his hand to wipe his face and suddenly understood as the first rays of sunlight dripped like fire from his fingers. He leaped to his feet.

"Jake!"

"I'm here," Smilin' Jake answered from a pile of rubble where he had been thrown.

"Bill! Ox!"

"We made it," Ox replied. He helped Bill to his feet. The smaller man was limping badly.

"Lynch?" Lorn called. There was no answer.

"Lynch?" he called again.

Lynch crawled from beneath a pile of bleached bones. "That was too close."

Relief flooded through Lorn. They were torn and bleeding, but they were all alive. He sat down and rested his shaking hands on his knees.

"What about you?" Jake asked.

"I'll live," Lorn answered. He nodded at Lynch. "Did you get all of 'em? The Wizards?""

Lynch looked troubled. "One escaped."

"Did you get Marsten?" Lorn asked hopefully.

"He was never here," Lynch replied. "And the man who escaped was a stranger to me."

"But Marsten was involved, wasn't he?" Lorn asked.

Lynch nodded. "Marsten and his second have been behind almost every skirmish you've been sent to straighten out for the last three years." He sat heavily next to Lorn and surveyed the carnage. "What a goddamn mess."

"Is it over?" Smilin' Jake asked. "The spell, I mean?"

"I reckon so," Lynch replied. "Since all but one of the Wizards it took to cast the spell are laying in a hole up there, looking frighteningly similar to these Slayers," He nodded at the bleached bones, devoid of even a scrap of hide.

"Then let's get out of here," Lorn suggested. "Bill, can you walk?"

"I'll carry him," Ox replied. "I just want to get away from here. This place gives me the spooks."

The torn and battered *magii'ri* and one very disheveled Wizard slowly made their way down the long slope to the sea, and the waiting ship which belonged to the Wizards who cast the spell. Once they had secured the ship, Lynch insisted they build a fire and clean their various wounds. He grimaced when he saw the tattered flesh of Lorn's forearm.

"How does that feel?" he asked.

"It don't hurt much," Lorn admitted. "As a matter of fact, it feels cold already, like it's already dead."

Lynch carefully bathed the wound then tended to Bill's leg. "The Slayer's aren't the cleanest animals. I'd feel better if you'd let me cast a healing spell on both of you."

"One more won't hurt, I reckon," Lorn replied. "This time, that is."

Lynch muttered a few words in a tongue none of the others understood, and Lorn felt warmth creeping back into his battered arm. He flexed his fingers and wondered at the power of Dark Magic.

"You both need to sleep, to let the spell work," Lynch said. "I reckon Jake can keep an eye on me." He added with a grin.

"You've more than repaid your life debt," Lorn answered. "You're free to go as you please." He stifled a huge yawn. "Besides, I've seen how your friends end up."

"Former friends. They doublecrossed me. Now, sleep," Lynch urged. "We can talk about that later."

Lorn and Bill found bunks in the Captain's quarters and within minutes both were sound asleep. Smilin' Jake and Ox made a thorough examination of the ship then returned to the main deck.

"I owe you an apology," Smilin' Jake said suddenly to Lynch. "You saved my life when it would have been easier to let that bastard bite me in two."

"Then who would I have had to exchange witty remarks with?" Lynch replied with a grin. He was feeling good, there was no doubt about that. "You owe me nothing, Jake."

"I read you wrong. I reckoned you were bad, through and through."

"You were right about that," Lynch assured him. "I am definitely bad. I have done things…things that would curdle your stomach. There is nothing I can ever do that will atone for those things. And I really don't care."

Smilin' Jake laughed. "You just keep on tellin' yourself what a bad man you are, Lynch. I know there's good in you yet."

Lynch stared out at the calm sea. "Would you like to know how I became so powerful?"

Smilin' Jake merely shook his head. "Not really."

"I'll tell you anyway," Lynch pressed on. "There is a ritual of Dark Magic. To perform it, I kill lesser Wizards and eat their hearts. Then their power becomes mine."

Jake shrugged. "Lorn's ancestors did the same thing. If they killed a brave man in battle, they ate his heart to become more courageous themselves."

"You crazy bastard," Lynch said. "You were ready to blow my guts out a few days ago. Why can't you accept this now? I am bad, evil if you will."

"Oh, I know you're a Dark Wizard," Smilin' Jake responded. "And I have no doubt you've done some terrible things. I reckon I would lose my breakfast, if I'd had any, if you told me all you've done. But deep down inside you, Lynch, some of the man you were before all this remains. And he was a *good* man." Jake abruptly turned away. "Hey Ox, what do you think about the Isle of Serpents for our retirement cabin?"

# CHAPTER SEVEN

LYNCH WAS CONFUSED. FOR the first time in perhaps a century he did not know what course to take. A month ago, which felt like a lifetime, he had been plotting to absorb the strength of the Gray Hunter named Roark to further his own ambitions of strife and even greater malice, and now he truly did not know what direction his next step would take. He leaned back on a coil of rope, tipped back the bottle of rum he had liberated from the rich stores of the ship, and watched the *magii'ri* Warriors as they slept soundly. Graywullf had nearly run them all into the ground, himself included. But Lynch felt no fatigue. Indeed, he felt invigorated after his encounter with his fellow conspirators. Former conspirators, he corrected himself with a grin and a salute with the rum bottle. No one crossed Lynch and lived. No one.

On a sudden whim, Lynch helped himself to several more items from the ship's hold then busied himself in the galley. He had explored every hiding place, every barrel and crate, while the Warriors slept the sleep of total exhaustion. The ship was virtually a floating paradise, and he fully intended to partake of everything. When he was finished in the galley, he filled a cup with coffee, then poured a third of it back in the pot and replaced that with a dollop of rum. He carried it back to the Captain's quarters and waved it back and forth under Lorn's nose. On the second pass, Lorn's eyes flew open and he sat up.

"Did I smell coffee?" he asked in amazement.

"And more," Lynch replied smugly. He handed the cup to Lorn, then roused the sleeping Warriors. "Come on, wake up. Look at that amazing sunrise!"

The Warriors rubbed sleep from their eyes. Lorn took a sip of spiked coffee and glanced reproachfully at an unrepentant Lynch.

"Breakfast is served in the galley," Lynch said.

The Warriors all but fell over each other in their eagerness to fill their bellies. When they saw the spread which Lynch had prepared, they stood openmouthed in shock. Platters of salt pork and bacon, eggs and biscuits lined the table, along with containers of butter and honey and several kinds of jelly. They dove in like starving wolves, and Lynch matched them, fork for fork. Finally, Lorn sat back and sighed.

"Where did all this come from?" he asked.

"It's good to be a *magii'ri* Wizard," Lynch replied. "They travel like kings. All of this came from the ship. Barrels of eggs cradled in sawdust, hams hanging from the beams, and crates full of every delicacy that you, my good Warriors, have not even smelled in two years. Maybe even in your entire life."

Smilin' Jake dropped his fork with a metallic clang.

"Are you gonna finish that salt pork?" Ox asked.

"Go ahead," Smilin' Jake told him. Ox speared the last piece with his fork and began gnawing at it.

"We been eating horse meat and drinking water that smelled like piss from a stinking skin for two years, Cap'n. Why did they do that to us?" Smilin' Jake asked.

"I reckon this is your story, Lynch," Lorn said. "As my people used to say, my ears are open. Finally."

Lynch told the tale of a twisted plot, led by Marsten, the ruling Wizard of the Council. He wanted to eliminate the *magii'ri*. Without the heavy hand of justice administered by the Gray Hunters, men would show their true nature and revert to dark, mindless savagery. Rape, murder and thievery, graft, bribery and greed would rule the land. But an open revolution was too risky. The *magii'ri* Warriors could possibly prevail in a pitched battle, so he had resorted to subterfuge and trickery. Marsten had split the Warriors into small bands and sent them on missions with a high possibility of failure. At the very least, the Warriors would be weakened by attrition and less able to resist when they returned. The conspiracy ran deep, involving both Warriors and Wizards alike.

"I still don't get it," Bill said. "What would Marsten gain with the Warriors gone?"

"Think about it," Lynch replied. "If the Warriors were gone, who would have all the power? The Wizards. Marsten could take whatever he wanted and no one could stop him."

"Was Marsten in on this little spell, the one that brought forth the Slayers?" Lorn asked.

"He was," Lynch admitted. "This was sort of a side job, you might say. I did enlist the aid of several of the lesser Wizards and Marsten knew about it."

"You enlisted the aid of lesser Wizards? How did you do that?"

"Captain Graywullf," Lynch replied, "I have been in Norland many times, under one guise or another." He turned toward a hatch and let the sunlight fall directly upon his face. Lorn studied his features.

"You were a cook in Marsten's kitchen," he finally said.

"Bravo!" Lynch said with a mock salute.

"No, that ain't right," Ox interrupted. "He was a guard at the main gate. But his name was…Hell, I can't remember."

"As I said," Lynch reminded them, "I was there under many different guises. I even sat on the revered Council of the Staff for a time."

"But Marsten was in on the revolution?" Lorn asked.

"Absolutely," Lynch replied. "He recruited me."

"Recruited you? How did he even know you existed?" Smilin' Jake asked.

Lynch pressed his hand to his suddenly throbbing temples and shook his head. "Have any of you ever read any of the books in the vast library at Richfeld?" To his surprise, the *magii'ri* Warriors looked taken aback.

"The thing is," Lorn replied slowly, "we was never taught to read or write." Many things became much clearer to him in that moment. "Marsten said the Council didn't think it was necessary for Warriors to waste time being taught letters."

"You can't read?" Lynch asked in amazement. "None of you?"

"It ain't just us," Smilin' Jake replied. "None of the Warriors I know can read or write."

"How do you know the Code, the laws you uphold, where to go if you can't read a map?"

"We memorized it," Lorn replied. "It didn't take long when Fowler was ready to knock our teeth down our throats if we messed up."

"Good ol' Fowler," Ox interrupted. And things became even clearer to Lorn. When he was younger he had thought that Fowler was a sadist, beating the hell out of them if they didn't remember something. Now he understood. Fowler had known, even then, that there was something rotten in Norland and he had prepared them for it. But they had awakened too late.

"He knew something was up. Fowler knew there was evil afoot, so he made damn sure we memorized everything we possibly could. I've been blind as a bat!" Lorn muttered in disgust.

"Now your eyes are opened, as well as your ears," Lynch said. "It's been said that history repeats itself, that events which happened many years ago can happen all over again, simply because mankind can't seem to learn from their mistakes. In your case, it's because you were deliberately misled."

"What would we have learned about you?" Smilin' Jake asked.

Lynch sighed. "That's a long story. I have walked this World for several lifetimes of mortal men," he finally answered. "But I didn't always use the same name. For seventy years I was known as Count Oliver Bastille, a very rich man with an unhealthy interest in torture. Later, I was the chief executioner in the court of King Bern, during the First Ogre War, while Bern was occupied on the battlefield. It's said that the courtyard at Bernfeld is still stained by the blood of my victims even now. I've visited from time to time, and it's all true. After that I graduated to inciting riot and revolution. It's much more effective than killing victims one at a time. Eventually I took the name of Lynch."

"You skipped a chapter," Smilin' Jake insisted. "You know, the part about being *magii'ri.*"

"I did that deliberately," Lynch agreed. "But since you won't leave me alone and we have a long sea voyage ahead of us for you to continue badgering me, I'll tell you. I was born *magii'ri* and it was discovered that I had talent in both magic and the skills of war. I served as a Warrior for many years. That was before I took the title of Count Bastille. We were taught to read and write then, not like it is now. I was sent on a mission to capture a priceless treasure, but that's not what I was told. I was told it was merely a book of *magii'ri* history and spells of the Light which had fallen into the hands of Dark Wizards. My men and I were ordered not to let them speak, lest they cast a spell upon us." Lynch's face grew dark and savage. "We killed all of them, men, women and children alike. I found the book bound in gold and sealed shut. Then we burned the place to the ground with their bodies inside. I carried the book, but could not resist the lure of its contents. That night, by the light of the moon I broke the seal and began to read the book. It was called the Book of Runes." Lynch grinned mirthlessly at the Warriors' reaction. "You've heard of it. It contains every spell of Dark Magic known. So I asked myself, why did the Wizards want that book so badly? The answer, whether true or planted by the very spells I was reading, was that the Wizards wanted it to practice Dark Magic themselves." He paused so long that Ox actually rose and refilled his cup with rum. Lynch took a deep draught. "I was in a quandary. If I returned to Norland bearing the book, I would be rewarded greatly, but the Light would be diminished. Believe it or not, I was true to the Warrior's Code at that time, and the preservation of the Light was my top priority. If I returned without the book, my head would quite literally roll across the courtyard when my men reported that we had found it. Then, as now, I valued my hide quite highly. I wrestled with my dilemma for weeks while we trekked across the desert, but each night I read more of the book." Lynch drained his cup and stared into space. "It consumes you, you know that. With each spell I read I thirsted for more and eventually I realized that I could not part with the book, no matter what the consequences would be." He fell silent.

"What did you do?" Bill finally asked.

"I did the only thing I believed I could," Lynch replied. "I offer no excuses, although the Dark Magic had a strong hold on me by then. That night I killed my own men. I was tormented…it had to end one way or another that very night! I could not survive another day with my mind being torn in two, so I told my men I was deserting them and I was taking the Book with me. They tried to stop me, and I killed them…down to the last man. Only my brother stood by me. I became a Dark Wizard that night, although I didn't know it. I read the entire book then hid it in a place where it will never be found. I returned to Norland with a tale of defeat, after counseling my brother to disappear. The Wizards sensed a change in me and they sent one who could not be corrupted to find the truth. Malachi Graywullf, his name was, and the story he brought back disgraced me forever." He stood so abruptly that Lorn actually drew on him. Lynch grinned. "The time for that is long past. The sire of your sires caught me by surprise and captured me. I was an Outcast, even from the people who prided themselves on being Outcasts. What did that leave me? I was imprisoned and scheduled to be hanged, but the Magii'ri Wizards underestimated the Dark Wizard Lynch. I escaped, and here, after travels that would only confuse you, it would appear that we have come full circle."

"Son of a bitch." Lorn muttered.

"Exactly," Lynch laughed. "It was quite an adventure. And your very own High Wizard Marsten wants that book above all else."

"No, I mean you are one cold blooded son of a bitch," Lorn said with a slow shake of his head.

Lynch looked at the deck and scuffed his foot. "I do what I can. I mean, I'm sure there are others who are more efficient, more polished or more powerful than I, but I do have a certain flair for mayhem."

"You killed your own men. Did you feel any remorse at all?"

"Of course! They were some of the most valiant men to ever serve the Light. Good men, every one. Well, not every one, but most were. But as you know by now, I value my own existence, miserable as it may be, above all else."

The Warriors fell silent. Each one was thinking about times they had taken lives to defend their own.

"How far has it gone?" Lorn eventually asked.

"The Revolution?" Lynch replied. "I have no idea, since I spent the last eighteen months in your time dodging bullets. I haven't been to Norland itself in years. The corruption runs deep. The one tiny seed of discontent that I sowed has sunk its roots into every level of society in Norland."

"So…we won't be welcome back in Norland," Lorn mused. "Marsten and the Council have been turned against us and in turn have poisoned the minds of the people against us. We been gone too long, and people have a tendency to forget the good and remember the bad. Hell, they might openly attack us. So, I'm not gonna ask you to come with me, but I have to go back."

"Count me in," Ox said around a mouthful of eggs.

"I'm in," Bill added.

"You idiots," Smilin' Jake grinned. "You know we're probably gonna get killed, don't you? Outnumbered ten to one, the people you swore to protect turned against you, and if we do win, there's no reward for it. We'll die poor and alone. Outcasts from our own people, just like Lynch." He shook his head. "You'll have to kill half the Wizards on the Council. Maybe all of 'em."

"Wizards can die at the end of a blade or a bullet just as easily as any man." Lorn said, disbelief at the mutiny of his best friend flooding his mind.

"How does that set with you, Bill?" Smilin' Jake taunted. "Instead of one curse we'd have dozens."

"What difference does another curse make?" Bill answered. "We been cursed before."

Smilin' Jake threw his head back and roared with laughter. "What about you, Jonny boy?

"For the boy," Ox answered. "I'll do it for Luke."

"So we're going to face almost certain death, not once, but many times. The best part, which none of you have realized, is that we don't even know who might be enemies and who might be an ally. Let me see. Very little chance of survival, probably no reward, and we'll be remembered as renegades, if we don't die in a hail of bullets when we step off the ship. I reckon I'm in."

"Yer a crazy bastard, Smilin' Jake," Lorn laughed. "And I'm damn glad to have you."

"You're all crazy," Lynch interrupted. "Why go back at all? With this ship you can go anywhere in the World. Let the Wizards rot in their own filth." An idea suddenly struck him. "As a matter of fact, I'll join you. We make one hell of a team."

Lorn stared at Lynch until the Wizard actually looked away. "I ain't doing it for the people of Norland, not anymore. And I damn sure ain't doing it for the Council or the Code. This is for my son."

Lynch opened his mouth to speak then clamped it shut. Now he understood.

Hours later Lorn and Smilin' Jake sat atop the Captain's quarters with a stiff breeze blowing their hair back, watching as Jon and Bill tried to catch fish for dinner. Lynch tended the wheel, and Jake noticed that Lorn's eyes were never far from the tall Wizard. Fluffy white clouds scudded overhead. Below, Ox cheered as Bill hauled in a sizable flounder. Then they both flung themselves on it, laughing, as the doomed fish flopped across the deck. Bill knifed it and the two rebaited their hooks.

"Why did you act like you were bailin' out on me, Jake?" Lorn asked suddenly.

Smilin' Jake nodded in the direction of Bill and Ox. He drew a deep breath and released it in a gusty sigh. "Cap'n, you know I'd follow you through fire and flood without a question. Hell, I'd die for you and those two meatheads down there. I just wanted to make sure they knew what we were in for."

"What do you think we're in for?"

"Blood. A river of it. And most likely some of it will be ours." He turned to scowl at the growing waves. "We ain't gonna make it through this'n." Then he laughed. "Looky there. Ol' Jonny boy finally caught a fish."

"Don't come with me," Lorn said suddenly. "Stay on the Isle of Serpents. There's plenty of water on the far side, and game to hunt. Live out your days here, the three of you, in peace."

"Can't do that, Cap'n, We took an oath, and the *magii'ri* blood is still stout enough for us to honor that."

"Forget the oath, forget the Code. Save your lives!"

"Save yer breath, Cap'n. I parted enough pretty legs to guarantee that ol' Jake Sipowicz won't be forgot, not for many years. My seed's been planted. Now, you an' me both know that this feller who got away from Lynch has to have some influence on the Council. Who be you thinkin' of?"

"That's the Hell of it," Lorn admitted. "You were right, the entire Council may be in on it."

"So we'll just have to go back to Norland and find out, won't we?" Smilin' Jake replied

"I reckon so," Lorn agreed. And, he hoped fervently, we better get there in time.

# CHAPTER EIGHT

THE CAPTURED PIRATE SHIP was still hopelessly grounded on the sand bar they had struck in the storm, and with the low tide the sand flat extended nearly up to the base of the Citadel. They worked relentlessly, and by sundown all of the ship's cargo was safely stored inside. The Guardians did not reappear. Lorn took one last look around at the gunpowder and bullets, flints and crates of rifles and pistols and cases of giant powder, as well as chests of pure gold coins ferom the pirate ship. It was enough to start a war, or at least blow the Citadel and a good chunk of the Isle completely to Hell.

"Last chance," Lynch said from the doorway.

"What are you talking about?" Lorn asked.

"Last chance to load those back up. You could arm a regiment, overthrow the Wizards and put yourself in power with those weapons."

"I don't want any of that," Lorn replied as he turned away. "I'm only going back for my son."

"Think about that," Lynch replied in a low, persuasive tone. "With this weaponry and two ships, we could have the run of the seas. We could travel anywhere we wanted to go, bedding down exotic women in every port, eating only the finest foods and drinking the best liquors. Dabble in piracy and you'd have gold enough to leave this part of the World far behind. And I can show you how to do that."

"You keep forgettin' one thing," Lorn replied with a flat stare right into the Dark Wizard's bottomless black eyes. "And it's time for you to get it straight. I'm goin' back for Luke. Once I see that he's safe," the Warrior paused, "well, I might just take you up on that. Until then, gettin' back to Norland and finding my son is the only thing that matters to me. Not you, not even Jake, or Bill or Ox mean as much to me as Luke. If I have to throw you overboard to make it to Norland, you'll be takin' a long dip."

Lynch grinned. "That's what I wanted to hear. Let's get on with it."

"You'll be comin' with us then?"

"I reckon so," Lynch answered with a grin. "Life is definitely exciting around the *magii'ri*."

They boarded the ship. Smilin' Jake crossed the deck to stand beside Lorn.

"We're ready to cast off," he mumbled, then grimaced in pain. His face was swelled up like a pumpkin, and his brow was slick with sweat. Even his trademark grin was absent. Lynch glanced at him then looked again.

"You've got a broken tooth, don't you?" he asked.

"That Guardian might have knocked one loose," Jake admitted.

"Let me see," Lynch ordered. "A bad tooth can lead to a lot worse."

Smilin' Jake grudgingly opened his mouth. Lynch grimaced. One of his teeth was broken off just above the gumline and was obviously infected.

"I can help. That tooth has to come out."

"Can't you just cast a lil' spell on me?" Smilin' Jake asked. "There's no need to go fishin' around in my mouth with a pair of pliers, is there?"

Lynch had already ducked below deck to rummage through the ship's surgeon's supplies. He emerged with a wicked looking pair of pliers.

"Hold still," he ordered. "I'm under strict orders not to use any more Dark Magic, you know."

"One more little spell won't hurt, will it Cap'n?" Jake begged as he backed away.

Lorn nodded to Ox, who stepped forward and wrapped Smilin' Jake in a bear hug. Jake struggled and cursed, but he couldn't move. Lorn forced his jaws apart and Lynch grasped the offending tooth with the pliers. With one quick jerk he wrenched it free. Blood and pus erupted from the empty socket.

"Oooh," Smilin' Jake groaned in relief. Ox reluctantly let him go. He rushed to the side and spat, then turned back to his fellow grinning Warriors.

"Ox, I think you have seriously damaged your chances of staying in my retirement cabin." He paused and gingerly felt his face. The swelling was already going down. "Then again, that's been bothering me for days." He grinned. "How do I look?"

"It's a lucky thing you already planted your seed, Jake." Bill offered.

Jake turned to Lorn. "It ain't that bad, is it?"

"Hell no, it's an improvement," Lorn observed.

"Yeah, Jake," Ox agreed. "You look real nice."

"Screw you," Smilin' Jake responded. "It has to look better than your beat up mug."

Lorn laughed. "That's enough. Let's get the sail up. We wasted too damn much time already."

Later, as the Isle of Serpents slipped steadily out of sight, Lynch joined Lorn by the wheel.

"Jake said you wanted to see me?"

"I reckon," Lorn replied. "I need to know everything you can tell me, about the Revolution and…that spell."

"You want to know if the Slayers had time to reach Norland."

"Yes," Lorn answered. "I need to know."

Lynch pursed his lips in thought. Finally, he shrugged. "I might be wrong, but I don't think they had time to reach across the sea."

"So there's a chance that Luke will be alright when we get there."

Lynch knew that the Warrior needed to reassure himself. "I'm sure he's fine." He sucked in a deep breath, and released it in a gusty sigh. "You'll never stop the Revolution. You know that, don't you?"

"There's always a chance," Lorn replied.

"You amaze me, Warrior. After all you've been through, you still honor the Code."

"It's all I've got. It's all any of us have got." He nodded towards the remaining Warriors. "They don't have any families at all. None of the Warriors do any more. It took me a long time to realize that, even after the trouble I got into when I married Luke's mother. This isn't just a revolution, is it? It's an extermination."

Lynch blinked back his surprise. "Perhaps it is," he admitted. "I was only interested in the potential profit."

"Then you forgot one very important thing," Lorn reminded him.

"What's that?"

"They know you're *magii'ri*."

Understanding blossomed across Lynch's face and he grinned widely. "I'll be goddamned. Double crossed again." He laughed, then shook his head and laughed again. He clapped Lorn on the shoulders. "Don't you see it? Oh, what poetic justice!" He laughed again, until tears streamed down his face and he gasped for breath. Finally he regained control. "Oh," he gasped. "This is too much. I made a career out of double crossing my partners, and now…" he laughed, "now I have been doublecrossed by everyone *except* the men who should be my sworn enemies!" Then his face grew dark and savage. "Marsten has no idea what a terrible mistake he made this time."

Lorn grinned into the darkness. He had made his point. "I reckon so." He thought for a long minute. "Lynch, I have a favor to ask you."

Lynch held up one hand. "Stop. I joined you because I like a good fight. That's all. Let me kill some people, maybe mutilate Marsten, and I'll be happy. But I draw the line at going back to being a loyal little *magii'ri* Warrior."

"It ain't that," Lorn argued. "You are what you are, I accept that. I just want you to try to stop using Dark Magic, even for a little while."

"Oh, is that all?" Lynch asked sarcastically.

"No, it ain't all," Lorn continued. "Jake and me have an agreement if something happens to me he'll take care of Luke. The only other favor I'll ever ask of you, is if me and Jake should both happen to get killed, is for you to make sure Luke is alright."

Lynch shook his head. "Sweet mother, Graywullf. Can't you think of a better role model for your son?"

"Damn near anybody," Lorn agreed. "But I can't think of anyone better suited to protect somebody, and to teach them to protect themselves, than you. And if you'll lay off the Dark Magic for a while, I think you'll feel better," Lorn continued. "Who knows? You might even forget to hate yourself for a little while." He lashed the wheel and went below.

Lynch hawked a gob of phlegm and spat it over the rail. He summed up all his feeling s in one word. "Shit." Then he leaned back against a pile of nets and stared at the stars.

They pointed the ship West and sailed on, and Lynch kept up a running commentary telling Lorn everything he knew about Marsten. In time he came to the Black Queen Mordant. Lorn's attention was commanded at the mention of Mordant, and he found himself with a suddenly painful erection.

"So Marsten is just using the Black Queen?" he asked as he turned away from Lynch and adjusted his breeches.

"I reckon. Unfortunately, she thrives on the same diet as I do, and her power is growing. In time she'll be at least as powerful as the man who made her. She will eventually become a Dark Sorceress. Then Marsten will have to contend with her, as well." Lynch studied Lorn quizzically. "Are you alright?"

"I reckon," Lorn said uncertainly as his pelvis thrust forward at just the thought of the Black Queen. Lynch took a half step to Lorn's right, and Lorn turned to face away again. "She's a crafty bitch," Lorn said, but his mind dwelled more upon the physical effect she'd had on him on the beach, as the thought of her was having on him now. "So there's two very powerful enemies already near Norland, dug in like a bunch of hogs," Lorn said. "I guess it's up to us to root them out." He called the other Warriors over and summarized what Lynch had told him.

"Ah, yes, the life of the *magii'ri* Warrior," Smilin' Jake offered. "Train under slave drivers from the ripe age of seven, learn the most efficient way to kill a man by the age of ten. Hone your skills by traveling to foreign lands and meeting people of vastly different cultures and killing them as well. Keep the World safe, only to return home and find the end of the World has begun under your nose."

"It ain't that bad," Lorn argued. "We eat good, most of the time…"

"Horse meat," Ox grunted.

Lorn laughed. "And I know how many pretty girls you've bedded in foreign ports, Smilin' Jake. Hell, you were just bragging about that a few days ago."

"It's a good thing he was so drunk with most of them," Bill added. "Their likeness could scare crows off a garbage pile."

"You were right there with me," Smilin' Jake countered.

"I reckon I was," Bill agreed. "It seemed like a good idea at the time."

Lorn grew sober. "Here's the situation. We don't know who we can count on, so we have to suspect everyone. From what Lynch told me, not all of the Warriors or Wizards are in on it, so we can't just go in with guns blazing and cut 'em all down either. Yet again, I'm not too anxious to get ambushed so we're not gonna announce ourselves by sailing right into Elanderfeld. We'll head for the old garrison at the mouth of the Muddy River, then cut across country and try to pick up whatever information we can along the way." The Warriors nodded in assent. "We ain't droppin' anchor until I can see Norland, so that means we'll each take a shift at the wheel. Our course is due West. Bill, you take the first shift."

For fifteen days the ship fairly flew across the waves, and Lorn kept the crew busy inspecting every gun aboard. The cannons were cleaned and readied. Lorn was taking no chances at being caught unprepared. Besides, the activity took the edge off the nagging worry that he was already too late. Too late to stop the end of his world, and too late to save his son. The nights were the worst, when he lay awake, staring at the timbers above his head, regretting all the years he had already lost, years in which he could have gotten to know his only son. But in the evening, Lynch did his best to educate them, as he put it.

After the evening meal, they gathered around the wheel, and while one of the Warriors tended it, Lynch told them many things.

"Do you know the story of the beginning of the *magii'ri*?" he asked.

"Aard selected our ancestors to enforce his laws," Lorn answered. The others murmured their assent.

"Not exactly," Lynch corrected them. "In the beginning, Aard and the lesser gods, the god of the River and the god of the Sea, enforced their own laws. But they grew tired of constantly intervening in the lives of men, who it seemed couldn't follow the laws on their own. So Aard decided to hand pick men to serve him. He traversed the realms of time and space and even other Worlds in his search for just the right breed of man, one who could be ruthless yet completely loyal. The men he found were your ancestors. They were men from different Worlds than this, and different times. He brought them here, gave them the gift of unnaturally long life and magical knowledge and trained them in his ways. And yes, he also gave them superiority in weapons. Aard's laws eventually became the Code by which you live."

"Whoa, wait just a minute," Smilin' Jake demanded. "Are you tellin' me that our father's fathers came from other Worlds?"

"I most certainly am," Lynch replied, relishing the moment. "Aard, the Mountain God whom you blindly follow, kidnapped your ancestors, enslaved them and brought them to this World to serve him."

"And how did he do that?" Lorn asked.

"There are doorways," Lynch replied. "Magical doorways, that lead to other times and other Worlds."

"Bullshit," Bill scoffed. "Why ain't we ever seen these doorways?" The other *magii'ri* agreed.

"Magical doorways," Lynch repeated. "Do you suppose they stand in plain view with signs painted on them, 'Enter here to go to another World'? Of course not. They're very well concealed." His voice took on a conspiratorial edge. "But I have found some of them. I have been to other Worlds. There are Worlds that would take your breath away in awe at their wonders in one moment, and terrify you with their savagery in the next."

"Have you been in the jug again?" Smilin' Jake asked. But deep inside he felt the truth of Lynch's words. He looked around at his companions. Their language was a blend of different dialects, an amalgam of regional slang, and no trueblood *magii'ri* even looked like another. He rose abruptly and went below deck. When he emerged he carried a case of rum. He casually broke the top of the crate and silently handed out a bottle to each man. He popped the cork out of his own and raised it.

"Here's to knowin' the truth, even if it hurts sometimes," he said. Lynch, Bill and Ox followed suit. Finally, Lorn did the same.

"I reckon so," he said slowly. He took a long pull from the bottle and let the fiery liquid course down his gullet and warm his belly. He knew that the *magii'ri*, even the World that he knew, would never be the same. "Someday, Lynch," he said, "When this is all over and peace ain't so hard to find, I want you to show me those places you've been."

A strange expression shadowed Lynch's face. "Someday I will, Warrior," he agreed. Deep inside he knew it was not meant to be. Shame at his part in it nearly overtook him, but he shrugged it off as he had so many times before. "By the gods, ol' Marsten owes us all a drink!" He tipped his bottle back and the liquor flowed freely. By midnight they were all falling down drunk. Then the wind, which had been favorable since the start of the voyage, slacked off and eventually died. The ship glided silently across the glass- smooth surface of the sea, barely moving, while the sails hung nearly empty from the mast. When the others finally awoke at midmorning with a foul taste in their mouths and the heat of a blacksmith's forge in their heads, Lorn stood at the wheel, his mouth drawn into a grim line. Lynch joined him.

"What do you make of this?" Lorn asked.

"It's not good," Lynch replied.

Lorn rolled his eyes. "I know it ain't good. Do you think it's natural?"

"I'm no seaman, but it don't seem natural to me."

Lorn grunted an obscene reply. "We're still six or seven days from Norland, maybe more. If it ain't natural, then..."

"Then there is a very powerful Wizard trying to prevent us from ever reaching port," Lynch finished.

"I hope that ain't it," Lorn said fervently. "Me and the boys can sail a ship, but we ain't sailors. If he decides to blow up a storm, it could get ugly fast. Can you do anything about it?"

"Like what?" Lynch asked. "Conjure up a wind? Maybe that's exactly what he's doing. Combine the two and we'll have a hurricane. I haven't traveled across the planes of space and time to drown, Warrior. My revenge is not yet complete."

The ship had all but stopped dead in the water.

"Well, we have to do something," Lorn replied as the other Warriors climbed to the top deck.

"I don't like this," Ox offered.

"None of us do," Smilin' Jake interrupted. "What the Hell is goin' on now?"

Lorn shrugged. "Your guess is as good as mine. I reckon we just have to wait it out." He lashed the wheel and left the others.

"He's worried," Bill mused. "I ain't never seen the Cap'n at a loss for ideas."

"Yeah," Ox agreed. "He ain't the same."

"You numbskulls," Smilin' Jake said. "He's worried about Luke." He looked at Lynch. "Ain't that right? He's worried those goddamned Slayers made it to Norland."

"I reckon so," Lynch agreed. "But I'm almost sure they didn't."

"Almost," Smilin' Jake said, "ain't very good."

"It's the best I've got," Lynch retorted. Then he, too, left the upper deck.

Eight days later the ship turned in aimless circles, and the sun seemed to grow hotter with each passing hour. The *magii'ri* sought out any shelter they could, but the hold was like an oven. Finally, as the sun sank below the horizon Bill leaped to his feet, ran to the nearest lifeboat and began to untie the lashing. Lorn dropped one calloused hand upon his wrist and stopped him.

"I can't stand it no more," Bill cried. "We're gonna run out of water!"

"Calm down, Bill," Lorn ordered. "We have plenty of water for another week or ten days. This will break."

"But we could row to land in ten days, takin' turns," Bill argued. "It'd be better than sittin' on our asses doin' nothin'!"

"Even Ox couldn't row us to land in ten days," Lorn said quietly.

"I could do it," Ox interrupted. "Why are you bein' so hard on us, Cap'n? We'll die out here, and there's plenty of fresh water on the coast." He paused. "Wait just a minute. Maybe you don't want us to make it."

Lorn was truly confused. "What the Hell are you talkin' about? I have to make it for Luke."

"It's Dark Magic," Lynch cut in. "It has them confused."

"And you," Ox turned towards Lynch. "Everything we do has gone to shit since you joined us." He advanced towards the Wizard, drawing back one massive fist as he did. But there was a crack, and he fell limply to the deck. Jake stood behind him wielding an oar. Bill began to move towards Lorn, his hand on the hilt of his knife.

"Stop this nonsense," Lynch shouted. "Stop it! Can't you see? This is exactly what your enemies want. This is what they need!"

Bill stepped back like he had been hit in the face with a bucket of cold water. Smilin' Jake dropped the oar.

Lynch sighed and shook his head. "I'll go. I'll take one boat and row to the coast and see if I can find the Wizard responsible for this. He has to be on the coast close by."

"No," Lorn stated flatly. "If any of us goes, we all go."

Lynch grinned. "Do you want to be trapped in a lifeboat with Ox when he wakes up? I don't."

"Just the same, we'll wait for him to wake up then we'll decide." Lorn turned to Bill. "Hand over them knives. I don't want to wake up with my throat slit." Bill reluctantly did as he was ordered. "Jake, tie Ox to the mast. And tie him good, dammit."

Lynch helped Smilin' Jake drag Ox to the mast and prop him upright as Lorn and Bill went below deck once again. Jake stepped back and stood upright as he finished tying Ox's hands. "That should hold him," he observed.

"Sorry, Jake," Lynch said suddenly. Smilin' Jake looked up in surprise as Lynch's iron hard fist crashed into his jaw. His eyes rolled up in his head and he collapsed beside Ox. Lynch ran lightly to the lifeboat and finished untying it, then lowered it silently into the sea. He threw in a cask of water then followed it over the side. In minutes the ship was a rapidly shrinking spot on the horizon.

# CHAPTER NINE

LYNCH MUTTERED THE WORDS of the spell and bent his back into the oars. Under the influence of Dark Magic his body was a machine, impervious to weather, heat or cold, and after spending weeks with the *magii'ri* his strength was at its peak. He gritted his teeth and settled into a rythm. It looked like it was going to be a long night.

As he rowed he let his mind wander. In his imagination he relived the pursuit by Ned Roark, the endless frigid nights as he longed for a warm bed and a hot meal. He felt the helplessness that had encompassed him when he had felt himself falling for the second time. He had expected to feel his life force driven from his body at any second by a crushing impact then he had plunged deep into the inky black water of the sea off the coast of the Isle of Serpents. He had welcomed the suffocating blackness that followed, the slow drift into unconsciousness before the final long sleep. But it had been interrupted when Lorn Graywullf had pulled him from the sea, pulled him from the most peaceful dreams he had experienced in centuries. Graywullf had saved his life, there was no doubt, maybe he had even saved his soul. Lynch actually stopped rowing at that. Better not get too carried away, he thought with a short bark of laughter. The soul of Lynch was a tad beyond salvaging. But he had paid the life debt, and the *magii'ri* were fighting a battle they could not possibly win, so who could blame him for saving himself? He began to row again, and the light boat skimmed over the placid water.

He only stopped to drink, and any observer would have thought the craft was borne on the back of a serpent it flew so fast over the waves. In a mere three days he reached the coast. He drained the last draught of stale water from the cask he had stolen then stood on wobbly legs as he looked up and down the coast. He heard water flowing. Despite the *magii'ri's* inability to read or write, they had navigated accurately. The mouth of the Big Muddy was within a half mile from where he stood. He felt an unfamiliar pang at the thought. Dammit, they were good at what they did, and they did it not for any reward, but because they believed in it. Lynch shook his head. He was getting soft. No matter. He was free of them, and they of him. He had corrupted them quite enough. Lynch stretched and ran on light feet towards the river.

When he reached the river, he turned and followed it inland, pausing only to get a drink of fresh water. There were villages farther upriver, and he intended to have a hot bath, a good meal and a woman before the night was over. The he saw the light. He shook his head twice and pawed at his eyes in disbelief. Surely no Dark Wizard would be so incompetent as to make camp right next to the river in open sight. And to have a fire, while he was working a spell? Unless he felt himself to be completely safe, Lynch reminded himself, well within the borders of Norland. And a slow, wicked grin eased onto Lynch's face.

He tested the edge of his heavy bladed knife and looked at the moon. The Dark Wizard Lynch was never one to look a gift horse in the mouth, he thought. Or something like that. He almost giggled at the thought.

Lynch crept forward stealthily until he was within thirty yards of the fire. Only one man sat near it. He made a slow circle all the way around the campsite to make sure there were no guards. He encountered no one. Doubt crept into the back of his mind and crouched there. What if this was not a Dark Wizard, but some poor traveler waiting for a boat? Or a trader sent to watch for a ship? What did it matter, Lynch thought angrily. He was Lynch. He had killed innocents before, and not just men, and he probably would do so again. He swept into the camp, and his doubts disappeared the instant the man seated by the fire raised his expressionless eyes to greet him.

"We've been waiting for you, Lynch."

The thrill of fear that Lynch initially felt at the sound of the seated man's voice gave way to a rapidly growing curiosity. Still, he crouched at the edge of the firelight with his heavy bladed knife in his hand, ready for a sudden attack.

The seated man smiled warmly. "Come over to the fire and have a draught with me." He filled two tin cups from a mellow brown bottle and Lynch caught the scent of rum. He licked his lips.

"I don't know you," Lynch replied.

"You don't recognize me?" the seated man said. "I'm hurt." He caught the snort of disbelief that erupted from Lynch's mouth. "No, really, I'm deeply hurt. After all the time we spent honing our craft together, huddling in bywater inns hatching plans and drifting across the countryside creating mayhem together, now you don't even recognize me?"

"I didn't say that," Lynch corrected. "I said I don't *know* you." He recognized a Wizard when he saw one, even an incompetent one. Outwardly he appeared calm, but inwardly his thoughts were in chaos. "What's your name?"

The seated man laughed. "Good ol' Lynch! Trying to sneak an answer to a riddle that has been safe for centuries. Men have tortured me for that answer, I doubt I'll hand it freely even to you. Call me…Le'el."

That was no help, Lynch thought. "Funny name," he responded. Le'el cast a dark look his way as he sat down opposite him and accepted the cup of rum. He sniffed deeply before he raised it to his lips. Le'el laughed again.

"It's not poisoned." As if to prove the point he tipped the bottle back and took three long swallows. He lowered it, gasping. "Whew! Next best thing to poison, though."

Lynch stared into Le'el's eyes. They were dark, fathomless pools, even after he had stared into the fire his pupils nearly encompassed his entire eye.

"How did that business with Roark turn out?" Le'el asked casually.

Lynch showed no indication that he had even heard, or if he had, that the question was even important enough for an answer. He shrugged. "I'm here. He's not." Inwardly, he knew with dead certainty that the man who called himself Le'el was a Dark Wizard. Or one of the new breed, he thought grimly, who called themselves Wizards of the Light but plied the trade of evil behind closed doors. No one but the *magii'ri* and King Elander knew who had been sent to hunt him down. And this gent did not look like a member of King Elander's court. But he didn't look smart enough to come in out of the rain, let alone cast a spell over miles of open water.

"At least he didn't get the Book of Runes, eh?"

"The Book of what?" Lynch asked in return as he leaned across the fire and helped himself to the rum. He felt the cloying, invasive presence of a spell, and casually crafted one to repel it.

"I can't believe I let you talk me into hiding it in the Land of Ice," Le'el continued as if he hadn't heard Lynch's response. He shifted position slightly and Lynch caught the gray glint of gunmetal partially hidden by Le'el's blanket.

Lynch didn't bother to reply. He merely grunted an unintelligible response. He felt the presence of another invasive spell, no stronger and even more obvious than the first. Again, he crafted one to repel it with almost no effort. Across the fire Le'el began to sweat. Lynch allowed himself an inward grin. Suddenly he felt good, so good he grew careless. The next spell was much stronger, craftier and infinitely more dangerous. He actually felt the foreign presence of Le'el inside his mind before he expelled him. Still he showed no sign of strain. Indeed, he seemed oblivious to the efforts of Le'el to read his mind.

"How goes the Revolution?" he asked.

"It has been put in motion. There's no stopping it now," Le'el answered despite his every intention not to. He glared at Lynch, who looked back innocently. "Stop changing the subject. Where did you leave the Book of Runes?"

Lynch fingered the white scar on the side of his head, and the crooked one across his forehead. He feigned confusion "I seem to have forgotten." He crafted his own spell to loosen Le'el's tongue even more.

A tiny tic appeared in Le'el's left eyelid as he strained against Lynch's magic. Lynch was instantly suspicious and delved much deeper into Le'el's consciousness. He saw Le'el's intent and instinctively used a great deal of his own power to counteract any spell, and a cricket under his seat kicked out into the light and died. Lynch grinned. Le'el looked sick to his stomach. His hands shook so severely rum sloshed from his cup. He hastily sat it down.

"They didn't tell you much about me, did they?" Lynch asked. "What did they tell you? I wonder." He rose and walked around the fire to Le'el's side. The lesser Wizard recoiled from him, but Lynch stayed him with a gesture of his hand. He cupped his hands palms down over Le'el's greasy black hair for only a moment.

"They told you I was a thief…who had stolen The Book of Runes and that I would be no challenge to one of your power." He looked quizzically at the trembling Wizard. "You are what passes for a powerful Wizard? What have the times come to in Norland?" He concentrated for a moment again. "Still, you are well studied in spells, especially weather spells. So it *was* you!"

Le' el leaped to his feet and frantically clawed at the short sword which hung at his belt.

"Enough of this!" Lynch roared. He chopped one hand down on Le'el's forearm and as the lesser Wizard dropped his sword, Lynch buried his knife in his solar plexus. He gave it a savage twist then threw Le'el to the ground. "Power only in weather spells is still power to be taken," he growled savagely while Le'el's last breath rattled in his chest. Lynch delved deep into Le'el's chest cavity and came out with his heart as it still pumped. He held it aloft in the unnaturally bright moonlight and said the words, then brought it to his mouth. He held it there, inches from his lips for several long moments. Then he lowered it only to raise it once again, opening his mouth as he did. But he could not complete the ceremony. He growled in disgust at himself and lowered his gory feast to one side.

"Coward,' he muttered. "This is no time to grow soft!"

He clutched the other Wizard's heart until it grew cold and the moon faded. Abruptly, he rose and hurled the congealed mass into the river. As he did, he felt a cool sea breeze. He laughed despite himself.

"I do believe it's going to blow." He said softly.

He rifled through Le'el's clothing and came up with three copper pieces in a threadbare pouch. "I'm guessing Wizardry isn't paying too well in Norland these days," he said. He removed Le'el's cloak and glanced at the fallen man's bloodstained shirt, then at his own tattered rags. That would not do. Tonight he wanted to be another anonymous traveler, to eat a hot meal and sleep in a real bed. Bloodstained clothing always drew the wrong kind of attention. He drew the cloak tighter about his waist and belted it with Le'el's belt then washed the Wizard's blood from his hands. Almost as an afterthought he exchanged boots with the dead man. Finally, he turned his attention to the object hidden in Le'el's blanket. He withdrew a rifle, finely made and well cared for, with the initials L.G. carved into the stock. Lorn Graywullf's rifle. "Well, I'll be goddamned," he whispered. So that was the plan Marsten had come up with, the final straw that would turn everyone against the *magii'ri* Warriors. He debated taking the rifle with him, then decided against it. He had no powder and bullets, and if his suspicions were correct, anyone caught with that rifle was certainly as good as dead. He threw it after the heart and listened with satisfaction to the splash that signaled it's disappearance. Someday perhaps, a lone fisherman might hook it and drag the rusted mass to the surface, but it would be unrecognizable by then. Humming softly to himself he turned and began walking up the river.

Lynch reached the village at the old garrison within a couple hours. He entered the first inn he came to. Once inside he paused and drew a deep breath. He cataloged smoke from at least three different kinds of tobacco, the faint scent of opium which came wafting through cracks in the floorboards, the scent of beer, whiskey, rum and sex. Over it all lay the stench of human sweat and woodsmoke. Lynch savored the aroma of one of his favorite places on earth. He shouldered his way to the bar.

"You got a bathhouse?" he asked the saloonkeeper.

"Out back," the mutton chopped, baldheaded man answered.

"How much?"

"One copper for the bath, one for a meal and one more'll get you a bed for the night."

Lynch stared hungrily at the bargirls. The saloonkeeper laughed.

"You got more than one kind of hunger tonight, eh? But a girl will cost you three coppers, with another one for the Council so I can keep runnin' this place. You got that kind of money?"

Lynch removed his stolen purse from his belt and fingered it absently. "Nope," he said suddenly. "I reckon not." He sighed and reluctantly walked from the inn.

He wandered aimlessly through the village and located three more inns, each larger, noisier and more raucous than the last. Finally, he came upon a beggar sitting with his bony knees drawn up close to his chest, leaning against the outer stockade fence. The gate guard was nowhere in sight. The beggar heard Lynch approach and turned sightless eyes towards him.

"Spare a coin for an old man?" the beggar asked. He held out a grimy wool cap. Inside, Lynch caught the gleam of silver.

"Of course," Lynch answered. He dropped his three copper pieces inside the beggar's cap then deftly pulled the silver piece out between his thumb and forefinger. "Better take shelter, old timer," he advised. "There's a storm comin'."

"I reckon so," the beggar replied.

Lynch wheeled around and walked swiftly back to the nearest inn. The old beggar turned his milky eyes to track his progress.

"I reckon so," he repeated thoughtfully. A crooked grin twisted his scarred face as he turned and walked away.

Inside the inn, Lynch waved the silver piece under the innkeeper's nose. "I want a bath, the biggest steak you have, a bottle, a room and a woman. In that order."

"Yes sir," the innkeeper's eyes lit up at the sight of silver. He snagged the coin from Lynch's open palm and stashed it in his own pocket. He turned away to yell at a servant boy to draw a bath then began to lumber down the bar. He was stopped by Lynch's iron hard grip upon his shoulder.

"I think you forgot something," Lynch said quietly.

"No, no," the innkeeper protested. "I was just getting' yer change, good sir!" He hastily dug into his pocket again and dropped two copper pieces into Lynch's outstretched hand.

"That's more like it," Lynch said with a slight smile. He was so preoccupied with his thoughts he failed to notice the old beggar, standing straight and proud now, as he watched from the entrance.

Three hours later, Lynch lay back on the lumpy mattress, his appetites finally sated. A sudden gust of wind rattled the grimy glass in the window frame and was followed by the sudden pecking of raindrops. The storm struck in earnest and the entire building shook on its foundation. Lynch draped one arm over the comfortably pillowy form of the bargirl in bed with him and slowly drifted into an uneasy sleep.

# CHAPTER TEN

"**H**E'S GONE."

The words jolted Lorn from an uneasy slumber. "Who's gone?" he growled. But he already knew the answer.

"Lynch. He socked me and took a boat," Smilin' Jake responded.

"I knew it," Bill said, nothing more than a voice from the dark confines of the crew's quarters. "As soon as it gets tough, he skipped out."

"What about that bit of action back there with the Slayers?" Lorn asked tiredly.

"He took on the Dark Wizards all alone, too," Smilin' Jake reminded him.

"Did he?" Bill asked. "We wasn't watching him, you know."

"It don't matter," Lorn said through gritted teeth. "He's gone. How's Ox?"

"Listen," Smilin' Jake replied.

Through the heavy slabs of oak that formed the deck they could hear a bawdy drinking song. Ox finished the song in his awful baritone and there was a moment of silence.

"Is he drunk?" Lorn asked.

Smilin' Jake held up a hand. A moment later they could plainly hear Ox cursing and threatening to kill whomever had tied him up in dozens of creative ways.

"He ain't drunk, he's out of his head."

"Let's go above deck," Lorn ordered. He and Smilin' Jake climbed the ladder, but as soon as Jake's legs cleared the hatch, it slammed shut. Lorn leaped back to it and tried to open it, but they could plainly hear Bill latching it shut as he muttered unintelligible curses.

"What the Hell is goin' on here?" Lorn asked in disbelief.

"You dirty son of a bitch," Ox's voice broke in. He strained against the heavy ropes that bound him to the mast. "When I get loose I'm gonna rip yer head off and throw it to the sharks. I'll tear your arms off at the shoulders and stomp yer guts out!" His eyes bulged with fury as his massive arms strained against his bonds. The mast actually creaked from the strain.

"It's Dark Magic," Smilin' Jake explained, as if to a child.

Lorn simply shook his head. "What do we do now?"

"Sweet Mother," Smilin' Jake muttered. "Am I the only one on this ship who's got any brains left?" He led Lorn to a patch of shade next to the captain's quarters then found a canvas tarp to rig some shade for Ox. They were crazy as bedbugs, but he wasn't going to let them die of heatstroke. He looked thoughtfully at Ox as the huge man strained against his bonds. Then again, he wasn't about to let him go so he could carry out his threats. Smilin' Jake valued his life and limbs too much for that. He returned to sit beside Lorn, who looked as forlorn as a lost child, until the sun sank below the horizon.

For the next three days Smilin' Jake kept his companions alive and cursed the heat, Dark Wizards and magic in general. The first night Ox had knocked his tin cup of water out of Jake's hands. Smilin' Jake could only watch in disgust as the precious liquid stained the deck then rapidly disappeared into the thirsty wood. Ox struggled against his bonds and kept up a steady stream of curses all night, but by morning he gratefully accepted his allotment of water. As soon as he had swallowed the last drop he resumed his invectives. Smilin' Jake had grown used to it, and simply turned a deaf ear to his friend's ramblings. When he tapped on the hatch with an offering of water, Bill cracked it open and took the water with a quick, slim dark hand then secured the latch immediately. Apparently, he had decided to spend whatever time he had left in the pitch black of the hold. Lorn watched all the activity with complete detachment. He drank his share of the water and resumed staring at the empty sea.

On the evening of the third day, Smilin' Jake sat beside his lifelong friend and Captain, watching the sunset. They had enough water for a few more days, and Ox had finally worn out his voice. Smilin' Jake had taken to sliding a crate over the hatch at night, and he was musing that it was about time to perform that chore. He had no desire to wake up with his throat cut, and Bill was likely to do anything under the influence of Dark Magic.

A sudden breeze chilled the sweat that beaded his forehead as he leaned into the side of the crate. That breeze felt good, he thought. A breeze!

"Cap'n!" he shouted. As he did, he saw flashes of light on the distant horizon. He had no way of knowing that the Dark Wizard Le'el had just made a fatal mistake. Lorn stood and ground the heels of his hands across his eyes. He looked like he had awakened from a week long drunk. Ox stared in dumbfounded silence at the heavy ropes that bound him hand and foot. Bill began thumping at the underside of the hatch.

"Lemme outta here!" he shouted. "I can't stand to be closed up like this!"

Smilin' Jake shoved the crate aside and leaped back as Bill erupted from the hatch, his eyes wild.

"That ain't funny, lockin' me up like that when you know I can't stand it," Bill said indignantly.

"Yeah, and why did you tie me up?" Ox asked in a hurt tone of voice.

Smilin' Jake looked in disbelief from one to the other then threw his hands in the air. "I give up," he muttered. "Don't you fools remember anything?" he asked as Lorn cut Ox free.

"We was arguing about taking a boat," Bill said. "Because somebody put a spell on us and we're stranded cause there ain't no breeze." Another gust ruffled his dark hair.

"The spell's broke," Lorn said in sudden understanding. "Raise the canvas. Let's get this damn thing moving!"

The crew leaped at his orders. The ship groaned as the wind filled the sail. Lorn stood at the helm, watching the dying flashes of light that signaled Le'el's death at the hands of Lynch. Jake joined him when everything was lashed into place.

"We owe you, Jake," Lorn said gruffly.

"It was like waterin' plants," Smilin' Jake said dismissively. "Except for Ox. That was more like waterin' a bear."

"We still owe you. You're charmed, you know that?"

"What do you mean?" Smilin' Jake asked.

"Dark Magic don't hit you like the rest of us. It's got me thinkin'. I need to ask you something, Jake. If I don't make it…"

"You'll make it," Jake interrupted.

"If I don't make it," Lorn continued, "I want you to take care of Luke for me."

Smilin' Jake stared out at the sea and ran one rough, work hardened palm over his face. The sandpapery sound it made as it rubbed across the bristles on his chin was plain in the night air. "Cap'n, I don't think I'm the right choice for that." He clasped one of Lorn's hands in his own and held it up in the moonlight. The contrast between Lorn's pale skin and his own mahogany palm was obvious. "There's some folks who wouldn't understand. He'd probably be better off with Bill, or even Ox."

"I'm askin' you, Jake. Not them."

Smilin' Jake took his time answering. He shook his head. "I don't want to be saddled with a kid, Cap'n. You know me better'n that, I like to live free and easy. That ain't no way to raise a child."

"You're the best man I know, Smilin' Jake, for all your bad habits. I need you to do this."

Smilin' Jake ran his hands over his head, then dropped them as he gave up. "Alright. If something happens to you, then I'll take care of Luke. I just want you to know," he added hastily, "that the only reason I'm agreeing is because I know you're going to come through this just fine and I won't have to do a damn thing. Raising a boy would cramp my style."

Lorn was visibly relieved. He had a bad feeling about things. It was just a tiny, gnawing worry hidden in the corners of his mind, but no matter what he did or how he tried to change things it wouldn't go away. Just knowing that Smilin' Jake would look after Luke made it a little easier to bear. The wind picked up and the ship lurched forward, plowing through the waves and sending a salty spray over the crew. Lorn gauged their progress against the Evening Star. His eyes widened. They were fairly flying over the waves! Sudden fear hit him like a punch in the guts. They were going too fast, with that much speed any maneuver would swamp them for sure.

"Drop canvas!" he shouted. He scrambled down with Smilin' Jake immediately behind him. "Drop it! Drop it now!"

Ox and Bill stood with their arms askance, looking at him as if he had gone mad.

"We're going too damn fast!" Lorn shouted. The wind whistled through the ropes as the crew lowered the canvas, but the ship slowed not at all.

"When we reach shore I'm going to shoot every Wizard I meet," Lorn growled. "Hang on, she's out of our hands now!"

The ship rocketed forward, raising high on each wave before beginning a sickening plunge into the tough of the next one. The bow plowed deep then shot ahead, dousing the helpless crew with a spray of sea water each time. They watched in awestruck silence, clinging to anything solid.

"Will she hold together?" Bill shouted above the wind. No one answered. "How fast do you reckon we're goin'?" he persisted.

Lorn and Smilin' Jake exchanged glances. "I ain't never gone this fast before," Lorn replied. "Have you?"

"Nope," Smilin' Jake replied. He turned to face full on into the wind. "Come on! Is this all you've got?" Crazy laughter echoed over the growing waves.

"Maybe that ain't such a good idea," Ox shouted. The wind grew stronger, whipping the words from his mouth.

"Bring it on!" Smilin' Jake shouted even louder. "We'll be in Hell by dinnertime, boys. Let's not keep the devil waitin'!"

Bill shook his head and clamped his lips shut. Ox looked imploringly at Lorn, who simply shrugged. "Ride it out," he said with a sudden grin. By the gods, why not? He laughed. Suddenly, he knew. He knew exactly what he had been born to do. It was time to get on with it. "Let 'er rip," he shouted. Then louder, "Let 'er rip!" His own laughter drowned out Smilin' Jake's who stared at him in sudden understanding. His grin grew wider. Their fate was out of their hands, if it had ever been in them. Call it destiny, fate or just plain bad luck. It was time to play out the hand.

The planks of the ship creaked and groaned under the strain, sounds that were audible even over the roaring of the wind. Ropes as thick as a mans wrist snapped like threads, until the canvas was ripped from the mast and was whipped from sight within seconds. Lorn and Smilin' Jake stood together alternately laughing and cursing the storm, daring the gods of the sea to do their worst. The ship plowed ahead, faster than any mortal man aboard it had ever gone, even as pieces of it were torn away to spin crazily out of sight or sink to the depths. Bill and Ox had long since given up and took shelter in the hold. All through the night and the next day the wind screamed. And just as suddenly as it had come up, it stopped. At sundown a sliver of land appeared on the horizon, and the ship glided silently towards it like it was guided by an unseen, giant hand. Lorn let it run right into the shallows, then dropped anchor. It came to a gentle halt. Bill and Ox emerged from the hold, and all four stared at the land they had called home in uneasy silence.

"I'm only gonna say this once," Lorn announced. "It was damn good serving with all of you, even when we had our differences."

One by one the *magii'ri* Warriors filed by and shook his hand. Once again they stood as a group.

"You're free to go as you wish," Lorn said. "I ain't asking any of you to go where I am headed."

No one answered.

"You're all damn fools," Lorn said gruffly.

They lowered the one remaining lifeboat and threw in their personal effects. In minutes they stood on solid ground. The beach was swept smooth, totally devoid of tracks, but the sounds of flowing water led them to the mouth of the Muddy River. Like Lynch had done the night before, they trekked up it to the nearest village, bypassing Le'el's ill fated campsite. The storm of the night before had erased any sign of it.

They came to the village. Water still ran in coffee colored rivulets down the center of the street and the boardwalks were coated with mud. Lorn halted at the edge of town.

"It don't look like much," Smilin' Jake commented.

"They never do," Lorn answered. "Let's get on with it."

The four friends waded through the mud of the street and stopped on the boardwalk in front of the first inn. A few people braved the mud, going about their daily business. None paid any mind to the four ragged men. Lorn shrugged and ducked inside the inn. There were three men seated at the bar, and a total of five more at various tables. None appeared to be armed, and after the first curious glance when he walked in, they studiously ignored him. Each of his men received the same cursory glance when they shouldered their way through the doors and joined him at the bar. The barkeep approached.

"What'll you have?"

"Whiskey," Smilin' Jake said.

"Stay that," Lorn interrupted. "We'll have food first, and maybe a little information." He casually flipped a silver piece between the fingers of his left hand then deftly covered it with his palm when the barkeep reached for it. "I want beefsteaks all around for us, the best that you got. None of that dried up whang leather you've had hangin' for the last month either. Butter fried mushrooms and baked sweet potatoes. How much will that run me?"

Smilin' Jake's grin got bigger.

"Two copper pieces each, if yer goin' to run down the reputation of my food and make yer own menu," the barkeep growled.

Lorn flipped him the silver piece, which the man caught deftly in midair.

"Keep the change, if you'll answer a question or two," Lorn suggested.

The barkeep's eyes gleamed with greed. Times were tough in the old garrison town. "What do you want to know?"

"I'm lookin' for a friend of mine," Lorn said. "A tall man, two scars on his head. One looks like a lightning strike, and he's got mean eyes."

The barkeep's eyes widened in recognition. "Sure, sure! I remember him. He came in night before last. He wanted a meal and a woman, but he didn't have enough money. To tell you the truth, I was glad to see him go. No offense!" he said, suddenly realizing what he had inferred. "I just mean, he looked …well, he looked like trouble to me."

Lorn and Smilin' Jake exchanged nods. That was Lynch, no doubt about it.

"Did he stay here?" Lorn asked.

"Nope, he just kinda smiled, a really spooky smile, and walked right on outta here. I can send one of my boys to the other inns if'n ya want. They'll ask around about him."

"I reckon not," Lorn replied. "We'll meet up with him another time." He changed tactics. "To tell you the truth, we been out to sea for several months. Is there any news we mighta missed out on?"

The barkeep's face darkened. "None but the usual." He cast a quick glance around the room. "The blasted Council keeps raisin' taxes on everything from booze and food right on down to the whores. It's getting' so a man can't make an honest livin' anymore. They're even skimming off the gambling tables!"

"So don't pay it," Smilin' Jake suggested.

"Don't even be sayin' that," the barkeep begged. "I pay my levy. The last innkeeper that refused to pay the levy ended up floatin' down the river, while his wife and kids burned up with the inn."

"What are you saying?" Bill demanded. "The Council burned down a man's inn and murdered him and his family?"

"Hell no, it wasn't the Council. It was them hard eyed Warriors, the Council's private hit men that did it." He glanced into Lorn's eyes and suddenly turned away. "I better get you fellas some grub. Marie!" he bellowed into the back of the inn. "That damn girl's deaf, I tell ya." He shuffled out of sight.

"What do you think?" Smilin' Jake asked as soon as the barkeep was out of sight.

"He knows we're *magii'ri,*" Lorn suggested. "You can guess the rest. The Council is using Warriors to enforce some pretty unpopular laws. The good news is that they don't know anything at all about the Slayers." His relief was plain to see. Ox leaned over and gave him a congratulatory punch on the shoulder which nearly toppled him off his barstool. He regained his balance and shook his head at Ox, and said, "I'd say the Revolution is still in the stewing stage. If we can get to Richfeld and Marsten, we can still stop this."

"Cap'n, we haven't had a decent night's sleep in a real bed for two years, not countin' the ship's bunks, which weren't that bad but they wasn't real beds, and then you go and order the same meal Lynch was dreamin' about back on the Isle..." Bill rambled on.

"He's right," Smilin' Jake interrupted. "We need a good night's rest." His eyes were locked on the feminine charms deliberately put on display by the bargirls.

"How much rest are you gonna get, Jake?" Lorn asked.

"Yeah, Jake are you lookin' to sow some more of yer seed?" Ox asked.

"Don't tell me you ain't thought about it," Smilin' Jake replied with a good natured grin. "It's been two years for me. Now I know ol' Bill spent a lot more time with the horses than he needed to and Ox probably damn near wore out his gun hand, but you just can't beat female company sometimes."

"What's he talkin' about?" Ox asked.

"Never mind," Bill said, shaking his head. "He gets the smell of fresh cooter in his nostrils and he just goes plumb crazy."

"Shut up, all of you," Lorn ordered with a grin. "We'll stay here one night." He let his own eyes follow one of the bargirls for a moment. "In the morning we'll get some new clothes and head for Richfeld."

The barkeep and a serving girl burst through the back door and slapped steaming platters of food in front of the Warriors. Lorn felt saliva spurt into his mouth at the scent of fresh beef. He carved off a huge bite and chewed slowly, savoring every flavor.

"Not to interrupt yer meal," the barkeep whispered. "But I can see now that yer *magii'ri*. I only ask that you don't harm my family."

Lorn swallowed. He stared long and hard at the man. "We are trueblood *magii'ri* Warriors and you know we would never intentionally harm innocent people. We've been at sea for two years, so you should know we have nothing to do with whatever is going on here."

"Two years you say?" the barkeep whispered in a wonderstruck tone. "By the gods, you be one of the few of the old breed that are left then."

"What are you talkin' about?" Lorn asked around a mouthful of food. He swallowed and took a huge draught of beer. "I told you we're Truebloods, like nearly all of the Warriors."

"Like they used to be, you mean," the barkeep said quietly. He leaned closer to Lorn. "I'd tone down my voice when you mention bein' Trueblood, if'n I was you. Ever since Marsten started servin' an alien god, the Trueblood's started disappearin', if you get my drift."

"The *magii'ri* serve Aard," Lorn replied gruffly as a cold lump of worry in his stomach threatened to ruin his meal. "There are no other gods."

"Yer right!" the barkeep agreed quickly. "I been tellin' everyone that this feller ain't a god. But strange things have been happenin' here in Norland…" he let his voice trail off. Lorn followed his eyes to the door as the batwings slowly swung inward. Five men filed in, muddy and ragged, with the dark stubble of beard along their jaws. They carried staves of hardwood and each had a saber in a scabbard on their belt.

"Cover them hoglegs, Ox," Lorn ordered without raising his voice. Ox casually stretched and when he relaxed his coat tails covered his holstered pistols. Lorn caught the barkeep's frightened eyes. "Them fellers that just came in, who are they?"

"Marsten's new Warriors," the barkeep stuttered. "Nobody's allowed to carry guns in Norland any more, and they's talk of disarming the whole population of swords and bows to boot."

"What the Hell?" Smilin' Jake asked darkly. "How's a man supposed to defend his home and family?"

"Marsten says the Warriors can do that job better if'n they don't need to worry about a farmer with a sword, cuttin' 'em down by mistake."

"What about guns?" Lorn asked.

The barkeep shook his head. "I gotta go serve 'em. You got rooms here, and whatever else you want for tonight. Come midnight I'll meet you in your room and tell you everythin'."

The barkeep hastily crossed floor to serve his new customers and tried vainly to detour their attention away from Lorn and his men. One of the new arrivals cocked his head around the barkeeps' burly form then impatiently pushed him aside with one thick forearm. He examined the Warriors at the bar with a cold stare.

"Recognize him?" Lorn asked.

"Nope," Smilin' Jake asked. "I don't know any of the others either."

Bill and Ox just shook their heads. "Somebody should tell him it ain't polite to stare," Ox added.

"I reckon you'll get your chance soon enough," Lorn said with a resigned sigh.

The barkeep hustled by and ordered the cook to fix up five more plates, then placed a bottle and five shot glasses on a tray. He leaned close to get the bottle from under the bar. "They're Martsen's men. Leader's name is Rand. Give 'em a wide berth, they get mean when they drink whiskey."

Lorn nodded as he sopped up the last of his gravy with a tough biscuit. Smilin' Jake started to get up but Lorn halted him. "Sit. Have a drink, let your supper settle. I'll have a word with our boys over there." He leaned close to Ox as he seemed to adjust his coat. "Five to four, Jonny boy. That means only two for you. No more than that, ok? We all want to get our licks in tonight." Ox grinned. "And don't kill any of 'em." he added as he began to walk away. He turned again. "And no serious injuries either. Just knock 'em out and have done with it." Lorn stopped again. "Come to think of it, don't break any bones either."

"Why don't I ask if I can powder their behinds while I'm at it?" Ox complained.

"Alright," Lorn relented. "Just don't kill anybody."

Lorn approached the table where the five sat with a slight grin on his face and a lift in his step. Slowly but surely things were beginning to become clearer, and these men were most certainly his enemies. He intended to have a word with them, learn what he could, then run them out of town. He stopped at the end of the table where the apparent leader sat. The man slouched in his seat and stared at Lorn insolently.

"What do you want?" he asked without a hint of cordiality.

"Maybe a word with you," Lorn replied.

"Make it quick. Me and the boys have had a hard day. We're tired and don't want to be bothered."

"You work for Marsten?" Lorn asked, bored with the man's brusque attitude.

The man was suddenly on edge. He sat up straighter, and he and his men reached for the wooden staves they carried. "He pays us to keep order. There's lot of riffraff this close to the sea."

"What happened to the *magii'ri*?" Lorn asked.

Rand, the leader, laughed as the barkeep cringed and backed against the wall behind his bar. The serving girls ran from the room. "We are *magii'ri*."

Lorn suddenly lost interest in the game. He wrapped Rand's wrist in a steel hard grip and jerked his sleeve back. His forearm was bare. Without another word Lorn jerked the sleeve downward and it ripped free at Rand's shoulder. There were no identifying marks, brands or tattoos that marked him as a true blood *magii'ri*.

"You're a liar," Lorn accused quietly.

The saloon went silent. Such an accusation often ended up with one man or more dead. Chairs scraped across the wooden floor as Rand's men stood. Rand stood and slapped his stave lightly into his other palm.

"I've killed men for less than that."

"Then have at it," Lorn laughed, and hit the man with a driving punch square in the solar plexus. He put all the power of his shoulder behind it, twisting his body to lend the punch even more inertia. Rand's breath exploded from his mouth as his face went slack and his lips worked like those of a fish. He dropped to the floor as the others leaped towards Lorn, but only one man made it. The rest were knocked to the floor as Ox's massive shape hurtled into them. By the time Lorn had that one staggering out the door, Ox had knocked out two of the others and carried the last one out by the collar. He unceremoniously threw his limp form into the muddy street. Smilin' Jake and Bill sat at the bar, sipping beer from foamy mugs. Neither man had moved.

"Thanks fer the help," Lorn said sarcastically.

"There was only five of 'em," Smilin' Jake replied.

"Fine," Lorn replied. He knelt by Rand, who still struggled to draw air into his tortured lungs. He found an iron keyring full of keys and tossed that to Jake. "Now you two can haul 'em down to the garrison and lock 'em up."

"But there's five," Bill protested. "We'll have to make two trips."

Lorn rolled his eyes. "Ox, give them a hand."

As his men gathered up the imitation warriors, Lorn returned to the bar.

"By gods," the barkeep exclaimed. "That's worth a free drink for everyone! It's about time someone put Rand in his place."

Soon the citizens of the old garrison town were gathered around Lorn and, when they returned, his fellow *magii'ri* Warriors. Everyone wanted to buy them a drink and asked who they were. Lorn explained that they were Trueblood Warriors, returning from duty.

"That's Lorn Graywullf," Ox proclaimed proudly after several rounds of free drinks. "Remember that name! They'll write songs about him someday."

The night passed in a murky haze. Lorn vaguely remembered too many hands patting his back and pumping his hand, and way too many drinks being passed his way. The memory of the saloon girl was a bit clearer, as was the thrill of pleasure she brought to his tired body again and again. The girl finally curled up next to him as rain once again beat against the window panes and Lorn's world went black.

A sudden torrent of ice cold water roused him back to consciousness. Lorn jerked upright, slammed his head solidly on something that rang like steel and promptly fell back onto a straw littered floor. He lifted his aching head and pried his eyes open. Rand stood in front of him, separated by steel bars, still holding the bucket he had used to douse the blacked out Warrior. Lorn's vision swam and blurred.

"Why do you have fur?" he croaked in a voice he didn't even recognize as his own.

"I don't have fur, you dumb son of a bitch," Rand replied. His voice sounded like it was coming from the bottom of a deep well.

"Just go away," Lorn muttered. His head ached something fierce.

Another bucketful of icy water soaked him and he rolled to a sitting position, coughing and sputtering.

"Leave a man be," Lorn begged. His tongue felt thick and he found it almost impossible to think straight. He never felt that bad after a night of drinking. He leaned over and puked.

"We got you this time, Graywullf," Rand continued. "You'll swing from the gallows for sure."

Lorn became dimly aware of an insistent clamoring of a large group of people. He looked carefully around and discovered that he was in a cell in the old garrison. "What are you talking about?"

"King Elander's dead," Rand told him with obvious relish. "You shot him, and when you had to make a fast escape you left your rifle behind. It's even got your initials carved in it."

"Elander's dead?" Lorn repeated.

"That's right. Shot in the back by a coward. As if you didn't already know that."

"How could I know? I've been gone for two years. Just got back last night," Lorn replied. Elander had been shot? With his rifle. How? Dread filled him. Norland would be plunged into chaos. It all came together then. "My rifle was stolen from me on the Isle of Serpents. I was set up."

"Save it," Rand said in disgust. "Yer gonna be tried first and then hang, if I can get you by that lynch mob out there."

"What about my men?" Lorn demanded. He was sober now, but he still felt hollow inside. Somebody must have drugged him, he realized.

"You better worry about yourself," Rand suggested. "Don't fret about them. They's being taken care of too." He inserted a huge key into the door and stepped back from the bars as two more men rounded the corner. They were armed with Lorn's pistols. "We're takin' you out of here today. Give me one tiny reason and we'll blow your treasonous guts out." He swung the door open and stepped back, jerking his head at Lorn to leave the cell.

Whatever Lorn's intentions may have been at escape, those notions were immediately dispelled when he felt the weight of heavy irons clasped around his ankles. He shuffled out of the cell, where Rand clapped irons around each wrist, then he turned down the dank hallway. The sounds of the gathering crowd grew louder with each step that he took towards the lighted end of the hall. When he reached the outer office the sounds grew into angry roar. He couldn't make out individual words, but he could actually feel the hate emanating from the crowd. Lorn peered out the door and saw a prison cart backed up to the steps leading to the office. The rear ramp was down, and several more men stood guard. Someone in the crowd caught sight of him, and the roar grew into a deafening din. Rotten fruit and stones began to rain down on the guards. Lorn guts twisted in sudden fear. He was totally helpless with his hands and feet bound in iron.

"Unlock my legs, at least," he suggested. "If they rush me I'm dead, bound in irons like this."

Rand threw the door open and shoved him hard enough that he barely kept his feet. "Get movin'!" he ordered.

Lorn kept his head down and shuffled as fast as he could across the open space to the covered prison cart. Several objects struck him in the body, then a stone half the size of his fist clobbered him above the ear. He reeled and nearly fell, then lunged into the wagon. He rolled over on the filthy straw that littered the bottom of the wagon and peered out a gap between the wooden slats that covered the bars on the sides. The crowd was nearly mindless with rage. Lorn recognized the barkeep from the night before, waving a heavy hammer, spittle running down his chin as he shouted at the guards to hand over the prisoner. The serving girls were there too, shouting for justice. A bottle shattered against the side of the wagon, then was followed by several more. Blood trickled into Lorn's ear, and he hastily sat up. Rand was screaming at the crowd to back off, then the wagon lurched into movement. The crowd rushed the wagon as soon as the guards were aboard and began to shove against it, trying to overturn it. The wagon slowly picked up speed as Rand mercilessly whipped the team, but bottles and rocks continued to rain down on it. It seemed like an eternity to Lorn before they finally left the crowd behind.

"Stand up," one of the guards ordered.

Lorn looked at him in confusion.

"Stand up, damn you!" he kicked Lorn in the side.

Lorn rolled away from the kick then gained his feet. He looked warily from one guard to the other. Both wore bruises from their encounter the evening before. One man slipped a chain through his wrist irons, then looped it through the roof of the wagon. He pulled out the slack and hauled Lorn's arms up above his head. Both guards holstered their captured weapons. He dodged the first few blows, taking most of the power out of them, then one punch caught him above the left eye. Lights exploded in his head and he sagged in the chains. The two men moved in, raining blows down on him until he slipped into unconsciousness.

A sharp jolt from the wagon prodded Lorn awake. He ached everywhere, but when he tried to stand and took some of the pressure off his arms it felt like they were being cut off at the shoulder. He groaned involuntarily, then gritted his teeth and forced himself to loosen his cramped muscles. He didn't seem to be seriously injured, but he had no doubt he was bruised fom head to toe, and one eye was swollen halfway shut. The guards were riding up top with Rand, so he supposed they were well away from the garrison town.

King Elander was dead. That thought still shocked him, even more than the fact that he was being set up to take the blame for it. Someone had taken his rifle from the Citadel, waited until they were sure he was in Norland, and then used it to kill the King. His goose was worse than cooked, he realized. It was roasted, the meat stripped off the bone and the carcass thrown out to the dogs. Just like his carcass was going to be after his trip up the gallows, or more precisely, after his trip *down* from the gallows. He never thought that he'd hang. The idea did not appeal to him. Of course, they could just turn him loose and a lynch mob would tear him to bits. He shook his head again at how quickly the people of the garrison town had turned against him. Never again, he promised himself. If he survived this he was done putting his life on the line for others. *Just have to survive this*, he thought.

It took nine days to reach Richfeld. The first three nights the guards had gathered to beat the hell out of him, then they had grown bored with it. Or so he supposed. Either way, he had three teeth knocked out, numerous bloody gashes on his face and head and not one spot on his body didn't ache. He thought there just had to be a special place in Hell for men who beat helpless victims. But when they reached the outskirts of Richfeld he'd had enough time to begin feeling human again.

The wagon stopped without explanation, and stayed out of sight until dusk. Then Rand and the guards threw a moldy tarpaulin over the wagon and lashed it in place.

"Not a peep out of you," Rand warned. "If a mob rushes us we'll be leavin' you for 'em."

Lorn nodded.

They were challenged at the gate, but Rand had papers authorizing a delivery to the Council, so they were let by. Lorn could feel the fear from the guards. He had no doubt they would abandon the wagon at the first hint of trouble. But none came.

The wagon rumbled to a stop, then Rand clumsily backed it to a dock. After one last fearful glance, Rand dropped the ramp and released Lorn's hands from the roof. His legs were so stiff they would barely obey him, but Lorn managed to stumble across the dock into a building. The door slammed shut behind him before a light illuminated the interior. He stood before David Flannery, Inquisitor General of the *magii'ri*.

"That will be all," Flannery told Rand. "Your job is done. Go get cleaned up and get some rest."

Lorn felt a ray of hope as Rand and his men disappeared, but it was quenched seconds later when another group of guards appeared.

Flannery sighed when he looked at Lorn.. "They were only supposed to deliver you for execution, not half kill you in the process."

"No problem," Lorn replied. "I always wanted my arms to be a couple inches longer."

"This is not a joke, Graywullf," Flannery said. "The evidence against you is insurmountable. You killed the King and after a fair trial you will hang for it."

"So after my fair trial I'm all set to hang, eh? And you already built a new gallows. That doesn't sound all that fair to me." Lorn said. Flannery looked away. "I didn't kill King Elander," Lorn finished.

"Then who did?"

"I don't know," Lorn answered. Flannery rolled his eyes. "Look, you've known me for years, Flannery. I did not kill the king. Someone took my rifle from the Isle of Serpents and is using it to frame me."

"I have known you for years," Flannery conceded. "Hell, your reputation is spread far and wide. You killed a Wizard when you were fourteen. You abandoned your post and deserted when you were seventeen, when you killed yet another Wizard. You spent more time in prison than out between the ages of eighteen and twenty one. If the *magii'ri* needed someone killed, they called upon Graywullf." He stopped suddenly, aware that he had said too much.

Understanding dawned in Graywullf's eyes. "And now it's time to be rid of me."

"This isn't the way I wanted things to be. We were friends once. I would have much rather that you just never returned from a mission."

"I can't believe that you're in on it," Lorn exclaimed.

"You and your men are among the last of those who are *not* in on it," Flannery responded. "Goddammit, the old ways just don't work anymore."

"For who?" Lorn asked. "For you and Marsten? For the rest of the Wizards? What about the villagers that my Warriors and I protected for years?"

"It's over. The old ways are gone. The Revolution will cleanse the country and we will begin again. Some sacrifices have to made," Flannery insisted.

"Sacrifice yourself," Lorn replied. "I'm not a believer."

They came to a cell. Flannery opened the door. "It's clean, and there will be no more beatings. I'll have fresh water and food sent down, and a healer to look at your wounds."

"Yeah, it'd be a damn shame if I died before you got a chance to hang me."

Flannery slammed the door shut with one last exasperated glance at Lorn Graywullf.

His cell had a window port, and that was how he kept track of the days. It was much too high up in the smooth stone walls to see out of, but at least the sunlight could filter in and dispel the darkness of the night. That was how Lorn knew it was the morning of the fourteenth day when he had a visitor. David Flannery had been true to his word. A Healer had come in and plastered his various wounds with a poultice that stank of vinegar and bitteroot and after two days of that he had been allowed to bathe. The meals had been regular, and they even brought him a change of clothes. He figured it was so he could look respectable when they hanged him. Then Marsten came to visit.

The old Wizard looked exactly the same as he had three years earlier, when Lorn had seen him last. Lorn had no regard for Marsten at all, and the Wizard knew it. But another man accompanied him, a man who kept his face hidden behind the shadow of a hood. Lorn felt a threatening aura even before they approached his cell. He kept trying to get a look at the man, but he was careful to keep his face hidden. Marsten broke the silence.

"You finally snapped, eh, Graywullf?" he asked, not expecting any answer.

"Nope," Lorn replied. "You know better'n that. As many times as you tried to break me, you know you just ain't got what it takes."

"You're going to hang," Marsten said, "for the assasination of a King. Consider yourself lucky we don't torture you first."

"Bring it," Lorn replied. "You know I'm going to die laughing in your face."

"I had nothing to do with this, Graywullf. You shot the most popular King of our time in the back. We found your rifle where you abandoned it as you fled the scene. Then you showed up in Garrison Town spending coin fom Elander's treasury. It's an open and shut case. We have witnesses."

"You forgot one detail," Lorn replied resolutely. "I didn't do it."

"Come now, Graywullf," the other man interrupted. "Admit to it."

"Who's yer friend, Marsten?" Lorn asked, ignoring the other man's comments.

"That's not important," he said smoothly. "Just admit to killing Elander. Consider it your last role in the Revolution."

"Shove your damn Revolution up your ass," Lorn retorted. "I have no part in it."

"Oh, you played many parts in it," the man in black laughed. "Perhaps you just didn't know it at the time."

"I did my duty," Lorn conceded. "It was your underhanded dealings that twisted it to serve your own ends."

"The people of Norland won't see it that way," Marsten interjected. "They only see the *magii'ri* Warriors killing innocent people seemingly at random. After years of heavy handed justice, the people you protect *hate* you and your kind. Of course they will revolt." He laughed. "Your life isn't worth a plugged nickel, Graywullf."

"Just the same, I'll never admit to something I did not do."

"You have a son, is that correct?" the dark man asked.

Lorn lunged for the door of his cell and shook it violently. "You stay away from my boy! Lay a hand on him and I'll kill you. I promise you, I'll come back from the Abyss if I have to!"

Marsten and the dark man stepped back involuntarily. "When the time comes," the dark man insisted. "You will admit to killing Elander, and maybe your son will be alright."

They left him alone with his thoughts. Lorn stood at the door of his cell, grasping the bars so tightly his knuckles whitened. Despite every effort he made, it seemed that his actions were destined to harm Luke, not protect him. He released the bars with a disgusted sigh. Hell, it seemed that everyone associated with him was destined for a bad end. First his wife died at the age of eighteen. Then his heavy handed instructor, Fowler, the man who much later became his friend, was found poisoned. Now his men and even his own son were in harm's way. He sat down on his bunk and sank his head into his hands in despair.

"Feelin' a bit sorry for yourself, eh?" A familiar voice asked.

Lorn jerked his head upright. "Lynch?"

"Why don't you say that a bit louder, so the guards can hear?" Lynch replied. "I'm sure they'd love to capture me, too."

"How in the Hell did you get in here?"

"Did you forget who I am?" Lynch said with a chuckle.

"Then bust me out of here," Lorn demanded.

"I can't do that. If you escape all of Norland will think you're a murderer."

"I'll deal with that, but I can't do a damn thing in here! If you bust me out I won't run. I'll find a way to clear my name," Lorn insisted.

"I think I already have a way to do that," Lynch replied. "But you must go to trial so we can expose the Council in a way they cannot deny."

"I knew you were crazy," Lorn said in reply. "They stacked the deck against me, Lynch. They have all the proof they need."

"Do they?" Lynch scoffed. "They have nothing. But, they don't know that I know that. You must challenge them at your trial and call their hand." A sound echoed up the stone hallway and Lynch cast a suspicious glance in that direction. "You have to trust me. I'll do the rest. Can you trust me that far?"

"I reckon I don't have a choice," Lorn said.

"That's right," Lynch said. "So just relax. If they don't have you killed in here within the next three days, you will appear before the Council for your trial."

Lorn shook his head at that remark. "I hadn't even thought of that. I'm helpless in here. If they try to kill me I'm a dead man for sure."

Lynch grinned in the half light, and a shiver went up Lorn's spine. "They don't know who they're messing with," he laughed softly, and Lorn decided he really was crazy. Then Lynch held out his hand, palm down. "Take this."

Lorn reluctantly held out his own hand and Lynch dropped a very small, round stone object into it.

"It's a talisman," Lynch explained. "It contains very powerful magic." Lynch caught the hard stare Lorn shot his way. "Yes, it's Dark Magic. Do you have a problem with that?" Lorn shook his head. "Keep it safe and always touching your body. I suggest you swallow it. It will defeat any spell cast your way for three days. Remember that, three days only!"

Graywullf took the object with a skeptical shake of his head.

"I think they'll try to keep it quiet, that's why you need a defense against magic. This," he held out a small knife, "is just in case it gets rough. I think you know not to use it unless you have absolutely no other choice."

Lorn grinned and nodded as he tested the edge of the blade. It felt good to be armed again, even if it was with a knife small enough to use at the dinner table. When he looked up, Lynch was gone. Graywullf leaned back on his bunk and stared at the crosshatch pattern of the steel bars that formed the ceiling of his cell and wished for the hundredth time that he hadn't been so blindly loyal to the *magii'ri*. It was obvious now that the Revolution had been planned for years, dating back to the time when he was still an apprentice. One by one the old timers had been singled out and eliminated. Fowler was first, since as the headmaster of the Warrior sect he was obviously the most dangerous and wielded the most influence. The position of headmaster had been left vacant for years, with those duties being delegated to much younger Warriors. Now Lorn could see that those Warriors had been loyal to the Wizard sect of the *magii'ri,* and they had given the older Truebloods the most perilous assignments, many of which were destined to fail. The older Truebloods were removed from the sect by attrition, and in the process they had unknowingly enriched the Wizards and secured their position even more. Every mission they had been sent on had taken wealth from those who earned it and redistributed it to the wealthy Wizards. Even the legitimate missions had yielded wealth, power or territory for the Wizards. Lorn had counted many of the old Truebloods as friends, and the longer he thought about it the angrier he became.

Those Truebloods who were still loyal to the *magii'ri* Code of Honor had become few and far between. He knew without a doubt that his men were loyal, but beyond that he had no way to be sure. Lynch's words came back to him. The simplest way to avoid a trial would be to simply kill him, dispose of the body and claim he had escaped.

He unclasped his left hand and studied the ordinary round pebble that Lynch had given him. Could he trust the Dark Wizard? Now that it was apparent the Wizards of the Council were corrupt, his distrust of magic was even stronger than before. He had no choice. He took a dipper of brackish water from his bucket and tossed the pebble into his mouth. His spit dried up, and even with the water he could barely force himself to swallow the pebble. It finally went down, and then he felt no different than before. He grunted a disgusted curse, then hid the knife in his boot. He only hoped whatever spell they tried on him wouldn't kill him right away, so he could stick that little blade up some Wizard's ass and open him like he had a zipper. With that thought to comfort him, he stretched out and tried to rest.

That day and the next passed slowly, so slowly Lorn could actually hear the ticking of some distant clock inside his head. He willed the sun to set, and when it finally did he breathed a sigh of relief. Then he heard footsteps in the passage. He gritted his teeth and forced his racing heart to slow down. Somewhere, far away from his cell, a door slammed shut with a crash and Lorn nearly pissed himself. He'd never been in such a position, relying so totally on another, nearly helpless against an attack. Always before he had been able to defend himself, sometimes with nothing more than a club or his bare fists. But this…he almost wished an attack would come, just to end the interminable waiting.

So suddenly he thought he was dreaming a darker shadow appeared in front of his cell. He heard the slight whisper of a man breathing and smelled a sharp unpleasant odor. Then he realized his visitor was muttering under his breath and panic overtook him. He lunged for the steel bars and thrust his hand through them, clawing futiley for the other man's throat. He saw stars and his muscles weakened. He cursed Lynch then his world went black once again.

Lorn Graywullf woke to the tumult of many voices raised in alarm. Rough hands shook him, and he realized he was being carried.

"It's damn shame he's dead, too," a strange voice said. "I wanted to watch him dance on the end of a rope."

They thought he was dead. For just a moment he considered letting his captors carry him right out of the prison, but then he realized his body would probably be handed over to the villagers. He opened his eyes to slits, and despite his predicament a slight grin curved his lips.

"Good morning," he said loudly. The next thing he knew he was falling. He landed hard on his back. The prison lackeys who had been ordered to remove his body scattered, running into each other in their haste to escape. They tripped and fell down, only to scramble back to their feet once again. Unintelligible screams echoed down the passage as they got as far from the 'body' as they could. Lorn wanted to laugh, but he was too busy trying to draw air back into his lungs. He leaned back against the bars of another cell until his breath returned. One of the lackeys finally peeked around the corner, jerked his head back, then peeked again.

"He ain't dead," he solemnly announced.

"No, I ain't dead," Lorn agreed. "Can't a man sleep in peace around here, even on the morn of his hanging? Why in the World did you think I was dead anyway?"

The lackey approached. "You wasn't breathing, and Marsten, he sent us down here to remove the body. But when we got here they was two bodies, you and another guy outside the cell. That other guy, he was dead for sure. I think," he added quickly.

"Don't you think you better put me back in my cell?" Lorn asked.

The lackey suddenly realized his prisoner was free and unfettered, for even his wrist irons were gone. His face paled. "You ain't gonna kill me are ya?"

"No," Lorn replied in disgust. He stood, and the lackey jumped back and made a run for the corner. "I'll be in my cell," Lorn called. "Run along and tell Marsten. No wait!" he shouted. He actually heard the man's boots skidding on the stone floor. "That other guy, what killed him?"

The peasant didn't return, but he did call out back around the corner. "He was burned to a crisp."

Lorn listened as the peasant's footsteps retreated up the passage. At least he'd had the guts to come back, unlike the other three.

Lorn returned to his cell, loathe as he was to do so. He slammed the door shut violently.

"Now you're thinking," came that familiar voice from a cell next to his.

Lorn jumped a foot in the air. "Dammit, stop doing that."

Lynch chuckled. "You played that hand very well. Keep it up and you'll walk out of Richfeld a free man. Despised by many and hated by your former allies, but free."

Lorn ignored that part. "What happened?"

"They sent a Wizard with a killing spell, just as I suspected. My Magic is more powerful than any they have encountered and the spell was reversed. He actually killed himself."

"One less," Lorn murmured.

"Not all Wizards are bad, Graywullf," Lynch stated. "Besides, you can't kill them all."

"I can try," Lorn argued. "I ain't met a good one yet. Are you tellin' me that you're not bad?"

"On the contrary," Lynch replied. "I've already assured you that I am most definitely the baddest of the bad. Rotten clear to the core. You tried to talk me out of that."

"So why are you helping me?"

"I'm just playing a different hand," Lynch said. "Not only a different hand, I'm actually playing a completely different *game* than all the rest of you, but that's not important."

Lorn wearied of the banter. "Today's my trial. I hope you didn't forget that you're going to be there to clear my name."

"I'll be there," Lynch replied. He walked from the cell and down the passage. Actually, he wouldn't miss Graywullf's trial for the World. He was completely recovered from his hardships in the Land of Ice, and Lorn Graywullf played a major part in that. His powers were at their peak and he was enjoying the buildup to expose Marsten immensely. He would never forget that Marsten had had a hand in double crossing him. Helping out Lorn Graywullf along the way was a pleasant diversion.

Lorn knew Lynch was gone. He felt it. Lynch was not joking when he said he was bad. Lorn felt that too. He didn't know everything the Dark Wizard had done in his exceptionally long life, but he suspected it went well beyond his imagination. However, the Dark Wizard was helping him now, and that was all that mattered. For all his shortcomings, Lynch's word was good.

Marsten's voice rang down the passage, slicing through his thoughts. "What do you mean he's not dead? He has to be dead."

Booted feet echoed down the corridor and soon Lorn's cell was surrounded by hard eyed, armed men wearing battle armor. One soldier called out the all clear and Marsten shoved his way through them. The man in black was close behind him. Lorn grinned at them.

"You!" Marsten spat. "How…? I was assured you were dead. Why won't you just die and leave us be?"

"Mornin', Marsten," Graywullf said with a nod. "I reckon we better get on with the trial. We don't want to keep the hangman waiting."

Marsten cut loose with a string of curses. He stepped closer to the cell and waggled his finger at Lorn. "You will hang today, mark my words. When you're dancing at the end of the rope, then I'll finally be rid of you for good." He turned and spat on the charred remains of the Wizard assassin he had sent the night before, then stormed up the passage. The man in black leaned in very close to Lorn's cell and eyed him suspiciously. His hood slipped back just far enough for Lorn to catch a glimpse of skin whiter than a fish's belly and one ghostly, milky colored eye before the man in black slipped it into place once again.

"Perhaps we underestimated you, Graywullf," he said thoughtfully. "Not that it matters. You will go to trial and you will hang. Bring him," he ordered the soldiers. He wheeled about with a flourish of his cloak and followed Marsten.

His cell door was unlocked and Lorn was prodded down the passage with a short sword.

"How long you been taking orders from the likes of him?" he asked with a nod in the direction the man in black had gone. None of the soldiers responded. "Don't the *magii'ri* still rule Norland, and enforce the laws of Aard throughout the World?" His answer was a vigorous prod with the short sword that sliced a three inch gash along his ribs. With a low growl Lorn wheeled and chopped his hand down on the wrist of the nearest soldier, then caught his sword as it fell. He flipped it, and brought it crashing down on the next soldier's blade with enough force to disarm him. The soldier who had prodded him stared at Lorn with eyes that had gone wide with sudden fear. Lorn clapped him on the helm with the flat of the sword so hard he crumpled in a heap on the floor. Then Lorn stepped back and lowered the sword.

"I care not who you serve, but hear this! I am a Trueblood *magii'ri* Warrior, loyal to the Code, and I will not be treated like common street scum. Escort me to trial, hang me if I am found guilty, but *never* disrespect me!" With that he dropped the sword and continued down the passage. He knew the way well enough from years of service as a young Warrior escorting criminals down that same passage. The stunned soldiers scurried after him.

Lorn waited long enough for the soldiers to catch up, allowing them to save face by entering the great hall of justice as a group. The Hall was packed, and as soon as the door swung open the crowd began to shout insults at the prisoner. Graywullf walked stoically to the set of wrist stocks built on a raised platform in the center of the Hall and allowed his hands to be locked in place. All observers were thoroughly searched before being allowed entrance to the Hall, but Lorn felt extremely exposed and very helpless. If another attempt was made on his life he knew would be joining his ancestors at the Feast well before dinnertime. He examined each face as he came to them, looking for some hope of leniency, but each observer seemed more crazed with rage than the last. Finally Marsten entered through the Council door, followed at a respectful distance by the other Wizards of the Council of the Staff. Lorn only recognized two of the Wizards. Lynch had greatly thinned their ranks on the Isle of Serpents when he had crushed their spell of darkness. And where the Hell was he, now that he was sorely needed?

"Silence!" Marsten ordered. A few of the observers continued to curse the prisoner, and the soldiers went into the stands. The crowd immediately went silent. Marsten nodded to himself. He was in his element, the center of attention. "Lorn Graywullf, you are charged with the assassination of King Elander the Good," he began.

Lorn felt a foreign presence for a split second and felt a momentary bout of dizziness then a lesser Wizard seated in the stands leaped to his feet.

"I did it! It was me!" he cried. He jerked spasmodically and fell to the floor.

Lorn stared in disbelief then slowly realized the Wizard must have been crafting a spell aimed at him, which had been reversed by Lynch's talisman! He breathed a huge sigh of relief.

"Remove that man," Marsten ordered. "Seal the doors! We will have no more interruptions."

Out of the corner of his eye Lorn saw the man in black as he hastily left the stands. He was stopped briefly at the door by the guards then allowed to leave. *Rats always know when to leave a sinkin' ship,* he thought. Lorn shifted his attention back to Marsten just in time to see a look of alarm tinged with fear pass across his face. *That rattled 'em,* he thought. The crowd slowly settled back into an uneasy silence.

"Lorn Graywullf, you are charged with the murder of King Elander." Marsten again intoned. "How do you plead?" he added reluctantly.

"Not guilty," Lorn answered in a clear, strong voice.

"Let it be noted," Marsten announced. "The Council of the Staff will show beyond any doubt that you did commit this heinous crime."

A steady stream of witnesses followed, so many their testimony became a blur to Lorn. An ache settled in at the base of his spine and radiated outward. After what seemed like hours, Rand was called to the stand. He testified that Lorn Graywullf's rifle was found at the scene. The crowd roared for justice.

"Silence! Silence!" Marsten shouted, but a satisfied smile had settled on his features. The crowd slowly complied. "The evidence against you is damning, Lorn Graywullf. Do you have any rebuttal?"

"How do you know it was my rifle?" Lorn asked.

"It has your initials carved in the butt, and fancy beadwork, like those savages once did." Rand answered. "Everyone for hunnerds of miles knew it was your rifle."

"So where is it?" Lorn asked.

Rand shrugged and muttered an answer under his breath.

"I can't hear you," Lorn said. "Speak up."

"It has been destroyed," Marsten interrupted. "As all guns will soon be, and good riddance!"

"Destroyed?" Graywullf echoed. "You destroyed the one piece of evidence that could place me at the scene of the murder?"

"We have many, many witnesses who saw you there," Marsten assured him. "We can go on with testimony all day, if necessary."

The door swung inward with such force the soldiers guarding it were flung across the polished stone floor. Lorn nearly laughed with relief. A tall, forbidding figure filled the doorway. "That will not be necessary," Lynch announced. "My client is innocent, and this trial is a farce."

"I told you to seal that door! Can't you do anything right?" Marsten shouted. "Who are you? No one is allowed entry once the trial has begun."

"I am Lorn Graywullf's representative," Lynch replied. "I was held up by circumstances beyond my control. So, where were we?" He allowed his true appearance to become visible.

"You?" Marsten nearly shouted. His face blanched and he cast a worried glance to the doorway, as if gauging his chances at escape. "Guards! Disarm that man!"

"Easy now," Lynch said to the guards in an even tone as he cautiously handed over his weapons. H looked like a wolf that had already opened up a fine young deer and was preparing to sink his teeth into the choicest morsels. "I have no problems complying with the laws of this court." He proceeded to the platform, carrying a long, leather wrapped package under one arm. "Mr. Graywullf," Lynch said with a nod in Lorn's direction..

"Took you long enough," Lorn replied. "Where the Hell you been?"

"Clearing your name," Lynch said conversationally. "And arranging for a secondary plan if needed."

"That is enough." Marsten ordered, recognizing that his control of the situation was rapidly eroding.

"As I walked in," Lynch said, ignoring the Wizard, "I could have sworn I heard you say the murder weapon, purportedly Lorn Graywullf's rifle, was destroyed. How was that done?"

"It was melted down, as I watched," Rand replied, before Marsten could stop him. "Ain't nothing left of that rifle but a pile of slag."

"And it was a a very distinctive rifle?" Lynch asked.

"Only one of its kind," Rand replied.

"Is that true?" Lynch asked Lorn.

"I reckon so," Lorn answered.

"So this very recognizable rifle owned by Lorn Graywullf was found at the scene of the murder and destroyed by you, Mr. Rand, and you are under direct orders of whom?"

"Mr. Marsten gives me my orders," Rand replied sulkily.

"So Marsten ordered you directly to melt down Lorn Graywullf's rifle?" Lynch asked.

Rand stared hard at the floor while Marsten tried desperately but discreetly to take his attention away from the imposing figure of Lynch.

"He did," Rand finally answered.

"Then what is this?" Lynch exclaimed loudly as he whipped the leather covering from the package he had carried in. Gray gunmetal reflected the light streaming in from the window ports.

"My rifle," Lorn answered.

"Exactly!" Lynch crowed as he held the rifle high over his head and turned so all the spectators could see it. "This is Lorn Graywullf's rifle, which Mr. Rand and Mr. Marsten both claim was in their possession until they destroyed it. But I am here to tell ALL of you that I took this rifle from a renegade Wizard who was in Garrison Town the same night as Lorn Graywullf. This rifle was stolen from Lorn Graywullf on the Isle of Serpents months before the King was shot."

"Enough of these lies," Marsten protested weakly.

"I speak only the truth here today," Lynch stated flatly. "It is you, Marsten, who has twisted the truth from the very beginning of the accusations against my client. You never had the rifle, and your witnesses were all told to repeat the same story as coached by you and your fellow Wizards."

One of the witnesses who had given false testimony rose surreptitiously from his seat and began to slink towards the doorway. Several others followed him, but Lynch pinned them to the spot with a loud shout.

"You!" he yelled. The first man straightened up and pointed a shaky, questioning finger at his own chest. "Yes, you." Lynch repeated. "Did you give false testimony here today?"

The man began to speak, but suddenly grabbed at his throat and began to choke. He fell to the floor as reddish foam seeped from his clenched lips.

Lynch shook his head. "We can go on until there are no survivors if that's what you want, Marsten. Or," he added, "we can cut through this bullshit and you can drop the charges against Graywullf."

"Bah! You have nothing," Marsten retorted. "A rifle which you copied with Graywullf's instruction and cheap magic tricks more suited to a parlor game than a court of law. At this point the only way Graywullf could possibly prove his loyalty to Norland would be with the head of the Black Queen in a gunny sack!" He made a chopping motion with his left hand and archers rose from their places of concealment all around the balconies and buttresses. Every one aimed an arrow at Lynch. He froze in place, a look of utter disbelief on his face.

Lorn rolled his eyes at the Dark Wizard. "Is that the best you could do?"

"He can join Graywullf," Marsten announced. Five of the archers lowered their weapons and approached Lynch.

"It's not over yet," Lynch said in a low voice.

At that moment the door to the High Wizard's chambers burst open with such force they were torn completely off the hinges. Ox came charging in, flanked by Smilin' Jake and Bill McCurry. Ox wrapped one massive arm around Marsten's body and with the other hand he grabbed Marsten by the throat then lifted him completely off the floor. One of the archers released an arrow, which thunked solidly into the stock inches from Lorn's face.

"Anybody makes a wrong move, I'll rip his head off," Ox announced.

The remaining Wizards and guards were caught flat footed. One guard started towards Ox, who grinned and increased the pressure on Marsten a tiny bit.

"Stop you idiot!" Marsten squealed. The guard froze.

Smilin' Jake and Bill took the weapons from then guards nearest to them.

"Everybody shut up!" Smilin' Jake shouted. "Looks like a standoff," he continued as the crowd quieted down. "What do you say we make a trade? We'll take the cap'n and Lynch and mosey on out the back here, and we'll leave Marsten on the edge of town. What do you think about that, Marsten?"

Marsten's eyes bugged out and he nearly choked with rage and the ever increasing pressure of Ox's ham like hand on his throat. "Yes," gasped.

Lynch held out his hand until the head guard dropped the keys to the stocks into it. He released Graywullf

"You cut that close," he muttered to Lynch. "Marsten!" he shouted. "Tell your men to drop their weapons."

Marsten managed to nod, and his men dropped their weapons to the floor.

"Now what's the plan?" Lorn said in a low tone.

"To be honest," Lynch replied, "this is as far as I got with plan B."

Lorn rolled his eyes. He drew a deep breath and ran his hand through his hair. "Marsten," he began, "you put me and my boys through Hell and you showed yourself to be a yellow bellied coward and a traitor. I reckon there's not much I'd like more than to run you clean through and see if you bleed yellow."

The color drained from Marsten's face as Smilin' Jake grinned.

"But," Lorn continued. "I am a Trueblood *magii'ri* Warrior, sworn to loyalty to Norland and the laws of Aard. For that reason alone I'm gonna let you live. This time," he added. He let his eyes sweep over the audience. "Some of you know me. All of you know *of* me. I have always been and will always be loyal to Norland. I did not kill King Elander. The problem is there's no way to prove who did it, unless they confess." He swung his gaze back to Marsten, who began to look panicked and tried to shake his head.

"I know you didn't do it, Marsten," Lorn said in disgust. "You don't have the skills. But I think you know who did it. My point is I'll do whatever it takes to clear my name and find the real killer."

Lorn and Lynch scooped up weapons discarded by the guards and the entire group retreated through Marsten's chambers. Lynch led the way out of the chamber and down first one narrow hallway, then another and another, shutting and barring each door as they went. The entire infrastructure of the great hall was a maze of hallways and tunnels. They finally emerged in an alley.

"That'll buy us some time," Lynch said. "But you're all wanted men now."

"Same as you, I reckon," Lorn replied.

Lynch grinned. "I'm used to it."

"Can I kill him now?" Ox asked. He held Marsten out and shook him like a rag doll. Marsten cursed furiously.

"Sorry, Ox," Lorn answered. "We need him alive for a little longer." He turned back to Lynch. "This is still your plan. Can you get us out of here?"

"Follow me," Lynch replied.

He led them down back alleys and garbage littered dirt lanes to a rundown stable at the edge of the city where they took refuge. Lynch wasted no time grabbing a horse and beginning to saddle it.

"Word's gonna spread fast," he said when the Warriors hesitated.

"So now we're horse thieves," Smilin' Jake said with a rueful shake of his head. "Ain't it funny how times change?" But he caught his own horse and began to saddle up.

"Ox, tie him to a post," Lorn ordered the big man. "Tie him tight, and gag him."

"Wait," Marsten began to plead.

"Shut up," Lorn said in an even tone. "Somebody'll find you. Now… there ain't no audience here so you can talk freely. Me and you both know I didn't kill Elander. If you tell me who did, I'll find him and kill him and we can put this whole mess behind us. Kind of a fresh start. Of course, you'll have to turn over a new leaf, so to speak, and actually start running Norland according to the Code. Or," he drew his borrowed blade from its sheath and tested the edge with his thumb, "I reckon this is sharp enough to bleed you out."

A speculative gleam lit Marsten's eyes. "You'd swear on your honor that you won't reveal anything from the past?"

"I would, if you swear on whatever's sacred to you that me and my men will get a full pardon when we're done."

"We have an accord," Marsten agreed. "The man who killed King Elander is Timon Blackhelm. You saw him in the dungeon. He fled during your trial. I would imagine he sought refuge with the Black Queen Mordant."

Lorn snorted. "Mordant, eh? The Queen of Black magic and sworn enemy of Norland and the Light." He chuckled. "I'm guessing she still has an army of followers, so that might get a bit tricky. Still…a small group might sneak in and grab one man without being caught." He extended his right hand, and after a long pause Marsten shook it. "We have an accord." Lorn agreed.

They tied Marsten and hurriedly fled the stable on stolen mounts. After pushing the horses hard for several miles, Lorn slowed the group to a walk. Smilin' Jake rode up beside him.

"I'm beholden to you, Jake," Lorn began.

"I reckon," Smilin' Jake replied. "But that don't matter. You know Marsten agreed to your accord way too fast. He's got somethin' up his sleeve."

"I reckon he does," Lorn agreed as Lynch eased his mount up to listen in.

"So do you think this Timon Blackhelm really shot Elander?"

Lorn remembered the man in black from the dungeon and the cold, hard gleam in his eye. "I reckon so." He turned to Lynch. "Yer awful quiet, Lynch. That ain't usually a good sign."

Lynch grunted an unintelligible curse. "That's because I know Timon Blackhelm, and he is definitely capable of killing a king. But I also know the Black Queen and for this group to oppose her in her territory is nothing less than certain death."

"I have no choice," Lorn replied. "The rest of you do. I won't ask you to come with me. Hell, I got a better chance sneakin' in there alone than with a group."

Smilin' Jake snorted. "Bullshit. You ain't no better than me. I'm goin'."

"Me and Ox are in," Bill chimed in.

"Idiots," Lynch muttered. "And what about your son, Graywullf?"

"Well, Lynch," Lorn answered. "In case you didn't notice we're circling Richfeld now. I left him with a farmer named Hudge and we're gonna pick him up then disappear for a while."

Lynch digested that information. "So you're taking him with you?"

"No," Lorn replied. "But I ain't seen him in two years. I'm gonna spend time with my son, Lynch, and teach him a thing or two before I go."

"I see. Now…do you really think Marsten will hold true to his word?"

It was Lorn's turn to shrug. "Nope. But if Timon is the killer, and I bring down Mordant along with him, I reckon that'll prove my loyalty to the people of Norland beyond a doubt."

"You are a stubborn son of a bitch, Lorn Graywullf," Lynch responded. "You're free! Take your son and your men and turn your back on Norland forever. Begin a new life on the other side of the World, somewhere the Wizards can never reach."

"And then what?" Lorn replied. "Raise my son as a coward with no honor?" He spat in the dust. "Besides, you know as well as I do there's no place the Wizards can't reach."

Lynch's face darkened. "Better to be a live coward than a dead hero."

"I told you before, I ain't doin' this for the people of Norland and I ain't doin' it for the reputation I might get. I'm doin' it because it's the right thing to do."

"They'll turn on you again, Graywullf, just like they did so easily in Garrison Town. Hell, for a copper piece they'd have torn out your guts right here not more than an hour ago," Lynch argued. "If they catch you they still might."

Lorn couldn't deny the truth in those words. The images of the hate filled faces of the residents of Garrison Town were burned into his memory. They had turned on him and his men with only a word. Most likely all the people of Norland would do so again.

"I'm honor bound to complete the quest," he said. "Once that's done I can cut and run if I have to."

"I'll have no part in foolishness such as this," Lynch replied. "You're a good man, Graywullf." He extended his hand and Lorn shook it. "Too good a man to throw your life away for people who will hate you before the sun rises another day."

"Where will you go, Lynch?" Lorn asked.

Lynch shrugged. To tell the truth, he had no idea where his course might be. In that way he actually envied Graywullf, who's path never seemed to deviate. He swung his horse to the side of the trail.

"Fine," Lorn said over his shoulder. "Didn't need you anyway." He gigged his mount into a trot.

"You really ain't goin'? Ox asked as he walked his horse around Lynch, who merely shook his head. When Ox looked back again, the Dark Wizard was gone.

# CHAPTER ELEVEN

Marsten flung the door to his private office open so hard it thundered against the wall behind it and ricocheted back into him. He cursed loudly and kicked it. Then he cursed again. Timon Blackhelm reclined stoically in Marsten's own chair, his booted feet propped on the polished teakwood of Marsten's desk and a thick, black cigar trapped between his sparkling white teeth.

"You lost control of that rather quickly," Timon said as he thoughtfully studied the glowing end of his cigar. "I am beginning to wonder if I chose the right man for the job."

"Wonder all you want," Marsten replied as he flung his robe across the room. "Lorn Graywullf is as good as dead, along with his men."

Timon chuckled. "How many plans have failed? Three? I have to tell you I am losing patience very quickly."

"Too many," Marsten was forced to agree. "But now I have him."

Timon dropped his booted feet to the floor with a loud thump. He leaned forward eagerly at the sound of confidence in Marsten's voice. "How?"

"I'm sending him right into the enemy's hands, and he agreed to do it. Lorn Graywullf has accepted a quest to restore his honor. He is going after the Black Queen herself. Oh, and you, of course."

Timon grinned. "You set me out as bait? This is good. Very good." He rose suddenly. "I will raise an army that will annihilate him and his men, and the ensuing animosity will keep Mordant busy for years to come, giving us all the time we need to increase our power." He chuckled. "I like it."

"Don't forget Graywullf bested you twice already," Marsten said. He regretted the words immediately. Timon leaped across the room and wrapped one hand around Marsten's throat and flung him against the wall and held him there.

"Never forget who you're dealing with, worm," Timon threatened. "Graywullf got lucky. This time there will be no guns and no giant powder. Just my steel against his."

He released Marsten. The Wizard choked and coughed, then managed to whisper, "How did he defeat the killing spell?"

"Indeed," Timon agreed. "How did he? Someone is helping him. I wonder who would be stupid enough to help him now?"

# CHAPTER TWELVE

LORN SAT IN THE shade of an immense cottonwood tree and watched as Smilin' Jake led his son through an intricate series of defensive moves. Each was armed with a wooden stave the same length and approximate weight of a shortsword. Luke learned quickly, and Lorn was glad of that. The days had passed far too fast for his liking, drawing ever nearer to the time when he had to leave. Luke made one small misstep, and Smilin' Jake prodded him gently in the ribs with his stave. Then they began again, and Luke performed the series flawlessly. Lorn grinned. Jake was a good teacher and a hell of a lot gentler than any who had taught them. A mistake under Fowler's hand had often resulted in a ringing openhanded blow that sent the student home for the day. Jake joined him while Luke ran off with the boundless energy of youth.

"He's a natural," Smilin' Jake told Lorn.

"I reckon so," Lorn said wistfully. "I'd like to see how good he is when he grows up."

"That's easy," Smilin' Jake replied. "Abandon this fool quest. We'll hijack a ship and be back at the Isle of Serpents before winter."

Lorn eyed his friend reproachfully. "What kind of lesson would that teach Luke?" He nodded at Jake's silence. "But you could take him, Jake. This ain't your fight."

"I'll see it through anyway," Smilin' Jake answered. They'd had the same argument at least once a day. They both knew the outcome. "But Luke is good, as good as any I've ever seen. And he's just a boy."

Lorn Graywullf grinned. Luke was good at everything they'd taught him. Lorn had instructed him in the way of the gun, using a decrepit old training revolver with the barrel clotted shut with rust. From Smilin' Jake and Bill McCurry he'd learned about blade work. And Ox had taught him hand to hand fighting. The boy had amazed them all.

"He's got something extra," Lorn conceded. "He'll be better than any of us. Maybe the best ever. He's smart, too."

"Must come from his Mother's side," Smilin' Jake grunted. Lorn chuckled. "You told him about the Citadel?"

"Yep. He knows about bullets and charges, and even the giant powder. And he could find the Citadel without ever looking at a map."

"Then we should be getting on with it."

Lorn sighed. "I reckon so." he paused. "Jake, have you ever wondered how many of those fellers we sent to the gallows was actually innocent?"

"I never did until I faced it myself," Smilin' Jake admitted. "But it's been botherin' me since."

"That's why you're comin' on this damn fool quest, ain't it?" Lorn pressed.

"You ain't the only one who feels honor bound," Smilin' Jake answered. "Maybe if I have a hand in bringing somebody who is really, truly bad to justice it'll even things out a bit."

"You know it's an ambush," Lorn stated flatly. "We ain't meant to come back at all."

"I've been telling those two knuckleheads that same thing," Smilin' Jake said. "Damn stubborn fools won't cut and run either." He climbed to his feet and walked back to Ox and Bill. "Get your shit together. We're leavin' in the morning." He glanced around at the swiftly running stream, the cool green of the hay meadows and the refreshing shade of the cottonwoods. "Ox, I do believe we have found the perfect place for our retirement cabin." His teeth were bared in a grin, but it resembled a grimace. He didn't laugh.

# CHAPTER THIRTEEN

"Luke, you do as Hudge says until I get back, ya hear?" Lorn Graywullf was dressed in light chain mail, with his massive battlesword slung over his broad back. No helm covered his unruly hair, which was carelessly tied back with a strip of rawhide. He leaped astride his great black warhorse and looked down at the short, squat farmer on the ground with a hint of barely repressed savagery.

"Luke's a good boy, and strong. He'll help with the chores, and if you treat him good, there'll be gold when I get back."

Hudge bared his yellow teeth in a huge grin. "We'll treat yer boy right, Graywullf, like we always do. Godspeed to ya." He laid a grime caked hand on Luke's shoulder in a friendly, protective gesture.

Lorn locked eyes with his only son. "It's a routine patrol. We'll be back before summer's end."

The boy stared back and barely nodded. Lorn wheeled his mount, but before he could drum his heels into the beast's flanks, it came to a dead stop. The warhorses of the *magii'ri* were savage beasts trained to lash out at any but their master. Lorn glanced down in amazement to see his nine year old son staying a twelve hundred pound warhorse with one hand on its massive chest. Luke reached and laid his palm on his father's leg. Lorn leaned down and clasped it with his own, then he raised his hand and the squad thundered down the track in a cloud of dust.

"It's a fool's errand Marsten has sent them on," Hudge muttered. "The Black Queen Mordant is on the hunt. Everyone knows it. But Lord Marsten sends only a short squad to deal with it. Seven men against an army! It's suicide, I tell you."

"Keep yer voice down, Hudge," his neighbor warned. "Marsten's not one to take lightly. Word is there's a wind of change blowin' among the *magii'ri*. At any rate, it ain't smart to piss off anyone as powerful as Lord Marsten. Besides, you got another hand for the summer, even if he is a mite small."

"And another mouth to feed in lean times." Hudge muttered. "Look at the little feller. He ain't shed a tear, but you can bet he knows he might not see his father again." He raised his voice and turned back to the stoic little boy. "Come on down to the south field when he's out of sight," he called to Luke.

Hudge turned to walk away with the neighbor, a thin, stooped man named Billings.

"Don't you work him too hard," Billings said with a smirk. "I need some help in my fields too."

Hudge only grunted. He didn't really trust Billings, and felt that he may have already said too much. Billings was a widower with no children. He himself had three of his own, girl children all, with no wife to help care for them, and now the Graywullf boy. But Lorn Graywullf had always been true to his word, and the gold he brought back from each campaign carried them through the winter.

Hudge shook his head and sighed deeply. It hadn't always been that way in Norland, the home of the Holy Warriors known as *magii'ri*. Times were changing, and not for the better. Oh, the fields were still as fertile as ever and usually yielded more than a man needed. But since Marsten had risen to power, the levy to provide for the Warriors and Wizards had gone up five fold. Granted, they provided peace and security that couldn't be rivaled anywhere else in the World. Crime was not tolerated in Norland, the Warriors saw to that, and that was worth one third of his crop. But rumor had it there was another levy increase on the way. By god, how much of a burden did they think a man could shoulder and still stand upright on his own two feet? He shook his head and spat into the dust on the road. There was something amiss in Norland. Something *dark*. The thought made him shiver in the warm sun.

"What's troublin' you?" Billings asked. "If the boy is that much trouble, just turn him out."

"It ain't the boy. Don't you get the feelin' that somethin's wrong?" Hudge blurted out.

"Like what?"

"It's hard to explain," Hudge replied. "The sun still rises in the East, but when I watch it, I can tell it ain't the same. There's deer and boar in the woods, like there's always been, but they act a bit peculiar. I ate a rabbit stew last night, and by god it didn't taste like rabbit stew used to. My carrots and taters are growing, just like they always do, but they look *different*."

Billings laughed, but it sounded forced to Hudge.

"Yer imagination is runnin' away with you. Either that, or you need to lay off the jug."

"I'm not imaginin' things," Hudge said, a note of desperation appearing in his voice. He knew he should stop. He had to stop spilling his guts to this man in particular. But he just couldn't. "I never told anyone this, but I had trainin' as a Wizard. Matter of fact, I was a Wizard for nigh on ten years. I just didn't quite have the knack for it, but I *feel* things that others don't. I wake up at night sweatin' like a pig and see flashes of light at the base of the Anvil Mountains. The air is heavy and smells like summer lightning but there ain't a cloud in the sky. I asked around, and nobody else seen or smelt it. Or maybe it's just that nobody'll admit to it."

Billings was suddenly serious. "You need to speak to Lord Marsten about it. Hell, I think yer just spooked at takin' on another mouth. You got three already, don't ya? All girls?"

"Aye. Susan, Kate and Lizbeth."

"That oldest, she's what? Mebbe fourteen now?" Billings worked up saliva in a mouth suddenly gone dry and swallowed noisily. His oversized Adam's apple bobbed up and down like a cork riding a wave.

"Fifteen come midsummer," Hudge said distractedly.

"That's about marryin' age, ain't it? I took my first wife when she was fourteen." A sheen of sweat spread over Billing's brow.

Hudge was taken aback. "Hell, no. She's just a child."

"Better look again. She looks all growed up to me, an' if somethin' was to happen to you her man could take all of 'em in. It'd be better if it was someone they knowed, instead of a stranger, you know."

"Is that some kind of warnin'?" Hudge asked with anger darkening his face.

"Naw, it ain't no warnin'. I'm just tellin' you to think about your little ones."

"I'm ready to work."

Hudge whirled around. The boy stood there, a hoe in each hand.

Billings suddenly veered off the track. "I got chores to tend to," he mumbled.

Hudge watched him go. He had the feeling that something had been set in motion. Now all he could do was ride it out.

"I'll work for my keep, Mr. Hudge, or I can catch fish out of the creek and sleep in the barn. Either way, I won't be no bother to you."

"You ain't no bother," Hudge said gruffly. He laid a work roughened hand across the boy's shoulders. "Come on, let's go chop some weeds."

Luke Graywullf cocked his head and stared thoughtfully after the departing Billings.

"Was he sayin' what I think he was sayin'?"

Hudge turned around and scowled. "Prob'ly so."

"If he lays a hand on any of 'em, I'll kill him."

"That's enough talk of killin'," Hudge said wearily. But there was no denying the chill that he felt deep inside when the boy said it. He was like all of the trueblood *magii'ri,* Hudge thought. There was something savage and untamed in them, held in check only by their sense of honor.

"We got weeds to chop."

The work was a welcome distraction to Hudge, even in the afternoons when the sun beat down on them like a hammer and heat waves danced across the fields. The air was unnaturally heavy and muggy, and sweat cut grimy trails down his cheeks and soaked his faded shirt. For three days they labored, tending Hudge's small plots of corn and beans, and each day was hotter than the last. On the final day, Hudge had had enough. He stood and popped the kinks out of his back while he scanned the horizon. There was a storm coming, he was sure of it.

"Let's go get chores done," he called to his daughters and Luke. "It feels like rain."

Clouds built on the horizon as they walked back to Hudge's stone hut, built with fieldstone his Grandfather had pried from his own land and levered into place himself. By the time the chickens had been fed and the eggs collected and the cows milked, a wild west wind had kicked up.

Hudge closed up the barn and fastened the shutters on the house. Almost as an afterthought, he even closed up the interior shutters, built when attacks from half men had been common. Those inner shutters were iron-banded oak, made to absorb and turn blows from half-man battle axes. Luke watched with serious eyes.

"Expectin' trouble, Mr. Hudge?" he asked.

"Never hurts to be prepared," he answered. "And don't call me Mister. Just plain ol' Hudge will do just fine."

"It's blowin' like a wild bitch out there," Luke responded. "That's what my Dad would say." Then he flashed an easy grin. "I reckon I'll sleep with that fireplace poker easy to hand, if you don't mind."

Despite himself, Hudge grinned back. "You do that." Then he was serious again. "It's an ill wind, for damn sure."

They ate a quick supper, and Hudge herded his daughters off to bed.

"G'night, Luke," they said, almost in unison.

"Night," Luke responded. As soon as they had closed their bedroom door, a huge clap of thunder vibrated the entire house. The girls squealed, but didn't come out. Hudge poked his head inside their door and saw all three under the covers. He grinned. Another clap of thunder boomed and was followed by a brilliant flash of lightning. The girls jumped and squealed again, but stayed under the covers. Hudge turned back to the kitchen, and his grin disappeared. Luke was peering out of a tiny crack into the front yard, his back rigid and the fireplace poker gripped tightly in his hands.

"Somethin's out there."

# CHAPTER FOURTEEN

T HE LARGER OF THE two cats padded across the smooth granite surface in the entrance to his den, while the smaller lay uncomfortably on the stone floor. Her abdomen was distended, turgid with young, and she panted in discomfort. Her time was not imminent, but the days of her gestation were drawing to a close. Any physical effort left her winded and diverted her life force away from her precious young.

The whistle struck both of the werecats like a physical blow, and the big male curled his lips back from his elongated fangs in a snarl. The female rose and urged the male to follow, but he refused and ignored the call of the master. His mate needed to rest, and the master should know that. The whistle sounded again, too high pitched for human ears.

The female licked his curiously feline face, walked ten yards from the den and waited for him to follow. The male did snarl then, a low, menacing rumble, but he reluctantly left the safety of the den. The call of the master was unpleasant to him, but it was actually painful for his mate. That alone compelled him to answer the call. He took the lead and slowly trotted down the mountainside in the darkness.

They reached the walls of the City of Shadows and sought out the hidden opening known only to them and the Master. No sooner had the pair breached the wall when an iron grate slammed into place behind them. The male, Zagreb, growled again with his ears laid flat against his skull. Tight and narrow places made him nervous. He much preferred the open spaces of the plains, with the night wind ruffling his furry coat and the squeals of some unfortunate half-man replacing the shrill whistle that still tortured his sensitive ears. But that freedom was a distant memory, since he and Zastina had fallen under the spell of the Black Queen Mordant.

Zagreb and Zastina emerged from their secret tunnel and flitted like shadows through a city named for the same. Zagreb's sensitive nostrils caught and processed all the scents that wafted to him on the summer breeze. Some were faintly familiar, stirring memories of long ago hunts. The descendants of his former prey lived here and ironically served the same master as he and Zastina. A spurt of saliva drenched his lolling tongue and dripped from his six inch tusk-like fangs. It would be good to drift off into an alley for just a moment and indulge his appetite for meat.

The whistle sounded again, and Zastina stopped and threw her head from side to side in agony. Rage overwhelmed Zagreb like a red curtain across his vision and he roared a challenge into the night. All the normal night sounds ceased. From far across the city the light, airy laughter of the Master floated to them.

Zagreb ground his sizable teeth together and once again led the way into the heart of the city. Both werecats were well aware that heavily armed half-men had begun to fall in behind them at regular intervals. The escort, bristling with crude weapons, was the same every time Mordant summoned them. The Black Queen had them under her power, but she was still obviously not sure how firmly entrapped they were.

Zastina began to lag behind, and Zagreb slowed his pace accordingly. They were actually in sight of the palace when an overzealous half-man prodded Zastina with a huge, serrated blade. Zagreb wheeled and pounced right over Zastina's back before she had even finished recoiling from the painful blow. He crushed the half-man to the cobblestones and raked his fangs across the beast's leathery throat. He was rewarded with a spurt of shiny black blood and a choked, gurgling cry of agony, and he reveled in it. Even the punishing spell that sent him reeling from the carcass could not totally block out the primitive pleasure he felt. Tail whipping in the night air, he roared once again. All of the half-men fell back into the shadows of crevices built into the walls, and the Black Queen's cheery laughter once again floated in on the night breeze.

"Come!" she called from a parapet. "Come, my pets." Her voice was clear and pure.

Reluctantly, Zagreb rejoined Zastina and they continued into the palace itself. The half-men stopped just outside the door, hooting and whooping in excitement, until Mordant cast a quick spell to disperse them. The hoots were replaced with howls of pain as the half-men charged back to their posts. Half-men were not allowed inside the palace. Mordant much preferred to keep her distance form her filthy, moronic footsoldiers. The interior of the palace was guarded by two giants and a host of men who had long ago given their allegiance to the powers of the Dark. They were Nightriders, former truemen who now stared out at the world with expressionless black eyes.

Mordant approached Zagreb. He laid his ears back, but held his ground as the beautiful woman ran her hands lightly down the length of his back. Mordant was a tall woman, but her chin would barely clear the top of Zagreb's powerfully hunched shoulders. Zastina growled along with her mate. Mordant stared intently at the glossy female and her blue eyes narrowed in concentration. Zastina lay back on the floor and a deep rumble emanated from her chest. Zagreb felt the calming touch of this new spell, and soon he relaxed as well. Mordant smiled again, and rubbed her face in the luxuriant mane that spanned his shoulders.

"I have something I'd like you to do," the Black Queen whispered into Zagreb's ear. "There is a human in the village of Richfield, in the land called Norland."

Zagreb tensed. His muscles bunched up under the flexible silvery scales that covered him from shoulders to hindquarters and Mordant tightened her grip on his mane. Norland. The land of the Warrior Kings known as *magii'ri*. All creatures feared the *magii'ri*. All creatures, that is, except for the wolves.

"He carries this scent." One of the giants tossed a bloody shirt of crude weave at Zagreb's paws, and Mordant held it to his nostrils. Despite himself, Zagreb drew deeply of the scent. It was human.

"Drink it in," Mordant urged. "Remember it well. Find this human, and kill him. Kill him and all that carry his seed. Do it for me, Zagreb."

Little did she know that Zagreb couldn't forget the scent if he tried. Scents to the werecats were like colors, only no two were ever exactly alike. The scent on the shirt was a violent red, but not from the blood it carried. It was the color of a predator, a man born to violence and bloodshed.

Zagreb had scented this once before, when he was very young. The shirt and the blood that stained it belonged to a *magii'ri* Warrior. Mordant released Zagreb and climbed back to the platform that overlooked her hall. She reclined on her throne and abruptly rose into the air. Zagreb approached Zastina.

"No, my pet. Your mate will be much more comfortable here with me."

An iron barred cage dropped from the darkness above Zastina and imprisoned her. Zagreb bellowed his rage and slammed into the cage, but the bars were as thick as a strong man's arm and did not budge. Zastina began to whine and once again the red curtain dropped over Zagreb's eyes. His movements were so quick he was a blur, but he made no attempt to reach Mordant. Instead he leaped into the squad of Nightriders. He slashed with steel hard claws and sunk his fangs into any that got in his way. Growls burst from his chest even as he felt the punishing spell which the Black Queen hurled at him. His fury was so great that he shrugged off the pain of the spell and sliced open yet another Nightrider with one slash of his forepaw. One of the giants hurled a coarse net over him and the other leaped upon him and bore him to the floor. In moments he was trussed and helpless, but he still roared and screamed at the betrayal he felt.

The Black Queen lowered herself back to the floor and slowly walked towards him, surveying the carnage as she did. The giants hastily retreated from the struggling werecat, but Mordant only watched him with sorrow, not anger.

"Why don't you trust me, Zagreb? I'm only thinking of what is best for Zastina and your young." Her tone was soothing, her voice low and comforting. Zagreb ceased his roaring, but a deep growl still sounded from his broad chest. "Can't you see? Here Zastina won't have to hunt, or leave the safety of the whelping den while scavengers prowl nearby."

Zagreb's eyelids drooped slightly and the rumbling growl quieted. Mordant knelt next to the net and extended her hand. One of the giants took an involuntary step forward and made a half strangled sound of protest, but Mordant silenced him with a scathing look. She slid her hand inside the net and stroked Zagreb's flank.

"I will care for her and the babies, and protect them. It may be some weeks before you are successful and return. You understand, don't you?"

Zagreb's head drooped as he felt the power of the Black Queen. She held enough power in that one slim hand to crush him and his mate forever. Mordant stood and motioned for the giants to remove the net. They hurried to comply and quickly stepped back.

"Go. Seek out those who carry the seed of Malachi and destroy them!"

Zagreb dug his claws into the rock and bounded out of the palace. The last sound he heard were the low moans of his mate.

A short, very fat man emerged from a recess in the wall. He glanced left and right at the dismembered corpses of the Nightriders, then shook his head.

"That could have gone better."

Mordant laughed. "I would have expected something more profound from my High Priest, my dear Durbin."

"I'm sorry, my lady. But spilled blood has a chilling effect on my intellect. Are you sure the werecat will do as you bid?"

"Absolutely," Mordant cocked her head at the cage where Zastina lay.

Durbin nodded. "Just the same, I'd like to place a wager with you. I still say we should have sent a squad of Nightriders or perhaps Tarlow for the boy, and if your pet fails, then I win the wager and we will do just that."

Mordant sunk her hand into the folds of fat around Durbin's neck. "Don't forget your place, priest." Durbin's eyes widened in fear and Mordant flung him backwards. He barely regained his balance in time to remain upright.

He gathered the fine cloth of his cloak around him and bowed deferentially. "I am your servant, my queen. I merely wish to remind you that three full squads of Nightriders fell to the Graywullf and his six men. It would seem the blood of Malachi runs strong in their veins."

"All the more reason to destroy the boy now and to do it in a manner that does not cast suspicion upon me. I don't want any Trueblood *magii'ri* swearing an oath of revenge against me. Zagreb will kill the boy, and if he is seen, so what? Werecats have descended to the villages to feed since time out of mind." Mordant rubbed her temple. "Leave me," she said to the priest.

"As you wish." Durbin hurried from the hall.

The Black Queen motioned to the nearest of the giants. He rushed over and leaned down to catch her words.

"Tarlow, are you sure the Scribe said only one who descended from the seed of Malachi could harm me?"

Tarlow nodded. "He said the prophet Alanna wrote that the Black Queen would be defeated by one of the old blood. Malachi's blood."

Mordant rubbed her temples harder. One of the headaches, the really bad kind, was coming. "Not if we kill him first."

# CHAPTER FIFTEEN

 E ROSE FROM THE dust of a shallow grave, stripped of his armor and bared to the waist. His scalp hung in a ragged flap over his left ear and that side was bathed in his own blood, clear down to his belt line. He stared for long moments in stupid fascination at the stumps where the fingers of his left hand had been, and tried to remember who he was. Only the dust he had been buried in, as fine as any powder ever ground, had saved him from bleeding to death. It had caked over his many wounds until the blood stopped flowing, but he was weak from the loss of it.

The Warrior hunkered there, frowning in thought. His mind was clouded with agony and his thoughts came with terrible slowness. He remembered leaving Richfield, and being angry. But angry at what? Then it hit him. He was angry at the one who had sent them into the mountains after the Black Queen, even after he had argued vehemently that several squads were needed to deal with the threat of attack. Lord…*goddamn his head hurt*…who was the man who sent them? Lord Marsten That was it. The leader of the *magii'ri* had sent them, and he had gone willingly even after he knew it was a trap. When the highest ranking Wizard in the entire *magii'ri* clan sent his best Warriors on a suicide mission, it was definitely not routine. He had known what the outcome would be, and he had sent them just the same.

Lorn Graywullf sat heavily on an outcropping of rock. It was too hard to think, his head felt thick and full and he could see nothing with his left eye. He slid off the rock and lay gasping in the dust. He was supposed to die out there, with his men. So why fight it? He rolled over onto his back, ignoring the pain that ripped through him, and slipped back into unconsciousness.

He awoke in the chill of a high desert night, shivering uncontrollably, with the sound of a young boy's voice echoing in his mind. *Luke.* He had never told his only son they shared the blood of Malachi the Marauder, the very first of the Holy Warriors known as *magii'ri.* They would come for him now, and the sons of bitches would kill his son.

"No," he croaked. His throat was as dry as the dust he lay in and uttering that simple one syllable word made it feel like it was lined with broken glass.

With a low moan of pain he rolled to his stomach and forced himself to his hands and knees. He inched his way to each of his fallen men and methodically searched them as tears flowed down his gory cheeks. His worthless left hand kept getting in the way like a stubborn puppy, and he mentally cursed every time he reached for something with fingers that simply were not there. A careless movement caused him to jam the hand into a pumpkin sized rock and tear a scab loose from the stump of his index finger. Pain rolled up his arm in a wave so strong it caused his balls to draw up tight against his belly. He cradled his injured hand until the pain faded, then wrapped it in a filthy scrap of cloth. He collected everything that had been left behind, and under the last man he found a waterskin. He supported it with his left forearm and clumsily drank from it. The cloak that belonged to his second warmed his battered body, and he lay there among the corpses of friends. They were the last of the old breed and they were gone now, all of them. Gone to the Other Side.

Lorn Graywullf lay there until the faint light of dawn, gathering the memories from a hundred campaigns and the careless years before that He glanced down and to his left. There was John Duvay, a great bull of a man and the strongest of the *magii'ri* in Norland. He'd had a heart as big as he was, and a gentle side known only to his fellow Warriors. Now he lay with his huge chest torn open and that gentle heart ripped out. Near him was Bill McCurry, and not far away lay Jacob Sipowicz, his lieutenant and best friend. Smilin' Jake, the man who charged into a hundred battles laughing with the sheer joy of being alive, and who had gone down with his eternal smile twisted into a grimace. Lorn Graywullf looked closer. It was not a grimace. Smiling Jake had died as he had lived, laughing to the bitter end.

The Warrior didn't see them with their bodies twisted and torn. His mind drifted back to the year they had all turned fourteen, when they had entered into training to become *magii'ri* Warriors. Theirs was the last class under Fowler. He tried in vain to remember if Fowler had a first name or a second, but it didn't matter. He'd died in his sleep before that final class had been moved on, and after that things began to change. But that summer had been sweet. Right up until the very end.

# CHAPTER SIXTEEN

FOWLER STEPPED BACK, LIMPING badly, and Lorn followed up his advantage immediately. He feinted left with his ironwood staff and struck to the right. Fowler recovered quickly, and Lorn saw the ruse for what it was, but too late. The instructor blocked his attack and slammed his own staff home behind Lorn's knees. His legs flew out from under him and he crashed to his back. The air *whoofed* out of him and his face twisted up in agony. He still clutched his forgotten staff with both hands. The ring of fellow students was silent.

"Tuck up your knees, boy," Fowler ordered. "Get yer wind back."

Lorn did as he was told and his burning lungs gradually relaxed. He rolled to his hands and knees. A streak of spittle arced down from the corner of his mouth. He struggled to his feet and stood there swaying like a cottonwood tree in high wind. He pounded the end of the staff into the earth three times, signifying readiness.

"No more for today, boy," Fowler laughed. "I've not had a student die under my instruction yet. I don't want you to be the first. Never trust only one of your senses. You saw me limp, but was there a reason for it?"

"No, sir," Lorn answered.

"Next."

Lorn tossed the staff to the next boy, a lad he didn't even know. The boy held his own, and even slapped a light hit to Fowler's knee. The instructor immediately limped back, and when the boy pressed the attack, he slammed him to the dust also. Fowler stood there, glowering and shaking his head. When the boy rose to his knees, Fowler laid him low with a blow from his open palm, which was nothing but sinew and bone.

"Dismissed," Fowler growled. "Get yer chores done." He looked at his assistant. "If that's the best they got, we're in trouble. Dumb as a goddamn rock."

Two assistants carried the unconscious boy to the infirmary. John, Bill and Jake gathered around Lorn and they struck off towards the east pasture. The late summer sun wrung sweat from their bodies like an old dishrag.

"He hammered you," Bill McCurry said from the side of his mouth, careful to not let Fowler hear.

"No shit."

The other two boys laughed, and even Bill let a smile crease his serious features. His solemn dark eyes flashed.

"Let's cut through the trees and take a swim. We got plenty of time," Jake suggested.

He didn't wait for a response, but cut off from the cow path and into the dense growth of oaks and willows. It had become a ritual of the four friends to cool off and wash off the sweat of the day's training with a dip in the deeper pools of the creek. Lorn lagged behind, still shaking off the effects of his instructor's last blow. The day was coming when men such as Fowler and the other instructors would bow before him, and that day was not all that far off. He knew that as certainly as he knew the sun would set that night. He had held his own up until the last ruse, soon he would send Fowler crashing to the dust, and then he would move on. The thought left him feeling unsettled and out of place. He would become a Warrior, perhaps one of the youngest ever to pass the test, and he would have to mete out his own brand of justice, perhaps even at the end of a sword. But for now, he was still a 'prentice, and expected to join in the empty headed foolishness of his friends. He hawked up a gob of phlegm, the last effect of Fowler's well learned lesson, and spat it into the dust of the trail. It was somehow symbolic of the last days of his youth, like he had spat out the last bit of him that was still a child and when he plunged into the creek and surfaced, it showed plainly on his face.

They waited nearly too late to gather the milk cows. Lorn wanted to remember that last day of summer, to revel in it, so he didn't push the other boys to hurry as he usually did. The sun was all but gone beyond the western hills when they drove them into the barn, and the milkers soundly cursed them. Lorn only smiled, when at all other times he would have given back as good as he got.

"We have to take the shortcut and skip dinner to make evening lessons," he suggested.

"Aw, crap," John Duvay grumbled. "We're gonna miss dinner again?"

Jake laughed and poked the hulking boy in the midsection. "Won't hurt ya, Johnny."

John grinned and cuffed Jake on the side of the head. That one careless swipe nearly upended the smaller boy. He danced in front of the bigger youth and waved his fists playfully in the air. John swung at him again, but Jake nimbly dodged that blow. His easy laugh echoed down the alleys.

"Knock it off," Bill, the serious one, demanded.

"Bill's right," Lorn said with an easy grin of his own. "You two idiots can stand here and play all night, but I don't need another beating for being late. If you want to make it to the other side of the compound before roll, we have to hustle."

Without waiting for a response, he trotted away from the cluster of outbuildings, across the same pasture they had traversed earlier, and back into the trees. The night was hot and muggy, and Lorn felt his body become slick with sweat. They were fighting through a tangle of willows a half mile into the trees when a sudden scream rent the air. All four skidded to a stop. Lorn felt his heart beating through his ribs.

"What the Hell was that?" he whispered.

"Rock cat," John suggested, breathing heavily through his mouth.

"In the middle of summer?" Jake replied. "Don't be stupid."

The scream came again, and at the end, there was an abbreviated, strangled shout.

"Goddamn, that sounded human," Bill hissed.

Lorn couldn't explain what happened next, but he knew later that the final vestiges of his childhood disappeared that night. He wouldn't be tested for another six months, but that was the night Lorn Graywullf became a Warrior.

"Come on. Stay low and quiet."

The last scream had given him a bearing, and he led the other boys unerringly toward it. As he drew closer he could hear the sound of ripping cloth, low moans of pain, and finally heavy breathing and a strange grunting sound. Lorn picked up a smooth branch as big as his wrist. After a moment's hesitation, the other boys did the same. Without waiting to see if they would follow, Lorn crept ahead until he could see a blur of white in a tiny clearing. It took a moment for him to realize the blur of white was two people. He caught just a glimpse of a bared breast when the woman on the ground punched the man who covered her. He rolled slightly to the left, then drew back and smashed his own fist into her mouth. She lay still while his hips pistoned up and down.

Lorn rushed into the clearing on silent feet. He was beside the man before he even realized anyone was near. Lorn kicked him hard enough in the ribs to lift him completely off the woman, swung his staff in a tight arc and felt it thunk solidly into the rapist's head. He dropped to the earth, his erection pointing skyward like an obscene totem. Lorn rushed to the woman and discovered she was still breathing, even as his friends gathered around. He hastily covered her nakedness with her own torn clothing. Despite himself, he was becoming aroused from the brief sight of her bared breasts and the tangle of dark hair at her crotch. Looking at the tense faces of his friends, he knew they felt it too and were just as ashamed as he was. Smilin' Jake knelt by the fallen man.

"Holy shit, Graywullf! He's dead!"

"This ain't no time to be joking," John protested. "This is some serious shit."

"I ain't joking. He's dead as a post, and it gets worse." Jake held up the dead man by his hair so they could see his face.

They all recognized him. His name was Bertram, a lesser Wizard in the house of Marsten himself. His identity was obvious, even with half his face caved in.

"This is not good," Bill broke in. "Killin' a rapist is one thing, but killin' a Wizard? My Da' told me killin' a Wizard curses a man."

"Bullshit," Jake said with a shake of his head.

"It don't matter," Lorn replied harshly. "We're standin' around here jawin' like a bunch of old women. Bill, you're the fastest. Go on ahead and get Fowler. He needs to see this."

The slim, dark boy nodded. He gave Lorn a reassuring clap on the shoulder and took off.

"John, better strike a light."

"Aye." He busied himself gathering tinder and moments later a small fire lit the clearing.

Jake stood close to Lorn. "I'll come see you in the stockade."

"Shut up," Lorn snapped.

"I'm joking. A blind man could see what happened here."

"I'll see to the woman." He brushed past Jake, with visions of the rest of his life in chains clouding his mind.

Lorn knelt next to the woman. She was little more than a girl, he saw, despite the obvious maturity of her body. The Wizard had tossed aside a cloak. Lorn found it and covered the girl just as she awoke. Sheer terror washed over her face.

"Easy now," Lorn said in a quiet voice. "Nobody here means you any harm."

She sat up and pulled the cloak tighter around her. A spasm of pain caused her to grit her teeth. She nodded her head in the direction of the fallen man.

"Did he…?"

"He was tryin'," Lorn said as gently as he could. "I don't reckon he, uh…finished."

Thunder rolled in the distance and a light breeze ruffled her curly hair. Lorn tore his eyes away.

"Better build up the fire," he suggested. "It's comin' a rain."

They all heard breaking brush and saw the advancing line of lights carried by Fowler and his men. In moments they were surrounded by a half circle of hard faced men and one very serious young boy. Fowler walked a slow circle around the girl without even glancing at her.

"Beeson," he called. "What do you make of it?"

John Duvay interrupted. "We was comin'…"

"Quiet," Fowler never raised his voice, but there was steel in it. "Beeson?"

A long, lean, whipcord tough Warrior with a face of tanned rawhide walked his own quiet circle.

"The four pups was cuttin' through the woods and came upon this one," he negligently kicked the corpse of Bertram, "havin' his way with the girl." He glanced at Lorn's worn boots. "That one poleaxed him." He spat on Bertram's corpse. "Good riddance."

"I reckon," Fowler replied in agreement, and Lorn felt relief course through him. "But there has to be a trial. What were you four doing in the woods?"

"We were late, so we cut through the woods and skipped dinner to make it to evening lessons," Lorn answered.

"Skipped dinner?" Fowler grinned. "You skipped dinner to make it to lessons on time. There's hope for all of you yet. Why were you late?"

"We went swimming in the creek," Jake said, before Lorn could answer. He flashed his easy grin at his friend.

"What are you grinnin' at, 'prentice?" Fowler demanded. "There's a dead man here. That's pretty goddamn serious."

"He don't mean shit to me," Jake replied. The smile never left his lips.

Lorn cringed, half expecting to see Fowler knock out every tooth in Jake's head. But he didn't. Instead, the battle scarred veteran spun around to Bill McCurry.

"What do you think about all this?"

Bill glanced at the dead Wizard. "I'm glad he's dead. If Graywullf hadn't killed him, I would have." His solemn dark eyes flashed savagely in the flickering light of the fire. "Curse or no curse."

A tiny smile tugged at one corner of Fowler's mouth. "Warriors, it looks like we have four new names to add to the scroll." He lunged out of the firelight. "Take care of the girl and get a detailed report from her. Take her to Martin's. You four, come with me."

The trial was swift. The girl, a servant named Melinda, gave her testimony in a clear, strong voice. The entire Council was convinced well before Beeson even took the stand and all four boys were exonerated. Lorn fell in love that day, and six months later he was accepted as a trueblood *magii'ri* Warrior. A year after that he and Melinda were married and his three best friends joined him as members of his squad. That one sweet day was the last day of the summer of his youth. Then came the long rides and an endless succession of dusty towns, followed by the dark years. Melinda had stood by his side, even when the name Graywullf had been sullied and he was in one prison or another, until Death came and stole her away.

# CHAPTER SEVENTEEN

IT HAD BEGUN INNOCENTLY enough. Lorn and Melinda had been married less than three months, and he was stationed at Richfeld. It became Melinda's habit to shop the market each day, and that was where she encountered Trenton, a lesser Wizard assigned to the house of Marsten. She turned away from a display of fresh vegetables and bumped into the Wizard. He hastily caught her by the elbow, and pulled her much too close for propriety. She stepped back, murmured an apology and continued on with her shopping. By the time she returned home she had completely forgotten the incident. But Trenton had not.

He followed her throughout the afternoon, always maintaining a discreet distance, but keeping her well within sight. As he watched her, he became enamored of her. Her unruly black hair, which shone with vigor and youth, the sway of her hips, the fullness of her ridiculously ripe, full breasts. Before she left the market square he was obsessed. He followed her to the home she shared with Lorn in the quarters reserved for Warriors with wives and children, which was nearly deserted. From that point on he thought of nothing else. He planned his day around placing himself in areas where he could see her or encounter her again, until Melinda had become aware of his constant presence. She, of course, informed Lorn, and there had been a very short but bloody fight. Trenton nearly died, then spent three weeks in the infirmary and was warned to avoid the Warrior's quarters. Upon his release he immediately retired to the Wizard's library and spent his days in quiet study. The upper level Wizards assumed he had been taught a harsh lesson and thought the entire incident had blown over. But Trenton was inwardly furious and still obsessed. His studies were not to further his own knowledge. He was determined to have Melinda Graywullf one way or another. He turned to Dark Magic.

Lorn didn't know the details. He assumed Trenton allowed himself to stew over what he viewed as a public embarrassment until he was nearly insane. He had duties to attend to himself, and was soon sent on an extended mission. He was gone six weeks. He still remembered every detail of that fateful day when he returned home.

# CHAPTER EIGHTEEN

"**M**ELINDA," LORN CALLED AS he swung open the door. His pulse was racing, his breath was already short. They were young, they were in love, who could blame him for the intense physical need he felt racing through his body? The house, a small apartment really, was silent. He scanned the room, noting the dust on the mantel and dried up flowers in an earthen vase on the table. Flower petals littered the tabletop. Lorn's heart skipped a beat when he saw that, and he raced into the bedroom, which was also deserted.

"She's gone, Graywullf," came Marsten's voice from the doorway into the street. "She and that young fool Trenton have run away together, not long after you left."

Lorn felt as if he'd been kicked in the stomach. "She left me?"

Marsten nodded. "It happens, especially to Warriors," he replied. "Best to forget her and focus on your duty. Take a few days off, then report to me." He left as silently as he had arrived.

Lorn sat heavily at the kitchen table and stared at his trembling hands. Melinda had been happy. *They* had been happy. He knew that. Why would she do this to him? He sat there through the afternoon and into the evening as the house grew dark around him. Finally, Smilin' Jake came looking for him.

"She's gone, Jake," Lorn said as his best friend and lieutenant walked in. "She left me. She played me for a fool and then cut and run with that yellow belly Trenton."

"What?" Smilin' Jake replied in disbelief. "That's bullshit, and you know it."

"Why's it bullshit?" Lorn asked. "Look at me. I ain't no prize, and I'm gone most of the time."

Smilin' Jake grabbed Lorn by the collar and hauled him to his feet. "Listen to me. I've seen the way Melinda looks at you. She'd die for you, Graywullf!" He shook his head. "Nope, there's something mighty fishy goin' on here. She told you about Trenton in the first place, too."

"People change, Jake," Lorn responded. He shrugged. "Maybe I better just do what Marsten suggested and forget about it."

"Forget about it?" Smilin' Jake nearly shouted. "That girl loves you, Graywullf. If you ain't gonna be a man and do something about this, then me and the boys will." Lorn reached for him and Smilin' Jake shoved him backwards. Lorn hit the table and nearly upended it. The vase teetered and fell and shattered upon the stone floor. It was dry, and among the shards lay a scrap of rough brown paper with writing on it. Both Warriors saw it immediately. There was a crude drawing of a blacksmith's anvil followed by three jagged lines.

"The Anvil Mountains," Lorn realized suddenly. "She didn't leave me on her own. That snake is taking her to the Anvil Mountains." He pushed past Jake towards the street with the scrap of paper in his hands. "I have to tell Marsten. I'll take some leave and go find her."

"We'll go find her," Smilin' Jake corrected.

An hour later they stood before Marsten, High Wizard of the Council. He pursed his lips as he stared at the scrap of paper Lorn had presented to him. Finally he spoke.

"Even if this were true, your wife's been gone for three weeks, Graywullf. There's no way you can catch up to them before they reach the coast, presuming that's where they're headed. Your request for a leave of absence is denied." He held up a silencing hand as Lorn and Jake began to protest. "You are needed here, for the duties you swore to uphold with a blood oath. Rest assured I will send someone to investigate this matter. If," he glanced sideways at Lorn, "your wife was taken against her will my man will find her and return her to Richfeld."

Lorn Graywullf was speechless. His right hand dipped down and caressed the worn grips of his pistol, and Smilin' Jake's eyes flew wide open. For a moment he was sure that Marsten was a dead man. Lorn regained his self control and began to protest, but Smilin' Jake led him forcefully from the room.

"What the Hell, Jake?" Lorn exclaimed as soon as their boot heels hit the boardwalk. "I can't sit by while some man kidnaps my wife and the yellow skunk in there just tells me to go on home!"

"I reckon," Smilin' Jake responded. "But you were about three tenths of a second from blowin' his guts all over the floor, and that would be kinda hard to explain."

"I ain't gonna sit idly by," Lorn said again. "I gotta do something."

"I got a plan," Smilin' Jake said. "If'n you'll control your temper for a minute and listen to me, I think you can save Melinda."

Lorn stopped. "I'm listening."

"I don't know what's goin' on, but Marsten let it slip that they might be headed for the coast. You know every way station operator between here and Elanderfeld. If you leave tonight with nothing but a light pack and trade horses at every way station, I think you can catch them coming out of the foothills."

A grim smile stole over Lorn's face. He slid his knife from the sheath at his belt and tested the edge with his thumb. "And there won't be another time."

Smilin' Jake nodded.

Lorn Graywullf rode from Richfeld that night, under a cloak of darkness. He took only one full waterskin, his pistol and gunbelt loaded with bright brass cases tipped with stubby lead bullets, his knife and the clothes he wore. Smilin' Jake sent out a carrier pigeon with word to the way stations, and they each had fresh mounts waiting when Lorn thundered into their yards. He only stopped long enough to make water and stuff a handful of dried meat into his mouth, and in thirty six hours he had made what most would have reckoned to be an impossible ride. The final way station operator in the foothills of the Anvil Mountains held the reins of the last horse, a short buckskin. The operator was a lean, spare man, and Lorn never could remember his name.

"Seen 'em," he told Lorn when asked about a couple traveling alone. "They stopped here for the night, only two nights ago. The feller said they was married," he cast a sideways glance at Lorn, who stood impassively filling his waterskin. "He wanted to buy a horse, nearly killed theirs gettin' here. He got pissy when I wouldn't sell him one. Kept lookin' down the back trail, too. Real nevous feller." The operator paused. "They took the south fork. It ain't as steep, and they was gonna be afoot most of the way. Man with a good horse could catch 'em tomorrow, I reckon. They in some kinda trouble?"

"He is," Lorn corrected. "That's my wife he has with him."

The operator stared for a moment into Lorn's cold blue eyes and flicked his gaze down to the worn kingwood grips of Lorn's six shooter and the heavy bladed knife in his belt.

"I'll be lookin' for you and your missus on the way back."

The Wizard Trenton was scared spitless, that was plain to Melinda. He watched the backtrail more than he watched where they were going, and Melinda saw the worry in his eyes grow to near panic as the campfires on their backtrail grew inexorably closer. By the time they reached the Anvil Mountains it was obvious that whoever was trailing them was going to catch them, and soon. And Melinda knew as well as Trenton who was following them.

"He'll never give up, you know," Melinda mentioned casually.

Trenton whipped his head around to stare at her. "Are you sure it's him? Graywullf, I mean?"

"Who else would it be?" Melinda replied.

"Well, he can't trail me if he's dead," Trenton said. He actually giggled at that, and Melinda knew he was mad.

"I wouldn't bet on it," Melinda stated.

They rode on. The Wizard had forced her to ride behind him, and each time he tied her hands around his waist. The first several nights he had attempted to have his way with her, but each time his desire had deflated before he could even touch her. After that, he simply quit trying.

She didn't know how he got word out ahead, but when three shaggy men rose out of a hollow and Trenton slowed to meet them, she knew he intended to ambush Graywullf.

"He's behind us. Kill him," were his instructions.

Melinda felt their eyes on her as surely as if they were hands. Even if they succeeded Trenton was only trading one problem for another. She saw their desire plainly in their eyes. She sent a silent plea to the gods to warn Graywullf, but deep inside she knew he would win.

She was right. Less than an hour later three shots broke the silence. Three shots, then the silence once again ruled the mountain. Trenton's face went slack with fear.

"Leave me here and I promise you he won't kill you," Melinda told him.

"Leave you?" Trenton echoed. "Never. You're mine, as you should have always been."

"Then I offer one last chance," Melinda said coldly. "Leave me. Just walk away, and I promise you he'll kill you quickly."

Her meaning was clear. But Trenton was beyond reason. He pushed on, and by evening the horse stumbled then went to his knees, pitching them both to the ground. The Wizard struggled away from her, then sat dumbly. Melinda laid out her bedroll.

"I could kill you," Trenton said in a thick voice.

"And you'd wish you were dead a thousand times before he let you die," Melinda warned.

Trenton lapsed into silence and despite her fear, Melinda slipped into the deep sleep of mental and physical exhaustion. She awoke late that night with Trenton's breath hot in her ear. He had her wrapped in a tight embrace, and she could feel his desire hard against her thigh. Then once again, he went soft.

"I curse you," he panted. "I may never have you, but I curse you. If you bear his child, you will not live to see him become a man."

"You bastard," Melinda ground out. "You sniveling, weak piece of shit."

She struck him across the face. Trenton recoiled, then leaned back in. Suddenly, his head was whipped back and he was jerked bodily into the air. A string of rawhide encircled his neck, and drew tighter. He was lifted completely off his feet, and his legs jerked spasmodically. Lorn actually growled at the feeling of finally having his wife's abductor in his hands. He held the Wizard with one hand wrapped in the rawhide, then he whipped his knife across Trenton's throat so savagely he was nearly decapitated. Blood sprayed across his forearm, and he dropped the Wizard's lifeless body to the ground. The chase was finally over. Melinda flew into his arms, her heart beating wildly. Neither spoke for several long moments.

"I love you," Lorn finally said.

"And I you, more than life itself," Melinda said through her tears. Luke was born nine months later. Melinda never mentioned a word of the curse to anyone.

# CHAPTER NINETEEN

HEN DAYLIGHT CAME LORN searched the area on shaking legs and came up with a bow, which was useless since he could not grasp it, and a shortsword overlooked by the scavengers. He looped a strip of cloth around the hilt of the blade and draped it from his shoulder. He could see nothing with his left eye, and he explored it with trembling fingers. It was sealed shut with blood or some other fluid, whether he would see with it when he opened it was a question for another time. He closed his one good eye and ripped one of the lances from Ox's body. It was enough. It had to be enough.

He stumbled downhill, drawn by the faint sound of flowing water in the canyon below him. He had no idea how many times he fell, but he always got back up. The last time he fell into a slough of tepid water, and the shock of it against his torn scalp made his head swim in agony. He sat there in the water and gritted his teeth against the pain, and with shaking hands explored that hideous wound. He slid his scalp back into place and bound it there with a scrap of his cloak. It would fester, he knew that. He could feel the grit caught under it. But it didn't matter. He just needed it out of his way, so it would not impede his vision. He gently scrubbed his face, and was immensely relieved when his eyelid came free and he could see with his left eye again. It had been glued shut with dried blood. The water in the slough stilled, and he made the mistake of looking at his own reflection. It was not even a man who looked back at him. *Maybe I'm already dead*, he thought.

But the pain was real, and a dead man would not feel it. He stood once again and ran his hand down his legs. They, at least, were whole. At one time he had been able to run at a trot for a full day. Now he only hoped he could remain upright and keep walking.

He filled the waterskin at the stream, but did not bother to try to clean his wounds. The time for that was long since gone. A fire had started inside him, from the spark that was struck with the first slash of a Nightrider's blade. He glared in impotent anger at the red streaks that were already climbing inexorably up the back of his mutilated left hand. The wound was a death sentence, but how long did he have? He forced himself to think. They had been six days out of Norland on horseback, no more than a day or so from the City of Shadows. On foot it would take him three days. Three days to reach the city. Could he reach it before the poison from the Nightrider's blade reached his heart? There was only one way to find out. The lone survivor of the *magii'ri* squad turned his back on his fallen men for the final time. *I reckon I'll see you soon enough,* he thought, *and buy you all a drink in Hell.*

# CHAPTER TWENTY

ORDANT SLOWLY SPIRALED UP from the black pit of unconsciousness, her mind a calm, unfathomable pool. A sudden stench assailed her nostrils and she wrinkled up her nose in distaste. The stink rose in waves all around her, and with disgust she realized a good portion of it came from her own unwashed body. She opened her clear blue eyes and abruptly sat up.

She was naked. That fact didn't really bother her. But the fact that she shared her quarters with a handful of naked women, all as dirty and repulsive as she felt, did bother her. They stared at her with obvious distrust.

"Where are we?" she asked no one in particular.

The others just shook their heads and turned away. Mordant noted in growing alarm that they all shared the look of being used hard. There was something else they shared as well. Complete and utter hopelessness. Except for one. She was younger than the rest. Her breasts didn't sag and point at the floor, and her buttocks were still firm and round. She had at least made an effort to clean up a little, as evidenced by the fact that her skin wasn't completely stained with dirt, or worse. Mordant directed her attention at that one.

"Will you tell me where we are?"

"We been sold. I reckon they're takin' us to the coast."

"Shut yer mouth, you little tramp," one of the older ones hissed. "She's too high and mighty for the likes of us. Just look at them high class titties and her lily white ass. She never seen a day's work in her life, 'till they slammed her on her back, that is." She cackled with laughter.

Mordant rubbed her temples. She never knew where she might end up after one of the headaches.

"So you're whores."

"Don't be callin' names, missy." The older woman replied. "You took 'em one after the other until one gent slapped Moira." She jerked her chin at the younger woman. "Then all hell broke loose and we all got sold down the coast. You know what that means?" She leaned close to Mordant, her breath even more fetid than the scent of her unwashed body. "It means we go out to sea with a crew and we don't come back if they run short of food." She cackled again. "They pitch us overboard, ya see?"

With a shock, Mordant realized they were moving.

"How long have we been in here?"

"Two days," Moira answered.

"Two days! Driver! Stop the wagon! Now!"

Mordant crawled to the latched door as the wagon lurched to a stop. The other women crowded in a corner as far from the door as they could get. Suddenly the tarp covering the wagon was thrown back to reveal a tall, stooped man wearing an eye patch. He carried a short handled club in one hand.

"What the Hell's the ruckus about?" he demanded.

Mordant wrapped her hands around the bars encircling the wagon.

"Watch yer fingers, sweetie," Moira whispered frantically.

Mordant jerked her fingers back just as the tall man slammed his club against the bars. Her fingers would have been crushed to a pulp if she had been an instant slower.

"Get back, you crazy bitch! I told you all the rules," the tall man warned.

Mordant's lip curled back in a snarl. She extended her hands toward the driver and abruptly jerked them forward. He slammed into the bars with enough force to rock the wagon. Blood sprayed from his broken nose and the club dropped from his nerveless fingers. Mordant released him, only to bodily slam him into the wagon again and again until blood ran from his mouth and ears as well as his smashed nose. Then she held him tight against the bars. She advanced towards him, her head cocked to one side like she was examining an insect. She licked her lips as the driver's eyes rolled wildly in his head. The Mordant slid her hand up his leg and over his crotch. He made a strangled sound, and Mordant lifted the keys from his pocket. A sudden stain blossomed down one leg. Mordant calmly unlocked the door and swung it open. The driver dropped to the ground in a heap.

"Ladies?" Mordant gestured to the door as if she were welcoming them all to tea. "Care to join me?"

Most of the women simply stared, frozen in place by fear. Moira stepped forward quickly.

"Goddamn right, I do!" She hastily climbed to the top of the wagon and threw down a trunk filled with women's clothing. "Them bastards kept us naked so we couldn't run away, and kept us filthy so nobody'd want us enough to try to rescue us."

She handed Mordant a dress and quickly pulled a loose cotton shift over her head and cinched it at the waist. Her large breasts strained against the material. "It ain't camisoles and petticoats, but I reckon it covers the goods."

"Moira, get away from her!" The older whore's voice was shrill from inside the wagon. "She's gotta be a witch!"

Moira leaned very close to Mordant. "Are you a witch?"

Mordant placed her own lips right against Moira's ear. "Oh, no. I'm much, much worse."

Moira covered her mouth to suppress a giggle.

"Ladies," Mordant called. "I'll be needing that wagon. Empty, of course." She casually slipped her own plain dress over her head and wondered briefly what had become of her fine robes and jewelry. It didn't matter. What did matter was getting back to the City of Shadows in time for a very important meeting.

The wagon driver stirred, and Mordant relieved him of his knife and a bulging coin purse. She climbed to the top of the wagon and cut the ropes binding another trunk to the roof and kicked it over the side.

"Last chance," she called as she climbed into the seat. She stared pointedly at Moira. "Well? Are you coming or not?"

Moira hurried into her own place beside Mordant, who gave her a broad wink. The rest of the women hadn't budged.

"Idiots," Mordant muttered. "They prefer the security of captivity to the sweet nectar of freedom."

She cut the ropes that lashed the iron barred cage to the wagon frame and settled back into her seat.

"You better grab ahold of something," she advised. Moira clenched her fists around the rail of the seat as Mordant picked up the reins. She didn't lash the horses, but crafted a spell of panic and wafted it over them. All four horses lunged into the traces as one, and the cage lurched off the wagon in a cloud of dust. Within moments even the shouts of the older whores was lost in the distance. Moira climbed up to lean on the backrest with a huge grin lighting her face and her long blond hair flying in the wind.

"Serves 'em right."

Mordant laughed, like the tinkling of wind chimes. "Sit down here, girl." Moira did as she was bade. "This is very important. When and where did you first see me?"

"Three days ago, in a saloon on the outskirts of the City of Shadows."

"Goddamnit," Mordant hissed. "I'll never make it."

"Make what?"

"I had a meeting scheduled with someone very important, but I'll never make it back to the City tomorrow."

"Why not? You're makin' those horses fairly fly. We were in the cage two days, but we only been on the road one short day. It'll only take a half day to get back to the city."

Mordant laughed again and leaned over to kiss Moira on her filthy cheek. They would make it, if she had to run the team to death to do it. She lifted her spell of panic and cast one of endurance and hurled it at the horses. They would probably die when she lifted it, but she didn't care. They ran all the rest of that day, and into the night. By midnight she could see the lights of the city. Moira lay nestled in the hollow of her shoulder, fast asleep. Mordant jostled her in the ribs with her elbow. Moira came awake with a start.

"This is it. You can come with me and be a handmaiden to the Black Queen, or you can go back to being a whore. Your choice."

"I'll go with you," Moira whispered in a small voice.

Mordant nodded. She pushed the team even harder and gradually the lights from the City grew stronger until even the streets were illuminated. Mordant urged the team on like a lunatic, taking some corners on two wheels. She barely saw the man walking on the roadside in time to avoid running him down. She caught a glimpse of a stark white face with a dark smear of beard stubble, then the wagon thundered past. Only when they had gone by did a shudder of fear crawl up her backbone. She glanced back, but the man was gone.

"Did you feel that?" she asked Moira.

"I didn't feel nothin'," the girl responded sleepily.

Mordant shook her head and they pounded through the city directly to the palace gates. The image of the lone man stayed with her. There was something about him, a feeling she had but couldn't quite pin down. But she had no time for that now. Tarlow flung open the gate as the team skidded to a stop, and stood with their sides heaving and heads down. He caught Mordant as she jumped down. He hastily sat her down.

"My lady," he bowed. "We were worried."

"Is he here yet?" Mordant demanded.

"Not yet. Our scouts reported that he is camped just beyond the outskirts of the City."

"Then all is well," she snapped. "You did well, Tarlow. Bring him here, tonight."

Two of the horses collapsed, but the others were too exhausted to move. Mordant turned back to the wagon where Moira sat as still as stone, her eyes huge and round as she stared at the giant.

"Welcome home," Mordant said with a laugh.

"You...Are you her? The Black Queen, I mean."

"I am the Black Queen Mordant, and you have agreed to be my handmaiden." She turned away again. "Tarlow, show her to a room." She wrinkled up her nose. "And tell one of the servants to draw her a bath." Her tinkling laughter echoed behind her as she walked out of sight.

Tarlow extended a massive hand to the frightened young whore. "Don't worry, miss. No one will harm you, but you'll find that things are very different here."

# CHAPTER TWENTY ONE

IT WAS A TESTIMONY to his weakened condition that he hadn't been able to get off the roadway before that crazy goddamn wagon driver nearly ran him over. He did have enough sense to fling himself into the ditch at the roadside before she looked back, but he still felt that penetrating gaze. Maybe Bill McCurry was right. Maybe killing that snake of a Wizard all those years ago had cursed him. It sure seemed like it. After all, the one person he had come here to kill had almost killed him without a fight. But what the Hell, he thought. He was going to die, right here, tonight, at the ripe old age of thirty seven.

He clambered painfully to his feet and climbed back to the roadway. The lights from the city were strong enough that he could plainly see the red streaks as they marched up well past his elbow. Another day, maybe two, and he'd die screaming in agony as the poison from the Nightrider's blade made it's way to his heart. He held a hand in front of his face and felt the fire of the fever that burned within him. It was now or never.

He walked boldly up to the main gate, forcing his gait to remain steady. Music played within the walls. It was a sound foreign to his ears that gave the events to come a surreal cast. The blood was roaring in his head. At moments like these everything always seemed to move in agonizing slowness. One of the guards noticed him and jabbed his mate in the ribs. They both turned to watch him approach.

"I need to see the Queen," he slurred.

The first one gave a snort that may have been laughter. "She ain't takin' visitors. Especially no dirty, flea bitten beggar like you. Get yer ass outta here before I kick it up between yer shoulders."

"I need to see the Queen tonight," he insisted. His voice wavered.

"Gods damn him, Jenks, this bugger's sick. Can't ya smell it?"

Lorn Graywullf focused his lifetime of training into his right hand. He coughed and appeared to stumble forward, which brought him within striking distance of the first guard. He drew the sword from under his cloak and slid it between the man's ribs, jerked it back and slashed open the second guard's throat. They both died without a sound.

"Two for you, Bill," he mumbled.

He eased open the small door, slipped inside and stood there for a moment, letting his eyes become accustomed to the sudden light of many torches. The music was louder now, a lonesome, forlorn tune on an instrument he couldn't even identify. People jostled each other for position in front of several well lit, open fronted buildings, and Lorn felt himself drawn to the crowd. He concealed his sword by the strap and used his lance as a walking stick and joined them. The women wore plain colorless dresses and the men were clothed in homespun of the same faded out hue. He felt their glances upon him, and saw them turn their heads away in almost comical curiosity. Their eyes were pointedly glued to a raised, rough cut wooden stage where a young woman swayed in time to the strange music. Lorn stood a full head taller than the tallest man in the audience, affording him a perfect view. She shed her blouse as the Warrior's eyes touched her to reveal ridiculously ripe breasts and a perfectly flat stomach. Lorn locked eyes with her, but she saw nothing. The crowd began to sway with her, and when her hips thrust forward a collective moan rose from the audience. He broke away then, even as he felt the pull of the trance among the crowd, and staggered on up the street.

The streetside lamps had been lit, and glowed in an irregular line all the way to the magnificent building that had to be the main palace. He passed a table lined with old men playing cards, but none challenged him. Evidently they felt safe enough within their walled city with armed guards on the ramparts. He chuckled humorlessly. They were in for a surprise in the morning.

His breath came in short little gasps. He desperately wanted to sit on one of the benches and rest, but he knew if he did he wouldn't be able to get up again. A light breeze stirred dust from an alleyway and brought with it the scent of broiling meat. His stomach growled. It didn't matter. He knew he couldn't keep anything in his stomach anyway. Not after three days of fasting and the poison flowing through him. He concentrated on putting one foot in front of the other.

Three boys came running hell bent for leather out of the alleyway. He had the sword half out, but quickly slid it back under his cloak and stood there, swaying, as they nearly ran him down. He watched them go with bloodshot eyes. One stopped for only a moment to stare in openmouthed curiosity, then he ran to join his friends. Lorn bent tiredly and plucked his lance from the dust.

The crowd thinned quickly as he left the center of the city behind and began the climb to the palace. The long incline sapped what little energy he had left, and his head swam alarmingly when he reached the first guard station. It was manned by two soldiers who marched back and forth across the elevated arch over a slimy moat. The oil lamps sputtered and hissed and cast flickering shadows out into the darkness. He kept to one side, timing his steps with the guards. At the exact moment, one step before they crossed and would be perfectly aligned, he whipped his lance up and hurled it with all his strength. They never saw it coming. It struck both guards in the throat as their feet were coming down in perfect time and they fell to opposite sides.

He stopped to retrieve his lance. They were young, he saw. Very young, and probably inexperienced. He shrugged and crossed the arch. Hell, he was only thirty seven himself and when he was gone there would be only one sign that he had ever existed. *Luke. Luke, boy. You'll grow up straight and strong, and I know you'll set this right.* He blinked heavily and slowly surveyed his surroundings. There was a small door inset into the stone wall surrounding the palace. There would be a guard there, fat and slow, his head fuzzy with the need for sleep. He hoisted the lance and walked down in his foreign shuffle.

The guard was there just as he had imagined and Lorn dispatched him just the way he had seen it in his mind's eye. One swift thrust with the lance and it was over. The fat guard died with a foolish expression on his heavily jowled face. Lorn hoped he wouldn't go out that way when his time came. A key from a heavy iron ring unlocked the door and in no time he stood in the shadows, inside the main palace. It was all automatic now, no conscious thought was needed. Stay low, use the shadows, and always expect the unexpected. But what he saw next caught him completely off guard.

She was beautiful, there was no doubt about that, and the flimsy shift she wore did nothing to conceal the lush curves of her body. But none of that meant a damn thing to him anymore. He had come here to kill a snake, in his opinion, and if it was a beautiful one that didn't make it any less poisonous. The thing that nearly caused him to lose his concentration was the man she embraced. He knew the man. His name was Barnabas, and he was a minor Wizard who served as an adviser to Lord Marsten, High Wizard of the Council. All of his suspicions were being proven true.

Mordant stepped back from the Wizard. "Where is he?"

"Is that any way to greet a representative of the most powerful nation in the World?" Barnabas responded.

"Don't toy with me. He said he would come personally this time." Mordant's eyes flashed impatiently.

"He had pressing business to deal with. I am his voice in this matter."

The Black Queen wheeled around so quickly even Lorn was surprised. She held a stiletto firmly under Barnabas' chin. He swallowed noisily, but his hand was steady as he pushed the blade to one side.

"Don't kill the messenger. Haven't you heard that one?"

Mordant flung the stiletto aside and it slithered across the floor to stop directly in front of the pillar which Lorn stood behind.

"I fulfilled my side of the accord," she said in a low, dangerous voice. "The seven strongest warriors of the *magii'ri* are dead by my order. No one suspects that they were betrayed by their own leader. Now it is time for Marsten to hold true to his word. He sent them out, I had them killed. Now, I want my reward. I want to speak with him personally."

"That is not possible. He is tending to business across the sea."

A bell tolled three times outside the palace walls. Mordant's cheery laughter filled the air and chilled Lorn to the bone. But even more chilling were her words that echoed in his head. *The High Wizard himself had betrayed them.* Even after all that had happened, he had hoped that his suspicions were wrong all along and that Marsten was innocent.

The Black Queen reclined on a luxurious settee and stretched like a slinky cat. It was obvious from Barnabas' befuddled expression that he knew he had lost the advantage in the exchange, but he clearly didn't know how or why. He didn't have long to wait. Tarlow the giant entered through a side door, which Lorn had missed in his hasty study of the room, and one oversized hand encircled the neck of Lord Marsten.

Lorn went numb. How could it be? The High Wizard of the *magii'ri*, here, in the heart of the enemy stronghold? The muscles at the base of his jaw bunched as he fought to keep himself under control. He longed to give in to the first impulse he had, step from behind the pillar and run the bastard clean through. He had suspected Barnabas, or perhaps another lesser Wizard. Perhaps it was nothing more than a vain hope, but deep down he didn't think the High Wizard, the ruler of all of the *magii'ri*, would betray his own people. But it was clear that he had. And now there was a giant to deal with. His hands began to shake and a sudden weakness stole over him. His entire life had been dedicated to the service of Aard, the Mountain God, who he believed spoke through the High Wizard. And now it would be as if he had never existed, all because of one man's greed. Thirty-seven years, wiped out in an instant. Fury flooded through him, blocking out all reason, and with it came strength.

He gathered himself for a moment and tried to steady his shaking hands. They stilled of their own accord. He silently propped his lance against the pillar and stepped suddenly around it. He scooped up Mordant's stiletto by the blade, balanced it for a fraction of a second, and threw it directly at Lord Marsten. But Tarlow was no novice to violence. He swung the High Wizard to one side and the blade sailed harmlessly past. Or so it seemed. But it continued on its flight and slammed home at the base of Barnabas' throat. His eyes went round at the sight of the ragged creature who emerged from a half crouch at the base of the pillar, then went blank as he slid to the floor, choking on his own blood. *For you, Jake.*

Mordant leaped from her settee with her arms outstretched. Lorn felt the power of the spell she hurled at him, but he shrugged it off. Perhaps it was the fever that burned within him that made him immune to such magic, or it may have been the strength he drew from the *magii'ri* Code of Honor to avenge the wrongful death of comrades at arms, or even the remnants of the spell Lynch had cast upon him in the dungeon. Whatever the case, the Black Queen's magic could not stop him. He drew his sword once again and advanced upon the giant.

Marsten made a strangled sound in his throat as Tarlow hurled him bodily aside and drew his own blade. The giant lunged towards Lorn, covering eight feet with each long step. The Warrior let him come, feigning weakness, for now, in the heat of battle he felt none. This was what he was born to, and he had always done it well. The giant committed to his attack, raised his sword high, and brought it crashing down. But Lorn had already begun to move. He slid sideways, blocked the giant's sword with his own, and slashed the back of Tarlow's leg as he went by. The giant roared in pain but wheeled too suddenly and struck a backhanded blow that Lorn barely blocked. He had no movement of his body to soften the blow, and it sent needles of pain followed by a sodden numbness through his arm as his sword shattered.

Five Nightriders streamed into the room and surrounded the battered *magii'ri* Warrior. One overzealous Nightrider attacked. Lorn spun around and caught his attacker's sword in his cloak, and a sudden twist sent the blade spinning into the air. The Nightrider leaped for his blade, but Lorn merely stepped forward and slammed the jagged shards of his own blade into the Nightrider's back, just to the side of the spine. He went limp, and Lorn scooped the blade up just in time to fend off two more Nightriders. He dipped his shoulder and slashed one across the thighs, then slammed the blade home into the other's neck. He never stopped moving. With one short step he lunged just far enough to slice open yet another Nightrider, then step back and finish off the one who bled from his ruined thigh muscles.

"And then there were two," he breathed.

The final Nightrider hesitated, and Lorn cut him down with almost no effort. Tarlow watched with open admiration.

"You have my respect," the giant rumbled.

But he was already moving to attack. He used his size, reach and strength to force the *magii'ri* to give ground. Lorn backed away quickly. Sweat streamed down his face and the heat from the fire inside him was palpable to all who occupied the room. He maneuvered himself closer to the High Wizard, then suddenly stepped behind him and wrapped his left arm around Marsten's neck.

"Graywullf," Marsten muttered in a strangled voice. He clawed at the ironlike forearm around his throat but to no avail.

Lorn gripped him tighter, then tilted his sword threateningly at the High Wizard when Tarlow moved to attack yet again.

"I'll kill him," he warned. "Don't think I won't."

"Go ahead," Mordant urged. "Run him through."

Marsten made little mewing noises in his throat. Lorn slid the point of his sword a full inch under his ribs. Tarlow stopped so suddenly he nearly lost his footing, and Mordant half rose from her settee. She moaned in her throat and ran her hands down her bodice.

Lorn steered the High Wizard around the giant and backed towards the pillar. Tarlow watched like a hawk, alert for any opening.

"Why?" Lorn Graywullf choked out. He released some of the pressure on Marsten's windpipe.

"Why what?" the Wizard grated. "Why did you and your friends have to die? Or why do we spend our lives in service and die penniless, old and alone? I have held treasures of untold wealth in my hands and never got to spend even one copper of it. I peer inside the homes of wretched farmers while they make love to their wives, and I know I will never have any of it. I want it all, Graywullf. The time has come to serve a new god. I have seen the way it could be."

"You betrayed us for wealth?" Lorn asked in disbelief. "I swore fealty to you above all others except Aard himself! I would have gladly given my life for you and our Code if you had asked."

"The Code!" Marsten shouted. He spun away from Lorn's weakening grasp. "Look at yourself, Warrior. You will die with nothing because of your foolish Code!"

"I have my honor." He knew in that instant that he had struck a nerve.

Tarlow once again brushed the High Wizard aside and leaped to attack. Lorn dropped his sword, tripped and fell backwards. Tarlow did not slow. He intended to finish the fight. Indeed, he charged ahead so quickly he couldn't stop, even when he saw the lance in Lorn's hand and saw him plant it firmly at the base of the pillar.

It entered just below his belly button. The force of his rush drove it upward, through his diaphragm. It missed his heart by a fraction of an inch and erupted from his back. He dropped his sword and clutched at the shaft. A look of disbelief flooded his face as he sagged to one knee, and slowly toppled over on his side. His eyes were locked on the *magii'ri's* face. He touched the haft of the lance with a trembling hand, and stroked it like he was admiring a fine work of art.

"It would seem I chose the wrong side," he gasped. He raised a shaking right hand to his brow in a salute as Lorn fought his way back to his feet, sword once again in hand.

Mordant hurled herself to the floor and cradled the giant's head in her lap. Tears flowed down her face and her body was wracked with sobs. Lorn gritted his teeth and raised the sword for one merciful slash.

Something slammed into his chest. He staggered back against the pillar and looked down. A staff of gold, the High Wizard's staff, was sticking out of his chest. What the Hell was it doing there? How many times had he knelt before that staff in some ceremony or other? The strength drained out of him and he collapsed in a heap. Mordant didn't even notice, not even when the High Wizard looked down on the body of the last Trueblood Warrior in Norland. He leaned close to Lorn's grizzled face. Thunder rolled and a sudden breeze stirred the tapestries at the windows.

Lorn turned his head with agonizing slowness towards the window, where the fresh night breeze chased the flames in the lamps. "It smells like rain," he whispered.

# CHAPTER TWENTY TWO

Smilin' Jake rose slowly from a black pit of unconsciousness. He opened his eyes to a slit then abruptly closed them as the hot desert sun pierced them. Something tugged at his left foot. He kicked feebly at it then dropped his foot into the dust. Moments later, savage pain shot through his foot again and growling reached his ears. With sudden terror he jerked his leg back, and the growling stopped. With a long groan he rolled over and slowly raised himself to a sitting position. His entire body ached, but not as bad as his head. He tried opening his eyes again and was able to keep them open while using both hands to shade them. A rustling in the sand warned him, and his eyes flew open in sudden rage as he saw a coyote tearing into the flesh of Ox's upper arm.

"No!" He screamed, unmindful of the sudden agony in his throat. He lunged to his feet and fell flat. The coyotes closed in again. Jake's fist struck a smooth rock the size of an apple, and he hurled it at the nearest coyote in rage. His aim was good, it struck the beast squarely in the side of the head and it leaped sideways with a high pitched yelp. The effort caused Jake's head to swim and he saw black spots dancing before his eyes.

"Get out of here, you sons of bitches!" he whispered. Tears coursed down his face as he crawled to Ox's body and with a grimace, tore one of the lances free. Jake took a deep breath and stood. The sudden appearance of a man standing upright unsettled the carrion eaters, but they quickly recovered their courage. One strayed a little too close and Jake drove the lance completely through it with one hard thrust. The others raced off, their hopes for an easy meal dashed. Jake sagged against the lance then straightened as he spied a solitary figure coming towards him from across the plain. His image danced and flickered through the heat waves, inexorably eating up the distance between them. There was something familiar in that, in the unrelenting way the approaching man ate up the distance, as if no obstacle could stop him. Smilin' Jake readied his lance. Then he abruptly let it drop with a muffled sound in the dust.

"I'll be goddamned," Smilin' Jake muttered then he went limp and fell beside the lance.

He awoke hours later in the chill of twilight. The first stars were beginning to wink in the clear sky above, and Jake felt that if he could just lay there and stare up at them he would be happy. Then he remembered where he was and what had happened. With a low curse he rose to a sitting position, just as a man walked out of the darkness. It was Lynch.

"Come to finish what you started?" Jake whispered.

Lynch wordlessly offered him his waterskin. Smilin' Jake eyed it suspiciously, then grudgingly accepted it and allowed a few sips of the tepid liquid to roll down his throat. To him it tasted like the finest liqueur ever made. His head no longer housed that blinding pain and his vision wasn't blurred anymore. But that did nothing to temper the anger he felt.

"I asked if you came to finish us?"

"I had nothing to do with this, Jake," Lynch answered. "I tried to tell all of you it was a trap."

Deep down, Smilin' Jake knew the truth behind those words but in his anger he would never admit it. "Did they get Graywullf?"

"Looks like he's wounded and still heading to the City of Shadows by the sign," Lynch replied.

"Gotta go help," Smilin' Jake insisted as he clambered to his feet. He stumbled and almost fell. Lynch caught him and eased him back to the ground.

"You can't help, not in this condition." He cursed under his breath. "I'll go."

"You?" Jake sneered. "You run every time there's a fight. If you'd been here we might have gotten away." He dropped his head as he realized just how much he had revealed with that statement. Lynch dropped a hand to his shoulder.

"Graywullf knew it was coming to this, and so did you. Fate or destiny or a long forgotten curse, it was written. Tell me Jake, how many did you face?"

Smilin' Jake screwed up his face in an expression of total disbelief as he remembered the unending flood of enemies. "Scores upon scores. Hell no, more'n that! Thousands…"

"Nightriders," Lynch said distastefully. He had already read that from the sign left from the deadly battle. But Nightriders did not pick up their dead, and though there were many bloodstains in the sand not a single Nightrider corpse defiled the battlefield.

"I reckon," Jake agreed. "And half-men."

That was bad, Lynch thought, very bad indeed. Thousands of Nightriders had not been sighted in hundreds of years. Not, in fact, since one naïve Warrior had disobeyed orders and stolen the Book of Runes, which was necessary to conjure so many at one time. Bad times were coming. A return to the olden times, even, when Dragons soared the skies, ogres stalked the mountains and Demons arose to spawn with humans. Not good, he decided. Someone had discovered where he had hidden the Book of Runes and had used the spell to begin the Wilding. That was the only plausible explanation. Lynch realized with a start that tears trickled down Smilin' Jake's grizzled cheeks. He looked away in embarrassment while Jake regained his composure.

"I'll go," he repeated. Suddenly he knew what he had to do. "You must hurry back to the village and find Luke. Get him out of Norland! Bad times are coming, Smilin' Jake, worse than you can imagine. Worse than the old days."

"I have to tend to the dead," Smilin' Jake replied gruffly. "Warriors don't leave their dead for the carrion eaters." He struggled to his feet once again.

Lynch leaped to his feet and shook Jake by the shoulders. "Listen to me! This entire country is going to become a killing ground and if you don't get your ass back to Richfeld, Lorn Graywullf's only son will be one of the first to die!"

Smilin' Jake laughed bitterly. "Look at me, Lynch!" He swayed like a willow in high wind. "Maybe I can bury my two friends before I collapse and die with 'em. Maybe not. But there's no way on this World that I can walk back to Richfeld, let alone run that distance."

"There is a way," Lynch said hesitantly, and he hated himself a little more for suggesting it. "You and I, Graywullf, Ox and Bill…we ain't going to be the ones to win this fight. But if you save Luke, he just might be the one."

"Goddamn it," Jake cursed. He shook his head, then gave Lynch a resigned look. "They were the only family I ever had."

"I'll tend to them,' Lynch promised.

Smilin' Jake nodded. "You intend to use Dark Magic?"

"I reckon it's the only way, Jake."

"You told us once Dark Magic always comes with a price. You've done used it on me a couple times. What is my price going to be?"

"That's not for me to say," Lynch replied. "The price may not manifest itself for many years."

"But there's nobody else to save Luke," Smilin' Jake finished. Lynch nodded. He thought for a long moment. "I'll do it, but you have to swear on your *magii'ri* honor that you will help Graywullf."

"I will," Lynch answered.

"Swear it!" Smilin' Jake demanded.

"I swear on my honor that I will help Graywullf," Lynch muttered. "Even though my honor isn't worth a pile of horse shit."

"Your honor and my life are even up then," Smilin' Jake replied. A half grin stole onto his lips and a spark lit up his eyes. "Let's do this."

Lynch began to say the words, but once more Jake asked, "You sure you don't know what the price might be?"

Exasperated, Lynch replied, "Rest assured, Jake Sipowicz, I'll be several levels lower in Hell than you."

Smilin' Jake grinned at that. "That'll help some, if when I take a piss in Hell it trickles down on you."

Lynch said the words that tapped into his vast storehouse of Dark Magic and Jake felt his muscles come alive. Every sound, every sight, indeed every single sensation was amplified until Jake felt his head might burst trying to process all of it. He no longer felt pain, and his wounds actually closed as he watched. But deep inside he felt a sickness he'd never felt before as something foreign took root in his soul. This particular spell had no basis in the magic of the Light. He stared at Lynch with haunted eyes until the feeling subsided.

"Is that how you feel all the time?" Smilin' Jake asked.

"It doesn't matter," Lynch answered. "Run, Jake Sipowicz! Run like the hounds of Hell were on your heels!"

Jake couldn't have stopped himself if he had tried. His body felt like it was no longer under his command. He turned back to Richfeld and began to run.

# CHAPTER TWENTY THREE

HUDGE RUSHED OVER TO stare out into his own front yard, which was now a surreal landscape, foreign and threatening. Luke Graywullf stepped back from his vantage point with his arms hanging stiffly at his sides. Hudge took his place and studied the area as far as he could see in the blackness of the night.

"I don't see anythin'." He glanced over his shoulder at the boy as the first raindrops pelted the dust. He looked stricken.

"Luke, boy," Hudge said in growing alarm. He knelt and took the boy's rigid arms in his hands and gently shook him. "What is it? What's wrong?"

"He ain't comin' back," Luke whispered. "Not this time."

"What're you talkin' about? He'll be fine. Hell, there ain't a finer Warrior in all of Norland, even the World, than Lorn Graywullf."

Luke sighed. "It don't matter, Hudge. He ain't comin' back. There won't be no gold this time. I'll pack my gear and go down to live by the creek."

"No, you won't. I gave my word to your Father that I'd look out for ya, and by damn, I'm gonna do it."

"I don't want to be a bother."

"Goddamnit, boy," Hudge fumed. "Get this through yer head. You're stayin' here, and you ain't no bother. You got that?"

"I got it."

"Good. Now, tell me what you saw out there."

"I ain't sure, but it was bigger than a dog and it walked on all fours."

Hudge considered that as he turned to look outside. He couldn't see anything out of the tiny crack Luke had been peering through. He reached for the door, but his hand shook as he did and he jerked it away from the latch like it was a biter snake.

"Don't open it," Luke warned. "Step back."

The rain intensified. What had started as a gentle shower was turning into a downpour. Lightning flashed and threw crazy shadows through out the room. Hudge counted to seven before the thunder boomed after it. The heart of the storm was still seven miles away, and now the rain came down in solid sheets. It was going to be a real frog strangler.

"It's only rain," he assured Luke, who looked at him like he was totally crazy.

"It ain't the rain, it's what came with it." Luke suddenly grinned, and Hudge felt a cold prick of fear in his guts. "You got any weapons, Hudge?"

"Has it come to that?" Luke just stared at him and let him draw his own conclusion. Hudge stared back into those crazy blue eyes, so light they were almost colorless. The boy had the eyes of a predator, pure and simple. The eyes of a Dragon, his grandfather had called them. Time was that nearly every trueblood *magii'ri* had the same eyes. Not the color. No, they could be green or brown or black, just as easy. What they had in common was the way they looked right through a man. Like they had already let his guts out on the floor and were just waiting for him to fall. Even at the age when most boys would still run to their Momma with a bloody knee the truebloods knew they held the power to end life in each small hand.

"Here," Hudge left the door to delve into a hidden recess behind the fireplace. He pulled out a shortsword and a battleaxe with a large nick in the blade. He handed Luke the shortsword.

"It's Aarden steel, or so my grandpappy told me one night when he was deep in the jug and spinnin' lies."

Luke grasped the sword. It was very old, and the blade was covered with rust. He spun it once then slammed the flat of the blade down on the hearth. Hudge jumped a foot in the air and nearly wet himself as scale erupted in a fountain and rained down in tiny shards. The blade underneath gleamed with new life. He glared at Luke, who paid him no heed.

"It has an inscription on it." He held it to the light.

"That's a foreign script," Hudge remarked. "Do you know what it says?"

"I can't read," Luke said with a shrug.

"Let me see that."

Luke held it closer. Hudge ran his finger over the delicate lines of the script. His brow furrowed in thought.

"It's Elvish," he said in awe. "I haven't seen Elvish letters in years. It says: *Lucas Hudge, for valiant service to the Light.* By god, the old man wasn't lying."

"Them letters say that?"

"They do." Hudge shook his head in wonder. If the old man had served the Light so valiantly that the Elves rewarded him with this blade, then it was just possible that he also knew what he was talking about when it came to Dragons. And the likeness of the truebloods to those savage beasts. That was not a particularly comforting thought. Maybe the rumors were true. Perhaps, just perhaps, the *magii'ri* Warriors were becoming more like beasts than men. No. Trueblood *magii'ri* Warriors lived and died by the Code. They had one thing left when they pulled off their boots for the final time. Honor. The rumors were started by someone else, someone who could benefit from the demise of the Warrior sect.

He was shocked out of his musings by a jolt that shook the house to its foundation. For a moment he thought it was thunder. But there was no flash of lightning with it.

"What the Hell was that?"

Luke was already moving on silent feet to one side of the door. There was another jolt and the door bulged inward. A snuffling sound came through the thick slabs, then retreated. The rain was literally pouring from the sky now, and it pounded the house relentlessly, effectively drowning out all sound from outside.

"Get ready," Luke warned.

Another impact jolted the door so hard the latch exploded in splinters. The door was slowly swung inward, and a searching paw with wicked six inch claws pushed it further. Hudge's eyes went round and as big as a saucer.

"Dear god," he whispered. "Not my babies…"

That thought galvanized him. A hoarse cry burst from his throat as he hurled himself at whatever beast that massive paw belonged to. At the same moment, the werecat lunged into the room, his hunched shoulders filling the doorway and a low growl rumbling in his chest. He leaped at Hudge, who swung the battleaxe with all his strength. Zagreb the werecat caught it deftly with one paw and turned it so it sailed harmlessly past. It pinged off the floor and caromed to the side with a shower of sparks. He drew in great draughts of scent. The violent red hued scent he longed for was here, but it was different and confusing.

Hudge gathered himself for another attack. *Why did it hesitate?* He swung the battleaxe again, and seemed to take the beast off guard, but it glanced harmlessly off the scales on his back. He immediately regretted it, for then the beast turned its attention fully back on him. Hudge backpedaled swiftly until his buttocks slammed into the rear wall. The rockcat held him there with one careless paw.

"Let him go." The words were softly spoken, but it was clearly a command.

Zagreb reared in the air and wheeled around to face Luke Graywullf. Here was the scent he searched for. But this one was so small. Surely this was not the great Warrior that the Master feared above all else. He bunched his muscles for a final leap.

Luke never knew how close he came to the Other Side that night. He swung the shortsword up to the ready position and it flashed in the light. As it did, the rockcat recoiled. Luke immediately sensed his advantage. He moved the sword in a slow arc. Zagreb's eyes followed every move of the blade.

"A mere boy…" Hudge whispered in awe.

"It's not me. It's the blade, isn't it?" The last words were spoken directly to Zagreb.

The werecat looked into Luke's eyes. *She will kill my family if I do not kill you*

"I'll kill *you* if you try," Luke warned.

The scene before him was ludicrous. The boy didn't even reach the beast's shoulders in height. It could crush him with one paw. But it did not pounce. It dropped a scrap from its jaws.

*This belonged to your father.*

211

Luke slid his blade under the bloody shirt and held it up to the light. Without warning, the huge rockcat hooked the shirt with one paw and wheeled around to disappear into the night. A moment later, the outline of a man swayed in the open doorway.

"Jake," Luke whispered.

# CHAPTER TWENTY FOUR

MARSTEN BLEW OUT A gusty sigh. "I may have misjudged the strength of the *magii'ri* Warriors."

Mordant looked up from where she crouched with the fallen giant's head in her hands. "Get out," she hissed.

"My lady…"

"Shut up. Get out of here. Our agreement is broken. I will not ally myself with you, not for all the gold in the World."

Marsten began to speak, but snapped his teeth shut on the words. Now was not the time. He glanced around in disgust. All his plans had gone to Hell because of one pitiful caricature of a man who had emerged from the desert more dead than alive. He hurried out the side door and into the night.

Lynch stepped away from the concealment of the palace wall and paused to stare after the retreating Wizard for a moment. His brow was knitted in thought. He turned back towards the palace of the Black Queen then stared into the desert again. He shook his head in wonder. Life had been so simple before he met the Graywullf. He laughed. This was a Hell of a time to develop a conscience. The main gate boomed open, and Lynch watched as Mordant blindly ran down the path into the main settlement. He sighed deeply.

"I can't believe I'm doing this," he said aloud.

Lynch entered the palace and observed again the carnage wrought by one half-dead *magii'ri* Warrior. As he did, the girl who had come in with Mordant timidly approached the fallen Warrior. She clutched the shaft of Marsten's staff.

"I would not do that," Lynch warned.

The girl jumped back and her hands flew to her mouth as she stifled a scream. Lynch walked into the light.

"He may have enough life left in him to think you're an enemy. If that's the case, you'd be dead." Lynch said as he crossed the main room. "On the other hand," he knelt beside Lorn Graywullf, "if you remove that staff, you'll likely kill him." He felt the pulse in Lorn's neck. "He lives."

"How can that be?" the girl asked

Lynch grinned. "Dark Magic lasts a long time."

He didn't stop to explain himself. Lynch ran his hands over Lorn's sweat soaked brow and felt the heat from the poison trapped within him.

"Nightriders are such filthy beasts," he said with disgust. He held his open hands, palms down, over the inert form of the Warrior and conjured a spell of healing. Lorn's body went rigid and his limbs began to shake. Lynch grimaced as he surrounded the shaft of the staff with his hands and pressed firmly down on Lorn's chest. He allowed a tiny bit of his life force to enter the Warrior then abruptly jerked the staff free. Lorn's eyes flew open and for a moment he was lucid.

"Goddamnit, I told you no more Dark Magic."

Lynch grinned. "You can't shoot me now."

"Later," Lorn promised then he blacked out again.

A whisper of sound warned Lynch, and he spun swiftly. Yet another giant entered the room, followed by at least a dozen Nightriders.

"Oh. It's you," the giant said as he slid his half drawn sword back into the scabbard. "Is he dead?"

"Almost," Lynch replied. "He's done for." As he rose, he slid an eight inch wickedly curved blade from a belt scabbard beneath his duster. The words he muttered under his breath gave it the power to slice through muscle, bone, sinew, or even steel. He smiled in a friendly fashion as he approached the giant. The giant and the Nightriders relaxed.

"Good," the giant said. "He killed Tarlow. Never thought anybody could kill Tarlow."

Lynch didn't respond, he merely continued until he stood six feet from the giant. His eyes reflected the torchlight with a maniacal gleam. A look of alarm crossed the giant's face. He knew something was wrong.

"You look different," he remarked. He stepped backwards, fear evident in his eyes. "Are you feelin' alright, Lynch?" he asked.

"Fine," Lynch replied as took one quick step forward. His left hand swept from beneath his cloak with dizzying speed. The blade entered the giant's abdomen just above his belt and sliced upwards halfway through his sternum. The giant stared stupidly as his entrails slithered to the floor. But Lynch was already beyond him. He drew his sword with his right hand and flung himself into the milling group of Nightriders. Those closest to Lynch who were not immediately killed stampeded over their comrades in panic. Lynch was dimly aware that the girl was screaming in a high pitched, keening wail. His own voice rose in a primal scream as he clove his way through the remaining Nightriders. Then he was left standing by himself with the brassy scent of blood in his nostrils and the twitching bodies of Nightriders beneath his boots. His breath came in gasps for perhaps a full minute until he slowly returned to his senses. Lynch abruptly sheathed his weapons and returned to the fallen Warrior. He cradled the wounded man in his arms, but before he could lift him a shiny object lying on the floor caught his eye. He grinned suddenly, scooped it up and slipped it into his pocket. He'd seen that, often enough, on the cord around Mordant's neck. He lifted Lorn Graywullf and carried him from the palace. He looked back to see Moira following him.

"If you leave now, the Black Queen will be your enemy forever. Think about what you're doing."

"I want nothing to do with her," Moira answered. "That man needed help and they all tried to kill him."

"Do you have anywhere to go?" Lynch asked.

"No," Moira replied.

"Then come with me," Lynch ordered. "You can tend to him, while I tend to other business."

Lynch carried Lorn from the City of Shadows, and Moira followed. Now that his strength was entirely back, Lynch was a truly superb animal. His physical strength and endurance were unmatched, to say nothing of his magical power. They walked half the night, until Lynch found a secluded cave. He made Lorn as comfortable as possible with his own bedroll then dropped his waterskin and a small pack on the floor of the cave.

"There's water and food for three days if you're careful, two if you're hungry, and one if you make a pig of yourself. I suggest you do not show me you are kin to swine or you'll be plenty hungry when I do get back."

Moira's eyes betrayed her fear. "Where are you going?"

"I have business to tend to," Lynch replied. "Don't worry, I will come back. He will sleep, probably for several days. Don't try to wake him, he might be out of his head." He paused then gave Moira his sword. Without another word, he turned and left the cave.

A man on foot, young and in perfect condition can actually outrun a horse over distance. Lynch was not young, but he knew no match physically. He muttered a spell and began running.

# CHAPTER TWENTY FIVE

ARSTEN GROANED AS HE swung down from the saddle. He still could not believe that shadow of a man who had almost mystically appeared from the desert and single handedly destroyed his plans. His alliance with Mordant was shattered and his most trusted comrade was dead. He glared at the ground in distaste as lightning flashed and thunder rolled in the direction of Richfeld.

"I hate this," he muttered. "Everything is so dirty."

He kicked at the sand to level out a spot for his bedroll. He refused to accept failure. None of it was over. One more night and he would be back in Richfeld. Then he could complete the task of discrediting the *magii'ri* Warriors, albeit without Mordant's help, and have them totally disbanded. And, he thought with satisfaction, he would take a long hot bath, perhaps have a massage and a hot meal and sleep in his own bed again. He thought of the young stable boys he kept in constant fear for their lives. Maybe it was time he allowed one of them to share his bed. That thought comforted him. He made tea and ate some dried meat, then rolled up in his blankets to dream of his servants and his soft, comfortable bed.

He didn't know what roused him from his dreams, but when he sat up, someone sat on the far side of his fire. Marsten couldn't see his face, but there was something familiar about him. He fumbled fearfully for a weapon and simultaneously cast a spell of weakness at his visitor. The spell was rebuffed so forcefully it made him physically sick.

"You made good time," Lynch said thoughtfully. "You could have made it if you hadn't stopped." He absentmindedly took the shiny whistle from his pocket and blew into it. Marsten heard nothing. "Then again, I really wanted to catch you."

"Lynch!" Marsten exclaimed as relief flooded through him. "What are you doing here?"

Lynch shrugged. "It doesn't matter. You should have kept riding."

Marsten was ecstatic. "Now that you're back, we can return to Richfeld and make plans. Timon will remain loyal to the cause, but you know that for a fact. He has aspirations of actually ruling one day. What did you say?"

"If you hadn't stopped, you might have made it," Lynch mused. "I was becoming quite tired. Good thing I'll have a horse to ride back, and of course I finished your tea. Do you have any biscuits? I didn't have time to search your saddlebags yet. Did you say Timon?"

"Back where?" Marsten asked, thoroughly confused. "What are you talking about? Biscuits?"

"Back to the City of Shadows," Lynch replied. "Now answer my question. Is Timon Blackhelm here?" He blew into the whistle again. "Damn thing doesn't work." He shook it then tossed it towards Marsten. "See if you can get that whistle to work. I was in the mood for music with my biscuits, if you have any."

Marsten looked confused, but he distastefully picked up the whistle. "Yes, Timon joined us not long after you left. Didn't you know that?" Marsten wiped the whistle on his sleeve then blew into it hard and long. A distant caterwaul broke through the silence. Lynch turned and looked out into the desert. Marsten automatically followed his gaze. When he looked back to the fire Lynch was gone. The next thing he knew, a burning pain shot up his spine and his legs jackknifed out in front of him. He tried to rise, but his legs refused to obey. Lynch wrapped a gentle arm around him and lowered him down onto his side. He looked into the bottomless depths of Lynch's black eyes. The pupils were so enlarged his entire eyeball was nearly black. Marsten moaned in sudden terror. Lynch rose from behind him and wiped the blade of his knife on Marsten's cloak.

"I never did like you, Marsten," he said conversationally. "You're a predator of the weak, soft and spoiled, and most of all, you're a coward. And, you're greedy with your biscuits."

Lynch saddled Marsten's horse while the former lead Wizard of the magii'ri thrashed about in the sand, a growing stain of red under his body. He begged Lynch to help him, but Lynch acted as if he didn't even hear.

Lynch kicked sand on the glowing embers of the fire. Another caterwaul sounded, this one much closer than the last.

"Rock cats are about tonight," he said as he plucked the whistle from Marsten's hands and blew into it again. Sudden understanding erupted in Marsten's mind. He had called the rock cats into his own camp! Lynch swung up into the saddle. Marsten tried to rise, but only succeeded in rolling nearly into the embers of the fire.

"Thrashing around like that just makes you bleed more," Lynch mused reproachfully. "Draws predators of all kinds." He chuckled at the irony in that statement. "You know, they'll probably start eating you while you're still alive."

"No," Marsten pleaded. Terror flooded through him as he realized his legs were paralyzed.

"There's a sweet spot in the human spine," Lynch continued talking as if he hadn't heard. "A knife stroke there causes very little pain, but you'll never walk again. You also bleed like a stuck pig."

"You can't do this!"

"I already did it," Lynch replied. He shrugged. "I left you a sword. I think there's about a one in a thousand chance you'll make it back to Norland, if you crawl." Another feline scream sounded, this one was very close. Even Lynch felt gooseflesh rise on his arms. "Scratch that. You don't have a goddamn chance."

Marsten clawed his way towards the mounted Lynch. "You can't just leave me here," he pleaded. "I am a very powerful man! I can give you anything that you want."

Lynch kicked the horse away from the camp site.

"I am the highest ranking Wizard in Norland!" Marsten's voice carried out into the desert. "I'll heal myself and come for you!"

Lynch continued riding as he heard the tell tale growling of a hunting rock cat. "Only Dark Magic could save you now, and you don't know that, do you?" He whispered to himself.

"You can't do this!" Marsten's voice trailed away to screams, then to silence. Lynch rode into the darkness, nibbling on a biscuit.

# CHAPTER TWENTY SIX

"ARE YOU GONNA INVITE me in?" Smilin' Jake asked. He didn't wait for an answer. He staggered into the room and sat wearily at the table. Luke rushed forward to help and Jake reached out to grip his shoulder. Water ran down his face, dripped from his sodden clothes and puddled under his chair. Luke looked hopefully into his face until Jake averted his eyes.

"He ain't comin' back, is he?"

Jake shook his head. "I reckon not. He was gone when I woke up. I promised him I'd look after you and here I am."

Luke felt hollow inside. He dropped the shortsword from his trembling hands and sat heavily on the hearth of the fireplace. Smilin' Jake struggled to his feet and limped over to sit next to him, while Hudge righted another kitchen chair and sat at his table thoughtfully scratching his jaw with thumb and forefinger.

"Lorn Graywullf gone," he muttered. "It don't seem possible."

"We was ambushed," Smilin' Jake offered, sensing Luke's need to know. "Somebody knew our route and told the Black Queen. She sent Nightriders, half-men and a giant to ambush us. If it had been a fair fight we'd have cut 'em down." He shot a glance at Hudge. "It was Marsten that sent 'em. It had to be."

"The gossip mongers spread it around that Marsten left the city right after you did," Hudge said.

Smilin' Jake jerked his head upright. "Is that so? Maybe I should go wait on the trail for him."

"No," Hudge said. "You take this boy, right now, this very night, and you run for the hills."

"I ain't runnin' anywhere," Smilin' Jake responded. "Warriors don't run from trouble."

"No, they don't," Hudge agreed. "But they do honor their promises. You promised Graywullf that you'd look after his son and you can't do that here. If Marsten returns he'll be searching high and low for this boy. And if he don't, that low down snake Barnabas will take up the search."

Jake pondered that information.

"I don't need nobody," Luke interrupted. "You just go on and do what you want. I'll go down on the trail and wait for Marsten myself."

Smilin' Jake finally smiled. "You ain't quite all that just yet. I reckon Hudge is right. Can we borrow a horse?"

"I'll go saddle one now," Hudge promised.

"I have to eat," Jake told Luke. "Anything you got."

Luke hurried to the pantry and came back with the leftovers from the evening meal, which Jake devoured in moments. Luke returned to the pantry and brought back dried meat, then again with raw potatoes, turnips and carrots. Smilin' Jake ate all of it, then sat back and belched. Hudge had left his chewing tobacco on the table when he went to saddle the horse, and Jake bit off a wad of that and rolled it to the side of his mouth.

"I'm sorry, Luke," he began. Luke hurriedly turned away so Jake couldn't see his tears.

"Like I said, we were ambushed. Outnumbered maybe a hundred to one. Something bad is coming, Lynch told me that, so we have to get out of Norland."

"What about Hudge and the girls?" Luke asked. "They know where… he left me."

"Oh, Hell," Jake said. He hadn't thought about that. Hudge came back in soaking wet. "I hate to do this to you," Jake said to the farmer. "But you have to go back and hitch up a team. You can't stay here. Not now."

"I'll stay," Hudge replied. "My grandfather cleared this farm with his own two hands. I'll be damned if Marsten and his men can just come in here and take it from me without a fight."

"The *magii'ri* Warriors couldn't stand up to him," Jake said. "They hit us with over two thousand swords. They'll kill you so fast you won't even slow 'em down."

Hudge's eyes popped wide open. "I'll go hitch up the team," he replied as he headed back out the door. "Luke, wake the girls and get 'em ready."

Smilin' Jake and Luke shared a quick, weary smile. Less than a half hour later the girls and Luke were huddled under a tarp in Hudge's old covered wagon. Smilin' Jake rode up front with Hudge, and he kept the sword from Hudge's hut propped up against the seat next to his right hand. The road leading away from Richfeld was deserted when they started out. Most people seemed to be content to gather around a roaring fire in the comfort of their homes and ignore the storm. But as they left the city itself behind, deep ruts left by other wagons cut into the mud of the road as they converged from barely discernible cart tracks on each side of the road. Those were the tracks used by the hill people and farmers of Norland to take their wares into the city. But now they all turned away towards the coast.

Sometime around midnight the rain slowed, but the road itself remained a slimy quagmire. Several times on downhill grades Hudge slammed the brake lever all the way forward only to have the wagon jacknife and nearly overrun the tired old plow horses pulling it. Finally, the rain stopped and Hudge allowed his team to come to a halt on a low rise. Smilin' Jake squinted into the darkness. For as far as he could see, lanterns winked at regular intervals as they swung from other wagons just like the one they rode on. Luke peeked out between Hudge and Jake.

"What is it?" he asked, thick headed from exhaustion.

"We ain't the only ones leaving Norland tonight," Jake explained. "There's something evil here, I can feel it." He *did* feel it. Deeper than he ever had before. All the *magii'ri* seemed blessed with a sixth sense for danger, but this was different. Jake knew it was Lynch's magic, but he ignored that thought and hid it away in a dark corner of his mind. "I don't think it's only the Revolution that's got people spooked."

Hudge chewed thoughtfully on his wad of tobacco. "I reckon so. I can feel it too, but this team has to rest. Dead horses won't pull my wagon to the coast, and we worked them in the fields before hitchin' 'em to the wagon tonight."

"There's a grove of trees to the right," Luke commented, able to see better with his youthful eyes than even the *magii'ri* ranger.

"Pull off into it," Jake said. "We'll make a cold camp and let the horses rest then be on our way before light."

"Cold camp is right." Hudge complained, more to himself than anyone else. He blew a gust of air from his mouth and wasn't surprised to see steam. Cold air had ridden in with the storm, and it was early yet. Too early for some of the crops to withstand. "It's shaping up to be a first rate disaster," he said to no one at all. But he had thrown in plenty of food from the cellar when he had hurriedly packed. They would be alright. They had to be.

No one slept much in the close confines of the wagon. Hudge and Jake's wet clothing released a fragrant mixture of wood smoke, sweat and dirt as they warmed up. Jake slept the most. His wounds were healed on the outside, but he felt their effect inside. Finally, Hudge elbowed him awake.

He never saw the *magii'ri* Warrior move. One moment he was grouchily jostling him awake, the next he was flat on his back outside the wagon in the mud with Jake atop him with murder in his eyes. One hand held Hudge mercilessly by the throat as he searched for his weapons with the other. Luke leaped on his back.

"No, Jake! No! It's Hudge, he's a friend. Friend!" He shouted into Jake's ear.

Smilin' Jake was dimly aware of the shouting and little girls screaming. "Graywullf!" he shouted. "Cap'n, where the Hell are you?" What were they all yelling about? Then he heard the word *friend*. He came fully awake in time to see Hudge turning purple. He hastily released him, while Luke continued to pound on his back. "I'm awake, I'm awake," he muttered, coming out of a nightmare. Luke dropped off his back and checked on Hudge while Jake retreated towards the road.

The farmer gasped and choked for several minutes, then he told Luke in a raspy voice, "Tomorrow morning you wake him up!"

Luke grinned.

"Sorry about that," Smilin' Jake said. "I don't reckon I'm quite myself yet."

"Not at all," Hudge replied in a loud whisper, which was all he could manage at the time. "I should know better than to wake a Warrior that way. Next time I'll hit you with a rock."

Smilin' Jake grinned, but it hid a deeper pain that had awakened during the night. How many more nights would he see Lorn, Ox and Bill being torn to shreds? He shrugged and blew out a gusty sigh. "Ride back here for awhile," he suggested to Hudge. "Maybe you can rest while I drive, then we'll switch." He scanned the gray horizon, deep in thought. "I don't think we better worry about the hosses anymore. We need to make the coast as soon as we can."

Hudge nodded.

"Luke, you ride up here with me. I need your eyes."

By midday they caught up to the first wagon ahead of them. The driver was a stooped man wearing a huge, floppy hat. He turned and watched them for more than a mile, trying desperately to urge his team onward, but they caught up just the same. He reluctantly guided his team to a wide spot in the road and moved to the side. Luke noticed when they slowly passed by that he had one hand firmly wrapped around the handle of an axe, half hidden by a flour sack. Later, all he could really remember were the old farmer's eyes, desperate and haunted by an unreasonable fear. Smilin' Jake nodded as they went by, but neither man spoke.

Miles later, Luke asked, "Will he make it?"

Smilin' Jake needed no explanation. "I doubt it. His team was near wore out already, and we're miles from the coast."

"And if we took on his load we wouldn't make it either," Luke finished.

"I reckon," Smilin' Jake replied. He wasn't doing much smiling.

# CHAPTER TWENTY SEVEN

LYNCH NEARLY KILLED MARSTEN'S horse getting back to the cave where Moira and Lorn were hidden, but he knew before he dismounted that something was amiss. His lips curled back from his teeth in a feral grin when he caught the scent of a second woman. He scouted all around the cave and found her footprints, then he found where she had lain in the sand watching the cave for at least a couple hours. He knew her scent. It was Mordant, the Black Queen herself. He circled back to the cave entrance and stared at it for a half hour, but detected no movement at all. There was only one way to find out. He slithered down the slight rise and melted into the dark shadows at the cave mouth until his eyes adjusted to the lack of light.

She had been in the cave, but her scent was not strong enough to indicate that she was still there. Nonetheless, he slid his knife free of it's scabbard. Five steps further in he smelled another scent, the musky smell of sex. That made no sense at all. Moira was a choice little bit, but Lorn was in no shape to be rutting around, even after the potent dose of Dark Magic Lynch had bestowed upon him. A slight rustling sound warned him, and he caught Moira by the wrist as she lunged at him with a sword held out at arm's length. He easily disarmed her and held her, kicking, biting, scratching and screaming all at the same time.

"Easy there," Lynch grunted as he tried to control the wildcat he had cornered. She reached between his legs and grabbed him by the balls, squeezing hard. Lynch grunted again, this time in pain, and flung her to the other side of the cave. "It's me, goddamnit!"

The whites of Moira's eyes showed plainly. She was near complete panic. Lynch ignored the sickening pain in his crotch long enough to cast a hasty calming spell. Moira sagged against the wall and blinked several times.

"It's me. Lynch," the Dark Wizard said in as soothing a voice as he could muster, considering his testicles felt like they had been crushed. "It's alright now. I'm back."

Moira finally recognized him. "Lynch! Thank the gods! She came back! She took him…I mean, she made him hard and she had him right there in front of me. I thought he was going to die, but she just kept grinding down on him."

"What the Hell? Mordant did that?" Lynch asked in disbelief. Then it hit him. She wanted his seed, the seed of a *magii'ri* Warrior of the Old Blood. "Well, I'll be a son of a bitch. Where is he? Where is *she*?"

"He's here still, but he's in a bad way. It's like she took all his strength. The Black Queen is gone. She looked right at me but it was like she was looking through me. Then she just walked out into the desert. I was so scared and I didn't know what to do, and when you came in I thought she was coming back," Moira confessed in between sobs.

Lynch shook his head. "She won't be coming back. She got what she wanted." He hurried farther in to the cave. Lorn Graywullf lay beside a tiny fire. Sweat ran freely from his forehead and his exposed skin glowed with sickening heat. The water was gone, and damp rags lay scattered about. Moira had done what she could but the Warrior was too far gone. Lynch watched for a full half minute before he saw the wounded man's chest rise shallowly, then fall again. Goddamn her, Lynch thought. Damn her to Hell. She not only took his seed but most of his life force as well. He knelt beside Graywullf.

The wounded man's eyes flew open. "Took you long enough," he said in a hoarse whisper. "I been waitin' for you."

"I can help you," Lynch said. He laid one hand on Lorn's forehead, but the Warrior found the strength to brush it away.

"No Dark Magic," Lorn insisted. "I'm too far gone for that anyway, and you know it. Listen to me. I owe you ten life debts already, but I have to ask you again," he closed his eyes as a spasm of pain ripped through him. "Take care of my son…"

"Smilin' Jake is alive," Lynch replied quietly. "He'll do as you asked him."

Lorn actually smiled. "Jake made it? That tough son of a bitch. That's good, damn good to hear. But he'll need help."

"Not from me," Lynch argued.

"Whatever," Lorn replied. "Now I can die in peace. I nailed a few of 'em didn't I?"

"Nearly all," Lynch agreed.

"I always worried that I would go before my ancestors and be found wanting," Lorn said.

"You will stand tall among them," Lynch assured him. "You are a Warrior."

Lorn's body was wracked by a spasm of pain. "I reckon I'm gonna find out," he said with a tired smile. "I could use a shot of whiskey," Lorn appeared to become more comfortable. Lynch remembered that he had Marsten's horse, along with his saddlebags.

"I'll get you a whole bottle," he promised. He ran from the cave, past the cowering Moira and frantically searched through Marsten's saddlebags. He dug out a small bottle of fine whiskey and returned to the cave. "This is the best whiskey ever made," he announced as he drew near to Lorn's inert form. He stopped several feet away. The Warrior was dead. Lynch shook his head, screwed the cap off the bottle and took a deep draught, then raised the bottle to Lorn Graywullf. "To honor," he whispered.

# CHAPTER TWENTY EIGHT

"WE HAVE TO REST the horses, Jake," Hudge insisted. "Its all they can do to walk as it is."

Smilin' Jake came fully awake as the lurching of the wagon ceased. He'd heard Hudge, but it took a few seconds for the words to sink in. He had been through too much in the last few days, and that blow to the head had left some lingering effects. He only hoped it wasn't permanent. The old farmer was right, but Jake had a feeling they needed to get to the coast. Every time he looked back at Richfeld he had a bad feeling, like they were trying to outrun a wildfire. But they couldn't walk to Elanderfeld, not with him half sick and dragging three half growed girls along.

"Half a day," Smilin' Jake conceded. "Stop at the creek over yonder. We'll take on water, let the hosses graze, then hit the trail again."

Luke unhitched the horses while Smilin' Jake filled the waterskins and Hudge started a tiny fire and cooked bacon and biscuits. Then Luke rigged a fishing pole and walked up the creek, stopping at all the deeper pools. He hadn't gone more than a quarter mile before he had seven brook trout tied to his belt. Then he heard rustling in the brush behind him, away from the creek. He listened carefully and heard it again, along with what sounded like a small sob. Luke unfastened his belt and laid the fish down on a mossy rock and went to investigate. The sounds of a child crying grew stronger and convinced Luke that he was in no danger. He peered through the last bit of brush and was astounded to see a little girl seated under a tree all by herself. He stepped around the brush and the little girl whipped her head up. Luke caught a glimpse of blond hair and big dark eyes before she darted to her feet and disappeared behind the tree. He followed at a run.

When Luke got to the tree he slowed enough to look past it before blindly following. A game trail cut through the brush, too small for him to easily follow, but perfect for the little girl. Luke grunted in disgust, then shrugged and returned to find his fish. He retraced his steps perfectly to the mossy rock, but only his belt remained. The fish were gone. He shook his head again, and felt his face burning from embarrassment. He'd walked right into a trick and now there would be no fish dinner for any of them. He fastened his belt in time to hear Jake calling him back to camp with a low whistle. Jake gave him a sideways glance when he returned.

"No fish?" he asked.

"They weren't biting," Luke responded.

Smilin' Jake wrinkled up his nose, "Too bad. We seem to be running out of grub faster than we should." But he said no more about it. They ate the bacon Hudge had fried up, then sopped up the grease with his bullet hard biscuits. Two hours later they had the exhausted horses hitched up and were back on the road. Luke had learned a lesson, and kept a wary eye out the rest of the day. Once he thought he saw a flash of movement a hundred yards from the road, but even though he stared at the spot until his eyes burned it did not reappear. He tried to stay awake even when Hudge and Jake traded places, but he couldn't keep his eyes open. He slept as the wagon jostled down the road and his dreams were filled with images of a blond haired little girl with big brown eyes.

The following morning dawned clear, but the sun was nothing more than a blurred orange ball in the sky, obscured by smoke. Elanderfeld was burning. The scent of it filled the air as the breeze turned inland, an acrid, choking stench that stung the eyes. By midmorning, the first wagon fleeing Elanderfeld came into view. Jake stopped the wagon and waited, his hand on the hilt of Hudge's sword. The occupants of the wagon, two men, a grown woman and two children, were wild eyed and stained with soot.

"I'd turn back, if I was you," one of the men called out as the wagons drew abreast, ignoring the accepted formalities of greeting one another.

"What happened?" Hudge asked.

"The World's gone crazy, that's what," the man answered. "They's driving out the *magii'ri*. Killin' 'em if they find 'em."

"Who is "they"?" Smilin' Jake asked.

The man shrugged. "Everybody, seems like. It started a few days back. They hung the last couple Truebloods last night, then set fire to the town and started raidin'." He eyed Jake suspiciously. "Who are you?"

"Just a hired man," Jake said, cutting Hudge off before he could answer.

"Well, you better turn around."

"Are there any ships leaving port?" Jake asked.

"Some," the man admitted. "But they only take those that has gold to pay their way." He picked up his whip and released his wagon brake. "Take my advice, mister." He said to Hudge. "Turn that wagon around and head for the hills. They'll kill ya for sure." Then he laid the whip on the team and they rumbled off.

Smilin' Jake sat in silence, thoughtfully chewing some of Hudge's tobacco. He spat over the side. "Well, we didn't make it. No help for that now. Luke, jump down there and go into the brush, see if you can find them kids that've been trailin' behind us." He grinned at Luke's stunned expression. "I reckon I ain't so far gone I didn't know we was being trailed."

Luke dropped nimbly to the ground and hustled off into the brush.

"What are you doing?" Hudge asked. "We're turnin' around aren't we?"

"Nope," Jake answered. "We had a plan. The Cap'n always said you always stick to the plan."

"I only got the one gold piece that Graywullf left. That won't buy passage for all of us."

"I reckon not," Jake replied. "But we're going down and find out just the same. I can't be saddled with raisin' a kid."

Hudge stared hard at the *magii'ri* Warrior. "What are you talkin' about? You promised Lorn Graywullf you'd look after his boy."

"What do you think I'm doing?" Smilin' Jake replied. "You heard that feller. *Magii'ri* Warriors are about to become an endangered species. The best thing for Luke and all the rest of you to do is get as far away from me as possible."

Hudge shook his head irritably but said no more. He merely watched the swaying brush where Luke had disappeared. Inside the wide patch of brush, Luke paused to let his eyes adjust to the gloom, and almost immediately saw a set of footprints in the soft earth. He followed them slowly, his pulse pounding in his ears. He calmed down quickly, and moments later he heard whispered voices. Luke located the voices, sneaked in close, then suddenly stepped into a tiny clearing in the brush. A teenage boy and a younger girl sat huddled together, talking in low tones. The boy jumped to his feet between Luke and the girl.

"Easy," Luke said. "I didn't bring no fish this time." Neither replied, so Luke continued. "Smilin' Jake says for you two to come up and ride in the wagon. We're makin' a run for the coast. Elanderfeld is under siege, so if you want a way out you better come with us." He waited a few moments while the two conferred in hushed tones.

"Alright" the boy replied. "We'll come with you."

Luke nodded and set off. He could have run all the way back to the wagon, but he didn't. The other two caught up to him within a few yards.

"I'm Mathias," the boy said when he drew close. "This is Mariel," he indicated the young girl.

"I'm Luke," he smiled at the girl, and she smiled back. "Don't you have any family that could take you in?"

"I don't," Mathias responded quickly.

Mariel cast a curious glance at Mathias, then said, "Neither do I."

"Me neither," Luke replied. "Smilin' Jake's the only family I got left. We'll help you,"

Hudge and Jake watched them come out of the brush. "It's like a goddamned orphan train," Jake exclaimed.

"How did you know they was back there?" Hudge asked.

"They been stealin' food for about the last five days," Jake said with a laugh. "Didn't you notice? I found their tracks and could see they were kids."

Luke approached with the other two. "This is Mathias and Mariel," he said. "That's Hudge and Jake, and there's Kate, Lisbeth and Maryanne in the wagon."

Mathias approached Jake and held out his hand. Jake shook it with a solemn smile, then looked directly into the boy's eyes. He felt as if he'd been punched in the guts. The boy met his gaze with one blue eye, and one that was as green as sea foam.

"Ride in the back," Jake commanded. "Luke, you set up here with me and Hudge for awhile."

After they had set out again and the rumble of the wagon and jingling of harness covered their voices, Hudge leaned over and asked, "Did you see?"

Smilin' Jake nodded.

"See what?" Luke asked.

"He's marked as a Trueblood *magii'ri* Wizard," Jake explained. "They ain't more than a handful like him. If the renegades see him, he's dead for sure. Him and all his family."

"He said he ain't got any family," Luke said.

"They probably already killed 'em then," Hudge stated. "What is the World coming to?"

"Bad times," Jake answered.

"We can't let 'em kill them," Luke said decisively.

"We'll do what we can," Jake said. "I promise."

They approached the last downhill run to the coast and Smilin' Jake let the tired horses have free rein. The wagon picked up speed alarmingly fast, and Hudge reached for the brake on his side.

"Leave it be," Jake ordered. Hudge stared at him incredulously.

"What the Hell are you doin,?" he yelled above the rumble of the old wagon.

"We been spotted," Jake yelled back. He jerked his head towards the burning town, then turned his attention back to keeping the wagon under control. Hudge followed the direction of his nod. Five men on horseback raced towards them. Luke ventured a quick peek under the canvas that covered the wagon when he heard that, then dropped the tarp.

"Get down on the floor," he told the others. "and grab ahold of anything you can find, but don't look up!"

Smilin' Jake judged the distance to the coast and the nearest building. It would be close, too damn close, but it was better than being caught out in the open. A chuckle sounded in his throat, then built into a full fledged laugh. The panicked horses actually picked up speed, trying desperately to outrun the careening wagon. They hit a small rise and the wagon became airborne and slammed back to earth with a teeth rattling crash.

"We ain't gonna make it," Hudge moaned, terror-stricken.

"We'll make it," Jake replied. His old grin was firmly back in place.

Two of the riders cut off from the main group and skidded to a stop in the middle of the road. Both held lances.

"We ain't gonna make it!" Hudge yelled.

"We'll make it, dammit!" Jake shouted back.

Both horsemen raised their lances to the ready position and shouted at the incoming wagon to halt. Their horses pranced sideways as the riders fought for control. Jake guided the team directly down the middle of the road. The distance shrank between them, and one horseman gave in to his panic and gigged his mount so hard it went from a standing halt to a leap that carried it completely out of the road. The other rider was screaming at the wagon to stop. His mount wrested control from the rider and wheeled to flee just as the lead horse struck it broadside. In a fraction of a second horse and rider were sucked under the half ton wagon. It lurched sickeningly as the wheels struck the fallen horse and rider, but by some miracle Jake was able to keep it upright.

"Lifeboats!" Hudge yelled, pointing out to sea.

Smilin' Jake chanced a glance away from the road. Two lifeboats had been launched from the ship and were plowing through the surf towards the beach. He looked back, and saw the remaining horsemen charging down the hill. They were rapidly gaining on the fleeing wagon.

"We might not make it," Jake whispered under his breath. Then he heard a sound that made his blood run cold. It was the whine of approaching cannonballs then he heard the report of the cannons and saw the puffs of smoke from the ship. They were caught between the horsemen, the men on lifeboats and the ship. They would be shredded to bits. Although he would never admit it, Smilin' Jake closed his eyes for a fraction of a second and prayed.

The cannonballs whizzed overhead. Two plowed into the road not more than fifty yards behind the wagon and detonated, sending geysers of dirt fifty feet into the air. Another landed behind the horsemen, then one gunner got the range and a cannonball struck the first horseman dead center. The entire group vanished in a cloud of smoke. Elation coursed through Jake.

"I'll have to try that more often," he said out loud. Hudge stared at him like he had gone mad. "Slow us down," Jake shouted then he laughed again.

Hudge yanked with all his strength on the brake lever. The leather padded brake shoes slammed into the wheels and almost immediately began to smoke. The wagon slowed, but it was still going far too fast to totally control. Hudge leaned into the brake, and the handle snapped off. He stared at it blankly, holding it in his hands.

"Oh shit," Smilin' Jake said calmly.

The wagon hit one of the piers straight on and the racket of the iron bound wheels on the plank deck drove the horses insane with fear. They covered the last fifty yards so quickly all Jake could do was turn back into the wagon and yell, "Hold on!"

They were airborne once again. The world tilted crazily. Hudge leaped to one side, Jake to the other. Hudge's worldly belongings tumbled from the back. Then the wagon plunged into the sea.

Jake surfaced first. He dragged in a quick, ragged breath and dove. The normally clear sea water was clouded with bubbles from the wagon's plunge, but the trail of bubbles led Jake to it. As he kicked frantically towards the wagon, Kate and Elizabeth emerged from the wreckage and fought towards the surface. Moments later they were followed by the boy Mathias with Maryanne fastened on his back, her arms firmly locked around his neck. But Luke and Mariel were not to be seen.

Inside the wagon, Luke struggled to free Mariel from her pack. One strap was hung, impaled by a split wagon board that had missed the girl by scant inches. Finally, Luke cut the strap with his knife. Mariel fought to flee the wagon, but Luke dragged her upwards inside the cover. They popped into a huge air bubble trapped inside the heavy canvas tarp, where they both gasped for air. The wagon slowly descended towards the bottom of the sea.

"I can't swim," the girl sobbed.

"I won't leave you," Luke promised. "Wrap your arms around my neck, like Maryanne did with Mathias."

The girl did as Luke suggested.

"Take a couple deep breaths," Luke ordered. He dragged in as much air as he could hold, then kicked his way free of the wagon, towing Mariel with him. They cleared the wagon just as Jake reached it. He took one of Mariel's arms and together he and Luke thrashed their way to the surface. As they broke the surface, gasping for air, the lifeboats from the ship reached them. Mariel was lifted from the sea, followed by Luke. Jake's strength was waning. It was all he could do to float on his back, eyes closed, and draw in lungfuls of air.

"Give me yer hand, mate," a gruff voice ordered. Smilin' Jake blindly held out his hand and a strong, calloused paw enveloped his. He was nearly lifted bodily into the boat, where he flopped down on the floor. Jake lay there shaking from the adrenaline surge as well as the weeks of trouble until he felt the boat turn about and make for the ship. Hudge was the last one they pulled from the sea. He lay gasping on the floor of the lifeboat.

"Not much of a plan," he said to Smilin' Jake.

"It worked, didn't it?" Smilin' Jake replied. He studied the crew of the lifeboat as he recovered. "My thanks to you."

"Nothing' to it," the spokesman for the rescuers said. "Keep yer head down for a bit, young'un." he suggested to Mariel. She snuggled in closer to Luke and covered her ears as cannonballs whizzed overhead. The reports grew louder, and the acrid scent of gunpowder mixed with the smoke as Elanderfeld burned. Jake hazarded a quick glance over the gunwhales. A group of renegades had gathered at the end of the pier to try impossibly long bow shots at the lifeboats. The pier disintegrated into splinters as several cannonballs scored direct hits. No more arrows came from the shore.

"That'll settle 'em down some," the spokesman said. He was a grizzled fellow, missing one eye and most of the ear on that side of his head. He had a bushy gray beard that sported several bald spots where his face had been burned.

"Gunpowder?" Smilin' Jake said in a confused manner. "Where did you get cannon and powder?"

"We pick things up, here and there," the grizzled man said.

Jake digested that bit of news. "I'd speak to your captain, if I may," he requested.

"Ye already are," the grizzled man replied with a hint of a smile, which on his ravaged face was far from reassuring. "I be Captain Lamar Smythe, of the good ship The Undertaker, recently from the Southron Coast and anchored here for…ah…supplies."

The crew laughed at their Captain's last statement.

"You're pirates," Smilin' Jake stated.

Captain Smythe considered that. "Aye. I reckon we are. Once a pirate always a pirate. But we prefer the term buccaneers."

"Pirates don't usually rescue people," Smilin' Jake said with a hopeful glance at Captain Smythe.

"I reckon not," the captain agreed. "I think you'll find we are quite a bit different from your run of the mill pirates you might have known. We're always on the lookout for something that might…benefit us in one way or another."

Smilin' Jake grinned. "I think that could be arranged."

"Then we be glad to have you aboard," Captain Smythe said. "But first, if ye don't mind, I'd like to see the color of your coin."

Smilin' Jake nodded. He removed his plain leather belt and turned it over, then split a seam that separated two layers of leather. From that hidden pouch he produced three gold coins with a foreign stamp. Captain Smith's eyes took on a speculative gleam when he saw the gold. He took the coin Jake offered and examined it.

"I don't know the stamp," he said, "but to be honest, three coins won't buy you passage any farther than Garrison Town."

"I don't want to go to Garrison Town," Smilin' Jake said. "I want to go to the Isle of Serpents."

Captain Smythe and all his men laughed uproariously. "I reckon you might get there if you sprout wings and fly."

"I left a ship full of gold coins just like that on the Isle," Smilin' Jake said with a shrug. "But I reckon I can find someone else to take me there."

"Whoa, now," Captain Smythe said hastily. "No need to go off half cocked. I reckon we can come to terms for passage to the Isle."

"I reckon we can," Smilin' Jake said with a laugh. "I reckon so."

The ship was huge, far larger than any even Smilin' Jake had been aboard. A man just as large, in proportion to the ship, helped them aboard. Jake wondered briefly if he had giant blood.

"This is Mr. Dorsey, my first mate. If you need anything just ask him," Captain Smythe said. "Mr. Dorsey, show these fine people to their accommodations and explain the rules of the ship." Captain Smythe retired to his quarters.

"This way," Dorsey rumbled. He led them to a hatch that led below deck. "During the day you are free to come and go as you please, as long as you stay out of the way. At night you are required to stay below deck." He caught Jake's questioning look. "There are strange things about on the seas at night anymore," he explained. "Not fit for children's eyes."

They all filed down the ladder to the hold. At least a dozen more people occupied it already. Jake let his eyes get accustomed to the gloom, and saw that this hold ran one third of the length of the ship. Hatches to the other compartments were iron barred, double thickness oak, locked and chained. He turned again to question Dorsey with a glance as the huge man's bulk blocked out the daylight.

"The Captain has taken on other refugees," Dorsey explained. "We're a tri-deck, the bottom level is below the surface. That's where the galley and food supplies are kept. You won't be going down there either. Someone will bring you food and water. I trust this is all acceptable?"

"Don't have much choice, do we?" Smilin' Jake asked.

"None at all," Dorsey replied.

"Three levels? We won't be outrunning anyone, will we?"

"The Undertaker is much faster than she appears," Dorsey said. "Appearances can be deceiving."

"I reckon so," Jake agreed.

Dorsey cocked an eye towards the hatch. "Sunset is coming quickly. Settle in, you'll have supper soon. There's dry clothes in those chests," he indicated the chests with one ham like hand as he swung up the ladder. The hatch closed and the hold was cast into near darkness. The other refugees stared suspiciously, until one woman spoke up.

"Those children will catch their deaths if you don't get 'em into dry clothes," she said. "I'll help the girls find some clothes, you men get yerself changed."

"Thank you ma'am," Smilin' Jake said. "I reckon we're all in the same boat." He grinned widely. Hudge rolled his eyes and shook his head.

"You could have killed us all," he said. "Driving the wagon right into the sea! Who heard of such a thing?"

"Could have, but didn't," Jake reminded him. He turned to the others. "Is Smythe a man of his word?"

"Seems to be," one man replied as several others voiced their assent.

Smilin' Jake turned back to Hudge. "The it seems like we have passage to the Isle of Serpents." He looked around. "It might get a bit dreary, but it's better than the alternative."

Hudge shook his head again, then slowly grinned. "You are a crazy bastard, Smilin' Jake."

Jake grinned back. "I'm just getting started."

After they had changed clothes, Luke finally let out a long sigh of relief. He sat next to Mariel and Mathias. She stared openly at him with shining eyes.

"You're a Warrior," she told Luke. "Am I right?"

"Someday I hope to be," Luke replied. "My Father was, and his father before him."

"I'm a Wizard," Mathias offered.

Luke gave him a crooked grin. "I never had much truck with Wizards." He shrugged. "I guess you'll be the first."

The days at sea passed slowly. Smilin' Jake slept for nearly three days as Lynch's spell of Dark Magic healed his wounds. He awoke with a ravenous hunger and ate everything he could for another three days. Luke, Mathias and Mariel made friends with the other children aboard, but they spent many hours talking and playing games among themselves and slowly but surely they became friends. Mariel took to following Luke wherever he went in the hold or above deck during the daylight hours. Luke pretended to be annoyed, but secretly he wasn't. One thing that did annoy him, though, was being locked up all night. He found it hard to sleep, and sometimes as he lay awake he became aware that the ship had stopped dead in the water. Muffled voices could be heard topside, as well as clunks and other noises that sounded like the shifting of cargo. Everything aroused his curiosity, and that was how he found the old cannon port.

He had been bored, as usual, and was climbing a jumble of nets tied to the deck. He climbed behind the nets, and discovered a hatch that had been used to deploy a cannon at some prior time. Now it was only a hatch held in place by a hasp and locked with a rusty spike. He could smell the clean sea air rushing through the seams around the hatch. It smelled like freedom. Luke cautiously pried the spike from the hasp and lowered the hatch just enough to see out. He looked down. The sea lapped against the sides of The Undertaker some eight feet below him. The deck was six feet above him. He closed it quietly and fastened it shut with the spike. He mentioned it to no one.

Later that night, when everyone else was asleep, Luke returned to the hatch. He lowered it until it rested against the side of the ship, and prayed that it wouldn't flop and wake everyone up. He pulled his upper body through, found a handhold, and began to climb. In moments he slipped over the railing and stood on the deck. It was a moonless night, and the stars glittered brightly. Luke breathed deeply of the cool night air and reveled in his new found freedom. He had barely moved from the railing when the huge figure at the wheel turned and stared at the exact spot he had occupied only moments before. It was Dorsey, the first mate. Luke hid in the deeper shadows by a mountain of crates lashed to the deck and breathed a sigh of relief. He couldn't explain it, but the big man scared him. As a matter of fact, the entire crew seemed a little odd to him. Dorsey returned his attention to guiding the ship and a few minutes later a winking light appeared off the bow. Luke neither saw nor heard a signal, but the crew came silently out of their quarters and furled the sail. Dorsey dropped anchor and The Undertaker glided to a slow halt. Now thoroughly intrigued, Luke wedged himself deeper in his hiding place.

The other ship came up fast and quiet alongside The Undertaker. Someone dropped a gangplank from the visiting ship and the crew immediately began to ferry containers from the new ship to The Undertaker. Each container was three feet square and was carried by two men to the rearward hold. In a matter of minutes more than thirty containers were transferred. The other ship raised the plank and drifted silently away until the lights winked out entirely. Not one word had been spoken. The crew of The Undertaker raised the sails then filed back down the hatch to their quarters, except for Mr. Dorsey. He stood at the wheel, solid and huge. Without warning he turned and stared directly into Luke's eyes, but he gave no indication that he saw the boy crouching in the shadows. Abruptly, he turned back and stared out at the now empty sea.

Luke slithered over the rail, found his handholds and gingerly lowered himself back through the hatch. Once he was inside he fastened the hatch and leaned back on the nets, waiting for his heart to stop racing. The Undertaker lurched slightly as the sails filled once more and it began to glide across the waves. Luke wound his way among the sleeping forms that dotted the rough planks that made up the floor of the hold to his spot, then curled up and drifted off to sleep. He never noticed the glitter of Jake's eyes through his slitted lids.

That became Luke's schedule. He spent all day on the deck of the Undertaker, watching avidly as the crew performed their daily tasks. He stayed out of the way and didn't ask any questions, but he noticed when a crew member slacked off and found himself being berated by Mr. Dorsey. By the same token he noticed when a task was done exceptionally well and Mr. Dorsey granted the fortunate sailor with a clap of his massive hand across the shoulders and an extra dollop of rum in the evening. By night, Luke escaped the confines of the hold and watched the silent exchanges with growing curiosity.

The weeks crept by. One of the sailors had noticed Luke's interest in the ship and had given him a short length of rope and taught him a few basic knots. Captain Smythe nodded approvingly when he saw Luke practicing those knots, and he even deigned to teach him some foreign swordsmanship and explain defensive and offensive maneuvers at sea. Smilin' Jake watched the interaction between Luke and the crew and his smile grew ever wider. The boy had something special, some quality that set him above even the *magii'ri* Warriors. His aptitude for warcraft was unparalleled and once he learned something it seemed to be imprinted in his memory forever.

They drew closer to the Isle of Serpents, and Jake spent the evenings before they went to sleep outlining the coast and the Citadel in a rough drawing scratched into the deck planks of the hold. He explained where the *magii'ri* under Luke's father had hidden the Wizard's ship holding the foreign gold, and when he was sure Luke had it committed to memory he destroyed it. That same evening Luke decided to find out what the Undertaker was smuggling.

The previous nights that Luke had stolen above deck had been moonless. This night appeared to be the same, so Luke once again climbed up the side of the ship like a giant spider and slipped over the rail. He dashed into his hiding place and waited. At midnight he saw the telltale twinkling of light that heralded the arrival of yet another ship. As if on cue, the crew filed out, lowered the sail and took their positions as the Undertaker glided to a halt. The trailing ship drew close and stopped as if held by an unseen hand. The gangplank came down and just as the crew began to ferry the merchandise the moon broke free of the clouds.

Luke bit back a strangled cry of terror. In the moonlight the crew became almost transparent! He could see facial features, but he could look right through them to the backs of their hoods. When a coat blew open, he could count the buttons on the front and see the material in the back. If the coat was ripped, as most were, he looked right through them! Mr. Dorsey's hood shifted so Luke knew he was staring right at him. A wisp of cloud obscured the moon for a moment, and Dorsey's familiar features returned. He held a finger to his lips and cast a warning look Luke's way before the moon dissolved his face once again.

Luke heart pounded painfully against his ribs and he had to force himself to control his breathing. His pulse raced and he felt weak and lightheaded. By some scrap of iron will he managed to stop shaking and nestle deeper into his hiding place until the transaction was complete. The crew raised the sail and went below deck as they had done so many times before. Dorsey returned to the wheel, but as soon as Luke tried to slip back over the rail, he spoke.

"Not so fast, Mr. Graywullf," he said in a voice only slightly louder than whisper. Dread raced along Luke's spine. He searched frantically for a weapon. "You need not fear me," Dorsey continued. "I've been waiting for the moon to expose us as we truly are. Now I'll explain." He lashed the wheel and turned back towards Luke. "Yer frightened, and well you should be. The Undertaker is one of the few ghost ships with a crew as unique as ours." He sat beside Luke. "Most ghost ships won't take on living souls, and for good reason I suppose. But Captain Smythe has it on good authority that our curse can be lifted, and he is determined that one day we will find a living soul who can do it."

"Curse?" Luke managed to squeak.

The moon faded in time for Luke to see Dorsey's grin. "Aye, cursed we be, and that's for certain." He sighed. "We were pirates, lowdown scoundrels and salty seadogs. We preyed upon the weak and innocent. As Captain Smythe often said, we'd do anything for gold. And we did. One night in a far off port we were all deep in our cups and debauchery, finding our pleasures as we had grown accustomed. Captain Smythe made that very remark, and a dark and sallow man sidled up next to him. The air chilled, sound went silent, the dancing girls went still. This man asked us to pick up cargo at sea and deliver it to his specifications. Captain Smythe agreed. Well, all returned to normal. We had our time in port and set sail the next day." Dorsey paused.

"How did that curse you?" Luke asked.

"When we picked up our cargo and took the pieces of gold, we didn't know we had sold our own souls. That was our cargo. We deliver souls to Haan, the Guardian of the Abyss. Captain Smythe hopes that some day we'll rescue enough souls to balance the scales, and we might become human again."

"Your hold is full of souls?" Luke asked incredulously.

"Nearly," Dorsey replied. "A few more stops and we'll have to make a run for the Drop."

"The Drop?" Luke echoed.

"Aye. That's what we call World's End. We go over the Drop to Skull's Gate, and deliver our cargo into the Abyss."

Dread crept into Luke's soul. "I don't want to go there." He stated flatly.

"None do," Dorsey replied. "That's why the souls are held in sealed traps. All souls ache to return to their owner, and all bodies crave to be filled with their souls. And none wish to be condemned to the Abyss."

"Can't you run?" Luke asked. The moon reappeared and Dorsey's features melted away.

"Curses can't be outrun," Dorsey said. "We have no one to blame but ourselves."

"But you don't seem to be so bad," Luke protested.

"It matters not," Dorsey replied. "We were caught by our own greed." He shrugged. "It's been eighty years. This may be the last cargo of the living Captain Smythe takes on. He mentioned we might take your man's gold in return for your passage and make a run for the Southron Coast. It's rumored men practice magic there as well." He stood so suddenly that Luke cringed. Dorsey smiled. "Go below, Mr. Graywullf, and don't venture out after dark again." He went back to the wheel and stared intently out at the sea.

Luke hurried back through his hatch and stifled yet another scream when a hand firmly grasped his ankle. It was Smilin' Jake, and his teeth gleamed in the moonlight.

"Now that's something you don't see everyday," he said in a low voice.

"Y...you were there?" Luke asked.

"I've been keeping an eye on you," Jake admitted. "I figured they were smugglers."

"They ferry souls to the Abyss," Luke stammered.

"So I heard," Jake said. He studied Luke. "Does it matter? We paid for passage and they provided it. It doesn't matter if we're aboard a Ghost ship as long as Captain Smythe honors our accord. And so far I have no reason to think he won't."

"But Jake, he wants a ship loaded with gold to trade for magic on the Southron Coast!"

Smilin' Jake nodded. "I told you about that. Your father and me left a king's ransom on the Isle near the Citadel."

"I don't understand," Luke said. "With that much gold you could live like a king anywhere in the World. Why are you giving it away?"

"It weren't mine to begin with," Jake corrected. "So by trading it to Captain Smythe I bought us safe passage out of Norland and it didn't cost me a copper piece. That's a pretty good deal, if you ask me."

Luke was suddenly aware that most of the refugees were listening, including Mathias and Mariel.

"What do you think happened in Norland?" Luke asked.

Smilin' Jake dropped his eyes. In his mind he saw the faces of the people of Elanderfeld on that last wild ride down the slope to the sea. They had been twisted with mindless savagery and bloodlust. They might have been good people once, but something had corrupted them.

"I reckon there ain't much left," Jake said as gently as he could.

"What will we do?" Mathias asked. All of the refugees pressed closer. Many asked the same question.

"Whoa now, why ask me? I'm a wanted man. I can never openly go back to Norland again," Smilin' Jake said. "And why should I? I gave my life to those people and they doublecrossed me at every turn. I reckon I should say good riddance!"

"You don't mean that," Mathias interrupted. "You're angry, and hurt. But someday the *magii'ri* will return to Norland in victory and the old ways will return."

"You really believe that, don't you boy?" Smilin' Jake snarled. "You forgot one thing. You're *magii'ri*, and they want to kill all of us. Including our families. Men, women, kids, it don't matter to them."

"I have no family," Mathias replied stiffly.

"Makes no difference," Smilin' Jake said with a dismissive shrug. "The old ways are gone and I ain't going back. Those that want to stay with me are welcome."

"Actually," Hudge interjected as gently as he could, "the old ways may be coming back."

Jake gave him a murderous glare that shook Hudge to the bone, but he pressed on. "I don't mean the way things were a few years ago. I mean the *really* old ways."

"The Wilding," Mathias exclaimed. "Of course! This has all been written in prophecy."

"I should have seen this coming," Hudge muttered half to himself. "I had the training and I saw the signs. Taters and carrots that didn't taste like taters and carrots should, wild rabbit that was just a tad wilder than it should have been, summer lightning without a cloud in the sky over by the Anvil Mountains. I just didn't put two and two together. It's the Wilding alright. Damn me for an old fool."

"What the Hell is the Wilding?" Smilin' Jake asked.

"You tell it, boy," Hudge prodded Mathias.

"The Wilding is a prophecy recorded centuries ago. It says in a time of upheaval the *magii'ri* will tear themselves apart. A foreign presence of great evil will take root and flourish and the old ways will return," Mathias explained.

"What old ways?" Smilin' Jake asked suspiciously.

"Very old," Hudge replied. "If this is true…"

"It is," Mathias assured him. "All of the signs are there."

Hudge rolled his eyes at the young upstart. "It will be chaos. Ogres, trolls and were- demons will stalk the mountains. Creatures from the deep not seen in a thousand years will surface, and Dragons will once more rule the skies. Slagg, the Great Destroyer, will awaken from his long sleep. And he will be possessed of a terrible hunger from centuries of fasting," Hudge's voice trailed off.

"But the *magii'ri* will return, and with the Dragonspawn as their ally they will defeat the evil one and their world will be as it once was," Mathias finished excitedly.

The rest of the refugees were chattering among themselves so loudly Jake had to shout for order.

"Enough!" The hold became quiet again. "We are traveling to the Isle of Serpents. We'll be safe there. Am I right?" Smilin' Jake looked at Hudge, who acquiesced to Mathias.

"Not really," Mathias replied, nearly lost in thought. "The real danger, once the initial bloodletting is over, will be from the entities released by the evil one. Half men, Nightriders, and the most dangerous of all, Dragons. Of course, legions of ogres and trolls would be enough by themselves. So we must create the Dragonspawn…" His voice trailed off as he became deep in thought.

"Did you say Dragons would rule the sky?" Luke asked. Excitement sent chills along his backbone. Mariel slipped her small hand inside of his.

"I reckon so," Hudge sighed heavily. "Slagg's the worst of the worst, so the legends say. But there'll be plenty of lesser Dragons, unless he's killed them off."

"Shit," Smilin' Jake growled. "So all the old legends are coming back to haunt us?"

"I reckon so," Mathias answered.

"Tell me more about this Dragonspawn," Smilin' Jake said. "If he is supposed to rescue us then we need to find him right now, I'd say, and get on with it."

"You don't *find* the Dragonspawn," Mathias explained. "He must be *created*."

"The Dragonspawn is myth," Hudge argued. "And besides, even if we had the knowledge and the means to create the Dragonspawn, it's a very dangerous proposition."

"Whoa, back up," Smilin' Jake interrupted. "What do you need to create it? And what do you mean, it can be dangerous? I thought he was supposed to rescue us."

Hudge tried to silence Mathias, but the young Wizard spoke with increasing eagerness. "The Dragonspawn combines all the qualities of the strongest Warrior with the strengths of a Dragon. He has incredible strength, speed, vision, a sixth sense of danger and near immortality. If he is wounded, it heals incredibly fast. To create him we must have semen from a Dragon and a willing and fertile host of Warrior stock."

"You take the semen from a Dragon and you put it…in there?" Smilin' Jake asked in disbelief.

"And it must be done by a Dragonwitch who knows the spell," Mathias finished. "Really, it's the only way."

"You forgot the part about the Dragonspawn being ruthless, bloodthirsty, possibly immoral and unable or unwilling to distinguish friends from enemies," Hudge said, his voice rising with each word. "The Dragonspawn is a cold blooded killer. That is his main strength. And," he raised a hand to silence Mathias. "And, no living soul knows the spell."

Mathias' face fell. "I had forgotten about that," he admitted. "But you don't know that the Dragonspawn is a vicious killer. My theory…"

"Your theory?" Hudge shouted. "You may be born to be a Wizard, but you are not born with instinctual knowledge. The one and only Dragonspawn created over a thousand years ago did defeat Darkness. Then he turned on his allies and systematically began to destroy them as well!"

"My theory, based on years of study," Mathias glared at Hudge, "is that the Dragonspawn inherits much of his behavior from the man and woman who conceive him. The ancient one was merely a product of poor planning."

"You lost me again," Smilin' Jake said. "I thought we only needed a *magii'ri* Warrior woman and the Dragon's, uh, you know…to make the Dragonspawn."

"No," Hudge admitted. "The woman must be impregnated by a *magii'ri* Warrior and the Dragon's seed at the same time."

"Now that sounds a bit tricky," Jake said dubiously. "Especially since I been wondering exactly how you get that stuff from a Dragon in the first place."

"Why bother?" Luke interrupted.

"What do you mean?" Mathias asked. "The Dragonspawn is our best hope."

"Why go to the trouble of creating the Dragonspawn? Why not search out this evil one and kill him ourselves?" Luke asked.

Smilin' Jake actually laughed. "Spoken like a true Warrior, and the son of Graywullf. Why not indeed?"

"It's not that simple," Mathias argued. "There could be hundreds of enemies to slay, and all of them stronger than any Warrior ever born. These enemies will have the full power of the Dark behind them."

"That is not…" Hudge once again held out a silencing hand to Mathias. "That is not the point here. Since none here know of any Dragonwitches who just happen to know the spell to create the Dragonspawn, I suppose seeking out the evil one is our best course," Hudge said in agreement with Luke and Smilin' Jake. "Especially given the volatile nature of the Dragonspawn."

"You don't know that," Mathias muttered.

"It's settled," Smilin' Jake said decisively. "Forget about this Dragonspawn. We'll hole up on the Isle until the *magii'ri* can regroup. Then we can make further plans."

Wedged against the gunwhales of the ship at the rear of the group of refugees, none seemed to notice the relieved sigh that burst from the lips of a mutie, a young man who had lost the power to speak. He had tried everything he could think of during the discussion to convey his thoughts, but no one had paid him any mind. For a moment he had been certain the young Wizard would prevail and convince the others to follow him on his doomed quest to create the Dragonspawn. He alone knew the key to defeating the Darkness lay inside the young Warrior Graywullf, the descendant of Malachi. He knew it, because trapped inside the unspeaking hulk was the mind and spirit of Nish, the Seventh Scribe.

# CHAPTER TWENTY NINE

SMILIN' JAKE MAY HAVE convinced his fellow passengers of his desire to be rid of the *magii'ri* and Norland forever, but he hadn't convinced himself. Night after night he sat at the open port and stared out at the rolling sea and the stars that burned in the dark sky. He had been conditioned, groomed, trained, even *bred* for one purpose. To uphold the Code at whatever cost. He knew he couldn't do that hiding out a thousand miles from Norland. If he could just find someone to take care of the boy. "Dammit, Graywullf," he muttered. "Why'd you go and get yerself killed?" He heard movement behind him and hastily wiped his eyes.

"Is something wrong?" Hudge asked.

Smilin' Jake grinned. "Are you really that stupid?"

Hudge grinned back. "Sometimes I am a mite thick," he conceded.

Smilin' Jake shook his head. "How can everything go to Hell all at the same time? Corruption, then the Revolution, now The Wilding. I want the World to go back to being a normal place."

"It ain't over, you know,' Hudge replied. "The corruption is still there. The Revolution simply needs a leader, like a skilled surgeon, to slice out the corrupted flesh and save the patient. If that happens, The Wilding can be dealt with in time."

"You just had to point that out, didn't you?" Smilin' Jake said in disgust. "I have to go back. I know that. But I made a promise to Graywullf. I can't take that boy right into the line of fire."

"I'll take care of him. I'll take care of all of 'em," Hudge replied. "All the Revolution needs to be successful is a leader. You can be the leader who steers this fight in the right direction. Reorganize the *magii'ri*. Be ruthless but fair."

Smilin' Jake suddenly grinned, and it was like a grin from the old days. "Did you forget who I rode with and learned from? There was no better captain than Lorn Graywullf. We learned together. I just hope I can live up to bein' his friend."

Luke lay in his blankets, his eyes shining in the near darkness. Lying beside him, wrapped in her own bedroll, Mariel slipped her hand into Luke's and gave it a firm squeeze.

"So yer goin' back?" Hudge asked.

"I'm goin' back," Smilin' Jake conceded. "Why not? Dragons, ogres, half men, Nightriders…it ain't gonna be boring."

Two weeks later, Smilin' Jake watched as the refugees vacated The Undertaker with almost giddy happiness. If they had known of the cargo she carried, he mused to himself, most would have jumped overboard and disappeared into the depths. The last of their belongings was tossed ashore, and Mr. Dorsey stood at the head of the gangplank. Smilin' Jake nodded to him. Reluctantly, he turned to look at Luke.

Luke met his gaze unwaveringly. Hudge, Mathias, Mariel and Hudge's daughters gathered around. Jake glanced at them, then scuffed his boot in the sand.

"Graywullf told me there's farmers here. They'll help you out. And there's plenty of game and fish to be caught," he said.

"Don't worry about me," Luke said. "Watch yer back."

Smilin' Jake grinned. "Don't worry, boy. I ain't gonna kill all of 'em. And when you get a mite older, you and me are goin' back and set things right."

Hudge nodded. At least he understood, Jake thought.

"It's time, Mr. Sipowicz," Mr. Dorsey called.

Smilin' Jake sighed and turned to Hudge. "I'll bring back some gold." Hudge nodded. Jake laid his hand on Luke's shoulder. "You keep trainin', every day. And listen to Hudge. Ol' Lucas Hudge was a hell of a Warrior and I reckon Junior here ain't forgot *everythin'* he was told." He walked up the gangplank and stood aside as Mr. Dorsey raised it. "I'll be back for you one day. Be ready."

# CHAPTER THIRTY

LYNCH ROSE QUICKLY WHEN he heard Moira approach. He hurriedly dried his eyes and forced himself to regain his composure. What difference did it make anyway, one Warrior more or less? Lorn Graywullf had been warned and given an opportunity to change his course. That the Warrior had made the wrong choice and died for it was not his concern. But a part of Lynch envied him. The man had died heroically, albeit tragically as well. Who else could have survived such hideous wounds, walked for three days through the desert and still summon the strength to defeat all of his known enemies? It took an act of total treachery from a man he trusted to bring him down.

"Is he dead?" Moira asked.

Lynch nodded. "Help me gather wood. We can at least send him to the Feast in the manner of his ancestors."

They dragged brush and stunted cedar trees into the cave and piled it atop the body of Lorn Graywullf. Then Lynch sent Moira outside and ignited the fuel with an angry spell. His grief was giving way to anger. He watched the flames lick their way across the cedar logs and the firelight gave his eyes a reddish glow. Lynch turned his mind to thoughts of revenge.

The easiest way to summon half men and Nightriders in huge numbers required intimate knowledge of Dark Magic, knowledge that he knew Mordant did not possess. She was powerful, yes, but still inadequate to perform such a task. But someone, or something, Lynch thought, had found such knowledge. He only knew of one place to find such knowledge, and that meant he had to do something he had sworn he would never do. He had to make sure the Book of Runes was exactly *where* he had left it, and exactly *as* he had left it. He exited the cave to find Moira still standing there.

"Why are you still here?" he asked irritably.

"I have no where to go," Moira answered, visibly taken aback at the change within the Dark Wizard.

A thought occurred to Lynch. "Maybe you do," he said thoughtfully. He couldn't follow Mordant and check on the Book at the same time. But if Mordant had left in the manner which Moira had described, and Lorn and Lynch had silenced everyone else who had been present, the girl could return to the City of Shadows and simply wait for the Black Queen's return. Problem solved. Lynch stared at her incredibly full breasts straining against the flimsy material of her dress. She sensed his attention and tried to cover herself. Lynch shook his head. Even though she would make a delectable traveling companion, she had virtually no chance of survival accompanying Lynch where he had to go. Besides, he had been known to forget his direction when traveling with such a scrumptious piece.

"I'll take you back to the City of Shadows and sneak you back into the palace. They always lock down the palace when Mordant has one of her spells, so if they find you there just tell them you've been hiding. Mordant will come back eventually. She always does. Now, this is the important part," Lynch leaned in very close, and Moira felt her heart racing and her breath catch in her throat from the heat of his presence. "If I don't return and Mordant delivers a child, you must steal that child, take him into the mountains and kill him. Do you understand?"

"I couldn't," Moira stammered.

"You can," Lynch answered. "You can because you must. If Mordant has the child spawned by a Trueblood *magii'ri* he will grow to be a very powerful man, and being Mordant's son he will probably be a devoted follower of Darkness. You must do as I say. But," he continued. "I'm sure I will be back before nine months have passed. In that case I'll do it myself and save you the choice and the guilt."

Moira felt the intensity and the inevitable pull most women felt when alone in Lynch's presence. But even more than that she felt the persuasive power of his argument until her resolve melted.

"I'll do whatever you ask," she said.

Lynch merely nodded. He hadn't used any Dark Magic on the girl, but he wouldn't have hesitated to do so if she had resisted him. He felt a renewed sense of urgency. The more he thought of it, the more certain he was that the Book of Runes had been tampered with. He had thought the defenses surrounding it were impenetrable, but one never knew. The only way to be certain was to check for himself, the sooner the better. He cast a spell of endurance on both of them and set off towards the City of Shadows.

The City was shut down just as Lynch had suspected. He led Moira to an entrance even Mordant didn't know about, then led her on an unerring path directly to the palace. Once again he used an entrance so well concealed no one else even knew it existed, and Moira found herself in the wine cellar. Lynch considered using a tiny spell to erase Moira's memory of his personal entrances, then realized the poor girl would probably be lucky to find her own room from where they stood. He reminded her of her promise, pointed out the direction of her room and set off on his quest.

As he passed through the market area of the city Lynch helped himself to provisions and appropriated several waterskins. He then proceeded to the Queen's stables and selected a mount and a pack animal. They wouldn't last, he knew that. But much more than a couple of mounts hinged upon his completion of the journey, and a quick start might mean all the difference in the end. Besides, he figured the Black Queen owed him a lot more than that. He headed west, out into the desert.

The desert had never been a friendly place, but by the fifth day out Lynch could see a change in it, and it wasn't for the better. He crested a low hill expecting to see the glistening surface of a tiny creek below, but there was nothing more than a handful of crisscrossed deer trails. The next waterhole was dry also. In fact, the entire desert seemed as if the recent heavy rains had bypassed it completely. He made camp early that day and pondered his course. He calculated the remaining distance and gauged that against his remaining water supply. He might make it, but at least one of the horses wouldn't. The following morning he saddled up and turned the horses to the west once again.

At noon a stray dust cloud caught his eye and Lynch urged the horses behind a clump of stunted cedar trees. The dust cloud approached rapidly. He withdrew his spyglass, pilfered from another time and engraved with the name Swarovski. The spyglass was his pride and joy. One glance told him all he needed to know. Lynch retrieved his crossbow, cocked it and waited patiently. To a passerby he might have seemed like he was waiting for an old acquaintance, his demeanor was so calm. Finally, Lynch could make out two mounted men coming at a hard gallop. He selected another bolt for the crossbow and held it against the forearm, ready to be loaded. When the first rider came abreast of his hiding place, Lynch shot him out of the saddle. The other rider flung a terrified glance towards the cedar thicket, just enough for Lynch to confirm his suspicions. The Wizard carefully led the rider as the distance grew, then released another bolt. He heard it thunk home, and the rider tumbled from his saddle. Lynch calmly rode down to his victims and retrieved his bolts. He rolled one face up. They were sand pirates, pitiful husks of men who preyed upon anyone that ventured out into the desert. Strangely enough, they had been eradicated by the *magii'ri* Warriors nearly a hundred years ago. He caught one of the wild eyed mounts and examined the saddlebags. He found a torn blue dress, a few worthless baubles of crudely made jewelry, a rusty knife and a child's doll. To be riding at a gallop they couldn't have been going far, and that was definitely bad news for a lone traveler. Their dwellings had to be close, within a days ride. Lynch mounted and resumed his direction.

As he rode, Lynch let his mind wander. It was a skill he had mastered long ago, to turn his thoughts inward yet remain completely vigilant at the same time. The return of sand pirates and the fact that the desert seemed to be growing pointed to a conclusion he couldn't deny. The Wilding prophecy was coming to fruition. At one point in time, not so long ago, the Dark Wizard Lynch would have celebrated that fact. Now he wasn't so sure. One thing the Wilding meant for certain was chaos, a state Lynch had professed to love above all others. Perhaps total anarchy was not such a good thing, he pondered.

"You're going soft," he said aloud. The horse snorted it's assent.

The saddle horse died on the nineteenth day on the crest of a sand dune nearly three hundred feet high. Lynch felt the gelding going and managed to pitch himself free of the stirrups and land on all fours in the hot sand. The gelding stayed on it's knees, quivering, then toppled over next to Lynch. He rolled over to his seat, cast an eye on the already gathering vultures and struggled to his feet. He stripped his gear from the dead horse and made a shelter from his duster. Lynch slept in the pitiful shade cast by it until the sun went down. The pack horse remained tethered to the saddle horn on the dead animal.

At sundown Lynch rose, stripped the saddle from the dead animal, threw his almost empty pack saddle to the side and rigged up the pack horse. He had about half a waterskin left. He estimated how much distance he had left, then let the pack animal drink two thirds of the water. He examined his own dehydrating tissues with almost clinical detachment and decided he wouldn't need a drink until morning.

On the twenty-third day the pack horse stumbled and only regained its feet with a tremendous effort. Lynch slid from the saddle and weighed the waterskin in his hands. Then he lifted it and sucked the last cup of water from it. He left the pack horse where it stood, but he did take the waterskin, wrapped around his waist like an empty sausage casing.

On the twenty-fourth day, Lynch stood swaying at the base of an almost sheer cliff. He lay in the sand in the shadows cast by the rock wall and waited, gathering his strength. As the sun went down the sudden coolness of a high plains evening revived him. And as the moon rose the pillaged remains of a palace emerged, line by line, carved from solid rock. Lynch listened intently, every fiber of his being straining to hear the sound that he had to have to make the climb. Finally, after he began to wonder if a century had weakened the magic that surrounded the palace, he heard what he longed for. A trickle of water cascaded down from the rocks to disappear into the thirsty sand. Lynch lunged under the tiny stream, and as the first droplets hit his parched throat his head swam with relief. He drank sparingly, then sat back down again and rested. When he had repeated the process three times, Lynch knew he would survive. It had been close. The desert had grown in five hundred years and the few water holes that had been there before were filled with sand now. The desert had not only grown, Lynch reflected, it had become stronger. The Wilding had begun.

Even in his weakened state, Lynch took time to marvel at the palace, and the fact that he had been able to storm it with a squad of Warriors so long ago. Reluctantly, he began to climb the stairs to the huge main door. The magic embedded in the very stone he walked upon rejuvenated him. It had been too long. He should have come back for the cursed thing years ago and destroyed it. He felt the strength of the magic and wondered if it could be destroyed at all.

The main doors were closed. That was a good sign. Twenty feet high and the same across, the double doors were made of ironwood and banded with steel. They hadn't been strong enough to repel determined *magii'ri* Warriors, but Lynch suspected Dark Magic had been used to circumvent them. He'd been a Warrior then, not versed in the ways of magic. He raised his fist and struck the doors three times, then said a rune committed to memory. They slowly swung open. Stale air rushed out. Another good sign, Lynch thought.

He made his way quickly down the huge hallway from the entrance to the main hall. He gave the odd looking tracks separated by a furrow six inches wide and ten inches deep only a cursory glance. It was only a matter of minutes until Lynch stood in a side passage before a blank stone wall. Never a patient man, he nonetheless forced himself to remain calm. A breath of air stirred his long hair where it brushed the nape of his neck. Gooseflesh rose on his neck and a shiver went down his spine. A gust of warm air fluttered his hair and warm droplets struck the bare skin of his neck.

*"Who dares enter my den?"* the voice sizzled inside his head.

Lynch turned with exquisitely exaggerated slowness to stare into rows of six inch teeth so close he could see saliva dripping from them. Another gust of warm air from a nostril as big as his fist struck his cheek along with flecks of moisture. Smoke rose in lazy tendrils from the fire vent at the base of a long, sinewy neck. The creature's bulk filled the passage. Above his triangular head Lynch saw the end of a thirty foot tail as it whipped to and fro. His eyes were luminous, glowing in the semi-dark, with a reptilian pupil at the center which nearly consumed the entire orb.

"You've done well, Slagg," Lynch said, as if it hadn't been more than a half century since he had seen the Dragon.

The massive head dipped a fraction of an inch. *"Lynch. I wondered if you'd dare to return. I've fulfilled my task. Is my imprisonment over?"*

"Are you forgetting the final requirement?" Lynch asked in return. He slipped away from the Dragon and stopped ten paces from the wall.

Slagg drew in a deep draught of air and released a smoking stream of fire directly against the stone wall. Lynch repeated the words he had once vowed to never say again, and the wall vanished.

"Now you may go," Lynch said with a dismissive wave.

*"None dare disrespect Slagg, the Sky Rider,"* the voice warned Lynch.

The Dragon once more released a stream of fire, this time directed at Lynch. Any normal living thing would have been instantly immolated. The Dark Wizard Lynch was as far from normal as possible. Not a hair was singed. He turned to face the Dragon, his face screwed up in anger. "Are you done now? You would dare to break our accord?" He stared deep into Slagg's expressionless eyes, even though he felt the danger of that act in his own soul. "I can see the Sky Rider grows stronger every day, brother. Will you allow him to gain total control?"

Slagg ignored that comment, and Lynch knew Slagg's transformation was nearly complete.

*"You have not yet released me,"* Slagg's voice seethed and burned in Lynch's mind. The Dark Wizard reeled in surprise. Slagg had grown stronger through the centuries also. Nearly too strong to control any longer.

"As per our accord, you will be released when you take to the skies once more," Lynch reminded him.

*"The doorsss are opened?"*

"Aye, and they will remain so if my Book is where I left it."

*"I have not stretched my wings in centuries,"* Slagg said. *"Sssee how I have grown? My strength rivals yours, Wizard."*

"I wonder what you found to nourish such magnificence?" Lynch said, suddenly very curious and very aware that most Dragons can be led astray with a few well placed strokes to their ego. "What did you feed upon, down here in the dark, Slagg?"

*"Hate,"* came the hissing, burning voice. *"I long to feed upon the flesh of men, to tear and render their puny bodies. I need to feel the pulse beating in their throats before I silence them forever!"*

"Anyone I know?" Lynch asked innocently. "If you give me a clue, I'll give one in return."

Slagg leaped forward until his snout brushed Lynch's chest. *"You've ssseen him?"*

Despite himself, Lynch felt a thrill of true fear. Even Dark Magic and blood loyalty wouldn't save him from being ground into hamburger in those massive jaws. He placed a hand slowly between his chest and Slagg's snout and pushed the beast's head back.

"I know where he is," Lynch admitted. The wave of hate that flowed from Slagg was so strong Lynch was nearly overcome. "He is not here, as you already suspected. One day he will return, and you and I will crush him. Together, as we vowed. But it is not meant to be just yet."

*"I am Slagg, the Sky Rider. I am the Great Destroyer, last of the Old Ones. I need no man's help,"* Slagg hissed.

"Then go," Lynch replied carelessly. "You have forgotten your true self. We have each fulfilled our ends of the accord and I declare it void." The words stabbed his heart even as he said them so lightly.

Slagg disappeared from the chamber. Lynch listened to his progress for a moment then hastened to a stone table in the center of the hidden room. He could see the bulky outline of the book before he drew near and it called to him. His pulse was pounding in his ears as he stepped close and ran his hand lovingly over the cover. Then rage flooded him. An incoherent shout was torn from his throat.

"Doublecrossing worm!" he shouted. He extended his hands, projected the mental image of the door slamming shut and swept his hands back towards his chest. A distant boom was accompanied by another howl of rage so strong the mountain shook and dust sifted down from the ceiling.

"Uh-oh," Lynch muttered as he realized he had just locked himself inside a mountain with several tons of very enraged Dragon.. Perhaps he had acted a bit recklessly. He steeled himself for the confrontation. He didn't have long to wait.

Slagg announced his coming with deafening growls. His steel hard claws skittered over the stone floor and his progress was illuminated by flashes of Dragonfire. Lynch did the only thing he could think of. He grabbed the Book and held it to his chest.

Slagg burst into the chamber fully intending to tear the Wizard into tiny bits. He stopped so suddenly he actually choked on his own fire when he saw the Book. The power contained within that tome was unbelievable, strong enough to repel any single adversary acting alone. And there was more. Slagg needed the magic inside that book.

"Who was in this chamber?" Lynch pounced on his advantage.

*"None dared to enter here,"* Slagg replied.

"This Book was untouched for hundreds of years," Lynch said. "All about it the dust is a half inch deep. Yet the Book itself was clean. How could the Book be clean? I ask again, Slagg. Who entered here?"

*"Do not question me as if I were your lackey, my brother,"* Slagg fumed. *"It takessss both of us to open the chamber. None entered here."*

Despite himself, Lynch found himself believing the Dragon. Yet the Book had been disturbed. As the realization hit him, Lynch staggered and sat down. The Book had not been disturbed *during their time.* Someone had found a doorway. Suddenly it all made sense. He had a competitor. For centuries Norland had been his territory, his turf. Sure, he spread chaos far and wide, but it was at *his* discretion. To have someone come into his territory, right under his nose, and interfere with his business was the ultimate insult. An interloper was trying to overthrow him. Hah. *He* was the Dragonrider. *He* was the Executioner and Thief. This would not do.

"You're free to go," Lynch said suddenly. "I only shut the doors so I could talk to you before you vanished as your kind is so wont to do."

*"My kind?"* Slagg was instantly suspicious. *"You're hiding something."*

"No. I know you didn't let anyone in the chamber. I was mistaken," Lynch admitted. He stopped and chewed at his lower lip. "Slagg…join with me and destroy the Book."

*"NO!"* Slagg's voice scalded Lynch's mind. *"Destroy the Book before I am whole and I will remain thisss way forever!"*

"Maybe there's another way," Lynch said. "It takes both of us to open the door, it takes both of us to destroy the Book. Together we might find another way to defeat the Curse."

*"No,"* Slagg's voice came again, now smooth and smoky in Lynch's brain. *"The way to break the Curse is laid out clearly in the Book itself. We must…you must find him and we confront him together. Find him and bring him to me. Then and only then can we destroy the Book. Promise me, Warlock!"*

"I'll find him," Lynch promised. "We are bound together, Slagg. All three of us, sons of the same sire. I will find him."

Slagg was suspicious. *"As per our original accord. Open the doors, and leave them open thiss time. If I return again it will be to tear your heart out, Book or no Book, brother or not."* Slagg wheeled his immense bulk with incredible agility in the confines of the tunnels. Then he paused. *"Hide the Book well, Dragonrider. The one who has already read of it has strength to rival your own."* Lynch nodded thoughtfully.

Slagg vanished down the great hall once again and Lynch breathed a sigh of relief. He muttered the spell to open the doors so Slagg, the Sky Rider, could reaffirm his rule among the clouds once again. A tiny smattering of guilt plagued him for a moment, when he thought of the lives that would be claimed by Slagg before word was spread that the Great Worm was once again raiding. He considered killing Slagg, thereby ridding the World of a great pestilence, but he quickly realized there would be no profit in such a confrontation for himself. Besides, considering Slagg's immensely increased strength, it would be quite risky to his own health. The Sky Rider had a part to play yet anyway, and he couldn't do it as a decomposing hulk. And there was that small matter of sharing the same blood. Besides, Lynch mused, finding the man who had violated his book was the matter of greatest importance. Slagg might eat a few Nightriders and half-men, or perhaps a clan of sand pirates before word reached the settlements to be on guard. Then the most he could do would be to pick off a few of the braver, or perhaps less intelligent, souls who dared to settle in the Borderlands. Not much loss there, Lynch thought. If they were that stupid it was best not to allow them to breed anyway.

Lynch covered the Book of Runes with an ancient tow sack that was remarkably well preserved, probably from being in close proximity to the Book itself for all those years. He had a long trek ahead of him, and most of it underground to boot. Once he cleared the main passage Lynch had no worries of Slagg pursuing him, for the tunnels narrowed and shrank until a tall man such as himself actually began to feel claustrophobic. Lynch had never harbored any fondness for the dark and close confines so deep in the bowels of the World. Too many ancient beings existed there, forgotten for centuries, quietly growing stronger. And most had no qualms about dining on man flesh. Most scurried away as fast as their feet, or whatever they possessed, would carry them when they sensed Lynch's malignant presence. But he knew some watched from the darker shadows where even his magical light would not reach. Then again, this was the World of the Nightriders and half-men, at least when he began to emerge from the deepest recesses, and they would not hesitate to attack anyone down in their warrens where they felt safe. It should be an interesting trip, Lynch decided.

One thing Lynch forgot was the power of the presence of the Book of Runes. Coupled with his own aura, it projected a daunting field of energy that even the hungriest beast from the darkest nightmare found terrifying. Lynch, however, felt comforted and invigorated as he hadn't felt in years. For the first time since his harrowing adventure in the Land of Ice, Lynch's powers actually increased. Once again his step had a spring in it, his gaze was pure steel, his skin glowed with health and strength flowed through him. He knew with startling clarity once again that he was the Dark Wizard Lynch, Executioner, Dragonrider and Thief, born to create mayhem and chaos. But something was different. Previously, that knowledge and the wonderful feeling of power he now felt had been accompanied by a sense of something rotten inside his soul. That sick feeling had diminished. Could it be, Lynch wondered, that his assistance to the *magii'ri* really had rescued a miniscule portion of his tainted soul? How many years, how many centuries, had he considered himself beyond redemption? Even now he knew his only purpose in tracking down the reader of his Book was to kill the man. The revelation did nothing to darken the flickering light that burned inside him. He had used his powers, Dark as they were, to serve the Light. Some lives had been spared because of his actions. Did that mean he was not doomed to an eternity of meaningless existence?

Lynch stooped dead in his tracks and brayed laughter until his sides hurt. His existence, meaningless? Bullshit. His purpose in life would remain as it had even been, to serve Lynch first and foremost. He resolved once again to taste every delicacy in the known World, to bed a woman in every settlement of more than ten souls and to experience every sensation an immortal existence could offer. What more could there be? If people got in the way he would swat them like flies, good and bad alike. But a minute part of him, buried so deep he could not find it to eradicate it, kept niggling at him that he could find ways to make sure the good were spared and the bad paid the price for their actions. The laughter died on Lynch's lips. He was the Dark Wizard Lynch, but as they said in the World he intended to visit, he was a new and improved Lynch. It would make his existence doubly difficult, this conscience he had developed...even thinking of the term made chills go down his spine...but he knew he could weed out the truly bad and spare the good in his quest. The tiny light flared brighter for a millisecond, and Lynch soundly cursed it.

He found his way through the maze of caverns and passageways in the Underworld to the exit he sought. And so it was that Lynch stepped off a shelf of rock and dropped knee deep into the flowing waters of a sewer tunnel. Rats scurried away ahead of him to dash into their dens until he had passed. Lynch stoically ignored the things floating by him in the putrid water. This was the way he had to take, and so he would. After two weeks of the type of darkness found only at the earth's core, he would wade through solid shit for a glimpse of light.

This sewage system served the largest city anywhere in the known World. Lynch knew it was a village compared to some he had seen, but then they were not of this World. He had come to the port city of Elanderfeld, home to the late King Elander and many thousands of his subjects. With such a large population, there were also a large number of criminals to take advantage of the less wary. Or there had been, Lynch mused. He didn't know what was left after the Revolution.

He carefully pried open a sewer grate and took a quick glance around. He had lost track of time in the Underworld and was gladdened to see the gray light of dawn. Any more time spent in the fragrant air of the sewer would have been difficult to bear. Lynch loosened his knife in it's sheath, then bolted from the sewer into the shadows of a marketplace vendor's stall. He recognized the street and in a few moments he had his bearings. But Elanderfeld was not the same city he had last visited. The stench of charred wood hung heavy in the air accompanied by the odor of decaying bodies. As the light of the sun grew steadily stronger the heavens were filled with the sound of the rushing wings of thousands of carrion birds. Elanderfeld was dying. Not only the people, but the city itself. The Revolution had killed it.

Lynch swore viciously. His hand had been in this. He might as well have dropped the executioners axe on the neck of every soul killed in that damned Revolution. And now it may have cost him his only chance to catch up to the mysterious man who had been perusing his Book. He rose and trotted down the street. There was only one way to find what he sought.

It took longer than it should have. All of the old ornately carven street signs had been ripped down and Lynch had to rely on his memory to find the right ones. After several false starts and one completely dead end, he stood at the end of a cobblestone street lined with the burned out hulks of what had once been stately mansions. These were the homes of Elanderfeld's elite upper class, the sea traders and slave dealers, merchants and even a few retired pirates. The Revolution had been particularly violent there, as the philosophy of demonizing the rich espoused by Lynch and his cohorts had taken hold. Lynch paused for a long time. The ruins he stood in front of had belonged to a merchant, by all accounts an upstanding citizen. But Lynch knew he also traded in women, sold into slavery to the highest bidder. The home across the street, which was still decorated with the remains of the owner swinging from the archway, had been owned by the governor of the lower city. His men had often raided his neighbor's caravans, killing anyone who opposed them. Another home just up the street had a secret entrance directly into the sewer where crates of opium had been delivered for distribution. And so it went. Each home was more ornate, each owner had a station higher than his neighbor, but nearly all were involved in graft and corruption. The entire ruling class of Elanderfeld leeched off the working class they so despised, taxing them to the limit and demanding more every year. Many times in his years there Lynch had seen farmers and street vendors robbed and beaten by the governor's men.

Lynch bowed low to the swinging corpse in the archway. "Good day, guv'nor."

He walked away knowing that the driving force behind the Revolution had been right. The upper class had become too arrogant, too corrupt. Too many people wanted to live the life of leisure, producing nothing and growing fatter and richer every year while they looked down their noses at the working class toiling in the sun. A cleansing was needed. But they needed a leader who recognized the difference between wholesale slaughter and the selective surgery of removing the dead wood. No such leader had emerged and the mob had simply gone crazy. Still, he mused, some good had been done. It would be some time before corruption reached the previous levels. What the Revolution needed from the very beginning, indeed the only thing that would stop the carnage, was a charismatic leader.

The thought had never even occurred to Lynch that he should have been that man.

He entered the governor's mansion and found the master's suite. He built a fire and heated water, and after a hot bath and a change of clothes pilfered from the servant's quarters, Lynch settled in for the night. At sundown the endless commotion of the carrion birds finally ceased, only to be replaced by the growling and snapping of wolves and other nocturnal scavengers. Lynch cast a spell on his room and rolled up in his blankets. In minutes he had drifted into a dreamless sleep.

He was jerked violently from sleep by an unusual noise several hours later. He lunged from his bed and stood there swaying with his sword in his hand as he tried to gather his scattered brains. The noise had been faint, but somehow intensely insistent. It came again, and Lynch could not deny it. He gathered up his weapons and the Book and went back into the street. Coyotes and wolves scattered before him like leaves in a high wind. Lynch strained his ears for another hint of the sound, but when it came he realized it was *inside* his head. Now he was very intrigued.

The sound led him down several different streets, and soon he was loping towards it, heeding it's unearthly call. He only slowed when he heard another sound, the sound of raucous laughter and drunken jeering. But the other sound originated from the same place as the laughter, so Lynch continued on, his weapons at the ready. He finally saw the dancing lights of a campfire inside a courtyard, and he crept to the corner of the nearest building.

Firelight illuminated the courtyard. Lynch counted five men in a semi-circle around another figure in a crouched position. As he watched, one of the men reached down towards the figure on the ground. Lynch heard a ripping sound, and the standing men cheered as the man nearest the fallen person waved a piece of cloth. Lynch picked out two more men in the shadows, but as he watched a slightly built youth charged in from the darkness and crashed headlong into the man waving the cloth. They tumbled to the ground and the men cheered as their attention was diverted to the fighting men. Lynch caught a flash of steel just before the boy buried it to the hilt in the other man's stomach. He howled in pain and rolled away. The youth leaped to his feet and brandished the knife at the other men. The sound of ringing steel filled the courtyard as the remaining men drew swords. The lone sentinel in the darkness just watched silently.

Lynch studied the scene. He could walk away, or he could render them helpless with a relatively quick spell of Dark Magic. That would be the sensible thing to do, and much less hazardous to his own hide than an actual fight. But he had promised Graywullf he would try to refrain from that sort of activity. The sound of ripping cloth reached him. Lynch reacted as he always did to violence. He joined in. He loaded a bolt in his crossbow and shot the sentinel through the throat. He straightened his collar, quietly drew his sword and walked deliberately towards the group. The boy faced the gang bravely, and Lynch wondered briefly what had given him such courage. Then they closed in on him and he was clubbed to the ground.

"Is this a private party," Lynch asked, "or can anyone join?"

The four remaining men spun away from the boy on the ground. Blood stained his forehead, but Lynch was pretty sure he was alive.

"Do yerself a favor, pretty boy," one of the men growled. "Haul ass out of here, or you'll be joinin' the boy."

Lynch grinned and lowered his tow sack to the stones of the courtyard. The Book chose that moment to reveal itself. The men stared at it incredulously when the tow sack slipped back which gave Lynch a chance to glance at the person lying by the fire, and his mouth went dry. It was a girl of maybe seventeen years and she was naked from the waist up. Auburn hair tumbled about her bare shoulders and her full breasts heaved as she struggled with her bonds, but she was not giving up. Then Lynch looked into her eyes and he knew why the boy had risked his life.

"A book?" one man asked in disbelief.

"What are you, a librarian?" another asked. The rest guffawed drunkenly.

"Yes, I'm a librarian." Lynch deadpanned. "Have you ever seen a librarian when they get really mad?" he asked. He advanced upon the group with his sword at the ready. The men exchanged glances.

"Get him," one suggested. They attacked at once. Lynch let his instincts take over. He parried and thrust, and one man went down with his entrails spilling out onto the cold stones. But Lynch never stopped moving. The next man dropped to his knees clawing at the spot where his throat had been, another stared stupidly as he realized Lynch had already thrust his blade completely through his lungs. The final man stared incredulously for a moment then attacked. Lynch blocked every blow easily, without even seeming to try. He punched the would be rapist and broke his nose, then entangled his sword with his own and disarmed the man. He seized his wrist and spun, and the ruffian dropped to one knee howling in pain as his wrist bones shattered. Lynch swung his empty crossbow in a short arc and broke the man's opposite collarbone. He stared stupidly for a moment into Lynch's face.

"Who *are* you?" he asked.

"Does it matter?" Lynch asked in return. He stalked behind the man and silently broke his neck. His lifeless body tumbled limply to the cold stone courtyard. Lynch drew a deep breath and slowly composed himself. He walked quickly to the girl and knelt beside her. Her eyes darted wildly from side to side.

"I won't harm you," Lynch assured her. As soon as her hands were free she jerked the gag from her mouth.

"Don't touch me," she hissed.

Lynch grinned. "You're welcome." He handed her a blanket. "Cover yourself. That may help me think straight." He leaned in to adjust the blanket and the girl kicked him in the balls. Lynch hunched forward, hands on his knees. "Goddammit, what the hell did you do that for?"

"You stared a bit too long," the girl answered. She shook the ropes from her ankles and rose to adjust the blanket around her shoulders. She offered one hand to Lynch, who took it warily. "I am called La'Nay."

Lynch forced himself to ignore the agony in his groin. As he rose back to his full height, a shadow fell across him. It was huge. Then a crushing impact drove most of the air from his lungs and he was lifted from the courtyard and thrown ten feet through the air. He landed and rolled, then leaped to his feet and stood weaving like a drunk. Across the fire, his attacker loomed, hunching his massive shoulders menacingly. He stood at least eight feet tall, with legs the size of pine logs and a great shaggy mane of coarse black hair that flowed down to the middle of his back. Lynch observed that in a fraction of a second. He was certain the thing was only partially human, if any. Then it attacked.

Lynch was forced to give ground, dodging and blocking blows that should have dropped him in his tracks, and the entire time he searched for a weakness. The beast showed no fatigue. Lynch blocked a blow and slipped in close enough to drive three lighting quick punches into the beast's ribs. He felt the impact clear up to his shoulders, but the beast didn't even slow down. It grabbed Lynch by the collar and the crotch and flung him back over the fire. Lynch landed heavily, but was on his feet like a cat. His body went cold, and he saw everything with startling clarity. He felt no pain.

Lynch leaped the fire, then crouched low and swept his foot in a vicious kick to the side of the beast's knee. He felt the cartilage give, but the beast stayed on its feet. It looped a long punch which struck Lynch on the left side of his face. The beast's fist was large enough to break his nose at the same time. He felt like a boulder had dropped on his head. He rolled frantically away from the beast and struggled to his feet. Black spots danced across his vision.

"Fuck it," he growled. Lynch swept his cloak back and drew his sword, enchanting it with Dark Magic as it cleared his scabbard. The blade glowed brightly in the moonlight. Once again Lynch cast aside all physical impairment. He took three fast steps back towards the beast as it charged him. One strike cut off the left arm at the elbow, and as the beast howled in pain Lynch lifted his lips in an answering snarl and slashed the beast three times across the midsection. Its entrails burst out in glistening coils and the beast stared at them in disbelief. Lynch sliced open the beast's throat with a backhand slash and its lifeblood sprayed out in a fountain. Another swift strike severed the beast's head, and its body tumbled to the ground. Lynch dropped to one knee. His face felt like it was as big as a melon and he had lost the hearing in his left ear. Blood trickled from a gash left by the beast's hoary fist. A light touch on his shoulder startled him, and he leaped back to his feet with his blade drawn back. It was La'Nay, her hands held out to ward him off. She stepped back, frightened by what she saw in his eyes. Then he sagged back to the stones.

"Might have been easier if you hadn't kicked me in the balls," he muttered thickly.

The young man who had intervened earlier had risen up to one elbow sometime during the battle. "Who *are* you?" he asked.

"I wish people would quit asking me that," Lynch groaned. Then he slumped down onto the stones and slipped into darkness.

Lynch awoke a few hours before dawn. He was lying on a pad made of blankets, none of which appeared to be too clean, next to a crackling fire. The warmth felt good on his exposed skin. Visions of the fight flashed through his mind. He suddenly realized he felt *good*. Too good, actually. He ran a hand wonderingly over his face. There was no swelling. His nose felt crooked, but it didn't hurt either. He felt a ridge of scar tissue running from his left ear out onto his cheekbone. But he had healed. The girl was watching him. He cocked an eyebrow at her.

"I cast a healing spell," La'Nay said.

"You're a witch," Lynch replied. He wanted her. He also understood who had sent the plea for help he had heard in his sleep.

"I'm a Dragonwitch," La'Nay responded. "And who are you?"

Lynch rolled his eyes. "I wish people would stop asking me that. My name is L…Lemuel." He glanced at the courtyard. "Lemuel Stone." His glance fell on the Book, which was still partially visible. "I'm a librarian." He leaned over and covered the Book.

The youth approached with an armload of firewood. "A librarian?" He repeated in disbelief.

"Lemuel?" La'Nay said.

Lynch rose from the blankets and extended his hand to La'Nay. "Lemuel Stone, at your service."

La'Nay took his hand. The instant she did she felt desire pooling in her abdomen and spreading like molten metal through her groin and inner thighs. Whoever Lemuel Stone really was, he was definitely not a librarian.

"So what is that?" the youth asked. He pointed at the remains of the beast Lynch had slaughtered. Even as they watched the remains began to smoke and dissolve. Lynch shrugged.

"Looks like a Were-demon to me. Half man, half Demon. Sometimes they look more human," he said.

"How does a librarian know that?" La'Nay asked.

"You can learn a lot from the type of books I read," Lynch replied. "Who are you, boy?"

"Victor," the boy replied. "I joined up with…them," he indicated the dead renegades, "at the start of the Revolution. When they captured her I knew I had to set her free."

"That took guts," Lynch said. "But it wasn't real smart. Are there more bands of renegades here?"

"I reckon," Victor replied. "Since the Revolution renegades are thicker than flies. There's no more law, mister. The *magii'ri* are scattered."

"All it takes is one leader," Lynch had intended to plant that seed within this young man's mind and leave, but then he realized what an incredible, *unbelievable* profit could still be made from the Revolution. Not the spoils of an entire country, but here he stood at the ground level of a new government, and the magii'ri were still strong enough to restore order. And, he reflected, to handsomely reward those who helped their cause. He made his decision. "I'm just a simple man," he said as La'Nay and the boy exchanged skeptical glances. "But it occurred to me that this terrible, bloody Revolution may actually serve a purpose to benefit the common man. Did you know," he wheeled to face the boy directly, "that the Governor of lower Elanderfeld was involved in nearly every illegal activity that transpired in this fair city? The crown jewel, the shipping center of Norland, and the Governor himself was a common criminal. No wonder the honest law abiding citizens finally were outraged enough to take action! Now I have realized that honest men, good, decent, law abiding men such as myself must step forward and take on the responsibility of rebuilding this great country of ours."

La'nay stared at Lynch one eyebrow cocked. "You want to become a politician?"

"Oh, gods no." Lynch laughed. "But I might organize a few good men to begin restoring order until the *magii'ri* can take over." The more he thought about it, the more Lynch thought that his business with Timon could wait. He was probably already too far ahead to track. He might even already have found a portal and slipped back to another time. He stared at the young Dragonwitch and his resolve to punish Timon wavered. It had been a towering inferno, now it was a mere candle, guttering in its own wax at the end of the wick. Staying in Elanderfeld would be immensely profitable, and he *knew* if he stayed he would eventually part the pretty thighs of one incredibly arousing Dragonwitch. His decision was made.

"Are you a Warrior?" La'Nay asked, point blank.

"Umm, that is, I have been versed in combat. Yes," Lynch answered.

"Any idiot could see that," La'Nay said. "But I asked if you are a Warrior. Are you *magii'ri*?"

Lynch cleared his throat, rolled his eyes, and flung his hands up theatrically. "I was. I am a former *magii'ri* Warrior. There. Are you satisfied?"

"The *magii'ri* are not known for releasing their ranks. How do you come to be a former Warrior and still live?" La'Nay asked.

Lynch shrugged dramatically. "It's such a long story, and we have so much to do. It was nothing more than a misunderstanding really."

La'Nay chose to drop the subject, but it was far from closed. "What do you mean, we have so much to do?"

"I came here seeking a man," Lynch began.

"You don't seem the type," La'Nay replied quickly.

"Believe me, Dragonwitch, when the time comes you will know I am definitely not that type. But," Lynch continued, "I came here seeking an apothecary named Fergus, and I must see him before I can fully resolve my business and focus on the task of rebuilding Norland to surpass her former glory."

Lynch had to admit the sudden reversal of his plans, to profit from restoring Norland rather than simply looting and pillaging a deserted countryside, held much more appeal. It may even seem gallant, he thought, to certain female company.

"I also seek a man," La'Nay said.

"Ah," Lynch said knowingly. "A suitor? Perhaps even a fiance?" He scowled suddenly. "Certainly not your husband?" A husband or fiance' would complicate matters, but he had dealt with such men who stood in his way before.

La'Nay shook her head. "None of those. The man I seek is a legend, perhaps nothing more. He was an extraordinary Warrior and even a gifted Wizard."

Lynch stilled. "Why do you seek him?" he asked casually. Mentally he prepared for an attack.

"He...has something I need," La'nay answered. "The man's name is Slagg."

Lynch was blindsided. "Slagg?" he muttered. A huge grin stole across his face. "You wish to meet Slagg because he stole something of yours?"

"He has something I need," La'Nay corrected.

A chuckle escaped Lynch, followed by a bray of laughter that he could not contain.

"Do not have fun at my expense," La'Nay warned, her eyes flashing.

"I am sorry," Lynch apologized. "It's just that...well, I know Slagg. And I can't imagine him having anything a desirable young woman such as yourself might need or want."

"Wait just a damn minute," La'Nay said quickly. "You know him? You know Slagg?"

"I do," Lynch was suddenly wary again. Just how much of the legend of Slagg did this Dragonwitch know? *Idiot,* he chided himself. She's a Dragonwitch. Obviously she'd know the legend of Slagg. "I should say I *knew* him long ago," Lynch corrected himself. He winced as La'Nay raised one eyebrow at that statement. *Goddamnit,* Lynch mentally cursed. All this young siren had to do was sway her hips and shake her ample breasts and his mind went to mush.

"Boy," he called. "Victor?"

The young man had been watching this exchange with complete confusion.

"Yes sir?" he replied, suspicion that Lemuel Stone was a madman was strong in his mind.

"I'm going to clean up Elanderfeld," Lynch announced. His old dash and swagger was back. "You can be with me or against me," his gaze focused undeniably on the sooty stain where the Were-demon had dissolved. "Pass the word among the various Warlords to meet with me at noon tomorrow in the courtyard by the executioner's block." Victor hesitated. "Now." Lynch said quietly.

Victor nodded mutely and ran into the rapidly disappearing darkness.

La' Nay watched him go. "You're no librarian," she stated as her gaze swept over Lynch again. "If you knew Slagg, you must be a Wizard."

Lynch sighed. "The name I use is Lynch." He looked deep into La'Nay's eyes and saw several emotions. Surprise, yes. A slight touch of fear, definitely. But the last emotion was the one which aroused his interest the most. He saw desire, naked and hot, burning in her eyes. "Why do you seek Slagg?"

La'Nay smiled. "My reasons are my own, Wizard. And they shall remain that way. For now," she added. She nodded slightly in the direction Victor had taken. "You do know the Warlords will come for your head."

"I would expect no less," Lynch replied.

"Yet you still intend to meet them." La'Nay stated.

"I wouldn't say that, exactly. But to round them all up in one place is... ah...convenient," Lynch assured her. "It's the only way to begin restoring order to this land."

"And how can you restore order if they kill you?"

"Many have come for the head of Lynch and all have failed," Lynch responded. "If I have to kill the Warlords to restore order, I will. Once I have decided upon a course, nothing sways me." He locked eyes with La'Nay, his meaning clear in his gaze.

La'Nay stared at him. The look in her eyes was calculating, as if she was taking his measure. "I believe you, Wizard," she replied. "I have seen a sample of your strength. Perhaps, if you live to see another nightfall, I may suspend my search for Slagg, at least momentarily."

Lynch caught the promise in her words, and resolved to have her. He actually began to hope the Warlords would come itching for a fight. It seemed one particularly tasty young Dragonwitch had an intense attraction to power, and he fully intended to show her that he, Lynch, the Dragonrider and Thief, was the most powerful man she had ever known.

Lynch led La'Nay back to the governor's mansion. He carelessly struck a light in several lamps that hung from the ceiling and showed La'Nay to a separate room close to the one he had chosen. He even helped her to draw a hot bath, and waited impatiently for her to undress. La'nay stared at him in pointed silence until he surrendered and left the room. Only then did she step out of her filthy, torn dress and sink into the hot water with a long sigh. Lynch grinned on the other side of the locked door, tantalizing visions of La'Nay's supple body parading through his imagination. He returned to his own room and stowed his Book in a safe place, guarded by several killing spells. Then he slept dreamlessly until the first rays of sunlight illuminated the mansion.

Lynch paused at La'Nay's door only long enough to assure himself she still slept there then he searched the streets and deserted homes until he discovered a few chickens. In short order he found where they had nested and pilfered a half dozen eggs. He entered a store through the gaping hole where a window had been and looked around until he found a spilled sack of flour. Happy with his treasures, he returned to the governor's mansion and made hardtack biscuits and eggs in the gigantic kitchen. Then he carried it all back to La'Nay's room and knocked politely. La'Nays eyes widened appreciatively when she saw Lynch bearing a hot breakfast and together they devoured it.

Lynch arose and bowed grandly. "Thank you, my dear, for joining me. Now, if you'll excuse me, I have an appointment."

"I thought you told the Warlords to meet you at noon?" La'Nay asked.

"I did," Lynch agreed. "But since I am not a trusting soul, I think I'll go down a little early and have a look. You should wait here." The truth was, Lynch did not want the Dragonwitch anywhere near his meeting. She could cloud his thoughts with a glance, and knew he'd need his wits if as many Warlords and profiteers showed up as he expected. But he felt good. Better than he had in some time, in fact, and the old lust for battle and bloodshed was growing exponentially inside him.

He arrived at the Executioner's block from a secretive route and stood well concealed until he had examined every possible ambush site. Two such places were already occupied. Lynch grinned. These boys didn't believe in taking chances. He slipped back down the alley and climbed the back wall of one occupied building, slithered through the shadows until he stood behind one assassin, and killed him with a quick strike of his knife. Then he exited the building the same way he had come in, and dispatched the other ambusher in the same manner. He dragged the dead man from his chair and unceremoniously dumped his body in the floor then he leaned back in the same chair out of sight from the street below. Lynch sat motionless for nearly an hour when yet another assassin stealthily climbed to the second floor of a building opposite him and leaned a crossbow against the window jam. Lynch shot him through the heart with his own crossbow as he prepared to sit and watch the street below. He shook his head. They didn't take chances, but they were not very original.

As the sun neared its zenith, several men warily approached the square. Lynch knew they only waited for his death to resume their own power struggles, but for the moment they appeared to have come to a truce. Lynch chuckled. He wondered how long they had stayed up the night before trying to convince each other they wouldn't be ambushed at the meeting. He rose and stepped back from the window and checked the edge of his sword. He watched in satisfaction as Victor approached the group, assuring the Warlords that the man who had summoned them was indeed a Warrior of note. Lynch enchanted his sword with a quick spell and hurried to meet them.

Victor saw him coming, and directed the Warlord's attention to him. There were five of them, Lynch noted, which meant perhaps only two had not tried to have him ambushed before even hearing his intentions. As he neared the group, he carefully noted two of the men who surreptitiously glanced at the second levels of nearby buildings.

"I am Lynch," he announced when he was still some twenty feet away.

One of the Warlords broke from the group and ran. Lynch let him run until he was fifty yards out, then he shot him between the shoulder blades with his crossbow. Of the remaining four, two were those who had tried to set him up. Victor began to back away from the group.

"There's no reason to drag this out," Lynch stated flatly. "I already took care of your boys, so some of you might want to make a quick decision. Either you cut and run like your pal just did, which makes you lower than a yellow bellied skunk, or you do the job yourself." He opened his duster and indicated his sword.

Two of the warlords exchanged glances. Both were big, surly looking men, with knotted muscles and the scars won in hard fought battles. The taller of the two smiled slightly, then stepped forward as he drew his blade. The other man quickly followed suit.

"You don't know what you got yourself into, mister," the bigger man said confidently. "Jenks, you take him from the left."

They closed in swiftly, but nothing could have prepared them for the speed with which Lynch moved. Neither man even saw him draw his sword. It seemed to appear in his hand, and then they were both bleeding. Jenks knew he couldn't stand against that man, even on his best day, but he would not quit. Anger blossomed on the bigger man's features, however, he saw that he had been played for a fool. Then Lynch simply cut them down. He stood over their bodies, tall and menacing.

"The *magii'ri* will come back," Lynch said to the remaining two Warlords. "And their justice will be brutal. Stand with me in restoring order, and I swear you will be rewarded. Stand against me," he indicated the two dead men, "and you will join them."

The remaining men stared at him suspiciously, but neither had a death wish so they chose not to oppose him. Lynch could see the hate and distrust playing across their expressions. They would follow his orders for awhile, maybe as long as a few months. If the profits were high enough, they might follow him for half a year. But one day when his back was turned they both intended to rule once again. Little did they know of the man they now faced.

"I'll round up the boys," one said. The othe merely nodded his assent and they both left the courtyard.

Lynch breathed a gusty sigh of relief when they were out of sight. If they had chosen to attack him with their full force, he would have been hard pressed to escape with his life. But he had read his opponents accurately. They respected strength and courage, and they valued their own lives even more than Lynch did his own. He sat on the edge of the well and wished for a bottle of whiskey.

From across the courtyard, opposite of the direction the former warlords had taken, La'Nay watched intently. Her hands had gone first to her bodice, then to the juncture of her thighs, when Lynch had so easily mastered the two brutes who challenged him. Even now desire raged within her. Her entire body cried out with the need to be filled, but she slipped away before Lynch could discover her.

She hurried back towards the governor's mansion, and along the way she caught a young rooster and wrung his neck. By the time Lynch returned the maddening smell of frying chicken wafted from the servant's kitchen. La'Nay had also found a few dried apples, and made a pie with some of Lynch's purloined flour. Lynch spied the change in her immediately, and despite his hunger and the excellence of the food, he barely tasted it in his anticipation of what he hoped was coming. He didn't have long to wait. No sooner had they finished the meal than La'nay walked near to Lynch's chair, and he looped a long, sinewy arm around her waist.

La'Nay felt dizzy with lust, and when she felt the strength of Lynch's one armed embrace her desire burst into flame. She went to him willingly, and crushed her mouth to his. Their hands flew over each other's body, each seeking and finding evidence of the other's instant arousal. In moments their clothing lay scattered across the floor and Lynch held La'Nay, one arm pinned to either side of her head, spread eagled across the table. Their eyes met for an instant then he plunged into her. Their mating was fierce and passionate, and their hunger was so strong they did not relent until the sun dipped below the western horizon.

Lynch's days were filled with the activity of recruiting and organizing his own personal police force and his nights were occupied with La'Nay. He dealt with insubordination or resistance the way he always had, swiftly and lethally. In short order he amassed a deadly group of mercenaries who were totally loyal only to him. His one demand was strict adherence to the Code of the *magii'ri,* and through it all La'Nay watched him with her calculating gaze.

From time to time Lynch heard rumors of a dark and savage man with a constant grin who terrorized the lawbreakers further inland, and occasionally he sent men out to investigate. They always came back with the same story; the man claimed to be *magii'ri* and tried to convince others to follow him but none would. The *magii'ri* were almost universally reviled, and this man had that against him as well as the color of his skin. He never revealed his name, but Lynch knew beyond a doubt he was Smilin' Jake.

# CHAPTER THIRTY ONE

HREE YEARS PASSED, LONG years filled with hard work. Luke filled out, adding pounds of muscle to his frame. Hudge took Mathias under his wing and trained him and Luke together even though Luke showed the typical Warrior's clumsiness with magic. But even though he was still young, he showed an aptitude for combat beyond anything Hudge had even heard of. Finally, during one training session Luke inadvertently dropped the older man to his knees with a blow that he could not slow down. He grabbed Hudge by the upper arm, concern evident in his expression.

"Hudge!" Luke called frantically. "Hudge, are you alright?"

To Hudge, Luke's voice sounded like he was at the bottom of a well. Finally, the black spots ceased floating across his vision and he felt that he could breathe again.

"I'm alright," he grunted. "Let me catch my breath." Several anxious minutes later he did. He stood unsteadily. "That's it." he said with a final shake of his head. "No more. If I try to teach you any more you're gonna end up killin' me."

From that day on, Luke wandered into the forest on a daily basis, where he stayed until the sun was low in the sky, training until his body glistened with sweat. He ate whatever he could find, hunting and foraging, and his body responded well. He didn't know that his training regimen surpassed even that of the old Trueblood Warriors.

It was a fine spring day when Luke first met Lynch. He had just finished going through a series of maneuvers with a short sword and had finished off his "opponent", a bundle of tree branches, with a quick thrust. He stood with his blade buried within it, imagining it was one of the men who had killed his father.

"Not bad," a voice announced at his shoulder. He spun, blade held low, but then winced in pain as it was knocked from his grasp. He attacked the intruder with his fists and even managed to land a blow or two before he was knocked sprawling by a speedy, open handed blow. Luke prepared to lunge to his feet.

"Smilin' Jake got one thing right, there's no quit in you," his attacker said. "But you're training is lacking. Jake must be slipping."

"Jake ain't here," Luke replied, angered at how easily he had been bested.

"What?" Lynch said. "What do you mean, he ain't here? Did something happen to him?"

"He went back to Norland," Luke replied, hesitant to reveal too much to this stranger.

"Is that right?" Lynch mused. "When was that?"

"Three years ago. He went back to set things right," Luke said, "and when I'm bigger I'm goin' back to join him."

Lynch grinned, which sent chills down Luke's spine. He had been right, the renegade who terrorized the lawless element in the wilds of Norlad was Smilin' Jake. "My name is Lynch," he said as he offered his right hand.

Luke took it warily. The instant Lynch's grip closed on his own, he saw a flash of white hot light and his mind was clouded with confusion. He shook his hand free and stepped back. He knew the name, and now he knew instinctively that Lynch was a dangerous man, perhaps more dangerous than any he had ever known.

"I'm Luke," he said, keeping a watchful eye on the Dark Wizard.

"I know who you are," Lynch replied. "And you know me, at least by reputation. I made a vow to your Father several years ago, and since Jake ain't here I guess I'll have to keep it."

"What vow? What are you talkin' about?"

"Jake told your Father he'd watch out for you, and if he could not, then it was up to me. Since Jake ain't here, he ain't doin' his job. So," Lynch played his hole card, "I guess I'll just have to take you back to Norland with me."

"You'll take me back to Norland?" Luke asked. "No shit?"

Lynch grinned. "No shit."

"Let me get my stuff," Luke said. He started back down the trail to the village. Lynch trailed along, congratulating himself for accurately reading the boy's desire for revenge. As for his own part, he still wasn't sure. Was he interested in molding the boy into a defender of the Light, or did he just intend to use him as yet another tool? It made no difference to Lynch, he realized. The end result was what counted, not the reasons for obtaining it.

"My friends will want to come along," Luke announced suddenly.

"No," Lynch replied automatically. "One responsibility is more than enough."

"I ain't no responsibility," Luke stated flatly. "I can hold my own on the trail, and I know more than a little about sailing a ship. If they don't go, I don't go."

Lynch began to formulate an argument when they stopped in front of a hut and Mathias stepped out. He looked full into Lynch's face, and Lynch's mind recoiled while he held his body stock still. His face betrayed none of the emotions that roiled inside him. The boy was marked as a Wizard, that was certain. Not only a Wizard, but one of the Old Ones.

"I suppose one more won't hurt," Lynch said carefully. He wondered briefly how much of the natural ability this boy had tapped into already, and he decided he'd better not let his guard down. Then the girl followed Mathias out into the sunlight.

"How many friends have you got?" Lynch asked suspiciously.

Luke grinned. "Just two. Mathias and Mariel. We came over from Norland together, and we all want to go back."

"The way back is more difficult than the way here," Lynch assured them. "The seas are controlled by pirates, and my ship crashed in the storm. We'll take a skiff to Gryllis, then go overland across the Southron Desert to Bernfeld and that will take a very long time. Can you keep up?"

All three asserted that they could, and Lynch was secretly pleased. He wanted time, time to probe that young Wizard named Mathias, and time to teach young master Luke a thing or two not usually found in *magii'ri* training. He smiled again. Things were looking up. His old luck was returning, and not a moment too soon.

"Grab your things," Lynch said. "I have a man waiting with a skiff, but he won't wait for long." He tried to act indifferent, but inwardly he seethed at every delay. He did not want to be there when Hudge returned.

All three ducked into the hut and Lynch heard them rummaging around. In moments they returned. Each carried a small pack and they all had bows and a quiver full of arrows apiece.

"We should tell Hudge," Mariel said suddenly. "So he won't worry."

"I left him a note," Mathias answered. "By the tea kettle. He'll see it at supper."

"Then we're off," Lynch interjected. "We really must hurry."

He led the way, and they reached the beach quickly. The man with the skiff was a tall, bearded old man with unkempt, long, stringy hair that Luke recognized from his visits to bring supplies to the village. They cast off, and as the small sail filled with wind the little boat fairly skimmed over the waves.

"Ye barely made it," he complained to Lynch. "As it is we'll be til' dark comin' into Gryllis. I told you I don't want to be out here after sunset."

"Quit your bellyaching'" Lynch ordered gruffly. "I told you I'd pay double if we're out after dark."

"Gotta make it back first," the sailor replied. "I told ya, I seen things that ain't natural out here after dark."

"We'll handle it," Lynch said sharply.

"I reckon," the sailor said with a speculative look at Lynch.

As he had predicted, the sun sank below the western horizon before they could see land. Lynch hauled out a lantern, but the sailor shook his head.

"No light. It's best to slip by quiet and hope to remain unseen."

They glided along silently until dusk had settled in. Lynch nudged Luke, then held his finger to his lips and pointed below them. Far below, down in the depths, Luke could see a glimmering light. It became brighter and took shape as it closed the distance between them until Luke could see it looked like an octopus. But it was huge, and continued to glow with an unnatural light. It soared effortlessly through the inky black water and slowly reached one enormous tentacle to the surface. Lynch calmly placed his hand on the hilt of his sword. The tentacle missed the skiff by less than a foot, then splashed back into the sea. The octopus retreated until it was barely visible. Lynch grinned. He supposed he could have placed a concealment spell on the group, but with the boy Mathias being marked as a Wizard of the Light, he really didn't know how a spell of Dark Magic would have reacted. Finally the winking lights of a portside village became visible. Mathias started to speak, but Lynch silenced him with a glare.

The sailor didn't drop canvas at all. He let the small boat plow firmly into the sand, then he jumped out and ran up the beach, beckoning the others to hurry. They all followed him, and as they hit the beach a glowing tentacle rose from the sea and smashed the little boat to bits. Mariel screamed before Lynch could clamp a hand to her mouth. He scooped her up and ran for the treeline, but another tentacle wrapped around his leg and he fell flat. Mariel tumbled and rolled across the sand, then quickly sat up. Luke drew Lynch's sword and chopped the tentacle in two inches from Lynch's calf. Lynch made it to his feet and they scrambled for the safety of the treeline, where the sailor waited.

"Told ya," he said calmly.

"Shut up," Lynch replied. "We made it, didn't we?"

The sailor grinned. "Sort of. Ya might wanna cut that off, before it pinches yer leg in two."

Lynch grimaced as he sat in the sand and drew out his knife. He slid it between his calf muscle and the slowly contracting scrap of tentacle that still clung to it. He sliced it in two and tossed the pieces out onto the sand, where they began flopping towards the sea. He stood and fished out two gold pieces.

"A new skiff will cost me a silver piece," the sailor said hopefully.

"Fine," Lynch groaned. He dug out a bag and scooped out a silver piece.

"My riggin' is gone too," the sailor said.

Lynch shot him a murderous glare.

"Fine, fine," the old sailor said, backing away. "Can't blame a feller fer tryin'."

Lynch wasted no time leading his charges away from the tiny port village of Gryllis. He did not want to risk anyone seeing Mathias and recognizing him as one of the few Chosen Wizards. Most *magii'ri* Wizards were born to Wizards or Witches and had to be tested to determine if they had any aptitude for magic themselves. But not the Old Ones, recognized by the different color of their eyes. In all his years, Lynch had never seen one of the Old Ones. Until now.

Lynch pushed them hard, but at daybreak he conceded a short rest and a hot meal. He chose that time to begin his assessment of Mathias.

"Things have changed in Norland since you left," he began. "The Revolution left the country in near ruins. The *magii'ri* have been decimated, but enough remain to begin reorganizing the country and in time order will be restored, at least to the core areas. The Borderlands have returned to a wild state, thanks to the culmination of the Wilding."

"The Wilding!" Mathias exclaimed. "I knew it was coming. I saw all the signs. Have Dragons returned to the skies?"

Lynch looked at him with a speculative gleam in his eyes. "You knew about the Wilding, eh? And where did you learn that?"

"I…can't say, actually," Mathias replied. "It's just something I knew."

"And Dragons?" Lynch persisted. "What do you know of Dragons?"

"Very little," Mathias admitted, suddenly feeling very self conscious.

Lynch nodded, far from satisfied but willing to bide his time. "What would you say if I told you there are Dragons about once again?"

Mariel drew closer to Luke and the meager comfort of their tiny fire.

"My parents were killed by a Dragon," Mathias answered in a low voice. "I saw it, but I was powerless to help. I tried, I really did. But I couldn't move."

Lynch nodded. "Dragonmagic. Very few are able to withstand it. I can teach you, if you'd like."

"You can counter Dragonmagic?" Mathias asked eagerly.

"I can," Lynch answered sagely. "I have quite a few tricks up my sleeve. Was it a random attack?"

"What?" Mathias asked, caught off guard. He thought for a moment. "No, I don't think it was. It was looking for something."

"Something, or someone," Lynch mused. A faraway look came into is eyes and he seemed to drift off, then he roused himself. "Never mind that. I think that's quite enough about Dragons for now anyway. Think about them too much and it's like a beacon to them, drawing them right in. And we don't want that!"

"Jake's one of the Warriors fighting in Norland," Luke interrupted. "You said there was *magii'ri* trying to restore order. That's why Smilin' Jake went back."

Lynch nodded. "I was probably only a few days out of port from Elanderfeld when he was coming in."

"You said the Borderlands are wild now. Would that be where Jake might be?" Luke asked, and Lynch realized the boy was thinking ahead, trying to pinpoint Jake's location so he could find him if something went wrong. That pleased him.

"He probably is in the Borderlands," Lynch responded. "Still defending the people of Norland." He rolled his eyes. "Then again, I haven't heard any stories of him lately."

"He's following the Code," Luke asserted.

Lynch grinned. "I reckon so. What do you know of the Code, boy?"

"I know the Code. So do Mathias and Mariel." They nodded in agreement.

"So you know part of the Code is fealty to the King. But there is no King, and there will probably never be another," Lynch said.

"The Code is all about doing what is right and honorable," Luke said. "Nobody needs a King to tell them that."

"True," Lynch agreed. "But I know the Code as well, and I can tell you that the authors of the Code, your forefathers, never intended it to bind them or their heirs to the wishes of a ruling class. And that is exactly what happened. In the end, by following the Code to the letter, the *magii'ri* almost destroyed themselves. So listen close," Lynch drew a ragged breath, "the Code is flawed. The only thing that matters is what a man," he looked at Mariel, "or a woman can do and what they cannot do. In the end, survival is all that matters."

"Survival without honor is worse than dying," Luke argued, repeating it from memory.

Lynch stared at Luke for some time before replying. "I was a good friend of your Father's, boy, and I don't name my friends lightly. He was the most honorable man I have ever encountered. But it was his sense of honor that led him to his death. That blind reliance on the Code was taught just as the High Speech was pounded into every Warrior and Wizard. But the Warriors could slip in and out of the High Speech as circumstances dictated, an ability they could not transfer to their sense of honor."

"Are you honorable, Mr. Lynch?" Mathias asked.

Lynch shook his head. "I am not an honorable man. I take what I need from anyone who has it. The only law I live by is *my* law. I am the Master I serve."

"But can't a man live as you have lived, and still be an honorable man?" Luke asked.

Lynch grinned. "I suppose so. If a man of strong honor and rock solid will learned to embrace all the teachings of the Dark and the Light and bend them to serve only the Light, he would still be an honorable man. And perhaps a formidable man as well. As I said, I did nothing of the sort. I used Dark Magic indiscriminately for my own gain."

"Can you teach us?" Mathias asked. "To use it only for the good of the Light?"

Lynch grinned again. This had been far too easy. "I believe I can."

Two weeks later, he was forced to reconsider. Mathias took to his teachings well enough, but despite every effort, Mariel showed absolutely no aptitude for magic whatsoever. As for Luke, he steadfastly refused to even attempt to learn magic. In all his many years Lynch had to admit he had never encountered anyone as stubborn as the son of Lorn Graywullf. He had taken to any type of training that involved warcraft and he could speak the High Speech if he deigned to do so, but he seemed to revel in his crude Warrior upbringing. To Luke, the Light was the Light, and Dark was Dark. There was no in between. And anything he determined to serve the Dark was to be destroyed. Including those who dabbled in Dark Magic. He kept a wary eye on Lynch at all times.

As far as his training in combat, Lynch was astounded. Luke was proficient with longbow as well as the crossbow. He could fight with a knife hand to hand, or he could throw it accurately at surprising distances. His foot work was flawless when he and Lynch fenced, and he possessed uncanny speed. Lynch soon realized that the only physical advantage he had over the boy was size and strength, and even at that Luke was stronger than many grown men. In time he would become a formidable Warrior. But now they faced the most dangerous leg of the overland journey, the route through the tip of the Southron Desert.

Lynch had deliberately worked his younger companions harder than he thought necessary in an effort to toughen them for this part of the journey. Even he had no real idea what adversaries they might face in that vast, open space covered only by scrub brush and cactus, and broken by canyons that weren't visible until one was upon them. He did know water and game was scarce, and could even be more scarce because of the increasing strength of the Wilding. They were camped on the outskirts of the desert, waiting for a tiny spring he had uncovered to replenish, when Mathias brought up the subject of the Dragonspawn.

"Why is everyone so reluctant to enlist the aid of the Dragonspawn?" he asked, as he bent to draw a cupful of water into a waterskin as big around as his upper leg.

Lynch hesitated. How much should he tell this aspiring Wizard?

"The Dragonspawn is unpredictable, at best," Lynch said. "He could turn on the powers of the Light as easily as those of the Dark."

"I have studied the legend of the Dragonspawn for as long as I can remember," Mathias said. "And I have never found the spell necessary to create it."

"That is one spell I do not know," Lynch was forced to admit. "It's too dangerous, too unpredictable. I'm not sure the spell even exists anymore." But in the back of his mind, hidden from the outside world, it was like a light had burst into life inside his head. *She told you outright she was a Dragonwitch, you lust addled idiot!* Who else would be entrusted with a spell as powerful as that used to create the Dragonspawn? And she would know all about the prophecy. La'Nay had used him, and easily at that. The realization unsettled him. He had been all too willing to provide her with anything she wanted, including his seed. The seed of a Trueblood *magii'ri*. But she had not conceived. Was he not powerful enough? Preposterous! But then he thought of the day La'Nay had told him she was leaving, and the feeling of emptiness that followed. Another thought struck him. Did she actually have a Dragon's semen? There was only one bull Dragon left that he knew of, and that was Slagg.

"I am such an idiot," he muttered to himself. Of course she had visited Slagg, that was how his power had grown so suddenly. So she had the knowledge, she had the Dragon semen, all she needed was a Trueblood *magii'ri* to father her child. And he would be the Dragonspawn.

"It has to," Mathias voice interrupted his thoughts. "There is a prophecy which says the Dragonspawn will be created and will defeat the powers of the Dark forever."

"Better to focus on what *we* can do," Lynch argued. He couldn't believe that he was saying it. "Return to Norland and direct your energy into rebuilding the *magii'ri*. I am warning you, that will be a daunting task. The common blood citizens of Norland will not easily be convinced to trust the *magii'ri* again. But you must remain true, even if you have to live as outcasts in your own homeland." As for himself, he knew of a certain young Dragonwitch he would seek. He was certain that La'Nay was trying on her own to create the Dragonspawn, using herself as the host for the child. She would continue to search for a *magii'ri* strong enough to father the Dragonspawn with her, but finding such a man would be next to impossible. Lynch was certain of that. If *he* had been unable to impregnate her, who could possibly be strong enough?

"Suits me," Luke said. He thought about how quickly the citizens of Norland had turned against his father. He owed them no allegiance. His allegiance lay with following the Code and returning the Light to its former glory.

"The trail becomes harder every day from here on," Lynch warned. "We will have to rely on each other to make it through, and there will be no more time for me to teach you. I have to tell you we did not have one tenth of the time we needed for me to teach you everything I have learned. I take the blame for that entirely, but I know you could use my knowledge to reach your goals."

Lynch waited, seeming relaxed but genuinely disappointed that he could not impart his full knowledge to them. Inwardly, his entire being yearned for one of them to make the first move. Mathias obliged, driven by his unquenchable curiosity.

"Isn't there some way to…speed things up?" he asked.

Lynch smiled a tiny, satisfied smile. He hesitated for a calculated moment. "Well, there is one way. If we choose that way each of you will granted the full extent of my knowledge, which took me centuries to accumulate, in the areas in which you have shown aptitude."

"I would know everything you know about magic?" Mathias asked, suddenly extremely intrigued.

"Of course," Lynch replied smoothly, "and Luke would be more knowledgeable than any Warmaster. Even the *magii'ri* Warmasters of the old days were no match for my fighting prowess."

"And Mariel?" Luke asked.

"She will learn that which is most suitable to her," Lynch said.

"So what's the catch?" Luke asked.

"There is no catch," Lynch replied. "It's a simple spell of Dark Magic. The only price such a simple spell requires is your consent."

"I don't like Dark Magic," Luke said.

"You don't like magic at all," Mathias interrupted. "Think of it! I could be the most knowledgeable Wizard of the Light, and you could be the best trained, most knowledgeable Warrior in the history of the World! We could *make* history!"

Luke was dubious, and Mariel remained silent, pensively biting her lip. "No," she whispered.

"What was that?" Lynch whirled to face her.

Mariel cowered but did not back down. "I said no," she repeated. "You've brought us this far and taught us plenty, but we will not give you permission to defile us with Dark Magic."

"I'll be damned," Lynch said with a shake of his head. He turned and threw his tin cup into the darkness with all his strength. He started to speak several times and choked up, but he finally found his voice again. "Fine. Whatever."

"Whatever," Mariel repeated.

"What the…? Mariel," Mathias began.

"Stop," Mariel said steadfastly. "Just stop it, Mathias. You can be the most powerful Wizard the Light has ever seen just by applying what you already know. Leave it at that."

No more words were spoken. As had become their custom, Lynch took the first watch. He spent most of his time glaring furiously at Mariel. Mathias had been eager to accept what he offered and he knew he could have convinced Luke with promises of revenge. He had discounted the girl completely and she had been the one who resisted. He shrugged. It didn't really matter. It would have been easier and less dangerous for them all if they had agreed, but he could do it without their consent. After all, he was the Dark Wizard Lynch. He grinned and his unnaturally white teeth shined in the darkness as he crafted the spell to transfer his knowledge to the three sleeping teens. When they slept on undisturbed he knew it had been successful. If they had resisted, one or all of them would probably have thrashed about considerably. Before they died, of course. He awoke Luke for his turn at watch, and had to hide a satisfied smile when he saw a new gleam in the Warrior's eyes. Lynch slept soundly the rest of the night.

The going was easy at first, as Lynch knew it would be. But as the day wore on the terrain grew rougher. The scrub brush and cactus reached out with thorny hands to grasp at their clothing and even the shale under their feet seemed to slip at the most awkward moments. By late afternoon the heat of the sun had intensified and sweat ran in steady rivulets down the traveler's faces. Mariel stopped much too often to sip water from the skin which she carried slung about her waist, until Luke cautioned her to conserve what she had left. By the time they camped for the evening they were all exhausted.

Mathias began to gather sticks for a fire, but Luke stopped him.

"Best not do that," he said conversationally. "We been trailed most of the afternoon."

Lynch bared his teeth in a huge grin. "That we have," he agreed. "How many?"

"I seen four," Luke said. Mariel edged closer to him.

"That's my count, too," Lynch agreed. "What do you think we should do?"

"Post a guard," Luke said. "Take turns. Light out early come morning and walk until it gets too hot, then take shelter in whatever shade we can find. Then light out again in the evening. We can use the stars to guide us. If'n they follow through tomorrow or draw closer, we'll set up an ambush."

"Very good," Lynch agreed. "But why don't I just double back under the cover of darkness and kill them?" he asked the question in all seriousness.

"You don't know if they're friends or enemies," Mathias interrupted.

"Out here?" Lynch said as he gestured at the foreboding desert. He shrugged. "It's better than a fifty-fifty chance they're not ging to invite us for tea."

"We have to know. If they attack us, then we obviously fight back," Luke said. "We could scout them out, but they might catch on."

"My way is better," Lynch argued.

"The Code dictates that we must only engage enemies," Mathias said.

"And if there's no doubt, then we destroy them," Luke agreed.

"And that is the honorable way?" Lynch asked. He thought it was foolish to allow any unknown entity that close to their camp. It would be so much simpler to slip into their camp under the cover of darkness, knife them in their sleep, and continue on at a leisurely pace the next day.

"Yes!" the three youngsters answered almost in unison.

"Alright," Lynch replied irritably. "My answer was just a suggestion. Something so we could all sleep easier tonight."

"You don't get it, do you?" Luke asked later, as he prepared for his watch.

"What are you talking about?" Lynch said.

"You just can't go around killing everybody," Luke answered.

Lynch rubbed his bristly face. "I know, but sometimes I can't help my old habits. But you, my young friend, must realize that there will come a time, maybe many times in your life, that you can no longer tell friends from enemies. Then what will you do? Err on the side of self preservation and take a life that might be innocent, just on an off chance? Or put yourself and those you love in great danger by being too squeamish?"

Later, as Lynch sat in companionable silence, smoking a hand rolled cigarette as Luke kept watch, he asked, "What is it like, to kill someone?"

Lynch pondered that for so long Luke began to wonder if he would answer. Finally, he spoke. "I can't remember what it felt like the first time I had to kill a man in the line of duty. It was long, long ago, in a different World. After that, it came easy to me. Probably too easy. I know for a time I ceased to have a conscience, or any morals at all, and I will not say what I felt during that time. I know I speak lightly of killing now, and perhaps I have become nothing more than a beast myself." He stared into the darkness for several long moments. "I told someone not that long ago that killing was just what I did, like some men are farmers and some men are soldiers. I know that I'm good at it. I can look at a man or beast and I *know* where they are vulnerable. I know exactly where to sink the blade to kill or incapacitate them immediately. I don't even have to think about it. And I know when the time comes, master Luke, you will do what needs to be done. But it will mark you forever."

With that he wheeled away and stalked off into the night. The truth was, these young *magii'ri* were causing him to think too much, and too much introspection caused Lynch a great deal of discomfort. He was what he had become over centuries. Nothing would change that now, not even that tiny spark within him that was steadily trying to grow brighter. If he only could say one thing with certainty, it was that redemption was beyond him, and he was quite sure he didn't care.

The following day passed uneventfully, except for the fact that every step seemed to require a major effort. The sand shifted and sucked at their boots, and when they tried to stay in the rocks the shale slid and slipped and often left them falling to their knees. In short order their leggings were cut to ribbons and even their sturdy boots showed gashes in the tough bullhide. At noon they stopped in the scant shade of a scrubby mesquite to wait out the searing heat of the afternoon.

"We'll go on in the sand," Lynch ordered. "There's no way we can walk in the rocks in the dark."

"What about them fellers behind us?" Luke asked.

"I could eliminate them easily, but you won't abide by that," Lynch replied irritably. "So I guess we're just going to have to wait and see what their intentions are."

"They didn't draw no closer," Luke said. "And we didn't make very good time."

He wouldn't say it, but they all knew Mariel was slowing them down.

Lynch didn't answer, but he had noticed that the men trailing them hadn't gained any distance also. And that bothered him. He felt they were biding their time. But for what?

"Rest," Lynch said. "Nap if you want to. I'll keep watch."

Dusk came and went, and then full dark. Lynch rested, but he didn't sleep. The truth was, he didn't seem to need much sleep anymore. Instead he stayed awake and watched and thought. And as dusk deepened he saw the twinkling lights that could only be a village. There was one major problem. There had never been a village even in the tip of the Southron Desert. And these lights reached well into the night sky. That knowledge left him with an uneasy feeling wallowing around in the pit of his stomach. He nudged Luke and then Mathias.

Luke came awake quickly. "Why'd you let us sleep so long?"

Lynch pointed out the lights. The village was no more than a couple miles away. Then he pointed out that the men trailing them, or whatever they were, had split up into three groups. There were three campfires winking behind them, one directly behind and one off to each side.

"We're in it now," Lynch said quietly. "They're herding us right towards that village, and I can't say what we might find there. Besides, I never did take to bein' pushed." He rolled a cigarette. "The three of us could outrun 'em."

"There's four," Luke replied.

"Not if we leave the girl," Lynch said in a low voice.

"Not a chance," Luke stated emotionlessly. "You can run if you want to."

"Luke's right," Mathias agreed quickly. "I won't leave Mariel."

Lynch lit his cigarette. In the old days, and not so long ago, he would have left Mariel in the middle of the night to buy himself some time, and if the two boys had caused a fuss he'd have left them as well. Or killed them all. He let some of the tobacco smoke escape his nostrils. Actually, in the old days a comment such as Luke's would have had him in a murderous rage. Now he was quite surprised to note it barely stung his pride.

"Leaving her would not be honorable," Lynch finally decided. It was almost a question, but he didn't wait for an answer. He weighed that against his analysis of their chances of survival if they stuck together. "You three go on ahead, towards the village. But take your time. I'll double back and see what I can tell about the fellers trailin' us."

Luke agreed, and after a brief hesitation Mathias did also. Then Lynch was gone. One moment he stood next to them, the next he was just gone.

Luke bent and shook Mariel awake. Dark rings nearly encircled her eyes and she seemed groggy.

"We have to go," Luke said.

Mathias stood looking back at the campfires. "Do you think he'll come back?"

Luke shrugged. "Maybe. Maybe not. All we can do is push on." He gave Mariel his share of hardtack trail bread and several swallows of water from his waterskin.

"Let's go."

They walked slowly, on each side of Mariel. Both boys carried their swords at the ready, but no attack came. The gray light of dawn approached and the surrounding terrain slowly became distinguishable. The village came into view, but it was like no village any of them had ever seen. The tallest buildings any of them knew of were at the courtyard in Elanderfeld, and those were no more than three stories. Even at that distance it was obvious these buildings were much taller than that, and they were made of smooth faced bricks, not hand hewn stone. Realization hit Luke like a hammer.

"He's using us for bait."

"Oh shit," Mathias whispered fervently. "You're right."

They stopped at the outskirts of the village. Still no attack came, but Mathias felt the hair prickle at the base of his neck. Then, slowly, people began to emerge from the buildings. One noticed them and a cry of alarm sounded.

"Get ready," Luke said in a low voice. "Mariel, if it comes to a fight you cut and run back towards Lynch, fast as you can."

She nodded as the villagers gathered and approached them. They weren't armed with normal weapons, Luke noticed. Some carried clubs, others had axes or even dull garden spades.

"What do you think?" Luke asked.

"They look human," Mathias answered. "But it's hard to tell."

"I'd hoped for something more definite," Luke said as the villagers surrounded them. They *did* look human, and very young. Most were only a few years older than he. Some of the older men had heavy beard stubble, but they all looked relatively clean. Their clothing was made from a flimsy looking weave but the colors were amazing. Several of the men wore strange hats with bills in front, while a few others wore dark jackets over harsh white shirts. Over half of the group was black. Luke noticed that the blacks and whites seemed to split off from each other. As he studied them, he also noticed that while the suit wearers seemed open faced and rather scared, the rest, both black and white wearing short sleeved shirts and caps, had a gaunt and hungry look. There was no friendliness in their eyes. They seemed arrogant and aloof, and dangerous at the same time. Luke felt his palms begin to sweat. He targeted the most dangerous looking of the lot for his first strike, should trouble come.

"You speak English?" one asked.

"I reckon I understand you good enough," Luke answered. He had no idea what *English* was.

"Good." The young man who spoke seemed genuinely glad to see them. He was one of those wearing a dark jacket. "We've sent out search parties looking for help, but most of them never come back. Is your town close by?"

"N…" Luke began to answer, but a sharp nudge from Mathias' elbow stopped him.

"Not far," Mathias interrupted. "That's what he was sayin', not far. Sometimes he stutters." Luke shot him a murderous look, but Mathias ignored him. "How long has your village been here?"

"Village?" One of the men wearing a dark jacket laughed. "This isn't a village, it's part of the city of Denver."

"Denver? Never heard of it," Mathias replied. "Is it near Bernfeld?"

One of the cap wearers snickered. "Are you retarded? Denver is the biggest city in Colorado."

Luke looked around. He could plainly see the first and last buildings on each side of the village. "It don't look so big to me."

"It's big enough," the suit said.

"Shut up," one of the cap wearers said suddenly. "Here comes Bennie."

An enormously muscled black man approached them. He wore a short sleeved black shirt and a thin vest which bulged under each armpit. A shiny emblem shaped like a shield glittered in the sun high up on his left shoulder.

"What's the hold up?" he asked impatiently. "I told you to bring 'em in."

"Kid says they have a village close by," the first cap wearer said.

"Bullshit," Bennie said. "There's nothing within two or three days walk. We been that far."

He nodded in a friendly fashion at Luke, Mathias and Mariel. Broad gold hoops adorned his ears. When he smiled, a gold tooth winked in the sun. The smile never reached his eyes, which were cold and calculating as he surveyed the way they were armed. Luke studied him closely in return.

"Look," he said suddenly. "We can stand around out here until it's hotter than Hell, which don't seem to take long around here, or we can go in and talk in the shade." He looked slyly at Mariel. "We have water, too. Nice, cold, fresh water. Never runs out. Want some?"

Mariel pleaded with Luke with her eyes. She looked exhausted.

"Alright," Luke agreed.

"Yeah," Bennie said. "Alright. See?" he said to the cap wearer. "Was that so hard? We'll just go in and have a chat over a nice, cool drink."

Bennie led the way down the smoothest, flattest street any of them had ever seen into one of the tall buildings. Luke, Mariel and Mathias stopped just inside the doorway and stared in awe. The interior was a huge, open room paneled in dark wood and filled with tables and chairs. Glass windows filled the street side wall. A bar ran across one side. Bennie pulled out three chairs, then one for himself.

"Sit," he indicated the chairs. It was obviously not a request. "Now tell me boys, where are we and how in the Hell do I get out of here?"

Luke and Mathias glanced at each other.

"We're in the Sothron Desert. You have to walk to get anywhere," Luke answered with a shrug.

Bennie laughed mirthlessly. "You're a funny kid. No, I mean how do we get out of this *place?*"

"I don't know what you mean," Luke replied. "We were just tryin' to cross the desert. We don't mean anyone any harm. So, if you don't mind, we'd just like to fill our water skins and be on our way."

"I do mind," Bennie said. He reached under each arm with his opposite hand and brought out two very large pistols and sat them on the table. They were of a type Luke had never seen, but it was plain to him exactly what they were. Then he leaned back and allowed his vest to fall open. Luke saw at least three more magazines for each pistol.

"You see, we've been here long enough for all of us to get really damn hungry. And some of us got different types of hungry, if you know what I mean. There's no food and nothing' else except water. Now I don't know how in the fuck part of my neighborhood ended up in the middle of the fuckin' desert, but I'm ready to go back. Now you little shits are obviously not from Denver. That means you're from here. Which means you can tell me *how in the fuck I get out of this desert!*" Spit flew from his mouth as he shouted the last few words.

"That's exactly what we're trying to do, too," Mathias said calmly.

Bennie fixed his eyes on a spot above their heads. "He said you'd try to lie to me." He lowered his gaze to stare at Mathias. "He also said you'd have another dude with you. Tall guy, with a couple scars. Said he was a real bad ass and we better watch out for him. So if you won't tell me how to get out of this freaky damn place, then maybe you'll tell me where this bad ass mother fucker is."

"We told you all we know," Luke replied. "You said there was water here. If we fill up every container you got, you can walk out of here with us."

"May I please have a drink?" Mariel suddenly spoke.

"Somebody get 'em some water," Bennie commanded.

One of the suits walked into a back hallway and in moments the sound of running water was heard. He returned with a gallon sized jug and sat it in front of Mariel. She looked at Mathias, and he nodded. Bennie stared intently. She grabbed the jug and tilted it up. Luke felt his parched throat spasm involuntarily as he watched her drink, then she handed the jug to him. The water was cold and sweet. When he drank his fill he handed it to Mathias who did the same.

"See? I ain't so bad," Bennie said. "I just want to get back to where I was. The white dude told us you could show us the way."

"Where is this white…dude?" Mathias asked.

"Comes and goes," Bennie replied. "Ain't seen him in three days."

"Enough of this bullshit," one of the suits interrupted. "None of us have had anything to eat in more than a week. We gotta get out of here or we're all gonna die!" He stepped nervously from foot to foot as he spoke, and when he was done he slipped a small vial from his pocket, flipped open a cap and raised it to his nose. He snorted gently, and when he lowered the bottle a tiny patch of white powder remained under his left nostril. He wiped it away with the back of his hand, then licked it. He began to sniffle.

"You see," Bennie said thoughtfully. "This college boy here has one of the different kinds of hungry. Me, I just want things to go back the way they was."

"So do we," Luke said. "But we don't know our way out of here any better than you do, no matter what the white dude told you."

"Enough," Bennie replied. He motioned to some of the cap wearers. "Take 'em upstairs and lock 'em up." He scooped up one of the pistols and pointed it at Mariel's head. "Leave them knives here."

One by one they relinquished their weapons. When they were done, the center of the table was covered.

Bennie grinned, showing his gold tooth. "If we was somewhere else, I think I could like you kids." His grin vanished. "Take 'em away."

Two of the cap wearers shoved them upstairs. When they were gone from view, the sniffler turned back to Bennie.

"Now what?"

"I gotta think," Bennie replied.

"About what?" Sniffler asked. "Take the girl, just like the white dude said, and beat it out of her. You can do that, can't you?"

Bennie lunged quickly from his seat and wrapped one big hand around Sniffler's throat. He flung him against the wall.

"What do you think?"

Sniffler managed to nod slightly, and Bennie released him. He dropped to the floor gagging and coughing. Bennie sat down at his table and idly spun one of the pistols.

"I got no problem slapping the kids around," Bennie said to no one in particular. "But what's buggin' me is, where in the hell is this bad ass mother fucker what's supposed to be with them?"

Lynch, the bad ass mother fucker in question, was miles away. He had already visited two of the camps just after first light. The inhabitants of those camps lay stiffening in pools of their own blood. The members of the last camp had managed to start out before he could reach them, but Lynch wasn't worried. He knew he could easily surpass them and lay an ambush. In fact that was exactly what he was in the process of doing. He found a suitable ambush site and waited.

In less than thirty minutes three men stumbled into view. Lynch studied them carefully. They were all big men, muscular and tough looking, but young. And that made no sense at all. He made his decision, stepped from concealment, and shot the second man with his crossbow, dropped it and threw his tomahawk. It thumped solidly into the first man's spine. Then he leaped on the third man and bore him, screaming, to the ground. Lynch grabbed his chin and the back of his head and broke the man's neck with a violent flip of his wrists. The attack was over in less than ten seconds. Barely breathing any heavier than normal, Lynch approached the first man in line, plucked his tomahawk from the man's body and rolled him over with his booted toe. The man's eyes flew open. Lynch noted with some satisfaction that he saw no fear. Nothing but rage. This one would have been formidable in his own World, yet he had bested him easily.

"I reckon you know you ain't goin' home," Lynch said conversationally. The man nodded.

"So tell me what you're doing here," Lynch demanded.

"Makes no difference to me," the wounded man responded. "One minute we're all minding our own business, the next thing we know there's a flash of light and we end up here."

Lynch considered that. "You're not making any sense."

"Better be figuring it out," the wounded man replied. His voice grew weaker with each word. "The white dude said he brought us here and you could take us back, but we had to watch you cause you were a double crossing son of a bitch."

"The white dude?" Lynch mused. Was this part of the Wilding? But that wasn't quite right, and he knew it. These people were foreigners, but he almost recognized their style of dress. He frowned suddenly. He *did* recognize their manner of dress. *They were not of this World.* Someone had opened a portal and he had a good idea who it was. Timon Blackhelm. The white dude. He ground his boot heel into the wounded man's neck until he ceased struggling. Wherever the village had come from, it was obvious that the inhabitants were human. But that meant nothing. Lynch knew that. Humans could be worse than any evil creature ever spawned. He carefully searched his three latest victim's backpacks, hoping for more clues. But what he discovered only added to the mystery. There was spare clothing, a couple plastic water bottles which Lynch recognized from his trips through the portal, a small plastic box containing a syringe, several needles and a tiny bottle of clear fluid, which Lynch quickly discarded. At the bottom of the last pack, carefully wrapped in old rags, he found three pint bottles of Kentucky bourbon. He licked his lips. Just a taste, and he'd be on his way. One little taste wouldn't hurt anybody.

# CHAPTER THIRTY TWO

LYNCH JUDGED THAT HE was about half drunk. As usual, one little taste had led to another, and then another, and then a nice, deep draught. One of the bottles glinted in the sun where it lay empty beside his boot prints in the sand. He had a firm grip on the second, which he had not yet opened, and the last lay safely buried in his voluminous pack. Despite his inebriated state, he still possessed enough stealth to enter the city without being detected, or so he thought. He closed his eyes and sent out feelers casting for the dregs of energy left behind by anyone who uses magic and quickly picked out a faint trail left by Mathias. He heard a boot grate on broken glass and opened his eyes to slits.

"Hey old man," a muscular youth arrogantly addressed him. "Who the fuck are you, and what are you doin' back here?"

Lynch looked past him. There were five of them, all young, staring at him with hate filled eyes.

"You made several mistakes," Lynch said calmly. "First, you should never give an enemy of unknown strength even the slightest chance to defend himself. Second, you should have brought more men."

"So you think you're a bad ass," the leader said. "I don't think you're nothing. All talk." He glanced at his companions. "What does Bennie call it? Arrogance."

Lynch grinned. "It's only arrogance if you can't back it up. If you know what you're capable of, it's called confidence."

"Take him down," the leader said quickly.

He lunged at Lynch with a stubby knife, but the cagy Wizard had moved so quickly he was a blur. Lynch allowed his attacker to move beyond him then he grabbed his knife arm at the wrist and twisted it savagely up behind the youth's back until he actually heard the cartilage and muscle tearing in his shoulder. He flung the screaming youth into his companions, knocking two of them sprawling, and whipped out his own knife. By the time the two on the pavement had scrambled back to their feet, Lynch had dispatched the two who were standing. He lunged forward and plunged his knife into the nearest one's chest, withdrew it and sliced the other's throat from ear to ear. Then he leaned down and grabbed the leader by his shirt collar and slammed him head first into the brick wall, over and over, until he went limp.

Lynch felt stone sober now, but rage burned within him. He spat upon the bodies of the youths who had attacked him. He knelt and wiped his knife blade clean on one of his victims and made his way down the block to the building he had pinpointed earlier. A carelessly crafted spell of Dark Magic allowed him to hear voices on the opposite side of the solid brick wall nearest the alley.

Bennie was questioning his captives one last time and it was not going well. Finally, he walked casually behind Mariel's chair and leaned in close to her.

"Tell me what I want to know, little missy, or you and me are going to go back in one of those rooms that has a bed in it," he said it loud enough for Luke and Mathias to hear.

Luke leaped from his chair and lunged for the big man. Bennie let him come, and when Luke was close enough he hit him three times. Bennie's ribs felt like iron. Then Bennie slapped him with his open palm and sent him sprawling across the floor. To Luke it felt like his head had exploded. His ears rang and his vision blurred. He was only dimly aware of Mathias shouting at Bennie when the plate glass window shattered. Bennie drew both pistols and trained them on the broken window as he dropped into a crouch. All of his followers stared dumbly at the shattered glass. Then there was a whirring sound and Bennie's right hand dropped to the floor, severed at the wrist and still clutching his pistol. He stared stupidly at it for several long seconds then he screamed. As he continued screaming, he lunged to his feet and wheeled around to spray the bar area with most of the contents of the bullets in his second pistol. But there was no one visible. Luke rolled over and pried the pistol from Bennie's severed hand and slid it across the floor. It whisked out of sight behind the bar, and for several more seconds there was silence. Then Lynch jerked upright with the pistol in one hand and his bottle in the other. He fired three shots into Bennie's chest and jumped the bar as the big man was still falling. Then Lynch began firing wildly into the crowd of Bennie's gang, so rapidly the shots almost blended into one long roll of thunder. And just as rapidly, his pistol ran empty and the slide locked open. It was only then that anyone even noticed the half empty liquor bottle in his left hand.

Mathias had lunged forward and knocked Mariel's chair over with her in it. Now they scuttled for the cover of the bar as Luke rolled Bennie's prostrate form over and plucked three magazines from under his vest. He wondered for a split second at the unnatural outline under Bennie's black shirt, but he had no time to question or explore further. The remaining members of Bennie's gang were crowding back into the building, jumping through the broken window and shoving their way in through the door. Their faces were desperate masks of unreasonable terror. Luke threw one magazine to Lynch, who's hand was a blur as he sat his bottle on the bar, caught it deftly in midair and plugged it into the grip of his captured pistol. And then he mowed them down. Bennie's gang members tried desperately to reverse their course. It would have been comical, except that all the gang members in front were dropping with blossoming stains of crimson marring the gaudy colors of their clothing. Luke threw himself behind the bar and thrust another clip into Lynch's hand just as the second one ran dry. Lynch jammed it home and continued firing.

"Extras?" he shouted.

Luke slapped the remaining magazine into Lynch's waiting left hand.

"Go out the back!" Lynch shouted.

The three teenagers ran for the back door. Lynch coldly shot everyone in sight. He surveyed the utter destruction in the room for a moment, then safely secured his partial bottle in his pants pocket. Only then did he turn and run after them. They burst into the bright sunlight and draining heat of yet another identical day in the desert.

"Follow me," Lynch ordered.

He ducked and weaved across the street with the three young people directly behind him. As they neared the corner of the next building, Lynch dropped to one knee and skidded around it with his gun up. He fired two quick shots, then lunged to his feet and continued running down the foreign sidewalk. Luke, Mathias and Mariel followed. Two more of Bennie's followers lay in the street where Lynch had shot them. Luke ignored them. They caught up to Lynch at the end of the block. Nothing lay beyond but more desert, and now they were short three waterskins. Lynch took a quick second to analyze the situation.

Suddenly, more shots rang out and dust flew from the brick behind them, accompanied by the angry whine of ricocheting lead slugs. An entire volley of shots sounded as Lynch wrapped his arms around the whole group and simply fell backwards with them, out of sight behind the building. He grunted as a bullet slammed into the meat of his thigh, narrowly missing his precious bottle.

"Son of a bitch!" he groaned as he rolled back to his feet and plunged around the corner. He couldn't believe his eyes. Bennie was walking resolutely up the sidewalk holding his remaining gun in his left hand. His right arm ended at the wrist, cut off by Lynch's enchanted tomahawk. Lynch grinned and charged to meet him. When no more than fifty feet separated them he slammed to a stop and fired one deadly shot as bullets struck all around him. The bullet caught Bennie at the base of the throat and pitched him over backwards.

"Get up from that, asshole." Lynch taunted.

Luke, Mathias and Mariel watched in disbelief as Lynch continued stalking towards Bennie's fallen form. Just before he reached the big man, another man dressed all in black with a black hood leaped from the alley and plucked Bennie's gun from the dead man's grasp. He wheeled and in one movement he and Lynch covered each other. They stared at each other over the sights of their pistols for several long moments.

"Lynch," the other man said.

"Timon," Lynch responded. He took a step to the left and Timon did likewise.

Timon nodded towards the three teenagers without taking his eyes or his gun off Lynch. "What the Hell are you doing with them?"

"Doesn't matter," Lynch responded. He took another step to the left, and so did Timon. Both sought an opening, a millisecond of inattention from their enemy. Timon suddenly shifted his point of aim to Mariel and slapped the trigger. Nothing happened, and Lynch grinned and squeezed his trigger, expecting the satisfying buck and roar of a detonating cartridge.

None came. The slides of both pistols were locked back on an empty chamber. Both Wizards dropped the guns with a metallic clatter and drew their swords and leaped at each other. The sound of ringing steel filled the air as they fought. They thrust and parried with no apparent advantage to either side until both men were dripping with sweat.

"You can't beat me," Timon finally said.

"Nor you me," Lynch replied.

"But you have a weakness," Timon said suddenly. Lynch glanced at the three young refugees. "Ah, Lynchie," he exclaimed. "I see! You're trying to save them. You're a fool. Don't you know you can't save yourself? You can't undo what's been done for centuries. You can't unmake what you've become with one good turn."

"Perhaps," Lynch agreed. "So what now? Do we battle until the end of time?"

"You could surrender," Timon suggested.

Lynch laughed. "As could you." His eyes narrowed in thought. "Is this all just an elaborate trap? Are you really that frightened of me?"

He lunged and struck, and Timon parried.

"You're getting slow," Timon exclaimed. "That's what happens when you run out of challenges. Can't you see this World is coming to an end?"

"That IS it," Lynch said as realization dawned on him. "You've discovered a portal."

"Took you long enough," Timon replied. He struck suddenly and Lynch barely deflected the wicked blade. "Don't you recognize this street? We met here, at a laboratory, years ago."

"That was *you*," Lynch replied. By the gods, how could he have been so dense? "In the sleep deprivation experiment. How in the name of Aard did you manage to squeeze a city block through a portal?"

"It was an experiment," Timon admitted. "I theorized if I could move a city block into this World, I could move my army into the other World. It only partially worked, though. Parts of it are still connected."

"You intend to invade the other World."

Timon cast a sideways glance at Lynch's wounded leg. "You must be bleeding out. The old Lynch would have figured all this out long ago. Or maybe you're just getting soft. Whatever. Sure, I'm going to invade, after

I let Dragons and ogres and were Demons do most of the work. Oh, and the Slayers too."

Lynch thought of the carnage that would be dealt on an unsuspecting World if Timon succeeded. "You're a monster."

"Sticks and stones, my good fellow. You're a monster too, Lynch. Just like me."

"I am a monster," Lynch agreed. "Speaking of monsters, I should tell you I released Slagg from his imprisonment."

Involuntarily, Timon cast a quick glance skyward.

"He said if I should chance upon you to tell you Hello," Lynch continued. "Oh, and he fully intends to rip you apart, when he and I confront you. He's usually not far from me anymore."

"Nice try," Timon said with a nervous laugh. "But releasing him doesn't make you any less of a monster."

"I already told you, I am a monster," Lynch repeated. "But not like you!"

He lunged so quickly Timon had only one chance to react, and he was a fraction of a second slow. Lynch's blade sliced deep across Timon's chest at a diagonal angle and narrowly missed opening up his abdomen. His sword dropped from his suddenly nerveless fingers and his eyes flew open in amazement.

"Bravo," he groaned. Then he turned and ran into one of the vacant buildings. Lynch lunged to pursue him but only succeeded in crashing to the pavement as his weight fell on his injured leg. There was a flash of light inside the building and Lynch knew Timon was gone.

Lynch sagged to his knees then carefully sat with his legs outstretched. He jerked his knife from its scabbard and slit his pants leg all the way to his groin. He stared at the damage studiously for a few seconds. Blood still pumped steadily from a hole on either side of his thigh, but it was slowing. He was bleeding out, just as Timon said. Large caliber slugs had a tendency to do that. Luke, Mathias and Mariel ran to him. Mathias took one look and whipped off his leather belt. He encircled Lynch's thigh with it and drew it up as tight as he could. Lynch grimaced. Luke spied the neck of Lynch's whiskey bottle protruding from his pocket. He pulled it out, popped the cork, and upended it on Lynch's exposed thigh.

"No, no…not the whiskey!" Lynch began, but he bit off his words as the liquor hit his mangled thigh. His entire body went taut as he fought down the urge to scream. "Goddammit, you wasted the whiskey," He groaned. "I should have left you little shits," he panted as he fought to regain control of himself, "I try to do something good, and look what it gets me."

"You'll live, if we can stop the bleeding," Mathias said.

"I can stop the bleeding," Lynch replied. He cut two strips from the filthy material of his pants leg and wadded them into elongated balls. Then he gritted his teeth and jammed each one into a hole. His eyes rolled back in his head for a moment. "Son…of …a…bitch." He growled. "Wind some more around my leg, but not too tight. Then tie me up."

Mathias started to argue, but Lynch interrupted. "Listen to me! I'm gonna use Dark magic on myself. You drag me into one of those buildings and tie me up. Tie me good," he warned. "Until I come around I won't be my usual kind, gentle self. Now do it." He said the words under his breath and his body jerked spasmodically. "Don't stay here," he whispered. "Grab my pack and get out of here." Then he went limp.

"More magic," Luke muttered. Then he and Mathias dragged Lynch into the nearest building while Mariel stripped the nylon cords from the blinds on the windows. They bound Lynch hand and foot. Luke was particularly vigilant in drawing his knots up cruelly tight.

"No need for that," Mathias objected. "Cut off the blood supply and he might lose a hand or foot."

"It'd serve him right," Luke replied. "I think he was going to leave us, until he found out this place is from a different World."

"Maybe," Mathias agreed. "Maybe not. Lynch doesn't exactly follow the rules."

Luke rolled his eyes. "You Wizards all stick together. I'm going to look around." He stalked out the door.

Once out on the street Luke made a beeline for Bennie's body. He ignored the congealing pool of blood which was already drawing huge green bodied flies and rolled him over. In death the hugely muscular man seemed oddly deflated. But what interested Luke was the strange outline under his shirt. He stuck three fingers in one of the bullet holes and ripped the flimsy cloth to expose a thick vest of a foreign material, the likes of which he had never seen. He opened the rip further and saw where all three of Lynch's shots had struck in a cluster right over Bennie's heart. Each slug left a deep indention, but none fully penetrated the vest.

"So that's how he did it," Luke marveled. He thought about taking the vest, but it looked extremely hot. And, he reasoned, there was probably no more live ammunition in all of Norland and beyond. The magazine pouches sewn into Bennie's vest were empty. Luke retraced his steps back to Bennie's building. Once inside he moved carefully, listening so intently he could hear the sound of his own heartbeat. Lynch's tomahawk was embedded firmly in the wall, after its enchanted flight that severed Bennie's hand. Luke hesitated before slowly reaching a trembling hand to grasp the smooth wooden handle. It had a waxy, oily, foreign feel to it. Luke wondered briefly if Lynch had treated it with some type of tallow, or maybe resin. But deep inside he knew it was probably from something much more precious, at least to the person from whom it was drawn. It reminded him of a man from Norland named Oden. He was a dimwitted fellow with a huge potbelly. He never wore a coat, even in the coldest weather, and he always had his sleeves rolled halfway up his massive, hairy forearms. Oden was the man the villagers called upon when it was time to kill pigs, and he did it with a narrow headed hammer. Oden never needed more than one blow from that benign looking instrument for each pig slaughtered. Once he had sent Luke to fetch some of his tools, and they all had that same greasy feel on the handles.

He pulled it free. As he did, a tingling sensation shot up his hand and through his arm. He tried to drop the unfamiliar blade, but his fingers refused to do his bidding. The tingling was replaced with a strange warmth, and Luke actually felt the blood rushing into his muscles, swelling them with new found power. Black spots danced across his vision then his eyesight returned with amazing clarity. He sucked in a deep breath and tasted the acrid metallic flavor of the scent of blood as it emanated from the pool where Bennie's hand still lay. The remnants of the Dark Magic spell imparted by Lynch finished flowing into Luke, and he relaxed his grip on the tomahawk. But he did not drop it.

He knew what he felt was energy from a spell of Dark Magic. Part of him was repulsed, and he actually thought for a moment a gigantic hand might drop from the heavens or rise through the floor and squash him like a mealworm as punishment for betraying the Light. He knew in that instant that his allegiance could never be swayed, and he would go to his grave defending the Light. He also knew that no matter how hard he tried, no matter what sacrifice he made, Lynch was and always would be a creature at one with the Dark. The sheer power behind that one, simple spell was dumbfounding, and if that was evidence of the power of the Dark, then it was a formidable presence indeed. Timon was right. Lynch could not possibly repent. No one could embrace the Dark only to cast it off like a snake shedding its skin. If there was anything Luke knew, it was that the powers of the Dark demanded a price every time it was used. Anyone using it for centuries, as Lynch had done, would be contaminated by the Dark to the very depths of his being.

But yet another part, overwhelmed as it was by Luke's sense of right and wrong, still thrilled in the alien sensations he experienced. He craved that feeling of power, the thrill of holding a good blade. He could well imagine holding that blade to an enemy's throat just before the final blow. In his mind he actually saw Sniffler running away as he balanced that wicked implement in his hands, then threw it with unerring accuracy. He heard it thump solidly into Sniffler's spine, and his entire being cried out with the need to make that happen. And then he recognized the demons Lynch wrestled with every single second of his existence. He tucked the tomahawk into his belt, gathered up their weapons from Bennie's table, and hurried back to Mathias and Mariel.

The streets were literally lined with bodies, and Luke crossed and recrossed the street to avoid coming too close to them. He heard Lynch before he got there, even though the sounds coming from the building didn't seem to be human. Mariel was waiting for him outside the building.

"Mathias thinks something's gone wrong," Mariel explained.

Luke took a quick glance inside the door. Something had gone wrong indeed. Mathias had a piece of rope tied around Lynch's torso, but the Warlock was still dragging him around the interior with his struggles and leaving a crimson trail on the floor behind him. The sounds he made were unlike anything Luke had ever heard.

"What the Hell is going on?" Luke shouted.

"How should I know?" Mathias answered. He leaned back into the rope and brought Lynch to a temporary halt. "He just went nuts."

"Well, do something," Luke yelled.

"Like what?" Mathias replied.

Luke grimaced. He ran into the building, and as he neared Lynch the Warlock whipped his body straight, jerking Mathias off his feet. He landed hard on the unforgiving floor, and just as quickly Lynch jerked his torso the other way and lunged at Luke with his teeth bared. His jaws snapped shut inches from Luke's leg. Luke jerked the tomahawk from his belt and swung it in a short, powerful arc. At the last fraction of a second he turned the blade sideways and it thunked solidly against the side of Lynch's head. He went limp and seemed to melt to the floor.

"Like that," Luke said.

"Oh," Mathias said. "That works." He stepped back out of Lynch's reach. "Now what?"

"Leave him," Luke suggested. He knew, deep inside, that would be the wisest choice. He should put as much distance between himself and the Dark Wizard as he possibly could. But he knew what was going to happen before Mariel even spoke.

"We can't just leave him," she said from the doorway. "He did come back for us."

Luke knew Mathias' argument before he spoke also. "It would not be the honorable thing to do."

"Whatever," Luke replied. He heaved a loud sigh. "If we're not leaving him I better go find some way to carry him." He walked back towards the door. "If I were you, Mathias, I'd try some sort of spell on him before he comes to."

"I really don't know how that might react to the spell he's already tried," Mathias argued.

"What's the worst that can happen?" Luke asked.

Mathias had no answer.

"Exactly," Luke pressed his point home. "I don't think it can get much worse."

He brushed past Mariel who still stood in the doorway, her lips trembling.

"Don't you ever fret about Lynch," Luke told her brusquely.

# CHAPTER THIRTY THREE

HEY SET OUT UPON the desert as the sun dropped out of sight. Luke had found a gurney in one of the buildings and replaced the wheels with larger ones from wheelchairs. He had no way to know that was the same building where Lynch had encountered Timon. The same building, in a different World. The three of them managed to lift the Dark Wizards inert form to the gurney and strap him down with the restraints built into it, which was a handy feature, as far as Luke was concerned. Lynch's spell of Dark Magic had stopped the bleeding before it short circuited, and Mathias cast a healing spell of his own on the Dark Wizard. That spell of the Light seemed to calm Lynch but Luke no longer trusted him, even unconscious. As they left the pavement and set out upon the sand, Luke turned back to look at the foreign buildings one last time. They shimmered in the heat waves, then faded until only the barest outline was visible against the far horizon.

Luke navigated by the stars, and he and Mathias took turns pushing Lynch on the makeshift wagon. Before they set out they had filled all the waterskins and several plastic jugs of the same type used by the man Bennie sent to fetch water for them. They searched for hours, but found no food. In that, at least, Bennie had been telling the truth. They did find Lynch's pack stashed in a garbage can, and Luke loaded that on the gurney with the wounded warlock. He marveled at the weight of it, and wondered how Lynch could carry it so easily.

The high desert became almost chilled after sunset, and as the sun rose Luke killed an iguana that was too sluggish to escape. They built a small fire and roasted it with sage and a pinch of salt from Lynch's pack. Only after they had seasoned it did Luke feel a momentary doubt. What if it actually wasn't salt? But in the end hunger won out and he joined the others in feasting on the stringy, white meat. Then they slept in the scant shade of a scraggly cedar tree.

That became the routine. Travel at night, and when they stopped for the day Luke went out foraging. He usually returned with either a rabbit or iguana, only once did he come back with several quail. They soaked a worn handkerchief in water at every stop and wrung it out between Lynch's parched lips. Their progress was pitifully slow, and the hard labor was telling on all of them. The desert ate the spare flesh from all of them, leaving Mathias and Luke lean and tough. Mariel was even more drawn and pale, and they all knew something had to give.

By the morning of the fifth day the terrain began to change, and when the sun rose Luke ventured out into small hills that actually had a slight bit of vegetation covering them. He returned quickly with a jackrabbit while Mathias and Mariel forced a few drops of precious water between Lynch's clenched teeth.

"Any change?" he said with a nod at the Dark Wizard.

"None that I can see," Mathias answered.

"Can't you use more magic on him?" Luke asked.

"I've used all the healing spells I know," Mathias said. "Do you think I'd go on pushing that damn cart all day if I could get his ass up and walking? Besides, I thought you hated magic."

"I do hate magic," Luke replied. "But I took a look ahead, and if he can't walk, he ain't comin' with us."

"Why?" Mariel asked fearfully. "What did you see?"

"It gets rough, that's all," Luke said. "We can't push that wagon through it." He tossed a small branch into the fire and watched the sparks burn out in the morning air. "What about Dark Magic?"

Mathias looked away quickly. Too quickly, Luke decided.

"I don't know Dark Magic," Mathias said. But there was no conviction in his assertion.

"Bullshit," Luke snorted. "You and Lynch been tradin' secrets for two weeks and you mean to tell me he never taught you any Dark Magic?"

Mathias was caught and he knew it. "Alright, but he said never to use it unless it meant life or death."

"I reckon this qualifies," Luke replied. "At least for him. And maybe for us too, because I ain't so sure I can get all of us through this without his help."

Mathias nodded. In truth, Lynch had shared a great deal of Dark Magic with him, but it had always been accompanied by a strong warning. Dark Magic was *never* free. Not for the user and not for the recipient. Each spell had an undisclosed price, and Mathias had no desire to give up his soul so Lynch could walk the rest of the way to Bernfeld. He glanced at Luke again. Luke nodded in Lynch's direction, and Mathias surrendered. He spoke the words quickly but carefully, and before he even finished Lynch's taut muscles began to relax and color returned to his cheeks. He took a deep, sighing breath, and his eyes popped open.

"Where are we?" he asked.

Luke was astounded at the power of that one Dark spell. If such a simple spell held such great power, what chance did they have defending the Light? "Still on the way to Bernfeld," he replied. "Are you healed?"

Lynch attempted to sit up, but his bonds prevented it.

"I am returned," he said with a slight smile. "You can release me now."

Mariel and Mathias started towards Lynch, but Luke stopped them.

"Returned? Where, exactly, have you been?"

"Searching," Lynch replied. "I've been walking a fine line, trying to find myself. Whatever you've done, it appears to have pulled me back." He flexed the powerful muscles of his thigh. "I am healed, and you can trust me once again."

"I never did," Luke reminded him. But he unbuckled the straps that restrained Lynch.

Lynch swung his legs over the side of the gurney, then stood and stretched. He swept back the ruined tatters of his jeans from his wounded leg and carefully removed the crude bandage. A crimson, puckered scar marred the skin of his leg both front and back. But it appeared fully healed.

"Hurrah for Dark Magic," Luke said.

"Dark Magic?" Lynch said quickly. "Why did you not use the magic of the Light? There are many healing spells which I am sure you know."

"I tried them," Mathias explained. "It wasn't working. The spells of the Light actually seemed to make things worse."

Lynch seemed to mull that over. It was nearly a full minute before he spoke again, during which Luke and Mathias exchanged curious glances.

"Well," he finally said, "I am healed and we can be on our way."

"Not so fast," Luke replied. "You've been ridin' that wagon, and we've been doing the pushin'. It's time for us to rest."

"Of course," Lynch agreed. "For the second time I am indebted to a Graywullf for saving my life. And to both of you," he said to Mathias and Mariel. "I'll take the first watch so you can all rest."

He scooped up his pack without waiting for an answer and walked out to a high point where he could see the camp and the surrounding area.

"Something's different about him," Mathias whispered to Luke and Mariel.

"I reckon," Luke agreed.

"He's just not used to relying on others," Mariel said. "I think he's embarrassed because he charged in all swagger and bravado, and we ended up saving his life."

"Whatever it is, I don't like it. I don't like it when people change like that," Luke said. "I don't think we can trust him."

"Keep your voice down," Mathias hissed.

He needn't have worried. Lynch could feel the wave of distrust that surrounded the little band, but he didn't care in the least. He had his own demons to wrestle with after walking in the Shadows for five days.

Lynch found a secluded vantage point and wiggled his buttocks into the sand and soundly cursed the day he had encountered Lorn Graywullf. Prior to that day, Lynch had sailed through more than a century without ever being beholden to another living soul. He lived without a care, relying on no one and taking anything that pleased him whether it be a gold medallion or a merchant's wife or daughter. Or both. At the same time. In short, he thought he had truly given himself to the Dark. Then came that fateful day when a valiant servant of the Light had saved his life and he discovered that his soul was not entirely dead. He hated to admit it, but hope had sprung back to life within him, which was an emotion he thought to be as dead and forgotten as his soul. It was only then that he realized the true nature of his situation. He walked the thinnest edge of the sharpest razor, and on each side as far as he could see, were bottomless chasms. He was neither a servant of the Light *or* the Dark. He was an anomaly, a freak.

310

For no matter how hard he tried he could not vanquish that spark of Light within him. But, as the failure of the magic of the Light to heal him had so clearly illustrated, he could no longer entirely cast out the Dark either.

He stared morosely across the rough canyon country that lay before them. The Graywullf boy had steered them too far North. He should have turned West two full days earlier. But then, Lynch had not shared that information about the route when he was able, so he supposed he deserved whatever fate came their way. He dug into his seemingly bottomless pack and found the flat shape of the whiskey bottle he had secreted there, popped the cork and took a long, throat searing draught. Deep in his heart, Lynch knew that Timon had been right. Despite his own objections, he had been attempting to atone for his past. Of course, that had been an utter failure. He grinned without mirth and took another swallow of whiskey. It was painfully clear that he would never eradicate the malignancy in his soul which took root with his first foray into the Dark. That situation, at least, was permanent. Because of that void where the Light would never reach, the *magii'ri* Warriors and Wizards who had long since gone to the Other Side would not welcome Lynch to the table when he drew his last breath. There would be no Feast among the servants of the Light for Lynch. He tipped the bottle back and swallowed the fiery liquid.

But Lynch knew yet another tidbit about himself which would not be too obvious to anyone, even another servant of the Dark. He would never allow himself to be dragged back into the emotional oblivion that was his existence when he had sought to vanquish the Light and give himself entirely to the Dark. He had felt nothing, tasted nothing for far too long in the centuries before Lorn Graywullf had dragged him aboard that boat, and since then his senses had awakened once again. He had eaten feasts that a King would envy, but even that miserable broth made of dried horse meat in the Citadel tasted better after he had allowed himself to rejoin the human species. Certainly, he had bedded thousands of beautiful, wanton women and every time had been a thrill. But he had never in his lonely existence felt anything more than lust for anyone until he met La'Nay, and he had never felt such pain as when she had rebuffed him. He swallowed more of his confiscated sourmash. He had never loved as much or been hurt as badly until he had admitted to himself that he would never become a mindless, soulless servant of the Dark. And even at that he would not go back.

Lynch shook his head. "You have gone soft in the head," he muttered under his breath.

He tipped the bottle back once again and was surprised when it ran dry after only a few more swallows. He carelessly pitched it over his shoulder and glanced back at the camp. He blinked and rubbed his eyes, then without hesitation he hurled a spell of concealment on the rest of his band. The spell took effect in the nick of time, just as a mounted horseman rode within ten feet of Mariel. He was followed by three more mounted men, and half a dozen on foot. Hoods concealed their faces and they were all well armed. If they ventured to the far side of the dune Luke had chosen for cover for his camp, they could not miss the trail they had left walking in. Lynch leaped to his feet and grabbed for his sword. Too late, he realized it was slung under the gurney. He slapped the other side of his belt. His tomahawk was gone also.

All the hooded men saw his sudden movement and surged his way. Lynch gauged his strength and knew he could not use magic to defeat them, not as long as he had to maintain the spell of concealment. He delved into his pack and withdrew a crossbow. He cocked and loaded it in one smooth motion, then threw it up and fired a bolt into the throat of the nearest horseman. He chanced a quick spell to keep his companions asleep, hoping that it wouldn't have lasting consequences, then turned and ran. The hooded men gave chase.

Once he had gained some distance from the camp, Lynch ducked behind a boulder. When the first horseman appeared, he leaped on him like a big cat and knocked the man from the saddle. With a quick twist Lynch broke the man's neck and jumped into the saddle just as the rest of the men thundered around the boulder. He slapped his heels into the horse's flanks and plunged wildly down the hill. The mount surged into a full gallop, thrown into a panic by the unfamiliar rider and the fact that Lynch could not get his boots into the stirrups, which flopped maddeningly back and forth against the horse's sides urging it to even more speed. That suited Lynch just fine, for he wanted as much distance between these men and the camp as possible before his spell of concealment wore off. Somehow he doubted they would be willing to accept a surrender after he had killed two of their number without so much as a word of parley.

It quickly became apparent that Lynch had stolen the best mount, for he soon outdistanced his pursuers. That was not exactly what he wanted. He could not chance the men returning to the camp to find Luke, Mathias and Mariel sound asleep. He pulled back on the reins to slow his mount, but it had no effect. He reined sharply to the left, and in the next instant he was falling as the terror stricken horse lost it's footing and tumbled head over heels. Lynch kicked clear, tucked his head into his shoulder and rolled. Then his world went black.

Moments later his pursuers caught up. They surrounded him in a cloud of dust, weapons at the ready.

"Check him, Stubs," the leader ordered.

One of the foot soldiers did as he was told, probing Lynch's fallen form with a lance. Then he leaned in close.

"He ain't dead, Nash," Stubs replied. "But he's out like a light." He rolled Lynch over onto his back.

"Son of a bitch," Stubs yelped as he jumped backwards. "It's Lynch!" Most of the other men stepped back involuntarily.

"Well I'll be goddamned," Nash said wonderingly. "Now what in Hell are you doin' out here?"

"Do something, Nash!" Stubs yelled. "He's comin' to!"

Lynch's eyes fluttered open and he looked blankly around. Nash tossed a pair of handcuffs at Stub's feet.

"Cuff him, quick!"

Lynch suddenly lunged to his feet and stood swaying. He cast a murderous glare at Stubs, then at Nash.

"Hello, Nash," he said cordially.

"Lynch," Nash acknowledged.

"Enforcers, eh?" Lynch stated.

"Yep," Nash replied.

"Sent for me?"

"And others," Nash said.

"You didn't get the cuffs on me, Stubs," Lynch said with a wicked grin. "Want to try now?"

"Hell, no," Stubs replied, backing even further away.

"Relax, Lynch," Nash said. "You know how this works. You killed a handful of Warlocks, and now two of my boys. We have to take you in, and we have enough weapons here to do it. But if you put the cuffs on yourself, we're duty bound not to harm you, same as you're bound not to give us any more trouble. So what'll it be?"

Lynch gauged his chances, then shrugged. "Cuff me."

He held out his wrists and the man called Stubs slipped gleaming handcuffs over them and snapped them in place. Lynch felt the will to resist drain out of him. Stubs quickly stepped back out of his reach.

"I'll be goddamned," he crowed. "The infamous Lynch! And we caught you fair and square. There's no one in the World with a fatter price on his head than you, Lynch, and it's all ours. We just walked right in and slapped the cuffs on you, when nobody else could even catch a whiff of your back trail!" He slapped the dust off his hat. "We're gonna be rich, boys! And I'll wager we can make him pay on the trail back to…"

Lynch lunged forward and slammed the metal cuffs against the side of Stub's head. The Enforcer's mouth clamped shut and his eyes rolled back in his head as he pitched forward face first into the sand.

"Shut up," Lynch muttered.

Some of the other Enforcers began to shout in anger, obviously distressed over the failure of the enchanted handcuffs to fully contain Lynch.

"Yes, shut up," Nash said mildly. "I'm still the leader of this outfit, and I don't want to hear any more of that kind of talk until we're safely Under and I have that sack of gold in my hands."

"Under?" Lynch asked. "You said you were Enforcers, not bounty hunters."

"Enforcing don't pay too well," Nash explained. "It ain't personal." he hesitated. "Well, maybe it is. But the fact is we'll get a lot more for you if we go Under."

Lynch mentally cursed himself. First, he had placed his companions safety above his own, then he had willingly accepted the enchanted handcuffs. Even if the opportunity arose, he couldn't resist these men, at least, not enough to actually do them serious harm And they intended to drag him Under, where he could recall at least a half dozen Demons who would be incredibly pleased to skin him alive, an inch or so at a time, for about the next hundred years.

Stubs rolled to his feet, approached Lynch warily and looped a length of rope around the handcuff chain. He tied that to his saddle horn and gave Lynch a wicked smile.

"I hope you had a good breakfast, Lynch." Nash said. Several of the other riders chuckled.

Lynch shook his head. "I actually woke up with a stomach ache, and my leg's been botherin' me some…"

He bit off the words as Stubbs drove his heels into his horse's flanks and they took off like a jackrabbit. Only his instincts saved him from sprawling face down in the sand. He sensed what they were going to do and began to run before the horsemen. Even so, it was all he could do to keep up. Before they had gone a quarter mile his wounded leg began to ache and he was dripping sweat. Lynch gritted his teeth and growled deep in his chest. It looked like it was going to be a long day. No matter how he tried he was always forced right back into his old habits. He muttered the words and felt strength flow back into his body. *Damn them all to Hell,* he thought. He didn't know that was right where they were headed.

# CHAPTER THIRTY FOUR

LUKE WOKE FIRST. HE felt rested, but far from normal. He nudged Mathias and Mariel, and they both sat up slowly, staring owlishly. Luke saw the glare of sunlight off the empty whiskey bottle immediately and went to investigate. The first thing he noticed was the jumble of tracks left by the Enforcers as they passed with spitting distance of camp. He wondered briefly about that, but then his attention was diverted by the body of the man Lynch had shot in the throat. He rolled the man over onto his back and retrieved the crossbow bolt from his throat. He grabbed Lynch's abandoned pack and rejoined Mathias and Mariel.

"He's gone again," Luke said, cutting off Mathias' question before he had the chance to form it. "I can't explain it, but he was attacked by at least eight or ten men. He dropped one with this," he held up the bolt. "The rest took off after him."

Mariel shook her head. "Can't he stay out of trouble for even one day?"

"I doubt it," Luke replied. "What do you want to do?" he asked Mathias.

"We better track him," Mathias answered tiredly.

It didn't take long to reach the spot where Lynch had been taken. Luke and Mathias studied the sign.

"You reckon he's alive?" Mathias asked.

"I reckon so," Luke replied. "Who do you think they are?"

"With Lynch it could be anybody. He makes enemies out of everyone he meets," Mathias said. "But they didn't kill him, so it's probably bounty hunters."

Luke nodded. "Mathias, you're smarter than anyone I know. What's yer best guess about these fellers?"

Mathias pursed his lips in thought. "They could be Enforcers, but they don't usually mistreat their captives. Look, you can see where they made him run."

Mariel cringed at the thought of Lynch running on his barely healed leg.

"So they're probably taking him in for a bounty. Who might be offering a bounty on him out here in the desert is beyond me."

"Whoever it is, they have power and money," Luke observed. "So I better find him before they get where they're goin'."

"You mean we better find him," Mathias said.

"I reckon I said what I meant," Luke replied. "I have to move fast, real fast." He looked at Mariel. "I'm sorry, but you won't keep up, and I can't leave you here alone."

"We can leave him," Mathias reminded him.

"Don't tempt me," Luke responded as he dug out Lynch's tomahawk and crossbow. He rummaged around in Lynch's bag. It seemed bottomless. He pulled out a quiver of crossbow bolts, three knives, a short sword in a sheath, several items of clean clothing and a packet of six plugs of chewing tobacco. And there was more in the bag. "I gotta get me one of these bags," Luke said.

He took the tomahawk and the crossbow and bolts, then helped himself to one of the plugs of chewing tobacco.

"As soon as I leave, you light out and head west," Luke said. "You'll hit the coast. Follow it and sooner or later you'll see a ship. Besides, game will be more plentiful closer to the coast. Me and Lynch'll catch up."

"I don't want you to go," Mariel said suddenly.

"Mariel…" Mathias began.

"It's for the best," Luke said. "Besides, I'll be alright."

Mariel stepped forward and before Luke knew her intention, she kissed him squarely on the lips. He blushed furiously while Mathias grinned. Luke shuffled from one foot to the other then he just shook his head.

"I have to go," he mumbled. Before anyone could say anything more, he turned and ran down the trail.

# CHAPTER THIRTY FIVE

ESPITE HIS WOUND AND his own assessment of his perilous affiliation with the Dark, Lynch's reservoir of Dark Magic was enormous. The spell he cast allowed him to run until the Enforcer's horses were lathered with sweat and stumbling with exhaustion. His mind was clear, hovering about in critical detachment above his battered, tortured body. When the Enforcers stopped at the entrance to a cave, Lynch also skidded to a halt and watched the proceedings with increasing curiosity. Soon it became clear that the horses refused to enter the foreboding darkness of the cave. The Enforcers grudgingly stripped their gear from their mounts and prodded Lynch ahead of them into the unknown confines of the cave.

Lynch sent out feelers ahead of him, and was relieved when he didn't detect any magical beings or creatures that existed only in the Dark. He specifically sought for Demons creeping out from the bowels of the World to meet him, and he could not deny that he was glad there no such beings ahead of him. But a few minutes later, when Nash announced that they would rest for awhile, he turned back to the group. Immediately his senses hummed with a very clear, very strong presence of evil. Lynch was not superstitious, but neither was he stupid. He'd had his share of run ins with nearly every creature that existed. A man in his profession, as he called it, would inevitably cross blades with creatures of the Dark as well as those of the Light. But what he sensed here were definitely followers of the Dark. And that made no sense at all. Enforcers, even those who had stooped to collecting bounty, were not creatures of the Dark.

"Hey Stubs," he called.

"What?" Stubs answered irritably.

"You remember who gave you that nickname?"

"Son of a bitch!" Stubs cursed. "You swore you'd never reveal that to anyone." He stood and started towards Lynch.

"What?" Lynch replied innocently. "That most of your pizzle is nothing by now but a dusty Dragon turd?"

"Damn you!" Stubs yelled. "Bounty or no bounty, I'll kill you for that!"

Nash rose to stop him, but Stubs blew past him. In the instant before he reached Lynch, his clothing burst from his body. His human face disappeared and batlike wings sprouted from his back. His arms became elongated with huge clawlike hands, and his skin turned into scaly black leather. He swung one hand and even though Lynch saw the blow coming and tried to dodge it, the glancing blow sent him reeling across the cave. Then Nash metamorphosed and slammed his own grotesque body into Stubs, sending him crashing into the rest of the Enforcers. Soon, Lynch found himself surrounded by growling were-Demons.

"Interesting," Lynch stated quietly.

"So now you know," Nash said. "Is that what you hoped to accomplish? To make us reveal ourselves to you?"

"There was that," Lynch admitted. "But that story about how Stubs lost his pizzle is actually really funny."

Stubs once again lunged at Lynch, but Nash flung a scaly forearm into his chest and halted him in his tracks.

"Can't you see he's just raggin' on you?" Nash said in an exasperated tone. "I'm hungry. Go find us some meat."

Stubs cast a meaningful glance at Lynch, a look that promised a lot of pain at a later date. Then he growled and stalked back towards the daylight. Lynch waited until he was out of sight and the others returned to their camp site.

"So when did this happen?" he asked Nash, not really expecting an answer.

"Oh, you mean when exactly did a major Demon enter our camp and forcibly implant us with his seed?" Nash replied. "I have to admit I can't really remember the exact date. Time takes on a kind of fuzzy quality when you're living half in one World and half in another. I can tell you I wish I had died that night," he wheeled and returned to his companions.

Lynch watched in awe as they slowly returned to human form. One by one they all donned new dark robes. Only then did Nash walk back to where Lynch sat. He offered him a waterskin. Lynch cocked an eyebrow at him and cast a suspicious glance at the skin.

"Relax," Nash said. "Were-Demons don't usually resort to poison. It's not violent enough."

Lynch grinned. At least he could relate to that. "Who wants me, Nash?"

Nash actually laughed. "You mean which one, don't you? You made hundreds of enemies both above and Under. I could hold an auction for you, Lynch, and probably haul in more gold than I could carry in a wagon." He grinned, and for an instant Lynch could clearly see the were-Demon again. "But I won't because of the one who placed this particular reward on your head. It's Traegor."

Lynch nodded.

"How many of his spawn have you killed anyway?"

"I sort of lost count," Lynch admitted. "I tried to kill 'em all. But it ain't nearly enough. I'd have liked to eliminate his entire race."

Nash sneered. "Good luck with that. He wants you alive, so I guess you know what that means." He abruptly rose and went back to the fire.

Lynch did indeed know what that meant. Traegor, a very powerful major Demon, intended to torture him for killing many of his spawn, or any one of a hundred other reasons. That alone should frighten him into pissing down his leg, and he knew it. He focused for a moment. Nope, his breeches were bone dry. He'd just have to cross that bridge when he came to it. For now his mind kept wandering back to the moment Stubs had struck him. If the cuffs had been used correctly and were indeed magical, that same magic that was supposed to render him helpless also prevented any harm from coming to him. And Lynch found that very interesting. Perhaps Enforcer's magical handcuffs didn't work so well in the hands of a were-Demon. He drained half the waterskin and settled in to watch for his chance.

# CHAPTER THIRTY SIX

**L**UKE NEARLY RAN RIGHT into Stubs on the trail. The former Enforcer turned were-Demon was still in a terrible rage, and his growls and moans were all that warned Luke. Even with that split second of warning, he could never have been prepared for his first sight of a mature were-Demon. He did see Stubs a few seconds before he himself was noticed. That gave him enough time to draw back the crossbow and send a sixteen inch bolt slamming directly into the were-Demon's chest. Stubs dropped to all fours and covered the distance between them in two leaps. Then the beast was on him.

He fought as well as he could against an enemy that stood seven feet tall. The bolt had disappeared into Stub's chest, but the wound didn't appear to slow him down. Luke had enough time to strike three slashes with his knife, then Stubs knocked him head over heels with one huge, clawed hand and he lost consciousness.

Luke awoke some time late, hanging upside down with his head banging solidly into Stub's buttocks in perfect time to the rhythmic slap-slap of the were-Demon's bare feet on the solid sandstone of the canyon rim. His head ached fiercely and sticky blood covered one side of his face. He hung there in gauzy agony for several minutes until he realized his hands were free. That realization was followed immediately by the fact that Lynch's tomahawk still hung from his right wrist, secured there by a leather thong. The beast evidently thought he was dead and therefore didn't need to be disarmed and was hauling him back to camp, for whatever reason. As his foggy brain processed that, Luke realized there was probably only one reason a were-Demon would haul a carcass back to camp. The realization that he was about to become the main course at a were-Demon dinner galvanized him into action.

Inch by inch, Luke stealthily drew the handle of Lynch's tomahawk up by the rawhide cord until he could grasp it. From the moment it touched his flesh Luke felt a surge of strength. And there was something more, something he didn't identify until later. It was battle lust, the desire for carnage and bloodletting. Luke simply went with his instincts. He swung the tomahawk back and chopped at the tree like leg of the were-Demon with all his strength. The enchanted blade hacked through meat, bone and sinew like it was melted butter, and Stubbs, caught in mid stride, tried to plant a foot that simply was not there. As he tumbled to that side, his confused brain registered the searing pain but he still had no idea what had happened. Luke withdrew the tomahawk and struck again, faster than a biter snake. This time he drove the magical blade directly into his abductor's crotch. It sliced through Stubb's balls, cleaved his pelvis in two and erupted from his abdomen. He fell into the dust, his entire being suffused with utter disbelief and shock. The last cognitive thought he had was, '*What horrible enemy is this?*' Then Luke's borrowed tomahawk thunked solidly home at the base of his neck and his head rolled off the trail. Luke stepped back unsteadily, his blood singing in his ears and the lust for battle coursing like fire through his veins.

"Not so big now, are ya?" he whispered. With trembling hands he found Lynch's plug of tobacco and bit off a chew. His mouth was so dry it stuck to his tongue. When he had worked up a mouthful of juice he spat it upon the remains of Stubbs, and slowly walked up the trail. Adrenaline flowed freely in his blood, enough that his legs were shaking and his muscles twitching. By the time he covered the last half mile to the cave entrance, he had finally managed to calm himself. But now that he knew his enemies, he was uncertain how to proceed. Lynch's tomahawk made the decision for him. He had been carrying it by the rawhide loop, and as he wrestled with his fear, he grabbed the handle. His indecision was swept away by the urgent need to engage his enemy.

Luke crept into the cave and had gone no more than thirty feet when he encountered a snoring, hooded man with his back to a boulder. Suddenly, he faced another quandary. Was this man one of the band who had taken Lynch hostage? Was he even a man at all? Luke climbed the boulder and perched upon it, testing the edge of the tomahawk with his thumb. He knew what Lynch would do. But he wasn't Lynch.

An inhuman roar of rage echoed in the passageway and swept Luke's indecision away. The snoring man metamorphosed in an instant into another creature like he had encountered on the trail, and Luke swept the tomahawk in a backhand blow that decapitated that monster as easily as it had the first. He leaped from the boulder and charged deeper into the cave.

# CHAPTER THIRTY SEVEN

LUKE STARED IN TOTAL shock. The carnage in the cave was like nothing he had ever seen, even in his worst nightmares. Lynch was the only upright figure. Neither said a word as Lynch gathered everything he deemed useful. Only when they had gone back into the stark whiteness of the blazing summer afternoon did Lynch speak.

"I would have preferred that you didn't see that," he began, but Luke cut him off.

"It's time you quit playing your cards so close to the vest," he said. "You always have a plan, or at least an idea of what's going on, but you never tell anyone until it's too late to be prepared."

"I did not know we were going to be attacked," Lynch asserted. "I did the best I could at the moment to protect you. Why did you follow me?"

Luke was temporarily struck silent by the change the conversation had taken. Finally, he spoke.

"I might have left you," he admitted. "But I couldn't disappoint Mariel."

Lynch laughed. So he owed his life, quite possibly, to a slip of a girl and a teenage boy. Yes, he had bested those in the cave, but only he knew how much it had taken out of him. The final two that Luke had defeated may have been too much even for him.

"Come on," he told Luke. "Let's get out of this goddamn desert."

Seven days later they reached the coast. They walked along it for two more days when Luke spotted a sail. Even Lynch's eyes couldn't pick it out. He nodded approvingly. The boy was going to be good, there was no doubt about that.

"Can you see a standard?" he asked.

"Can't pick it out," Luke replied.

Lynch began kicking together a pile of grease brush. "Help me start a signal fire," he said. "Hurry now. I'm tired of this stinking desert."

Together the four kicked together a pile of brush three feet high, which Lynch set ablaze with a quick spell. Admiration shone in Mathias' eyes, which was a fact that caused Mariel's expression to darken in anger. But she had no time to say a word before the blazing greasewood sent a plume of black smoke billowing into the air. In moments it was obvious the ship had changed course and was making straight toward land.

"Now," Lynch said speculatively, "let's walk down and see who is offering us a ride."

It didn't take long for the ship to cover most of the distance and toss out the anchor. Before the longboats even hit the water, Lynch whistled under his breath.

"Well I'll be damned," he said with a chuckle. Then he waited passively with his arms folded across his chest.

"That's Jake," Luke blurted. "On the ship." He turned to Mathias and Mariel. "It's Jake's ship!"

Lynch grinned. This could be interesting. The men rowing the longboats didn't have much to say as they rammed the noses of the crafts into the sand and motioned for the small band to board. In minutes they were boarding the ship.

"Afternoon, Jake," Lynch said when he had climbed on deck, as if it hadn't been three years since the two had last spoken.

"Lynch," Smilin' Jake responded. There was no welcome in his tone. Then he spied Luke and his face creased in his trademark grin. Luke resisted the urge to run and throw his arms around him. "Luke," he said and as the boy drew near he clapped an arm around his shoulders. Luke felt as if he had finally come home.

"It's time," Lynch said.

Smilin' Jake glanced at Luke. The boy had filled out. "I reckon so."

Later, after the crew pulled anchor and they were well at sea, Lynch and Smilin' Jake sat in the captain's quarters.

"The *magii'ri* have regrouped," Lynch explained. "Mostly under my direction, at least at first. The people of Norland still hold them in contempt, but these are Truebloods, Jake. They have sworn to uphold the Code with no compensation."

"Is that so?" Smilin' Jake asked indifferently.

"You don't seem too interested," Lynch accused,

"I'm not," Smilin' Jake replied. "I tried to uphold the Code, to establish law and order and protect the people of Norland, and what did I get in return? Nothing. Everywhere I went people shit on me. They treated me like garbage. So I took a page from your book, Lynch. I helped myself. I've been ambushing pirates and thieves and relieving them of their plunder for more than a year now."

Despite himself, Lynch grinned. "I wondered what became of the renegade who was policing the Borderlands."

"I got smart," Smilin' Jake replied as he suddenly stood and went out on the open deck.

"And broke the Code a few times," Lynch pointed out as he followed him. "You're a wanted man, Smilin' Jake. Everybody from the outlaws to the *magii'ri* have a price on your head." Lynch baited his hook and waited to set it. "In fact, people are saying that the old time Truebloods were nothing but cowards and that you wouldn't have the guts to come back anyway."

Smilin' Jake whirled around so quickly Lynch took a step back. "Is that right?"

"It is," Lynch insisted. "Some of them claim to have run you out of the country personally."

"Such as?" Smilin' Jake asked.

Lynch knew he had him. He shrugged. "A few no name outlaws in Elanderfeld that I had in prison. Of course, I hung them. But they named a few others before they danced at the end of the rope."

"Who did they name?" Smilin' Jake demanded.

"A small time follower of Marsten named Billings, for one," Lynch said carelessly. He knew he had just signed the man's death warrant, but he didn't care in the least. "And a couple of *magii'ri* turned bad. Of course, most of them are returned to hide out in the Borderlands after you left."

"How many Warriors are there who remained true to the Code?" Smilin. Jake asked.

Lynch hid his satisfied smile. "Damn few," he admitted. "They have a hard battle ahead, and absolutely no help from the people. But they've started training Warriors in the Old Ways. I think Luke needs to join up."

"He's a mite young," Smilin' Jake pointed out. "And I ain't too sure I even want him to be brought up *magii'ri.*"

"Not too young," Lynch argued. "It's time, Jake. And you can't be seen in Norland. You're still a wanted man."

"I'll go with Luke. It's time I followed through on that at least," Jake replied obstinately. "Besides, it sounds like I have business back in Norland."

"You don't have to," Lynch replied with a grin. "I'll take care of Luke."

"That's what bothers me," Smilin' Jake said. "You're a bad influence, Lynch."

"I reckon," Lynch agreed.

Jake grinned as he made his decision. "We'll make for Norland. Anyone not wanting to land there better get off here."

"We all want to return to Norland," Mathias replied.

Jake nodded as he shook Mathias' hand and gave Mariel a brief hug. "Good to see all of you made it."

When the younger people had gone below, Lynch spoke again. "How well did you know them? Who were their parents?"

Smilin' Jake shrugged. "I never asked. The boy is obviously a Wizard. He says he took an oath to protect the girl."

"Why wouldn't he?" Lynch asked. "Brothers usually end up being overprotective of their sisters."

"What?" Smilin' Jake responded.

"They're brother and sister," Lynch assured him. "He thinks he's protecting her by denying that she's *magii'ri. "*

"What do you know," Smilin' Jake said with a shake of his head. "But… if Mathias hid that from us for so long, he had a reason. I'd appreciate it if you don't tell Luke."

Lynch had enough secrets to fill a book. "Whatever," he muttered. He was thinking about the boy with different colored eyes.

The voyage back to Norland was uneventful, but the closer they came to the coast the more agitated Lynch became. He paced the deck, sometimes muttering, but usually silent with a scowl on his handsome face.

"What the Hell is wrong with you?" Smilin' Jake finally asked.

"Strangers aren't exactly welcomed in Norland," Lynch replied. "I'm not sure if there's a hangman's noose waiting for me or if the people of Norland will be satisfied with simply stoning me to death."

"Maybe they forgot you," Smilin' Jake suggested.

Lynch rolled his eyes. "Preposterous. How could anyone forget me?"

"You're right," Jake replied after he'd thought that over. "So tell me the situation one more time."

"The *magii'ri* are regrouping," Lynch said. "But Truebloods are few and far between. Those who survived the Revolution have set up camp in the foothills of the Mirl Mountains, but I have to warn you Jake, the people of Norland want nothing to do with the *magii'ri*. They blame us, err…" he glanced at Jake to see if he had caught that slip. "They blame the *magii'ri* for everything. I've been among them…"

"You cast another Dark spell," Smilin' Jake interrupted.

"Yes, for a good reason," Lynch continued. Jake seemed to be growing more agitated by the minute. "I had to know if it was safe for Luke to continue his training. Now, the *magii'ri* have managed to push the Nightriders, half men and ogres back to the Borderlands, but it takes a strong force to hold them there. The people, meanwhile, refuse to accept that the *magii'ri* are upholding the Code. Halfbloods are now being accepted as 'prentices. The *magii'ri* desperately need more recruits, but the Council maintains that the age limits must be respected. Are you listening, Jake?"

"I'm listenin'," Smilin' Jake responded. "I knew most of that already. Who's in power?"

Lynch shrugged. "A handful of warlords feud over that regularly, but for the most part it's relatively peaceful between the people of Norland."

"So there is no King?" Jake asked.

"No. There may never be another King," Lynch said. "Norland may never recover completely." He spat over the side. "It wasn't supposed to be this way," he muttered.

"What wasn't supposed to be this way?" Smilin' Jake asked.

"Revolutions *cleanse*, not destroy," Lynch said, more to himself than to Jake. "All through history civilizations rebound from Revolution to become stronger, more vibrant and energetic, with fewer rules to bind the freedom of the people. This was not Revolution. It was butchery for the sake of butchery."

"Ain't that what you wanted?" Smilin' Jake asked. "No rules, everybody doing whatever they were strong enough to do. The strong survive, the weak are killed off and Lynch lives happily ever after."

"Say what's bothering you," Lynch said. "Don't dance around it."

The crew stopped their duties and watched, sensing trouble.

"You," Smilin' Jake responded. "You are what's bothering me, Lynch. Always lurking in the shadows where you won't be hurt while you lead others right to the gates of the Abyss. You wanted that goddamned Revolution, and it got Cap'n Graywullf, Bill and Ox killed."

Lynch started to turn away, and Jake lunged forward and jerked him around by the collar. Lynch thrust his forearms between Jake's and knocked his hands free.

"Don't do this, Jake," Lynch warned.

"I'm doin' it," Jake assured him. "It's time we got this all out, right now. Did you know Cap'n Graywullf was goin' to die that day?"

"I tried to stop it," Lynch began.

"You murderin' son of a bitch," Jake snarled as he lunged back at the tall Wizard.

Lynch stepped aside, but Jake was ready for that. He struck, fast as a biter snake, and Lynch recoiled as Jake landed two punches. Then he lunged forward and they stood toe to toe, slugging it out.

"Fight!" one of the crew shouted.

The hold emptied. Luke stood with Mathias and Mariel, dumbfounded as Jake and Lynch exchanged punches. Within seconds both men's faces were bloodied. Jake stepped forward and wrapped Lynch in a bear hug, and with his legs pumping he drove the Wizard backwards into a huge crate which splintered under the impact. Lynch grunted in pain, then drove a knee upwards, aiming for Jake's groin. The Warrior raised his leg to block it, but he answered Lynch's grunt of pain with one of his own as Lynch's knee drove into the meat of his thigh. Lynch slammed his hands between himself and Jake and threw him free, but both men were only able to make it to their knees before Jake looped a long punch that caught Lynch just above the ear. Lights exploded inside Lynch's head, but as he went down he drove his own fist into Jake's chin. Both men went down, groaning. The crew watched in shock. None had ever stayed even with Smilin' Jake, let alone nearly bested him.

"I tried to save him," Lynch gasped. "I tried to save all of you."

"What kind of Dark Wizard are you?" Smilin' Jake groaned as he lay flat on his back. "You lost three out of four."

"Yeah, well, I saved you didn't I?" Lynch retorted.

"Dammit Lynch," Jake said with a catch in his voice. "You should have let me die. They were the only family I had. There is no honor in surviving only because I ran from the fight."

"Was there no honor in saving Luke and the other refugees?" Lynch reminded him. "Luke is your family, and he's going to need your help."

Jake clambered to his knees. "He's going to need more than I can offer. He'll need the help of a Dark Wizard, or I miss my guess."

"I reckon so," Lynch agreed. He slowly climbed to his knees and offered his hand to Jake. Smilin' Jake looked at it for a moment then grasped it.

"So what can we do?" Smilin' Jake asked.

Lynch grinned, even though his lip was split and he had several cuts in his mouth. "Luke is going to become a Warrior, the greatest *magii'ri* Warrior ever known. And you and I are going to go back into the shadows and do some hunting. Savvy?"

Smilin' Jake's face creased with his first genuine smile in years. "I reckon so."

They landed at Elanderfeld. Smilin' Jake could not believe his eyes. Over half of the destroyed city had been rebuilt, and the rest was being cleared of debris to make ready for new construction. The place was abuzz with activity. Smilin' Jake even noticed a couple whorehouses lining the docks. Lynch caught the direction of his gaze.

"I have a man with supplies and horses waiting in the foothills," Lynch said as they disembarked. "There's no time for tomfoolery."

Smilin' Jake grudgingly agreed. Lynch's man, a lean young man with a hatchet face named Hoggins, met them at the designated spot with saddle mounts and pack mules. Smilin' Jake noted he had a firm grip and a hard stare. When they were well on their way, he turned back in his saddle to look at Hoggins, who rode the drag.

"Is he a Wizard?" Smilin' Jake asked.

"His father was," Lynch replied. "His mother was from Warrior stock. He's a 'prentice Warrior now."

"Is he any good?" Smilin' Jake asked.

"He's good," Lynch assured him. "Why do you ask?"

"I like to know who's got my back," Smilin' Jake replied. "That's all." He dug in his pocket and pulled out a plug of tobacco. He bit off a sizable chew and offered it to Lynch, who shook his head and shied away disgustedly. Jake situated his chew and spat. His horse rolled its eyes at him.

They made camp in a hollow deep in the foothills of the Mirl Mountains. Luke and Mathias ventured out with their slings and returned with five rabbits.

"I'll get them on as soon as you get 'em skinned," Smilin' Jake offered happily.

"I'll cook them," Lynch intercepted the rabbits. Luke sighed with relief. Jake was more than competent in most areas, but he was a terrible cook. Luke admitted to himself that he wasn't much better. After supper, Luke sat beside Jake while he smoked a pipe.

"It's good to be back," Smilin' Jake admitted. "I never thought I'd say that."

"What will we run into?" Luke asked.

"More than likely you'll be tested somehow," Smilin' Jake told him. He saw the worried expression that stole onto Luke's face. "Don't worry. You were trained by the best of the best. You know more than most of the trainers by now. The only thing they got on you is size and that's just cause they're older than you. But you got 'em all beat on natural ability." Jake paused and blew smoke rings for a moment. "There's one other thing, Luke. You got more heart than any ten men. I'm damn proud to ride with you."

Across the fire, Lynch hid a satisfied grin behind his hand.

Three days later they sat on their mounts on a low hill looking down into the Mirl Valley. Sentries had been posted, but so far they hadn't been spotted.

"You should ride the rest of the way without us," Lynch said. "Less trouble all around."

Luke and Mathias nodded.

"Hoggins will introduce you, but that's all," Lynch continued. "He's barely above the 'prentice ranks himself, so don't expect any favorable treatment just cause you know him. Just go down there and do whatever they ask." He stared hard at Mathias. "I know you have more ability than most Wizards, but don't show it off. They'll only question you and suspect you if you do that." He turned to Luke. "Most likely they'll think you're too young. The 'prentice age has been raised. It's up to you to show them you're ready. If you have to knock a few heads together, so be it." Luke nodded pensively.

Lynch and Smilin' Jake turned to go. "I'll be around," Jake said as he went by Luke. "If'n they jump you, don't hold back. But don't kill anybody either."

Lynch and Smilin' Jake rode down the back side of the hill.

"This ain't no time for joking," Lynch said shortly.

"Who said I was joking?" Jake replied. "Come on, we're burning daylight."

They rode for more than a mile in silence. The only sound was the occasional call of a quail, the grunting of the horses and the muted jingle of saddle hardware. Finally, Smilin' Jake reined in his mount and waited for Lynch to come alongside.

"You said we was going hunting," Jake said. "Might be easier for me if I knew what we was huntin'."

Lynch's face was bleak. "A boy child, borne of the Black Queen Mordant about nine months after you was ambushed."

Smilin' Jake didn't miss the importance of those words. "Nine months, huh?" He was silent for almost a mile. "That makes me wonder if you had time for a little ruttin' before the Black Queen escaped."

"He ain't mine, you dumb shit. Mordant managed to impregnate herself with *magii'ri* seed. The boy is Graywullf's."

Smilin' Jake wrenched his horse's head around so hard it shied and nearly went down on it's haunches. "The Black Queen got herself pregnant with Lorn Graywullf's baby? What the hell are we gonna do now?""

"We have to kill him," Lynch replied emotionlessly, but his voice lacked conviction.

Smilin' Jake spat in disgust. "Two grown men, both *magii'ri* Warriors, hunting down a boy of maybe three years? I can't do that, Lynch."

"He's Mordant's son," Lynch responded. "Bred for her purposes. She'll raise him to hate the *magii'ri,* and he'll hate them like only a halfbreed can."

"So he's Cap'n Graywullf's seed?" Jake asked.

"I reckon," Lynch answered.

"Then he's half good at least," Jake argued. "Why can't we give him a chance to show his stripes? If he's loyal to the Light, he'd be one hell of an ally. That old saw about taking a halfbreed to truly hate works both ways, I reckon."

Lynch was astounded. "By the gods. You Warriors are smarter than you look." He considered that for a moment. "Yes. I believe you may be on to something. There has never been a man more loyal to the Light than Lorn Graywullf. The Light may actually overpower the Dark. I'll tell you what, Smilin' Jake," Lynch said with sudden enthusiasm. "We'll find this boy together, and we will give him a chance." He gigged his mount around Jake and trotted down the trail.

Smilin' Jake watched him go for a moment. "You don't fool me," he muttered. "You never wanted to kill the boy in the first place." A smile was firmly in place on his lips as he trotted after Lynch.

# CHAPTER THIRTY EIGHT

L UKE SAT WITH MATHIAS and Mariel. Now that the time had come, returning to Norland seemed risky. Hoggins watched them for a few minutes, then shrugged and led the way down into the valley.

The outlying areas of the valley were dotted with farmsteads. The wheat fields were knee high and golden in the summer sun, and the sweet scent of ripening grain rode the warm breeze. Farmers were hard at work in the hayfields, scything hay for winter feed. Nearly all raised a hand in a friendly wave as the small group passed by.

As they neared the settlement, the homes became more concentrated. Here was where the merchants lived, tradesmen who supplied the *magii'ri* with everything they needed from clothes to flour. The center of the village was surrounded by a log stockade ten feet high and six feet thick. Pickets of gleaming steel lined the top of the wall. The *magii'ri* trained and lived inside the walls, except when they were out on patrol. Hoggins led them to a guarded gate, where they were admitted after a hushed conference. Then he led them straight to a squat stone building.

"The Council is inside," he told them. Then he rushed off.

Luke and Mathias looked at each other. "Might as well get this over with," Luke said as he swung down.

"Mariel, you better stay out here," Mathias suggested. He swung down and the two stood shoulder to shoulder.

The cool shadows of the interior of the stone building welcomed them. It was a relief after the heat of the day. Three very tall, stern looking men sat at a low stone table. They all studied the two young men with open interest. Finally, one stood.

"Hoggins signaled that you were coming in," he said. "I'm called Dobbin. The three of us that you see are serving as the Council until, well, until someone with more experience comes along." He looked behind Luke and Mathias. "So where is Lynch?"

"Left us at the coast," Luke replied. "Hoggins led us here."

"I see," Dobbin said. "And who are you?"

"Luke Graywullf."

The other Wizards exchanged glances.

"Well, Mr. Graywullf, don't expect to be admitted here simply because you are Lorn Graywullf's son," Dobbin stated. He shifted his attention to Mathais. "And you?"

"Mathias Bulwyn."

Dobbin nodded. "And the girl outside?"

"An orphan," Mathias said quickly. "If we're allowed to stay Luke and I will look after her."

Dobbin nodded thoughtfully. "The *magii'ri* are in an extraordinary position right now. We need men, but the key word there is men. Not boys. I'm sorry, Luke, but you're just too young. Mathias, we have some simple tests for you."

Luke stood dumbfounded. He wasn't even being given a chance. He wheeled and charged back out the door to the street. Mariel looked up in surprise as Luke ran by her. She caught up to him in the livery stable.

"Luke, what's wrong?" Mariel asked.

Luke swung a vicious kick at a bale of straw. "Coming here was a mistake. They won't even give me a chance. I'm going to try to find Smilin' Jake and Lynch and ride with them."

"I want to go with you," Mariel said.

Luke stopped. "I can't take care of you on the trail, Mariel. Here, I had a chance, with Mathias' help." Luke froze, looking over Mariel's shoulder at the stable doorway. Two *magii'ri* 'prentices swaggered in. Both appeared to be about sixteen years old.

"You Graywullf?" one demanded to know.

Luke looked from one to the other and nodded.

"Yer old man was a traitor," the second one sneered.

"And a back shootin' coward," the other added.

Luke saw no need for words. He charged the first teen and slammed his shoulder into the boy's belly. They both went down in a heap. The second boy aimed a kick at Luke's head that caught him in the ribs instead, and lifted him clear of the stable floor. Luke rolled with the kick and leaped to his feet. He ducked low and pounded three fast punches into the second boy's midsection. The first boy caught him by the ankle and pulled his foot out from under him, then leaped upon him. He outweighed Luke by thirty pounds. He bloodied Luke's nose and opened a gash on his cheekbone before Luke could throw him free. He was up fast, but Luke was faster. He stepped in and punched the older boy in one eye, then clubbed him across the side of the head. The second boy came up behind him and wrapped him in a bear hug, but Luke slipped down to free himself, then hammered his elbow back and felt the other boy's nose break. Both of his attackers were down. Luke felt blood trickling from his nose and his cheek and blood lust thrummed in his ears. Mariel screamed. Three more boys walked in. One carried a stave of hardwood.

Luke hunched his shoulders and charged, but before he completed three steps he was lifted clear off the floor. He writhed and struggled, but the man holding him was too strong.

"Let me go," Luke seethed. "I can take 'em."

The man holding him laughed. "I don't doubt you'd try. What's goin' on here?"

"Those boys said Luke's father was a coward and a back shooter," Mariel explained.

"Who's your father?"

"Lorn Graywullf," Luke answered. "He's dead."

The huge hand holding him relaxed a tiny bit. "I know. What are you doin' here?"

"I want to become *magii'ri*," Luke answered.

"Hmmm? You already *are magii'ri*. Come with me," the man released Luke and he spun around. He was looking at the biggest man he'd ever seen. He was even bigger than Ox had been. Luke hurried after him, and Mariel followed Luke. The 'prentices backed away and scattered as they tried vainly to disappear.

"I'm Colin," the big man said as his heavy boots beat a solid drumming on the boardwalk. They entered the stone hut and Colin stomped right up to the table with Luke in tow. He produced Luke from behind him.

"Thisun's ours," he said as his heavy hand dropped on Luke's shoulders. "He ain't got a lick of sense, but he can fight. And there ain't no quit in him. He's ours. He'll be a Warrior."

Dobbin glanced at his associates, then shrugged. "He'll be your responsibility then. If'n you want him, he's yours."

Colin nodded. Then he spun Luke around and herded him back out onto the street.

# CHAPTER THIRTY NINE

SEVEN YEARS PASSED. LYNCH and Smilin' Jake had scoured every inch of the Borderlands looking for the child of Mordant and Lorn Graywullf to no avail. The day came when even Lynch had to admit failure. Together they rode back with all the information they had accumulated while riding in the shadows to recruit the support of the *magii'ri*.

"There's no way the Black Queen could have amassed that many soldiers," Dobbin declared flatly. "My scouts haven't seen anything that would indicate the Black Queen is even in the area."

"That's what I've been telling you," Lynch repeated. "The Black Queen is gathering a huge force across the sea. There is only one reason she would do that. She means to finish what was started during the Revolution."

"Across the sea?" Dobbin said. "Mordant can't harm us if she's across the sea."

"When her force is strong enough she'll sweep over Norland like a prairie fire," Lynch insisted. "You must stop her now. Don't wait for her to bring the fight to your doorstep again."

"What did you say your name was again?" Dobbin asked.

"It doesn't matter," Lynch replied. He arose from his chair in front of the Council and returned to the street where Smilin' Jake waited. Jake spat in the dust off the boardwalk.

"Well?"

"They wouldn't listen," Lynch said. "Just like you said."

Smilin' Jake considered that. "Now what?"

"Find Luke," Lynch replied. "Time to see what he's made of."

"You, me and Luke against an army?" Smilin' Jake said. "I may be crazy, but I don't like those odds."

Lynch grinned. "Don't worry. I have a plan."

"I was afraid you'd say that," Smilin' Jake replied. "For the last seven years we been getting out of one scrape after another by the skin of our teeth, scrapes we got into mostly because of your plans." He worked his tobacco thoughtfully then spat a brown stream into the dust. "I guess one more won't hurt. What are we waiting for?"

They walked down the rutted street. As other groups of boisterous young *magii'ri* 'prentices passed by, Jake tilted his hat down and glanced away out of habit. It had been years since he'd last seen a wanted poster with his likeness on it, but it was better not to invite trouble. They approached a long rectangular water trough which drained into a muddy slough at one end. The 'prentices used it to rinse off the grime from a day of training when exercises ended for the day. Smilin' Jake glanced left and right, then placed a small white stone near the intake end of the trough. Then he and Lynch walked to the end of the square.

"Might as well get a drink," Lynch suggested.

"Kinda risky, ain't it?" Smilin' Jake responded. Lynch had never allowed them time for even a bath when they visited Luke.

Lynch shook his head and sighed. "Smilin' Jake, I do believe we have been forgotten."

Smilin' Jake was taken aback. "What are you talkin' about?"

"The Council has no idea who I am," Lynch said with a short bark of laughter. But it was obvious he was not amused. "After five centuries, I have finally outlived even my own reputation."

"Did you tell 'em yer name is Lynch?" Smilin' Jake asked.

"Hell, no!" Lynch replied. "If they're too wet behind the ears to recognize *me*, the Warlock who could have toppled an empire, then they ain't worth my attention anymore."

"Oh, so that's it," Smilin' Jake remarked. "Yer pissed because they ain't scared of you no more."

Lynch made a disgusted sound in his throat as they walked out of the town square and turned in to the first saloon they came to. Raucous piano music filtered out over the batwing doors, along with a mixture of tobacco smoke and a babble of voices. Smilin' Jake shrugged and followed him. Off duty *magii'ri* Warriors and Wizards alike lined the bar and sat at seven scattered tables. Lynch and Jake shouldered their way to the bar.

Smilin' Jake licked his lips. He hadn't had an open drink standing at a bar in years. Lynch ordered whiskey for both of them. When it came, he tossed his down and watched as Jake did the same.

"Whew! That came straight from the rock cat's kidneys," Smilin' Jake whispered. His throat felt raw.

"You just lost your taste for it, that's all," Lynch said sourly. He ordered another and turned to survey the room with his drink in hand. "Look at 'em," he snorted. "None of 'em dry behind the ears yet. And this is the cream of the crop, Jake!"

"Luke's younger than any of 'em," Smilin' Jake reminded him. He downed his second drink as his eyes watered. "What's eatin' at you?" he asked Lynch.

Lynch gulped down his third drink. His voice was hoarse. "We seem to have outlived our time, Smilin' Jake. Or rather, I have." He scanned the room. "Check that. Both of us belong to another time."

"What in the Hell are you talkin' about?" Smilin' Jake responded.

"This," Lynch gestured all around him. "It's all become so...predictable. In the old days, every day was a challenge! And I was so...so...enthused about even the simplest thing! Now, where are the challenges? What is there to make a man feel alive again?"

"Shit," Jake replied. "Is that what the last seven years have been? Just a way to make yer sap run again? Goddamn! When we rode into that last colony of ogres, I'm telling you my blood was singin'! If that ain't enough for you, then you're one crazy bastard, Lynch."

"Maybe I am crazy," Lynch agreed. "All I know, is when a man don't feel useful anymore, he ain't got much reason to live. I think maybe I'm about to that point."

"There's enough enemies in the Borderlands for another lifetime or two," Smilin' Jake said.

"That's just it. We could spend our lives here and not make a difference," Lynch said. "The next generation of Warriors will still be doing the same damn thing."

"You're drunk," Smilin' Jake said. "Or crazy. The Dragonrider wouldn't be sitting here in a saloon crying about being forgot."

"And neither would Smilin' Jake Sipowicz, Trueblood *magii'ri* Warrior," Lynch retorted. "Don't you feel it, Jake?"

"Keep yer voice down!" Smilin' Jake whispered urgently. "I'm not like you," Smilin' Jake continued. "I don't crave a spotlight shining on me all the time. You and me spent seven years doing necessary work. It wasn't flashy and nobody even cares that we did it, but we made a difference."

Lynch turned back to the bartender. "Did you know that me and this man right here," he clapped Jake on the shoulders, "have spent the last seven years traversing the Borderlands? We fought ogres, half-men, Nightriders, even a few were-Demons."

The bartender laughed. "Nobody rides through the Borderlands. I reckon you've had enough." He grabbed the bottle and continued down the bar.

Lynch turned back to Jake triumphantly. "See?"

"He's a bartender," Smilin' Jake replied. "I doubt he's been outside the village in years."

"I've had enough just the same," Lynch said. "I miss the old days when the name Lynch struck fear in the hearts of all he encountered. It's time to rekindle that spark."

"At what cost?" Smilin' Jake responded.

"Any cost," Lynch said. "If I go out, I'll go out with a blaze of glory."

"I think it's time you quit makin' plans for me, then," Smilin' Jake replied.

Lynch grinned. "Come on, Jake. One last adventure. Hell, I know you can't resist."

"What are you two planning now?" Luke asked. He had sidled up to the bar without being seen. Lynch and Luke had been so engrossed in conversation they didn't notice him. Luke had filled out. He was taller than Lorn had been, heavier through the shoulders and arms too. But he had the same eyes. Dragon's eyes. Emotionless and cold.

"Well," Lynch said loudly. "The Black Queen Mordant is gathering a huge force on the Isle of Serpents and me and Smilin' Jake here were trying to enlist the aid of the *magii'ri.*"

A few of the Warriors closest to Lynch glanced his way, then shook their heads and went back to their own business. Lynch stared smugly at Jake.

"You're serious?" Luke asked.

"As serious as death," Lynch answered.

"I wish you'd stop that kind of talk," Smilin' Jake said. He looked back at Luke. "You're looking good, boy. Bigger'n the cap'n was, taller too."

"Thanks, Jake," Luke said. "You look tired. Yer runnin' yourself into the ground. What's this about the Black Queen?"

Smilin' Jake sputtered in his whiskey glass while Lynch grinned.

"Told you," he said to Jake. "It's true. I tried to get Dobbin to send a force to intercept her. He all but laughed in my face. It's up to the three of us."

"Four," another voice interrupted. It was Mathias.

"Now we're getting somewhere," Lynch crowed.

"Hold up," Smilin' Jake said. He looked around then herded the rest of them out the doors. "I know you're just itchin' to die, Lynch, but four of us won't disturb Mordant's army one damn bit."

"We will if the entire *magii'ri* army is on our trail," Lynch replied.

"They won't send out the whole army for two deserters," Smilin' Jake retorted. "And you already said they don't give a rat's tail about you anymore."

Lynch shot him a dirty look. "They will," he assured Jake. "The entire World will be talking about Lynch very soon."

A week later they sat on the same low hill Smilin' Jake had plummeted down at the reins of an old farm wagon loaded with refugees from the Revolution. The port at Elanderfeld had recovered nicely under the watchful eye of the young Warlord who had cleaned up the city. Lynch counted eleven ships at berth in the harbor. Three of those appeared to be *magii'ri* military ships. Smilin' Jake noticed the special attention Lynch was paying to those particular ships.

"I'm liking this less and less," he whispered to Lynch.

"It's foolproof," Lynch replied.

"They don't have guns, do they?" Smilin' Jake asked. Lynch shook his head. "How about cannon? Do the ships still carry cannons?"

"They have cannon on board," Lynch replied. "But no powder. Without powder those big guns are useful as anchors and that's about it. We've gone over this a dozen times, Jake. If there is anybody in Norland who knows how to make gunpowder, he's not sayin' anything."

"I just don't want to get my ass shot off without a chance to fight back, that's all," Smilin' Jake responded.

Lynch grunted an obscenity. Suddenly he became animated. "The closest ship has been making ready all day, and now the crew is disembarking. This is it! They'll only have one or two sentries on board. Luke, here's your chance."

Despite himself, Smilin' Jake felt the first stirrings of excitement. Maybe Lynch was right. Maybe they had been wasting away in the Borderlands. Luke rose to leave and Jake placed a hand on his shoulder.

"Make it quick. If'n there's more than we counted on, bail out."

Luke grinned and slipped into the darkness. Smilin' Jake watched apprehensively. He could only see Luke for a few seconds then he was nothing more than a shadow among shadows.

Lynch grinned satisfactorily. "He's good. Damn good." A sound from the hillside behind them caught Lynch's attention. It wasn't actually a sound, he realized. It was a feeling, the same feeling he'd been having at regular intervals since their last foray into the Borderlands. Smilin' Jake saw the direction of his attention and studied the hillside. He saw nothing.

"What's got you spooked?" he whispered to Lynch.

"Somebody's been following us," Lynch replied. He turned back towards the ship just in time to see a lantern winking on the deck. "Come on. Luke's signaling us."

They hurried down the wagon road and walked boldly up the gangplank to the upper deck of the ship Luke signaled from. Luke and Smilin' Jake slipped over opposite sides and disabled the rudders of the other *magii'ri* ships while Mathias and Lynch made the ship ready to sail. As soon as Luke and Smilin' Jake climbed aboard, they ran up the sail and the ship began to glide out of port. The crews of the other ships shouted out the alarm and as the ship Lynch had chosen pulled out from between them, they attempted to give chase. Smilin' Jake stood at the helm with Lynch and grimaced as the other two ships collided with a sound of splintering timbers. Lynch waved and bowed grandly.

"I am the Dark Wizard Lynch," he shouted. "Remember that name!"

They sailed in silence for several hours. The shoreline faded steadily behind them, until the last light from the tallest tower blinked out. Smilin' Jake set a course for the Isle of Serpents then stood at the wheel, studiously chewing a huge wad of tobacco. Lynch catnapped then arose at dawn to relieve him. He stood at the rail and pissed overboard. As he fastened his breeches, he spoke.

"Ok Jake, something's bothering you. What is it?"

"This ain't just about restoring your reputation, is it?" Smilin' Jake asked. "We're doing this to defeat Mordant and get some revenge for the Cap'ns' death for the benefit of the Light. Right?"

"Of course," Lynch answered smoothly. He even managed to appear hurt. "I'm in this for the same reason you are, just like all those times in the Borderlands. If my reputation is polished in the process, all the better."

"But you ain't puttin' yourself first?" Smilin' Jake pressed.

"The old Lynch would have done that," the Warlock replied. "I'm the new and improved version."

Smilin' Jake grunted an unintelligible response as he climbed below deck to get some sleep. As his head cleared the deck he gave Lynch a thoughtful glance. "We'll see," he muttered.

The crossing was uneventful, and as they neared the Isle, Lynch became more energetic and animated. He also studied the coastline with his spyglass. It appeared deserted, but as they came closer he felt the fingers of apprehension. He kept returning to several dark images that looked like nothing more than heat waves dancing along the beach. As he watched they seemed to solidify. Realization hit him like a hammer.

"Son of a bitch," he whispered.

After seven years Smilin' Jake had become attuned to Lynch's moods. Whatever he had seen, it was bad. He merely shot a questioning glance Lynch's way.

"Bounty hunters," Lynch grunted. "On the beach. Looks like we attracted a bit more attention in the Borderlands than I had thought."

"Are they of the Dark or the Light?" Mathias asked.

"Probably Dark," Lynch replied.

"Sail up the coast," Smilin' Jake ordered. "Full sail, as fast as we can. We'll outrun them, go inland, then double back to the Citadel. Once we're inside we got it made."

The ship flew up the coast leaving the menacing shapes of the bounty hunters behind.

"So, Lynch," Smilin' Jake said conversationally. "Do you mind telling me what we're up against?"

"No bullshit?" Lynch replied.

"No bullshit," Smilin' Jake confirmed.

"There is a being here I have been tracking for centuries, among the gathering of Nightriders and half-men. I made a deal with Slagg, the Sky Rider to find this man, if man he is. Slagg wants him alive for a short time, then he'll probably tear him to pieces. I reckon he'll be along shortly," Lynch said matter of factly.

"Slagg? The Dragon?" Mathias interrupted.

"Yes," Lynch answered. "Slagg the Dragon."

Smilin' Jake kicked the gunwhales of the ship. "Exactly how long have you known this being was here?"

"I've been chasing him around the known World and even into other worlds for the better part of a hundred years," Lynch said. "I could never quite catch up when the odds were in my favor. Now…I think he wants me to catch up."

"Start from the beginning," Smilin' Jake suggested. "Is this being a man or what?"

"He was a man once," Lynch replied. "A very powerful Warlock named Blackhelm. "You know him, Jake, you and Graywullf went into the desert to destroy him all those years ago. He cursed Slagg, and Slagg sought my help to break the curse since I had the Book of Runes. I agreed to help if Slagg guarded my book. Blackhelm found a way around Slagg by traveling through a portal into another, parallel World. Now he is back here with intimate knowledge of my book. He was afraid of me because I have the means to destroy him. But now…he has aligned himself with the Black Queen and is using himself as bait to draw me into a trap where I may be safely killed."

Luke listened stoically, then reached into Jake's pocket and withdrew his tobacco. He bit off a sizable piece and began chewing. He spat a mouthful of juice over the side of the ship.

"So you led us into a trap?" Luke asked.

"No," Lynch hastily denied that. "I just put it all together when I saw the bounty hunters."

"We could put out to sea," Mathias suggested.

Smilin' Jake shook his head. "We'd never outrun the *magii'ri* now. No, we need to make a run for the Citadel. Once we're inside we'll be safe."

They continued up the coast under full sail. The *magii'ri* ship was a good one, and it plowed through the waves fast enough to leave a wake of sea foam behind. Just before nightfall they dropped sail and lowered the anchor. A fully loaded skiff was lowered over the side and they rowed ashore. Each man was armed to the teeth, and they all carried waterskins. As they set foot once again on solid land, Lynch spoke.

"Brings back memories, eh, Jake?"

Smilin' Jake merely grunted a reply to that. He pulled Lynch aside. "I got one last question for you. You said once that neither me nor Lorn or even you would be the one to put an end to this. Is that true?"

Lynch nodded. "It is, Jake. I've seen it. We all have parts to play yet, but you and I will not see Blackhelm defeated."

Smilin' Jake shrugged then grinned. "This may be the last stop for old Jake. I had the feelin' that I had cheated Death too many times already. We'd best not keep him waitin'. Come on."

Luke and Mathias had already started to climb the cliffs. The plan called for them to climb the cliffs, make their way a half mile back from the edge then double back to the Citadel. If they were lucky, the bounty hunters wouldn't smell them, and they'd arrive at the Citadel undetected. A ripple of fear made Jake's spine tingle. They'd be like flies on that open wall, waiting to be swatted.

Mathias and Luke reached the top safely, and crouched there with longbows ready to cover Lynch and Smilin' Jake. They also reached the top safely as full darkness fell on the Isle of Serpents. Jake's face shone with sweat in the moonlight and an unfamiliar ache had settled in his chest, but his trademark grin was firmly in place. He cleared his throat and spat, then stopped and stared. His spit was laced with red.

"How long do you think it will take us to reach the Citadel?" Luke asked Lynch.

Lynch glanced at Jake as the Warrior paused to catch his breath. "We might make it by midday tomorrow. Unless…"

"No," Smilin' Jake protested. "No more Dark Magic. Let's play this hand out with the cards we been dealt."

"As you wish," Lynch replied. "Lead on. I think you might still remember the way, even though your mind seems to be getting a bit feeble."

"Screw you," Smilin' Jake retorted. A spasm of pain shot through him as he shouldered his pack and set out towards the Citadel. He gritted his teeth and ignored it, but he could feel Lynch's eyes boring into his back.

They walked all through the night. As they drew nearer to the Citadel, Lynch took the lead and Smilin' Jake took the rear guard. Luke watched Lynch closely. At times the Warlock seemed to be more animal than human. His nightsight was superb, and Luke noticed how the tall Warlock's nostrils flared regularly, testing the breeze for scent. The eastern sky lightened, and Luke began to think they were going to make it.

At the rear guard, Jake focused on getting to the Citadel. Once they made it there he thought they had a chance. He coughed quietly, choking it off with the palm of his hand. When the coughing fit ceased, his palm was wet. He ganced at it as he wiped it on his jeans. It left a scarlet smear on the rough fabric. Jake stopped. Lynch looked back, and their eyes met. Lynch looked at the smear of blood on Jake's jeans, and Jake simply nodded when Lynch glanced up. The Dark Magic used so many years earlier was awakening and calling for payment. Lynch called for a halt.

"Don't stop on my account," Smilin' Jake growled.

"We all need a breather," Lynch responded. Luke noticed that Lynch hadn't even broken a sweat. He studied Jake closely. He could tell something was wrong.

"Jake, are you alright?" he asked.

Smilin' Jake smothered another coughing fit. His chest ached. "Fine. Here," he tossed his tobacco to Luke. "I'm gonna quit chewing that shit."

Luke tucked it into his pocket and turned back towards the sea. Far out above the waves, a huge shape glided on the wind.

"Lynch," Luke called quietly. "Did you say that Slagg would be arriving?"

Lynch leaped to his feet. He squinted, rubbed his eyes and looked again. Then he hastily dug out his spyglass and looked again. When he lowered his spyglass his handsome face was contorted with anger and fear. Not fear for himself, but fear for his companions.

"It ain't Slagg," he announced. He helped Jake to his feet. "Can you run?"

"What kind of dumbass question is that?" Smilin' Jake retorted. "By god Lynch, sometimes yer dumber than a pile of rocks. I ain't goin' anywhere." He unslung a quiver of arrows from his shoulder and nestled down among the rocks.

"What is he talkin' about?" Luke demanded. He took a step towards Jake.

Lynch stepped between them. "We have to go, Luke. That ain't Slagg. If we're all caught in the open we'll all die."

Luke caught the meaning of Lynch's words immediately. "No! Not for me! No one dies for me! I'll stay here with Jake."

"Go!" Smilin' Jake ordered him. "All of you, get the hell out of here." They stood as if rooted to the spot. "What the hell is wrong with you?" Smilin' Jake fumed. "If you die, all hope dies with you. Now go! Run!"

Luke angrily plucked his pack from the ground. He and Mathias ran towards the Citadel. The top turret was barely visible in the distance.

"I'm glad to have rode with you," Lynch said. Then he turned and ran after Luke and Mathias.

Smilin' Jake watched as the Dragon grew larger and larger as it hurtled towards the Isle. It began to veer after the fleeing *magii'ri*, and Jake leaped to his feet.

"Here! Over here, goddammit!" he yelled. He waved his hands and shouted until his chest felt as if it might explode. "You worthless fucking Worm!" he shouted as loud as he could. The Dragon straightened its course and ate up the distance between them. "That's better," Smilin' Jake said. "Come on over, Ol' Jake's got something for you."

Smilin' Jake stood tall among the rocks, his bow held firmly in his left hand and the fingers of his right holding an arrow in place. The Dragon swept over the edge of the cliffs and Jake could hear the wind whistling over its wings. He looked directly into the cold, expressionless eyes of the Dragon. He could hear his own heartbeat. A red mist settled over the scene. Jake drew back the bow, and when the Dragon was sixty yards away he began to fire. As soon as he released one arrow he placed another on the string, drew and fired in one continuous motion. The Dragon shrieked in pain as the arrows thudded solidly into his flesh, but none scored a mortal wound. Then he was upon Jake. One talon sliced open his shoulder and he dropped the bow from his suddenly nerveless left hand. The Dragon alighted, and reached for Jake with one huge, clawed foot.

"No!" Lynch shouted. He had returned in the middle of the fight. The Dragon whipped its head around as Lynch released an arrow. It slammed home in the giant worm's eye and black fluid spurted out. The beast writhed in agony, but it didn't attack Lynch. Instead, it lunged downward, jaws open wide. The massive fangs snapped shut on Jake's lower body as the Dragon whipped his head skyward once again. Jake dangled from the beast's jaws, his teeth gritted in agony. But his sword was clamped firmly in his hands. The giant worm's head dipped, and Jake plunged his sword to the hilt into the soft spot under the Dragon's weaker upper arm. The entire length pierced the Dragon's scales and sliced cleanly through his heart. The Dragon convulsed and whipped its head back violently. Smilin' Jake flew skyward then crashed to the earth in a broken heap. The Dragon fell with a thud that sent shudders through the soles of Lynch's boots. Lynch charged over to his fallen friend, mindless of the giant worm's death throes. Jake's eyes blinked open.

"Did I get the bastard?" he whispered. He choked, and blood rushed from his mouth.

"You got him," Lynch assured him as Smilin' Jake settled back against the ground. His face was twisted into a huge grin that settled into a snarl.

"Goddamn, that hurts." He glanced at the fallen Dragon. "Even Graywullf never killed a Dragon."

Lynch suddenly sprang to his feet as a foreign horn sounded. He stared in disbelief at the way they had come. As far as he could see a monstrous army sprawled over the Isle. His eyes flicked back down at Jake's mangled lower body.

"I'm afraid to look. How bad is it?" Smilin' Jake asked.

"Don't look," Lynch replied.

"I can't feel my legs," Jake said. "I knew it was bad." He twisted his head around to look at their back trail, the glanced down at his ruined legs. He summed it all up in one word. "Shit. Hand me my pack, will ya?"

Lynch handed Jake his ancient leather bound pack and marveled at the weight. Jake hefted it and chuckled a bit as he opened it. It was packed with dozens of sticks of tightly bound giant powder. Lynch whistled. The hard packed sticks glistened with an oily sheen.

"How long have you had that?" he asked in disbelief. "That's enough to blow up the whole goddamn isle."

"Maybe. I been carrying it for years." Jake replied. "Now do me a favor, you dumb son of a bitch. Light that chunk of wood on fire for me and get your dumb ass out of here. I got a little surprise for Blackhelm's boys."

"You're crazier than I am," Lynch said. He offered his hand to Jake, who gripped it fiercely. "I hate to leave you."

"I was done for anyway," Smilin' Jake responded. "If I was you," he said as he looked back at the advancing army, "I'd be runnin'."

Lynch ran. The words came unbidden to his mind and he uttered them immediately. The familiar flush flowed through him and his legs beat out a staccato rhythm on the hard packed ground. He caught up with Luke and Mathias. They both turned to give him a questioning look, but he said the words again and directed the spell at them.

"Run!" he bellowed.

They ran as if the hounds of hell pursued them, but despite the ground they covered Lynch still felt a desperate thrill of fear. That many sticks of giant powder in new condition, strategically placed, could blow up half the Isle. Crystallized as it was, it might be enough to vaporize all of them. Far behind them the first ranks of Blackhelm's half-man army reached Smilin' Jake. The army flowed around him until he was surrounded by rank after rank of growling half-men. Every soldier was armed with a spear or a sword or an axe. Several bent low over Jake and roared, their jaws open wide and flecks of drool spattering his face. Finally, the biggest half-man ever seen pushed them back a few feet. He glared down at Jake as he began to lower his flaming brand towards his pack. The half-man swept his foot to the side and kicked the brand away.

"I claim the first kill for the master," the giant half-man bellowed. His followers roared approval.

Smilin' Jake reached for a fist sized rock, which he clutched in his right hand. The half man general laughed.

"You fight with rocks?" he sneered.

"I reckon so," Smilin' Jake replied. His laugh carried all the way to the fleeing *magii'ri*. He slammed the rock down on his pack.

The entire plain erupted in a huge fireball that was a half mile across. The concussion knocked Lynch, Luke and Mathias off their feet. The whole World seemed to tilt crazily and the blast made their ears ring for days. Thousands of half men were killed outright and hundreds more were maimed by flying rocks. Smoking carcasses dotted the plain. The *magii'ri* stared in shock as they slowly climbed to their feet. A huge cloud of smoke billowed hundreds of feet in the air above a crater a hundred yards across. A few burning half-men ran crazily among their comrades and were quickly cut down by the fear crazed survivors.

"Come on," Lynch urged. "He bought us enough time to make it to the Citadel."

He turned away and began to run. Mathias followed, and after a moment's hesitation, Luke did also. His face was drawn and cold. Smilin' Jake had gone out like a Trueblood *magii'ri* Warrior should, but Luke was determined to see that he had plenty of company before the day was done. They ran down the same path Lorn Graywullf had used years before, and the stone door swung open as they approached. Luke and Mathias skidded to a stop and stared suspiciously as Lynch disappeared within the confines of the Citadel. Moments later his head popped around the doorway.

"Are you idiots coming or not?" he called.

Luke and Mathias exchanged glances and followed the Dark Wizard. He led them unerringly down the flights of stairs to the level where they had stashed the plunder from the Gray Goose and the pirate ship so long ago. Luke and Mathias paused in wonder at the crates which lined the room, stacked three deep in places. Lynch ran to the nearest one and pried it open with his shortsword. His face split into a huge grin when he saw the gleam of gunmetal, but it was shortlived when yet another foreign horn sounded, this one on the beach below the Citadel. All three rushed to the window port. Lynch grimaced.

"The Black Queen. Goddammit, can't anything go our way?" he cursed. His shoulders slumped. Was the entire World against them?

Luke stared out at the army assembled below him, while Lynch sat down, stretched his legs out in front of him, and leaned heavily against the wall. Nearly every square foot of beach between the Citadel and the sea was occupied by a foot soldier of the Black Queen. Luke saw Nightriders, half-men, giants, trolls, ogres and perhaps even a few were-Demons.

"We're trapped," Luke accused. "You led us right into it."

"Shouldn't we be doing something?" Mathias asked.

Lynch ran a rough hand over his grizzled cheeks. "It wasn't a trap. This is the only place on the Isle where you won't be killed instantly. The Citadel has a curse on it, remember?"

Luke turned towards the Dark Wizard. "No one else can get in, right?"

Lynch nodded. "Of course, they don't have to get in. They can just wait until we starve or die of thirst."

"Sounds like a trap to me." Luke turned back to the window and watched impassively as a group of Mordant's soldiers rushed the Citadel. They fell in waves, clutching invisible arrows that pierced their armor. It only took one charge before they retreated to a safer distance.

Luke nodded. "Uh-huh," he murmured. He bit off a chew of Smilin' Jake's tobacco and spat out the window port and reassessed the situation. "Alright," he said quietly, as he turned and walked purposefully to the crates and began to unpack rifles.

"You can't shoot them all, Graywullf," Lynch stated.

"I reckon not," Luke responded. He stoked one long rifle, thrust it through the window port, sighted carefully down the barrel and touched off a shot. A half-man flung his arms skyward and fell on his back. Luke grinned wolfishly.

"I always wanted to do that."

He loaded the long rifle again, picked a target and slowly squeezed off another shot. That half-man dropped soundlessly as the rest of Mordant's army began to mill nervously. Luke could imagine what they were thinking, caught out on the open beach, jammed in like sardines.

"Let me try," Mathias asked from Luke's left shoulder.

Luke shrugged. He loaded another rifle and handed it to Mathias. The young Wizard held it gingerly to his shoulder, glanced down the barrel and jerked the trigger with his eyes firmly closed. A half-man ten feet behind his intended target howled in agony and dropped to the sand, clawing feverishly at his midsection. Mathias opened his eyes.

"Not bad," Luke said approvingly.

"That wasn't the one I aimed at," Mathias answered.

Lynch muttered undecipherable curses under his breath. Mathias and Luke continued shooting at the massed soldiers on the beach until the room was thick with the acrid stench of gunpowder and Luke's head ached from the incessant recoil. The enemy soldiers retreated as far as they could, until they were just beyond rifle range.

"Are you done?" Lynch asked.

"For now," Luke replied. "Mathias is just now getting to where he can hit the broad side of a barn."

Lynch shook his head and blew out a gusty sigh. He leaned against the stone window port and extended his spyglasses. He studied the army from front to back, sweeping the glasses across and back and forth until he finally saw the one he sought. Mordant, the Black Queen. She was safely ensconced at the farthest point down the beach. Lynch noted that she had several giants as her personal bodyguards, and she had even brought a caged rock-cat. He was lowering his spyglasses when a familiar figure emerged from a tent next to Mordant's. Lynch caught his breath. It could not be! Not here. He studied the man carefully. It was him. Timon Blackhelm.

He lowered his glasses. Fate had delivered his most hated enemy into his hands. Never mind that an entire army stood between them. Lynch was suddenly elated. If there was only a way to get a message to Slagg. But he was trapped here, and Slagg evidently had troubles of his own, judging by his absence from an appointed meeting. He'd never been late before, and Lynch had to admit that bothered him a great deal. But, Slagg would have to find his own way to confront Timon, the Warlock who had cursed him. Lynch clenched and unclenched his hands as fury flowed through him. Timon was the one man who could have found the Book of Runes, and he was the only mortal who could challenge Lynch. That, coupled with the bad blood between them, made Lynch hate him with unreasonable intensity. Lynch raised his spyglasses again, and as he watched, Timon leaned back into his tent and dragged someone from within. Lynch caught his breath when he saw the flash of jet black hair. His body went cold. The person Timon held captive was La'Nay.

Lynch actually growled deep in his chest as Timon held La'Nay with one hand and gestured at the massive army with the other. Lynch could well imagine what Timon told her. He would tell her that no man could stand against such an army, and that soon the demise of the *magii'ri* would be complete. Along with one Dark Wizard, of course.

"No," he muttered.

Luke and Mathias exchanged confused glances.

Lynch whirled away from the window port and charged headlong across the room, leaving Luke and Mathias standing stock still and staring in disbelief.

"What the Hell is he doing?" Luke exclaimed.

"Follow him!" Mathias shouted.

The two ran from the room and followed the staccato sound of Lynch's bootsteps on the stone staircase.

"He's going down," Luke said needlessly as he and Mathias plunged after him.. They were far younger than the Dark Wizard and at the peak of their training, but they were no match for the fury of Lynch. He had called upon every Dark spell he knew to lend speed to his legs, and he quickly outdistanced them. Mathias lunged to a sentry port and called upon his own magic to lend his eyes superior sight. As soon as he caught a glimpse of the raven haired beauty he knew that Lynch would not stop, despite the fact that several thousand soldiers stood between him and La'Nay. He would be torn to pieces.

"Luke!" Mathias shouted as soon as the idea struck him. "Luke! Release the Guardians! Now, Luke! Say the words!"

Luke skidded to a stop two levels lower than Mathias and stared out his own window port for a few seconds. He had no idea what to say. He stared in disbelief as Lynch hurtled out the doorway and rapidly closed the distance between himself and the Black Queen's army.

"Brothers, I release you," he muttered, not really expecting anything.

Lynch was within ten feet of the nearest enemy soldier, a huge brute of a half-man, who eagerly raised his battle axe in readiness to chop the approaching human in two. Lynch charged on, and just as he reached the half-man the enemy soldier was flattened as if by a giant hand. The entire army parted as scores of half-men and Nightriders were flung aside by an unseen force too powerful to resist. Lynch charged on, unmindful of his near scrape with certain death. Still other enemy soldiers plummeted past the Citadel as they were flung from the cliffs above. For a moment Luke thought the Guardians might actually defeat Mordant's army. But there were too many. The ranks of half-men closed in behind Lynch and soon he was swallowed up by them. Then the huge mass began to surge towards the Citadel.

"Oh shit," Luke muttered as he realized he had just removed the only thing standing between them and thousands of enemies. He hurtled up the stairs two at a time. "Climb, Mathias, climb!" he shouted.

Mathias had recognized his mistake and was already four floors above him and climbing fast. Luke made it back to the level that contained the gunpowder, rifles and other crates from the plundered ship. He skidded to a stop.

"Well, why not?" he said to himself.

He bashed a hole in a keg of powder and ran a trail from the cache to the base of the next flight of steps. Then he ran back and knocked holes in several other kegs. He stopped just long enough to strike a spark with flint and steel, then his eyes widened as he saw how fast the powder burned. Once again he sprinted up the steps.

"Run!" he shouted as loud as he could.

Mathias burst through the upper doorway with his weapons drawn, but the path had been cleared by the Guardians. "Come on, Luke!" he shouted back into the Citadel.

Inside, Luke was too far down to hear Mathias urging him on. His lungs worked like a bellows and sweat poured down his face as he climbed desperately. The first half-men lunged into the smoke filled room. There was a flash of light, a deafening concussion and the Citadel disintegrated. All of the half-men in the vicinity of the storage room were obliterated. Luke felt the steps swell underneath him from the blast. He knew he couldn't make it, but he would not give up. His legs pumped furiously as he tried to outrun the blast. The Citadel was crumbling around him, and soon Luke was swallowed up by the heaving mass of debris.

Mathias was flung to the ground by the concussion, but he regained his feet in an instant. He wasted only a fraction of a second with one backwards glance at the ruined Citadel before it was covered with a curtain of gray dust. He leaped up the trail as rocks the size of cannonballs whizzed by, dislodged from the cliffs above. The entire Isle of Serpents rocked, and huge gaps appeared in the trail. A slab twenty feet long peeled away from the cliff with Mathias on it, and he knew his time was up. He leaped into empty space and braced himself for the inevitable impact. Instead of falling, a giant clawed foot curled around him and he was borne through the air. Mathias barely had the wits left about him to look up at the scaled underbelly of a mature Dragon. He was carried to safety some five hundred yards inland and unceremoniously dropped. Mathias skidded on his belly through a pile of rabbit brush before he stopped with a mouthful of dirt. He lunged to his feet, torn between confusion and fury, as he hastily drew his sword. Slagg carelessly knocked the blade from Mathias' grasp with one forefoot.

"Come on then," Mathias challenged. "Finish me!"

Slagg gave him a disdainful look then walked towards the edge of the cliff. He wanted to get a better look at the damage done by that horrendous blast. He was caught completely off guard by the hate filled spell Mathias hurled at him. Slagg growled in annoyance and shrugged off the spell.

*"I sssaved your life. Now go away and leave me be."*

Mathias felt the scalding voice of Slagg inside his head. It was nothing that he could ever have imagined. He stared in slack jawed, bulging eyed, impotent fury at the giant worm who treated him like an insect. He shook his head and reluctantly crept closer to the edge that he had been so recently rescued from.

Dust and smoke hung thick in the air. Mordant's army had surged forward as one, and most now lay lifeless, crushed by the avalanche of debris from the Citadel and the cliffs above it. The few survivors fled in abject panic from the Hell Luke had unleashed. Timon and Lynch had disappeared.

Mordant stared in total disbelief at the destruction of her army. She was only dimly aware of her surroundings at all, until La'Nay rose from the sand where she had fallen.

"You bitch!" Mordant shouted, venting her incredible frustration at the only living person who remained near her. "You were Timon's bait. That's the only reason I let you live. Now he's gone, and no one will save you!"

Mordant passed close by the upended cage that housed Zagreb, the rock cat. Her attention was focused on La'Nay. She raised her hands to direct a spell at her, but then she was crushed to the ground by an unbelievable weight. She never felt the immense fangs that encircled her neck and severed her brain stem. Zagreb raised his shaggy head to look once at La'Nay then he bounded off.

La'Nay stifled a scream with shaking hands. She shook her head at the incredible destruction that surrounded her. The Citadel lay in ruins. Huge sections of the cliff wall had been dislodged and even as she watched more debris rained down. Stone from the Citadel had rained down almost to the water's edge. The few survivors of Mordant's army were running down the beach, and nearly all of the half-men under Timon's rule had simply disappeared. She looked, then stared and shook her head. It could not be. One tall, broad shouldered figure emerged out of the dust and debris. He walked unsteadily towards her then when Luke Graywullf was a hundred yards from the ruins he turned and studied the destruction for a long moment. A feral grin, reminiscent of Lynch, split his grimy face. He raised his fists skyward and let out a great whoop.

La'Nay watched the sole survivor of the explosion, first in shock then in growing amazement, as he actually broke into a jig. She wondered for a moment if he was insane the she hid a smile behind one shaking hand at the boyish display.

"Luke!" Mathias shouted from the top of the cliff. He waved his arms and shouted, over and over, until Luke finally heard him. He waved back then he dropped his arms and clawed for a weapon when he saw Slagg. The Sky Rider, Slagg, watched in apparent indifference. The affairs and wars of men held less and less interest for him by the day as his Dragon side became stronger. Lynch had summoned him, and the Dark Wizard still held sway over him. That was the only reason he had come, and it was only because of Lynch's influence that he had saved Mathias instead of crushing him in his claws. Then he spied La'Nay. His uncanny eyes recorded every detail, and without warning he leaped from the cliff and soared down the beach. Luke and Mathias watched in disbelief as La'Nay raised her arms as if to embrace the giant worm, and he plucked her gently from the beach without missing a wing beat. With a few flaps of his wings he gained altitude and sped off into the setting sun.

Luke pitched forward onto his knees as his legs gave out. He knelt there, body shaking, as Mathias climbed down. He knew he had cheated Death, but it was an ongoing game, and Death always had cards up his sleeve. He toppled over and lay there in the sand until Mathias joined him. Mathias helped him up and they clapped each other on the back.

"We did it," Luke said over and over. "I don't know how, but we did it."

Mathias stared in the direction Slagg had flown, carrying La'Nay. "It ain't over yet."

"I reckon," Luke agreed. The image of the woman on the beach raising her arms to welcome Slagg wouldn't leave his mind.

Behind them the *magii'ri* warships glided silently towards the beach. The Warriors aboard stared in wonder at the destruction on two armies apparently wrought by only two men.

"Now what?" Luke asked.

Mathias also stared at the sky where Slagg had disappeared. A deep, smoldering rage had been awakened in him by his chance encounter with the Dragon, but there was more than that. He saw his path, his purpose in life. He would defeat the Wilding and lead the *magii'ri*, with Luke at his side, to their former glory. No matter what the cost. He would create the Dragonspawn.

Edwards Brothers Malloy
Thorofare, NJ  USA
May 18, 2015